Prai

MW01146479

Kathleen O'Neal Gear

"At heart a murder mystery. All questions are answered, but the evil remains."

— *Kirkus Reviews* on *The Summoning God*

"The Gears have done it again ... This crafty weaving of past and present is a wonderful journey of learning and adventure."

— *Romantic Times* on *The Visitant*

"A first-rate 'murder mystery, anthropological information on pre- European Native America, a slight dash of sex, and plenty of politics."

— *Booklist* on *People of the Mist*

"An exciting, skillfully crafted, and fast-paced story that also serves as an engrossing look at ancient culture."

— *Publishers Weekly* on *People of the Silence*

The Two Hearted

Also by W. Michael Gear and Kathleen O'Neal Gear

Big Horn Legacy

Dark Inheritance

The Foundation

Fracture Event

Long Ride Home

The Mourning War

Raising Abel

Rebel Hearts Anthology

Sand in the Wind

Thin Moon and Cold Mist

Black Falcon Nation Series

Flight of the Hawk Series

The Moundville Duology

Saga of a Mountain Sage Series

The Wyoming Chronicles

The Anasazi Mysteries

The Two Hearted
The Anasazi Mysteries Part Four

W. Michael Gear

Kathleen O'Neal Gear

WOLFPACK
PUBLISHING
— EST 2013 —

The Two Hearted
Paperback Edition
Copyright © 2023 (As Revised) W. Michael Gear and
Kathleen O'Neal Gear

Wolfpack Publishing
9850 S. Maryland Parkway, Suite A-5 #323
Las Vegas, Nevada 89183

wolfpackpublishing.com

Cover Image *A Hopi Man* provided by the Amon Carter Museum of
American Art, in Fort Worth, Texas.
Chapter Illustration by Ellisa Mitchel.

Paperback ISBN 978-1-63977-394-7
eBook ISBN 978-1-63977-395-4

Authors' Note

In an age of increasing AI generated text, we want you to know that you are reading 100% authentic fiction spun straight from our very human imaginations!

The Two Hearted

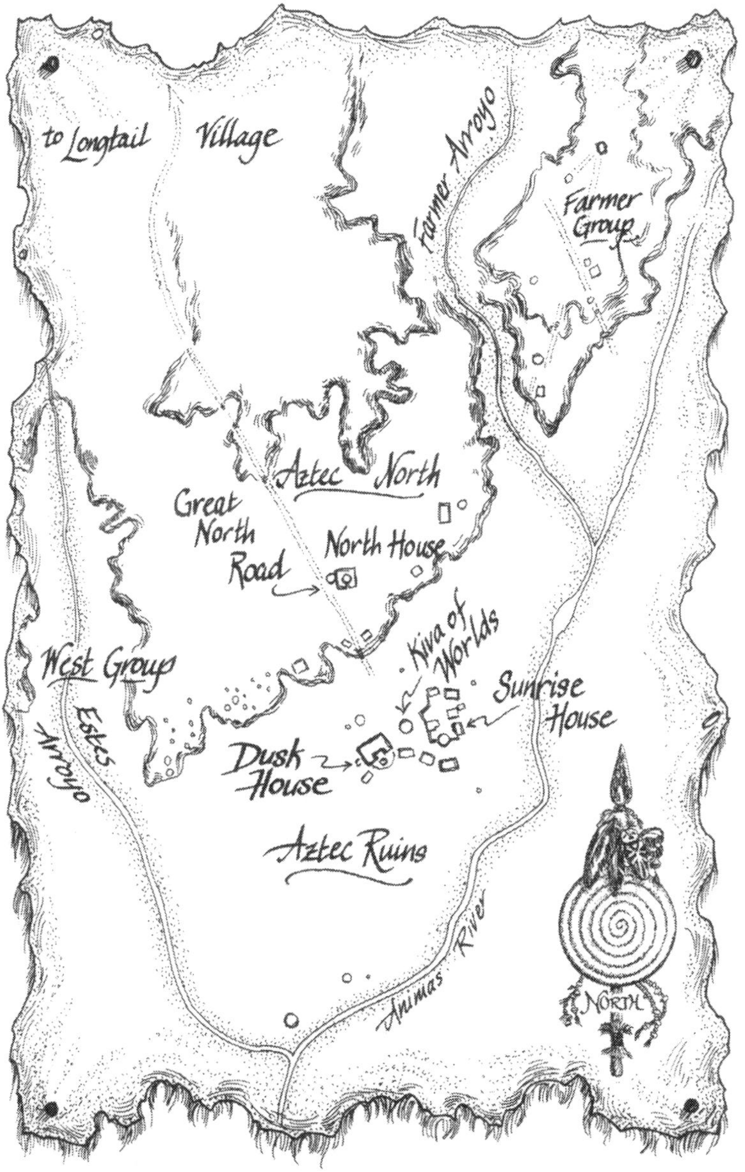

to Longtail Village
Farmer Arroyo
Farmer Group
Aztec North
Great North Road
North House
Kiva of Worlds
West Group
Sunrise House
Estes Arroyo
Dusk House
Aztec Ruins
Animas River
NORTH

The dream was so real...

Dusty cried out and jerked upright in his sleeping bag. Cold sweat prickled on his skin. He took a deep breath as the fragmenting tendrils of the nightmare broke around him. The inside of the camp trailer was black as pitch. What time was it? Midnight?

"Goddamn it."

He slung his legs out of the sleeping bag and perched on the edge of the fold-down bunk. Dale's trailer felt like an oversized coffin. In the silence, he could hear the faint sigh of wind through the junipers outside. A mouse skittered along the frame, its tiny claws scratching the metal.

The distant hoot of an owl sent a shiver across his soul. Most southwestern people had a wary respect for Owl. Even the Hispanic population was leery of *el Tecolote*.

Dusty pulled on his pants, slipped into his boots, and shrugged on his worn blue Filson coat. The trailer stairs squeaked as he stepped out into the night and looked up at the late October sky. A three-quarter moon hung in the east, setting the pale cottonwood leaves aglow.

The stories came welling up from his memory. Tales of selfish people jumping through yucca hoops to become witches. How workers of evil would pervert the ways of Power to achieve revenge, or their own ends.

His rootless childhood had been full of stories about witchcraft. While the Navajo Skinwalkers tended to be more colorful, the Pueblo witches had a nastier element. For years Dusty had believed that that element of their evil was descended from the Anasazi, particularly the Chacoans; some scholars thought they'd eaten people as a means of terrorizing subordinate villages. A sort of: "Be good or I'll send my elite warriors down to burn your town and eat your wife and children."

The idea wasn't far-fetched. Even the Hopi admitted that they had destroyed the villages of Awatovi and Sikyatki over witchcraft. Hopis killing other Hopis. To this day, Pueblo peoples were circumspect when it came to leaving loose hair, nail clippings, or sweat-soaked garments lying around. The Hopi elder who had been Dusty's mentor had urinated on rocks to prevent witches from later molding a doll out of that damp soil to use against him.

He thought about that as he walked silently through the camp and down into the shadows beneath the cottonwoods.

He stopped at the river's edge and looked out over the moon-silvered water. It seemed to dance and swirl, alive with the power of life. Like so many of the rivers in the Southwest, it had been flowing here when the

Anasazi had devoured themselves like the proverbial snake swallowing its own tail.

That long-ago night when the kiva burned, the gaudy light would have cast a red-orange glow over this water. Here, where he was standing, he would have heard the screams of the children. Were the parents shouting back, desperate to reach their sons and daughters? Or were they silent witnesses to the extinction of their hopes and dreams?

"Stewart?"

He started, wheeling, then sighed. "Jesus! You almost made me jump out of my skin."

Maureen stepped out into the moonlight. Black hair tumbled down her back like a midnight mantle. Her face was ghostly pale, her dark eyes like round holes in white cloth.

He said, "What are you doing up?"

"I think it was the jalapeno cheeseburgers. I didn't dare pick those peppers off. I would never have lived it down."

He sucked in a deep breath. "Sorry. I wasn't thinking. I just made them to my tastes."

She walked closer and examined his face. "Are you all right?"

"Fine. Just out for a walk."

"Uh-huh," she said as she folded her arms over her black coat. "Is something wrong, Dusty? You haven't been normal since I got here."

"The words 'Dusty Stewart' and 'normal' aren't generally joined in the same sentence, Maureen."

"Nightmare?"

He used the toe of his boot to squash a blowing leaf

and replied, "I get them on occasion." More lately than ever before.

She paused, took another step toward him, and gazed out over the river. "Well, after looking at the boiled skull, and the kiva filled with bones, I don't doubt it."

Dusty winced and closed his eyes. "Do you mind, Doctor?"

"Is that what you dreamed about? Burning babies?"

He nodded. "I was down in the kiva. The bodies were fresh, charred, the hair melted over the skulls until it looked like glass. Lips pulled back to expose cracked blue-black teeth. The eyes, my god, the eyes were popped out where the vitreous humor had boiled inside. I had been chased in there, had fallen among them. And my hand..." He held it out in the moonlight, studying it, feeling it alive and warm. "I kept trying to push myself up, and each time my hand pushed right through rotting bodies. They were all slimy inside."

"Then what happened?"

He rubbed the back of his neck, feeling odd about telling her his dreams. "I searched the kiva for the ladder to get out, and there was Dad, looking down at me, laughing. But the voice wasn't his. It was...it was..."

"Who?"

He shook his head. "Sorry, Doctor, I'm not about to feed more rumors about the Madman of New Mexico. Besides, I've always secretly been afraid that maybe insanity runs in my family."

"Oh, come on. Granted I didn't know your father, or what would have possessed him to kill himself, but I do know you." The moonlight added its magic to her beautiful face. "I may not always like you, but I've never seen anything that made me doubt your sanity. The quality of your soul, yes. Sanity, no."

He couldn't help it; he laughed. "Yeah, well, the next few sentences will make you reconsider. Do you know why I called you to come to this site?"

"Other than the obvious reason that I'm a physical anthropologist, no."

He bent down, picked up a rounded rock, and pitched it into the river. It splashed liquid silver in the moonlight. "This is really going to sound crazy, so brace yourself."

Maureen gave him a suspicious look. "I'm braced. Go ahead."

He waved a hand at the night. "It's all tied together. Everything. You, me, this site. I showed you that potsherd for a reason. I know it sounds delusional, but this site *is* tied to 10K3. Unless I can lift fingerprints from the pottery, I'll never be able to prove it, but we—you and I—are connected to these sites. And I think I know the reason."

She shivered before she could squelch it. "Okay, why?"

"You liked Magpie Walking Hawk Taylor, didn't you?"

She nodded. "We've been writing letters since I returned to Canada."

"Do you think she's crazy?"

"No, I don't. Why?"

He pitched another rock into the river. "Because she and I believe a lot of the same things. Funny, isn't it? She's an enrolled member of the Keres tribe, and no one thinks she's nuts because she believes in witchcraft. I'm a White guy who's lived on reservations off and on for most of my life, been initiated into a kiva—"

"But if you believe, you're a lunatic."

"The lady wins first prize."

She bowed her head, and long black hair spilled around her. The waves rippled platinum where the moonlight touched them. "So, you're telling me you believe these children died because of witchcraft?"

God, she was beautiful, straight and tall, with that perfect Seneca face.

Maureen tilted her head to look at him. "How long did you keep the basilisk in your house, Dusty?"

His stomach tingled. "Too long, I think. Had it in my house for about six months before I finished the excavation report and curated it along with the other artifacts we found."

She seemed to let it go as she looked out at the river and the full moon shining down. "It's beautiful here."

"It is. Just before you arrived, I was thinking about that, about this being *El Rio de las Animas Perdidas,* the River of Lost Souls. Just south of here is Aztec Ruins. When Earl Morris dug it in the twenties, it was littered with bodies, and just south of there is Salmon Ruins. Cynthia Irwin-Williams dug it in the seventies. It had another tower kiva like this one. Also filled with children."

"And you think witchcraft was the cause?" She didn't sound so skeptical now.

"One man's belief is another man's heresy. When someone dares to believe differently than you do, it always helps if you can label him as evil; that way people can hate him without feeling guilty. It's very convenient."

Maureen tucked her hands into her pockets and tipped her chin to look at the stars. "I recall that Hail Walking Hawk thought the basilisk was a witch's amulet. She said it was dangerous, filled with evil. Do you think you've been witched?"

Their gazes held.

"That's why you think we're tied to these sites, isn't it?" she whispered as though she feared someone might be listening. "You and I have been witched?" A smile tugged at the corners of her lips.

Dusty didn't see the humor. "Go ahead and laugh, but I recall that you spent a good deal of time touching the bones from that site, and even took home a pot of corpse powder. I'd get rid of that pot *pronto* if I were you. I'm surprised you haven't had the Blair Witch traipsing around your dreams."

Her smile faded.

Dusty caught the tension in the sudden set of her jaw. "Really? And you haven't told me about this before?"

She let out a breath, and it frosted in the air. "Actually, I thought about calling you. Or Maggie. But I just couldn't convince myself to do it—and I haven't had the dream since I've been out here."

Dusty studied her taut expression. "Which means you had the dream more than once in Canada? It's a recurrent dream?"

She sternly pointed a finger at him. "Yes, and if you tell anyone, I will mail the pot of corpse powder directly to you."

Dusty crossed himself. "No need to threaten. I'm good at keeping secrets. What's the dream?"

"It's"—she gestured awkwardly—"it's not a witch

dream. It's a ghost dream."

"Go on."

She tucked her hair behind her ears, stalling. "A wolf leads me to a cave in the mountains. In the back of the cave, there's a skeleton in a pool of water. While I'm standing there looking at it, four people come in."

"Four. A sacred number. Do they talk to you?"

"The old woman does. She tells me not to be afraid."

"I'm sure that calms you right down, huh?"

Maureen laughed. "Yeah, right. Anyway, it's not a scary dream, it's more like—"

"A Spirit Dream?" Dusty asked. "Like you're being called by a Spirit Helper?"

Maureen frowned at him. "I suppose some would say so."

"Which figure in the dream is calling you?"

"I don't know. Maybe all of them. The old man looks right at me, though."

"I could arrange for you to talk to some Puebloan tribal elders about it."

She gave him an incredulous look. "You're the one who needs a head session, not me."

The clipped tone of voice made Dusty's heart shrivel. "Just can't take the risk, eh? I assure you that nobody I recommend will blab to the American Association of Physical Anthropologists."

She balled her fists in her pockets. "You know what? This has been a lovely chat, but I think it's time to go back to bed."

She spun around and strode away.

Dusty sighed, spent a few seconds staring at the stars, then called, "Hey! Wait up. I'll walk you back."

"They're coming," Straighthorn said and stamped his feet to keep warm.

He and Jackrabbit, both young warriors, had been ordered to stand guard the morning of Matron Flame Carrier's funeral. The old woman, beloved of her band of Katsina's People, had been found brutally murdered. But then it was an age of violence, warfare, and witchcraft. Chaos, and the rise of new gods, like the katsinas, had reigned in the times following the collapse of the Chacoan empire and the abandonment of the great houses built by the First People in Straight Path Canyon.

The cold morning wind whipped Jackrabbit's shoulder-length black hair over his pug nose and into his dark brown eyes as he shifted to look. "Where? I don't see them."

"They are just leaving the plaza."

A purple gleam haloed the eastern horizon. In the distance, he could make out the shape of Longtail village. Gray forms emerged from the great kiva, and flute music drifted up to them, the notes sweet and mournful.

From their guard position on the knoll across the river, they would be able to watch most of the burial ceremony.

Redcrop led the procession, sprinkling the path with cornmeal to sanctify the way. Long black hair draped her white cape.

Behind her, six spectral figures Danced, twenty hands tall, with no arms or legs. They glided forward as if canoeing on air, and the rhythmic clacking of their carved beaks cut the stillness like knives. Buffalo horns curved upward from either side of the enormous empty eyes in their masks. Red-feathered capes covered their misshapen bodies. Part bird, part buffalo, and part man, the katsinas united the worlds of sky and earth, animal and human. They were moments of perfect harmony in a sea of chaos.

"I will miss our Matron," Jackrabbit said.

"She was a good leader. Was she your clan?"

"She was my *family,* Straighthorn." Jackrabbit rubbed his cold arms. "I have no knowledge of my clan. Three summers ago, i woke at the bottom of a cliff with my head bashed and bloody. I could remember nothing. Not even my name. I may have slipped and fallen or been in a battle. I wandered for days before I saw the Matron standing outside of Flowing Waters Town. She was looking up as if searching for me. I walked down, and she took me in. She fed me and clothed me." His voice turned brittle. "She gave me a home."

"I did not know her for long, but she was always kind to me. I will miss her, too."

The burial procession came slowly down the path

toward the river. Cloudblower followed the katsinas, and behind her, Springbank, Wading Bird, and Crossbill marched. On the elders' heels, War Chief Browser and Catkin carried Matron Flame Carrier's burial ladder. A large group of mourners assembled at the rear and fell into line as the procession descended into the cottonwoods.

Thirty people from Dry Creek village had come in for the ceremony late last night. Their campfires gleamed on the outskirts of Longtail village. They walked in the rear. Most wore bright yellow capes that contrasted sharply with the red and white capes of the Katsinas' People. The Dry Creek Matron, Ant Woman, had been a good friend of their Matron.

Straighthorn lost sight of them. Wind Baby shrieked across the desert and blasted the trees until they squeaked and groaned. A hurricane of golden leaves tumbled through the air.

Redcrop reappeared as the burial party moved toward the grave. She walked slowly, solemnly, her right hand extended to the path. The cornmeal falling from her fingers blew away in a glimmering haze.

Straighthorn whispered, "She must be dying inside. I wish I was there."

"Skink will relieve us at dawn. We will be there for the final Songs, my friend."

"I hope so."

Jackrabbit turned to look at him. "Oh, believe me, he will come. Skink may not be happy with you, Straighthorn, but he will not disobey the War Chief's orders. He values his skin too much."

The War Chief had a reputation for explosive anger, though Straight-horn had never seen it. In the past nine moons he had seen only a very solitary man, a man in mourning who dwelled on the deaths of his wife and son. Browser kept to himself, did what had to be done to protect the village, and retreated to his chamber alone at night. Many of the Longtail Clan widows had initially viewed Browser with interest, but he had politely shied away from them. The only woman he spent time with was his deputy war chief, Catkin.

Straighthorn had heard the story of how, two summers ago, Browser had sneaked into an enemy camp where Catkin was being held prisoner and rescued her. She'd been injured and was dazed. He killed the men raping her and carried Catkin out on his back. He'd rescued her again in Straight Path Canyon. Straighthorn wondered at that. Browser had risked his life at least twice to save Catkin, but he did not appear to be in love with her. Rather, she seemed to be his best friend.

Straighthorn said, "I should have kept my temper yesterday, Jackrabbit. I embarrassed Skink—"

"Everyone knew you were right. You had found the murderers' tracks. We should have followed them until we couldn't see our own feet in the darkness. Most of us wished to continue the search. The fact that you argued about it with Skink only improved your reputation."

Straighthorn gestured lamely. "Yes, but the argument diminished him. I fear he will find a hundred small ways to punish me."

"He is a very powerful man, my friend. You should be worried about the big ways he can get you. He is as cruel as a weasel, and you know it. If you turn up dead some morning, I'll be very disappointed in you."

Straighthorn sighed and looked up at the last of the

stars, the Evening People who glittered and faded on the western horizon. The stars known as Wolf Slayer and his brother Raven were always the last to go to sleep. They watched over the world until Father Sun rose into the sky and could guard it himself.

"You have only known Skink for a few moons, Straighthorn," Jackrabbit said. "He is very clever. If he decides to kill you, he'll make it look like an accident. 'Oh, poor Straighthorn, he slipped and fell on his own knife. I swear there was nothing I could do!'" Jackrabbit nodded for effect.

"You just sent chills up my neck."

"Good."

Straighthorn glanced over his shoulder, examining the path at the base of the knoll.

"You're going to have me jumping at my own breathing. Let's speak of something else."

Jackrabbit remained silent for a time, then he gestured to the rolling hills in front of them. "Do you think they're out there?"

"Who?"

"The murderers."

"No! Why would you think that?"

Jackrabbit shrugged. "I was in Talon Town when my friend Whiproot was killed. I heard his death screams. Later, the War Chief told me that Stone Ghost said murderers always come to watch if they can. I guess it gives them some"—he waved a hand—"thrill."

Straighthorn felt as if a nest of wriggling baby snakes had hatched in his hair. He pulled his war club from his belt and gripped it in a hard fist.

"I thank you, Jackrabbit. I was getting tired. Now I'm fully awake."

"Just in time. Skink is coming."

Straighthorn turned.

A shadow emerged from the brush and came toward them. The sound of feet crunching sand rode the wind.

Straighthorn sucked in a deep breath to prepare himself, and called, "A Blessed morning to you, Skink."

Jackrabbit lifted a hand and smiled. "We're glad to see you. It's been a bitter night."

Skink's buckskin cape swayed around his tall, lean body as he climbed to the top of the knoll. The pale morning gleam sheathed his catlike face. He did not even glance at Jackrabbit, but stopped in front of Straighthorn and looked down at him through dark cold eyes. "You saw nothing?"

"Nothing unusual," Straighthorn replied.

"Well," Jackrabbit clarified, "we saw the burial party leave the village and walk to the gravesite. That's a little unusual, but these days not—"

"Then leave. You are no longer needed here."

Straighthorn bowed respectfully, and he and Jackrabbit marched down the hill. They didn't speak until they had passed beyond the brush at the base of the knoll.

Jackrabbit said, "I don't think he likes us."

"It's me he doesn't like."

A sliver of brilliant pink light painted the east.

"It's almost dawn," Straighthorn said. "We'd better hurry if we're going to make it for the last Songs."

Straighthorn broke into a trot, and Jackrabbit followed him down onto the leaf-choked path by the river.

P iper clutches her cornhusk doll to her chest and slides forward on her belly, inching her way to the top of the hill from the hole where she has been hiding in the ground. She sees all of the people as shiny birds, red, white, and yellow. They can't talk. They squeak and squeal. Mother wears white, and stands beside another woman in white, but they are surrounded by yellow birds.

Piper puts her dirty finger in her mouth and sucks on it; it tastes bright and bitter, like licking a pyrite mirror.

New people come. Two men. They walk up from the river bottom and stand at the edge of the crowd, right behind Mother. But Mother does not see them. She is crying, her shoulders shaking apart. Or maybe it is laughing. Sometimes laughing looks like crying.

People lift the dead woman from the burial ladder and lower her into a hole. The Songs start. Human Songs. She can hear them. People live inside the squeals. As the masked Dancers spin around the edge of the grave, an old man lowers the burial ladder into the hole so that the woman's afterlife soul can climb out and go to the Land of the Dead.

Piper watches the children come forward, get down on their knees, and begin pushing dirt into the hole with their hands. There are many children. More than Piper has ever seen in one place.

The Songs stop. People hug each other and start to walk away. The old people move closer to the grave. Their hair is the color of rain clouds and snowflakes.

As if Mother knows Piper is spying on her, she lifts her head and stares at the hilltop.

Piper cannot move. Her body is frozen. She clutches her doll to her chest.

Mother has dead flying squirrel eyes. Black and bulging.

A small, terrible cry escapes Piper's lips.

She forces her legs to slide her backward down the hill, then she gets to her feet and runs, runs away fast, down the hill.

She stumbles through a tangle of rabbitbrush and takes a deer trail into the bottom of the drainage. The sand is wet; it squishes around her sandals. She runs, searching, her eyes moving until she sees a hole. An old coyote den dug into the wall.

Piper squirms in headfirst. It is big inside, big enough for her to turn around and stare out of the hole at the sunlight.

She listens. The birds have gone quiet. Not even Wind Baby dares to breathe.

"No one yet," she whispers to her doll. "It's all right. We're all right."

3

Dusty levered another shovelful of dirt from his excavation unit and tossed it into Sylvia's wheelbarrow. Despite the fact that the late afternoon temperature hovered around sixty-two degrees, he wore a short-sleeved gray T-shirt. Sweat matted strands of blond hair to his cheeks and soaked his armpits. October in the high desert was like nowhere else on earth. The patches of blue showing through the clouds glistened, and the air smelled like freshly plowed earth.

"Anything yet?" he called up from his meter-deep pit. To either side, the classic Chacoan walls of the structure caught the afternoon sun. The insides of the walls were rubble-filled, but the outer layer of stone consisted of flat slabs, carefully fitted together. Each layer was of a varying thickness, creating a pattern. More than once, while looking at such walls, it had struck him that they resembled the weft of weaving, as if the patterns were similar to those reflected in the occasional specimens of Anasazi blankets recovered from dry cave sites. The masonry workmanship was spectacular. During the time when the pueblo was occupied, that beautiful stonework would have been covered by thick mud plaster and painted with designs. Despite what modern people thought about brick and stonework, bare rock was anything but beautiful to the Anasazi.

"*Nada,* boss," Sylvia replied as she fingered through the dirt. A sweaty lock of brown hair curled over her forehead. She wiped a hand on her dirt-caked blue jeans and tugged at the battered canvas hat on her head. Still in her early twenties, Sylvia Rhone had worked for Dusty for years; she had just finished her BA in anthropology from the University of New Mexico. She looked like a field archaeologist, muscular and whip-thin; her brown hair, tied in a ponytail, stuck out through the back of her faded "Chinle Yacht Club" cap. The way she looked at Dusty, those bright green eyes contrasted with her worn and faded Levi's, frayed as they were at the hip from propping a sifting screen.

"Have I ever told you how much I hate clearing out room fill?" he asked.

"Maybe once or twice."

He bent down and tugged to remove another weathered chunk of toppled sandstone and heaved it into the wheelbarrow.

"Whoa!" Sylvia said. "That's a load!" She artfully turned the wheelbarrow and trundled it down the line of planks that crossed the rubble on the collapsed pueblo. At the edge of the ruin, she separated the rock and tipped the wheelbarrow to spill the dirt into a wooden-framed screen. He heard the unforgettable *shish-shish* as she worked it back and forth.

Dusty wiped his dirty face on his sleeve and took the opportunity to stretch his aching back muscles. "God, I think age is catching up with me."

"Yeah, I've heard thirty-seven is a real turning point. Like the storm surge before the hurricane. Just wait till next year." Sylvia lowered her screen and tossed the dregs—roots, insect hulls, and a few rocks—out onto the back-dirt pile. Then she wheeled her way back. "Okay, hit me again."

Dusty pried more of the tumbled stone loose and tossed it up into the wheelbarrow. Across from him, he heard Maureen and Steve talking in low voices as they worked over the bone bed in the bottom of the kiva. One by one, Maureen was mapping in the bits of bone, painting the more fragile pieces with polyvinyl acetate preservative, and removing them, many on their pedestals of dirt, to be cleaned later in the lab.

Dusty heaved another stone into the wheelbarrow and gazed out to the east. Beyond the cottonwoods, the Animas River flowed through the floodplain like a winding brown serpent. In every direction, hills rolled until they butted against golden sandstone cliffs. Just to the south, the land turned a drab shade of gray as the Animas snaked its way southwest toward the town of Aztec.

He bent to the task of freeing more head-sized blocks of sandstone and tossed them up into the wheelbarrow. The work couldn't be called anything other than nasty, but doing it by hand was the only way to be certain nothing important got damaged.

As Sylvia wheeled another load away, Dusty propped himself so that he could look over the wall. Steve Sanders was drawing in his field notebook. The bottom of the tower kiva had been cordoned off into a grid, yellow nylon string crisscrossing the floor in one-meter squares.

Steve, in his late twenties, was finishing his PhD at the department of anthropology at Arizona State. One of the few Black field archaeologists working in the Southwest, Steve had an IQ of one hundred seventy-six. His dissertation topic was "An Analysis of Chacoan Religious Philosophy Within a Jungian Context." A topic which required outside committee members from the philosophy and psychology departments, and was still beyond their comprehension.

Steve liked to break into an Uncle Remus accent, which he knew would drive Dusty half berserk.

Dusty's gaze lingered on Maureen. She sat on an overturned buck across from Steve, pulled her long black hair up and pinned it under her hat. The oversized black sweatshirt she wore declared an emphatic OH, CANADA! But his attention was on the way it conformed to her shoulders and stretched down to accent her slim waist. The snug black jeans she wore did really nice things for the rest of her.

"Uh, Boss Man? You working, or building up to a cardiac condition?" Sylvia asked.

Dusty turned. Sylvia stood behind the wheelbarrow, her arms crossed, green eyes amused.

"I didn't hear you come back."

"No shit?" She cocked her head. "You want Steve and me to cart rocks while you go hold the tape measure for Maureen?"

He pitched a rock into her wheelbarrow with enough vigor to make the steel ring. "Careful. I might start asking questions about your personal life."

"I don't have a personal life."

Dusty scratched the back of his neck. "Right. Sure. At dinner last night, I was afraid to seat you and Steve next to each other."

She rolled the chunks of sandstone to the back of the wheelbarrow. "Yeah, well, we went down to the river to talk. That's all. I mean, we didn't really plan... you know, that thing in Durango. It just sort of happened. We were trying to..." She shook her head. "I don't know, Dusty, it's just all so quick."

"Yep."

"Well, what do you think? I mean, about Steve and me."

"If you make it work, more power to you. If you don't, it's none of my business, and whatever you do is what you do."

"Gee, thanks, Dusty. That was really helpful."

He gave her a sidelong look. "I don't have to worry about assigning you to the same pit, do I? If that will be uncomfortable for either of you, just pull me aside and tell me, and I'll figure something out."

"Nah, we're cool. We're just going to take some time. See if we really like each other as much as we think we do. I mean, God, we've been friends for years. But Steve's not sure if this is a good thing."

"You didn't hit him with the baseball bat, did you?"

Sylvia grinned. "No. You know, I keep having to remind myself. I'll wake up at night and catch myself about to brain him, but so far so good."

Sylvia hauled off another load of rock and dumped it. Dusty had just about picked the floor clean enough to shovel again. Using a broom, he swept the shovel full, waited for Sylvia to return, and pitched it up into her empty wheelbarrow, then frowned at the hard-packed clay. He had finally found the room floor.

"That's it for fill. I'm down to the living surface, so from here on, everything's going to be *in situ.*"

"Got it, Boss man." Sylvia trundled away with the wheelbarrow.

He had just bent over to begin troweling when Sylvia called: "Yo!"

"What?" He looked up.

Sylvia brushed the twigs and rocks to the side in her screen and picked up a tiny bone fragment. As she held it up to the yellow light, she said, "Looks human to me."

She brought it over and handed it to him.

"Looks like a piece of deer skull to me, but let's ask the expert." He stepped over to the wall and called. "Dr. Cole, would you grace us with your opinion, please?"

Maureen said something to Steve, rose from the bucket, and tiptoed to the edge of the kiva. She stood in the shadow cast by the wall. He could see her Seneca heritage in every line of her face, her straight nose, full lips, the breadth of her cheekbones.

"Catch," he said, and tossed it to her. "And be careful."

She snagged it out of the air and frowned at the flat fragment of bone.

Steve watched Maureen thumb soil from the bone. His blue jeans had turned gray from the charcoal and soot, and the splotches of dirt-caked sweat on his brown shirt made it look as though it had been tie-dyed.

Sylvia said, "Dusty says deer bone. I say human. What's the verdict, Washais?"

Maureen turned the bone over in her hand. "I

think, Sylvia, you're a better archaeologist than your boss."

Dusty's brows lifted. "Yeah, why?"

Steve looked up mildly. "Don't I get to guess, *massa?*"

"No," Dusty said. "I'm not letting you make any more guesses until you learn to speak twentieth-century English."

"You mean like you do when you're drunk, Boss?" Sylvia asked.

Dusty scowled. "Okay, Maureen, what part of the human body is it?"

"The same part as your big 'bead,' Stewart: the skull." She leaned over the pit and frowned. "Where's the rest of it?"

"That's all we've uncovered. It was in the fill, but hold on."

Dusty jumped down into the excavation unit and picked up his trowel again. He didn't see anything on the surface, but he scraped around the place where he'd taken his last shovelful of dirt. The earth smelled damp and rich. In the corner, the soft soil indicated an intrusion in the prehistoric floor.

"Got a hole here."

Maureen and Steve climbed the aluminum ladder out of the kiva and perched on the wall next to Sylvia. All of them stared down at Dusty like vultures.

Dusty's trowel clanked on what sounded like a rock. He scraped the top of it clean, frowned, and began excavating around the object. Oblong, the quartzite river cobble had been battered on both ends.

"Hammer-stone," he said, then translated for

Maureen's benefit. "The ends took quite a bit of beating. Probably crushing nuts and seeds."

"What do you mean, probably?" Maureen asked.

Sylvia answered, "Well, we just found a crushed piece of skull, Washais." Maureen's Seneca name meant something scary like "ritual knife." "Somebody might have used that hammerstone to whack bone instead of acorns."

As he pulled dirt away from the artifact, Dusty added, "Don't forget that people ate each other down here, Doctor."

"The Cowboy Wash site is never far from my mind," Maureen muttered.

"Mark this one down in the books. She sort of agrees with me."

His trowel clicked in that distinctive way of metal meeting bone. Dusty reached for the brush sticking out of his back pocket and carefully whisked earth from around the smooth stone. A ring of bone beads, twenty centimeters wide, emerged.

He propped his elbows on his knees. "Well. Welcome to feature four. Sylvia, grab a handful of Ziplocs, the Sharpie pen, and the camera."

"On my way!"

Steve rubbed his jaw. "More evidence to support the cannibalism theory?"

"Not necessarily," Maureen said as she crouched on the wall. "Someone may have made beads out of the cranial bones, but that doesn't prove he ate the meat attached to the bones."

"Hmm," Steve said. "What do we have to find to prove they ate somebody here?"

"Two types of human blood in human feces would

be nice. Fragments of human bone would be even better." She paused thoughtfully. "Just like they found at the Cowboy Wash site."

Dusty said, "I always thought finding an intact foot in somebody's stomach would prove it conclusively."

Sylvia trotted up with the camera dangling from her neck, a wad of Ziplocs stuffed in her coat pocket, and the Sharpie pen hooked to her belt. "Here you go, Boss Man." She lifted the camera over her head and handed it down to him, then lowered the "feature kit" in its metal ammo box.

"Thanks." Dusty took the articles and positioned himself in front of the ring. He placed a one-by-two, painted black-and-white in centimeters, beside the feature for scale, arranged the north arrow, then jotted the details on the little chalkboard before adjusting the camera's focus. He took several bracketing shots.

Sylvia said, "That's a really strange feature. I mean, it looks symbolic, you know?"

"Symbolic?" Steve wiped his face on his sleeve. "You mean religious?"

"Yeah. Definitely religious."

Dusty handed the camera back to Sylvia, and said, "Plastic, please."

Sylvia pulled the Ziplocs from her pocket, gave him the wad, then handed Dusty the Sharpie pen.

Dusty troweled fresh dirt into a plastic bag for a floatation sample, and measured in the location. He reached for his line level and took the depth from the pit datum stake. As he pulled the cap off the Sharpie and labeled the bag, he said, "What makes you two think this is religious symbolism?"

Sylvia's freckled face seemed to light up. "Didn't

you ever read Mircea Eliade's book, *Patterns in Comparative Religion?* There's this really weird history of people connecting stones and bones. I mean, like, we all know that Southwestern tribes put rocks over the heads of people they don't like to keep their souls locked in the earth forever, but did you know that the Gonds tribe in India place a big rock on a grave to fasten down the dead person's soul? There are even people who speculate that we originally set a headstone on a grave to keep the soul in the body until the Second Coming. When the stone would be rolled away, a la Jesus, the person resurrected." Sylvia glanced around the pit. "Cool, huh?"

Steve gave her a deadpan look. "You took another philosophy class last semester, didn't you, Sylvia?"

"Religious studies," she corrected. "Anyway, this feature is even neater because many people associate stones with giving birth. Childless women among the Maidu tribe in California touch a rock shaped like a pregnant woman to get knocked up, and in parts of Europe young couples have to walk on certain stones to make their union fruitful. In Madagascar, women who want to have a child smear stones with grease."

Steve paused, and his bushy black brows pulled together. "Then what?"

Sylvia frowned. "What do you mean?"

"After they smear the stones. Then what?"

As his meaning dawned, Sylvia said, "Nah, I don't think so. I mean, if they do, nobody's ever recorded it. And somebody would have. Anthropologists are kinky."

"Kahunga!" Steve raised a fist, then jerked it downwards in approval. "By now they would have been nicknamed Mazola Rocks."

Maureen made a disgusted sound, jumped down into the room with Dusty, and edged him aside. "If you don't mind, could I take a look?"

"Why, certainly, Doctor. Besides, you're already here." He leaned back against the room wall.

Maureen's hair caught the sunlight. He took a moment to admire the way it glistened and wondered what it would be like to touch silky hair like that.

Her brows lowered. "These are virtually identical to the bone bead you showed me in Durango, Stewart, including the ground edges." She took his paintbrush, bent over the bone beads, and carefully whisked dirt away from the edges. "I'd say the bones were not cooked, though there are distinct cut marks on the larger fragments."

"You don't have to cook the bones to be a cannibal," Steve said. "You can crack the skull, shake out the brain, eat it, and toss the bones."

Dusty nodded. "He's right."

"Yes, well, you've still got to convince me this is a cannibal act," Maureen responded. "Even more curious is a cannibal who smashes the skull, grinds fragments into beads, then reassembles them around a large stone. As if they were a respresentation of a skull."

Dusty's smile faded. He dropped to one knee and stared at the bone fragments. "What are you talking about? The circle isn't in the shape of a skull."

"He didn't use all of the pieces, Stewart, just the callot, the upper part of the braincase." She drew a line across her own eyebrows and then around the back of her skull. "And these fragments are in anatomical order. Pieces taken from the frontal bone, parietals, and occipital all laid out in place."

Sylvia's green eyes widened. "Wow. I wonder what that means? Maybe the stone symbolizes a child in the womb."

"Or a rock for a brain," Dusty said.

"I'd guess a penis in a vagina," Steve suggested.

Sylvia squinted at the rock. "Boy, if so, that guy had real delusions of grandeur."

Maureen stood up. "I don't think we have enough information to speculate, folks. We need to finish the excavation. We've just uncovered the top."

"That's the first sensible thing I've heard." Dusty stuck his thumbs in his back pockets. "This has been here for eight hundred years. It could just be that freeze-thaw cycles moved the bone out from the stone."

Sylvia rose and dusted her pants off. "Why don't you let me dig for a while, Dusty? You've been pitching rock out of there all day."

Dusty braced his hands on the wall and climbed out over the unexcavated rubble filling the rest of the room. As he reached for his camo vest, he said, "Just keep in mind that the good doctor is going to be hanging over the pit. If you chip a single bone, I'll have to shove a stick in her mouth to keep her from biting off her tongue."

"I'll be careful." Sylvia leaped into the pit and pulled her trowel from her back pocket.

Dusty smiled across at Maureen, but she didn't see him. Two upright lines formed between her brows as she studied the ring of beads.

Dusty turned to Steve. "Hand me that bucket. Sylvia can trowel the dirt into it and hand the bucket up instead of using the shovel."

"On my way."

Steve followed the line of planks to where the bucket sat canted at the edge of the back-dirt pile.

Sylvia spent a few minutes carefully troweling down around the rock inside the bone ring. No one said anything until Sylvia's trowel struck something beneath the stone.

"Whoa, Sylvia," Dusty said, kneeling to get a closer look. "What did you hit?"

Sylvia reached for the brush and gently removed the dirt clinging to the object. "Looks like a pot rim to me, boss."

Steve bent forward and braced his hands on his knees. "The rock is resting on top of a pot?"

Dusty and Maureen exchanged a worried glance, memories of 10K3 resurfacing in their minds.

Maureen said, "You don't think—"

"I hope not."

Sylvia looked up. "I'll bet you five bucks it is."

"Is what?" Steve asked in confusion.

"Corpse powder," Sylvia said.

Steve straightened. "You mean, like among the Navajo? The stuff witches use to kill and make people sick? Why would you think that?"

Dusty said, "Remember 10K3? August before last we found a pot in a burial, and it was definitely filled with powdered people. Our local Keres monitor said she thought it was the work of a witch. But"—he pointed a finger at Sylvia—"that's purely speculation right now, Sylvia. You might just have a rim sherd. Keep working."

She gave him a military salute and went back to troweling.

"Powdered people? No kidding?" Steve's ebony

face shone with sweat. He wiped his forehead on his sleeve. "None of you died, I notice. Anybody puke their guts out?"

"Nope," Sylvia called up. "Mrs. Walking Hawk cleansed us in pinyon pine smoke. The evil spirits couldn't stick to us—" She stopped suddenly. "Hey, folks, I've definitely got a pot down here. See this?" She used the tip of her trowel to point to the rounded side of the black-on-white pot. "It's a little pot. About ten centimeters across."

Dusty gestured to the tape measure resting to Sylvia's left. "I'd like something a little more definitive, if it won't trouble you, Dr. Rhone."

Sylvia reached for the tape, measured the rim first, then the pot. "Yep! Ten centimeters. Am I a precision instrument or what?"

She set the tape aside, made notes in the unit notebook, and troweled around between the rock and the pot. When she'd moved enough dirt that everyone could clearly see the ceramic vessel, she said, "I'm not sure, but I think the rock is stuck to the top of the pot."

"Son of a bitch!" Dusty leaped into the pit with his trowel and said, "Move over, I need some room."

Sylvia shrank back against the fitted stone wall. "Careful," she warned. "That looks like pine pitch glue."

Dusty gently troweled and brushed until he'd exposed the base of the pot. "Come on, people. I need light." He went through the ritual of recording, then carefully lifted the small round pot out with the rock intact. "Sylvia, bag this," he said, and handed it to her.

"Gotcha." Sylvia slipped it into a Ziploc and used a

Sharpie pen to write the provenience on the outside of the bag.

Dusty climbed out and took the bag. Everyone around the partially excavated room went quiet, staring at him.

"What do you think it is?" Steve asked.

"I don't know," Sylvia said, "but I'm not sure we should open it up out here. You know, without adult supervision. Maybe we should call Magpie and have her bring out an elder—"

"I think we'll be safe on our own," Dusty told her. "This is probably a cache of beads or projectile points. Something harmless. Until we have evidence that it's a dangerous artifact, I'm sure we can handle it."

Sylvia whispered something to Steve from the corner of her mouth, and Steve's brows went up.

Dusty asked, "What was that?"

"Oh, I was just telling Steve about that time in Wyoming when you said you could handle big Bob Deercapture. Remember? He said he could pee farther than you, and you told him he couldn't. The problem was, it was fifty-six below zero, and Dusty turned kind of fast before he zipped and accidentally touched the side of the Bronco. I mean, who in the Southwest knows that warm wet parts will stick to metal when it's that cold?"

Steve shuddered. "Ouch. When I was little, my mother told me not to stick my tongue to ice trays or my head would freeze solid. I bet it's kind of the same thing."

"I *don't* think so," Dusty said, aware that Maureen's eyebrow had risen in a look of amazed disbelief.

Sylvia tucked a tendril of stray brown hair up under

her woolen cap. "Actually, it was no big deal. We just heated up a teapot and steamed it off. It would have gone a lot faster if Dusty hadn't been such a crybaby—"

"Good God, Sylvia," Dusty said. "Do you really have to go into the details?"

"But people can learn real-life lessons from stuff like this, Dusty. I mean, if your mother had told you about ice trays when you were a child, you'd have one less scar."

Maureen folded her arms. "A little like the incident in Cortez, eh, Stewart?"

Steve looked inquisitively from one person to the next. "She knows about Muffet?"

"Oh, come on!" Sylvia said. "Everyone in archaeology knows about Muffet."

Dusty got to his feet. It was the one and only time in his life that he'd danced with a stripper. And the last time he'd touched gin. "It's quitting time. Tarp the pits. Maureen and I will take the pot back to camp and get dinner started while you two clean up and stow gear."

Dusty climbed out of the room and stalked toward camp.

Behind him, he heard Steve whisper, then Sylvia said, "Yeah, well, he's really sensitive about that story. It's kind of the defining moment of his life."

As evening draped the land, the juniper grove behind their field camp went from dark green to black. Maureen sighed as she watched the world change. The long shadows began to disappear, fading into the night. The ancient pueblo became nothing more than a gray mound of rubble dotted with black squares of plastic.

"How are you doing with the lantern?" Dusty asked as he stepped into the trailer.

He had just finished arranging kindling for a fire after dinner. Tall and sun-bronzed, his form filled the doorway.

"I'm working on it, Stewart," she said as she picked up the matchbook. "Don't worry. I've started a few lanterns in my life."

"You pumped it up, right?"

"Right," she answered in irritation, struck a match, and held it below the mantles as she turned up the gas. The mantles caught in a *whoosh* and pulsing white light illuminated the artifacts and bones bagged on the square table. She smiled, suspecting that some of the most precious artifacts in southwestern archaeology had rested on the little Formica table.

"Thanks," Dusty said. "You want to get dinner started? Anything you want."

Maureen's brows lifted. "Anything I want?"

"Well, anything we have. Your selection is somewhat limited due to the fact that we did most of the shopping in Bloomfield. No caviar or escargots, I'm afraid."

She propped a hand on the table. "That's very creative, Stewart. I've never heard it pronounced *es-car-guts.*"

She walked out of the trailer and crossed to the supply tent. Boxes lined the walls. Each brimmed with different shapes and sizes of cans, bottles, bags of chips, and many things she couldn't make out in the dim light. She opened one of the coolers and peered inside. She found a package of meat, sniffed it, and cringed. The celery reminded her of Phil—really limp and sort of slimy. Giving it up as a lost cause, she turned to the cardboard boxes.

Stewart looked up when Maureen climbed into the trailer. Lantern light glinted in his beard, accenting his handsome face. "What did you pick?"

"Something called Dinty Moore's beef stew."

Stewart shuddered. "No wonder you get along with Sylvia."

"You don't like it?" She started to back out of the trailer.

"No, it's all right. I'll eat it. My backbone's rubbing my navel."

Maureen stopped in front of the stove and set the

supplies down. As she removed things from the pot and put them on the vinyl counter, Dusty said: "Isn't there a package of pork chops out there?"

"Remember the pot of powdered people from $10K_3$?"

He gave her a suspicious look. "How could I forget it?"

"The contents of that pot were in better shape than the pork chops in the cooler."

"Ah." Dusty nodded. "Right. We have to get ice the next time we go into town. Like tomorrow. We can wash our clothes at the same time." He looked around the trailer. "Let me see, what do we have to go with this stew? Crackers?"

"Not unless you like those awful little cheesy fishies that Sylvia prizes. That's the closest thing we have to crackers."

He opened the refrigerator and removed a loaf of dark rye bread. "Then I'm going to eat this." He set the loaf on top of the counter. "You can share if you want."

"Looks good to me."

Voices drifted in from the darkness as Sylvia and Steve washed off at the water jug outside. Someone smart, probably Steve, had a flashlight. The beam played around the camp.

Maureen used a match to start the stove burner, found a can opener in the drawer, and poured the stew into an aluminum pot that she had rummaged out of a cupboard. "Here come the hungry hordes."

Stewart nodded. "I see 'em. I'll bet Sylvia wants a Coors Light." He reached into the red ice chest and dredged out a dripping can of Coors Light and a draft

Guinness. He set the Coors on the table and popped the top on his Guinness. "Ah, the gift of the gods."

"Canned Guinness, Stewart?" Maureen lifted an eyebrow. "Sacrilege. Your genes should know it even if your tastebuds don't."

Dusty slipped into the booth and studied the black-and-white pot, propped so that the rock didn't overbalance it. He pushed the ratty brown cowboy hat back on his head and said, "Somebody had better get the coffee going."

Maureen's brows lowered. "Just who did you think that would be? I made the stew."

"You did not. Dinty Moore did. You opened cans and poured them into a pot. Besides, you're the coffee drinker."

Maureen sighed. "Good point. Okay, where's the coffee?"

He was staring at the black-on-white pot where it rested on the table, his blue eyes gleaming, but he pointed. "Cupboard to your right. You'll find everything you need on the bottom shelf."

She opened it, took out the battered, soot-coated coffeepot and red bag of New Mexico Pinon Nut Coffee. The water came from a six-gallon blue plastic jug on the floor.

Sylvia and Steve opened the flimsy aluminum door and stepped in.

"Boy, what a day," Steve said. He brushed at his brown nylon coat sleeves, and a sparkling fog floated up.

Sylvia coughed and waved at it as she walked through. "God. Quit that. I feel like Lawrence of Arabia."

"It's down to forty degrees, Rhone," Steve said. "I doubt that."

"Did you get the equipment stowed in the ammo boxes?" Dusty asked.

They used metal ammo boxes to keep most of their equipment safe: the trowels, brushes, dental picks, line levels, compasses, and the camera.

"Yuppers, Boss man," Steve said. He sank into the booth and pulled a bottle of Anchor Steam beer out of his pocket. Using his Swiss Army knife, he uncapped it.

Sylvia spied the Coors Light on the table. "A beer! I'm saved. Thanks, Dusty." She grabbed it and slid in beside Steve. Brown hair had escaped her gray knit cap and framed her face with damp ringlets. It made her pointed nose look long and sharp.

"Hey!" Sylvia blurted. "Where are my cheezy fishes? Aren't there any in the trailer?"

Dusty called, "Well, I guarantee I'm not the culprit. You'd have to tie me up and poke them down my throat with a stick before I'd eat one of those things."

A pause, then Sylvia said: "God. You don't think I ate them all, do you? There's nothing better than cheezy fishes in beef stew. You know, yellow and brown."

Dusty said, "You're the only woman in the world who evaluates food based on a Munsell color chart."

Steve smiled and turned to Maureen. "Are we going to open the pot tonight?"

"Ask the P.I." Maureen poured coffee into the basket, clamped the lid down, and set the pot on the burner.

Sand could be seen sprinkled in Steve's neatly

trimmed black hair, shimmering in the lantern light. "Mister Principal Investigator, sir?"

Dusty took a swig from his Guinness and said, "I thought once we had dinner going, we'd tend to it."

Sylvia shivered. "Gonna be a cool one tonight. God, I hate climbing into a freezing sleeping bag. The first few minutes are enough to make me change my major to accounting."

Maureen stirred the stew and turned from the stove with the wooden spoon in her hand. She aimed it at Dusty. "I don't understand why we can't go into town on cold nights like this and rent a hotel room. We're getting seventy-five dollars a day per diem, for God's sakes. Wouldn't any one else like a real shower?"

Sylvia stopped halfway through chugging her beer. "You mean you'd rather sleep in a stucco box, breathing recycled air, than in a tent where you can smell the cedar fire and sage all night?"

Steve added, "You'd rather wake up to the kids next door screaming than birds singing and coyotes howling?"

Dusty smiled at her, as if in victory. "Yes. Just what sort of uncivilized barbarian are you, Dr. Cole?"

Maureen shook her head. "Never mind."

She would never understand archaeologists. Oh, she loved nature, too, but not at the expense of frozen body parts. "It just seems silly to me that we—"

As if to mock her, somewhere out in the desert a lone coyote yipped, paused, then yipped again, and down in the river bottom a whole pack broke into song. Their beautiful lilting voices serenaded the night for several minutes, then the soft evening breeze replaced it.

Everybody at the table gazed at Maureen with wide eyes.

"I don't care," she said. "I'd still like a shower." She pulled at her waistband, feeling sand.

Dusty leaned forward. "I'll make you a deal. We need to pull the bone bed on the kiva roof. If we can do that, and open the kiva floor by Friday, I'll rent us luxurious rooms at the Holiday Inn in Farmington. What do you say?"

"I say, hallelujah."

"I don't know," Steve said. "That's a lot of careful recording to do in three days, boss, and a lot of that bone is burned. Delicate stuff. The old days of chucking bones into paper bags and calling it quits are long gone."

Dusty leaned back. "Yeah. Thank God. I still cringe when I think about the data they wasted back in the good ol' days."

Maureen checked the stove. "Well, the stew's boiling. I say we let it simmer for a few minutes, and open that pot."

Dusty took a long drink of Guinness, set his empty can down, and lurched to his feet. "I will assist you, Dr. Cole.

Maureen turned to the door. "I have to get my field kit."

She stepped out into the night and walked to her tent. White lantern light cast by the trailer windows threw beautiful patterns on the brown nylon walls. She kneeled, reached through the tent flap, and pulled her black field bag from the corner.

As she stepped back into the trailer, Sylvia said, "If we find dried flakes of humans in there, what are we going to do? Notify the regional tribes, or sew our lips shut?"

"My opinion is that we sew our lips shut and do the necessary scientific work to analyze it," Maureen said, and set her field bag on the table beside the small black-and-white pot. "This is private land, right? We don't have to abide by the same insane rules that we would on Crown land."

"That's *public* land here, Washais," Sylvia pointed out.

Dusty made an appeasing gesture with his hands. "Shh. If word ever got out that we'd discovered a pot of corpse powder and didn't tell anyone, I'd be accused by the traditionals of endangering the life of every person I came in contact with. I'd lose a lot of the trust that I've built over the years. People would run when they saw me coming."

"That happens now, Stewart," Maureen said.

He continued as if he hadn't heard: "If we find anything suspicious in that pot, I'm calling Maggie Walking Hawk Taylor."

Maureen opened her field bag. They'd had this argument before. But there was no sense in getting into a shouting match with him. Better to wait and see what happened.

"What?" Dusty said. "No scorching rebuttal from the physical anthropologist?"

"I'll fight that battle *if* the time comes, Stewart. For now, I'm more interested in what's in the pot than arguing with you."

Maureen pulled a stainless-steel scalpel from her bag. She lowered the sharp tip to the black ring of pitch that sealed the rock to the top of the pot, and the metal flashed in the lantern light. "Could you hold the pot still?"

He wrapped both hands around the pot, steadying it while Maureen scraped at the pitch. Their hands touched. Long hours in the dirt and sun had roughened his skin, but it felt warm against her cold hands. When she'd etched a hole through the pitch, she said, "Curtain time."

Steve and Sylvia leaned forward. Anticipation turned the very air electric. Sylvia's green eyes sparkled. Steve looked as if he were holding his breath.

"Well?" Dusty said. "I'm ready for the opening act."

Maureen wedged her scalpel in the hole and slowly worked around the edge, severing the rock from the pot.

"I could just twist that off, you know," Dusty informed her.

"I'm sure you could, Stewart." Very gently, Maureen sawed through the last of the hardened pitch and rested her scalpel on the table. She gripped the big rock with both hands and carefully lifted.

"What is it?" Steve asked, trying to peer inside. "What's in there?"

Dusty's blue eyes narrowed as he scrutinized the interior. He lifted the pot, tipped it sideways, then set it down again. "Nothing."

"What do you mean, nothing?" Sylvia braced her hands on the table and leaned over to look inside.

Maureen frowned at the clay-colored interior. She didn't even see any residue, though the poor light could be hiding many things from her view. She said, "Who's the hunched-over character painted on the bottom of the pot?"

Sylvia answered, "Kokopelli, the humpbacked flute

player. He's big in the Southwest, and much older than the katchinas. From about A.D. 200 to 1150, his image was everywhere, etched into rocks, painted on bowls like this one, even carved into kiva floors."

"Okay, but what is he? Is he a god?"

Dusty said, "Kokopelli and Kokopelli Mana, the male and female humpbacked flute players, apparently embody the creative power of the universe."

"Big medicine," Steve said in a quiet, reverent voice, "until the katchinas came along."

Maureen looked back at the pot. "I don't understand. They put a big rock on top of this pot, sealed it with pine pitch, and there's nothing inside? Why would someone do that?"

"Kokopelli's inside." Dusty ground his teeth for a few moments. "And maybe he's not alone, or I should say, he *wasn't* alone."

Steve's dark eyes went back and forth between Dusty and Maureen. "Is this some cultural tradition I don't—"

"Oh, I get it," Sylvia said, and grinned. "We just let a ghost out of the pot, right? A ghost that Kokopelli was supposed to be regenerating, or, maybe, reincarnating?"

Dusty fingered his beard thoughtfully. "Maybe."

"God, I love ghost stories," Sylvia said. "I hope it doesn't fly around shrieking and wailing. I'm really tired tonight."

Maureen set the rock down on the table and picked up the pot. She tipped it to the lantern light, studying the interior pot walls. "If you want my opinion, I think that whatever was in this pot evaporated. I'll let you know tomorrow."

"How?" Dusty said. "What are you going to do?"

"I'm going to scrape the interior of the pot and put it under my microscope, Stewart. It's a little scientific process that physical anthropologists use to kill ghosts."

The beef stew bubbled over and started spattering the stove top.

"Stew's ready, folks," Sylvia said. "Let's kill ghosts later."

Browser stood in the trees above the river, his eyes on Obsidian. She walked the trail below with another woman and a tall man. She was smiling, her white cape swaying around her tall body. Morning sunlight flashed from the wealth of long black hair that fell from her hood. She walked slowly, her gaze on the trail, but an eerie faraway gleam lit her eyes. The man and woman beside her proceeded with their heads down, as though grieving. Their white hoods hid their faces, but Browser might not have known them anyway. Many of the people who'd come for the burial were strangers.

Browser removed his white ritual cape and draped it on a branch to his left. His red knee-length war shirt would not keep him warm, but he needed to feel alive this morning. Death breathed all around him, stalking the land on silent feet.

Obsidian had stood rigid through the burial. She hadn't joined in the sacred Songs or Dances. She had made no effort to help send the Matron on a safe journey to the Land of the Dead. She'd caught Browser's attention when the katsinas Danced and everyone else had lifted their arms in praise. Obsidian hadn't moved. She'd stared unblinking at the Matron's body on the burial ladder.

Browser leaned a shoulder against the trunk of a towering cottonwood and wondered at that.

Obsidian and her friends passed through the dappled sunlight forty hands below, and the precious stones on her wrists glittered. She moved with uncommon grace for such a tall, slender woman.

As if she felt his gaze, Obsidian stopped, then tipped her pointed chin up. Her dark eyes met his like a clash of war clubs.

"Watching me, War Chief?" she asked in a voice just barely loud enough for him to hear.

"Watching the trail, Obsidian."

"Indeed? I would think any warrior could do that. A great War Chief should limit himself to more important duties, like guarding our village."

"Several of the elders are at the grave. I wish to make certain they have no trouble getting back."

"Then you are alone up there?"

"I am."

Obsidian touched the strange woman's hand, then tugged up the hem of her white cape and climbed the bank toward Browser; her steps were as fluid as those of a Dancer. Her hood waffled in the breeze, shielding her face. The strangers continued down the trail toward the village.

Browser straightened and lowered his arms. The idea of being alone with Obsidian tore at his insides like talons. He tried not to rest his hand on his war club. As she approached, he called, "How may I be of service?"

Obsidian halted two paces away, her huge, haunted eyes on him, jet black and warm, very warm. He did not know what to think of her. He had never known a woman whose mood could change so quickly. One instant she could look at him like this, and the next instant she could turn to ice. She threw back her hood and tiny turquoise pins twinkled through the endless midnight of her hair.

Browser said, "What is it you wish?"

"Just to talk with you, War Chief."

She walked closer and loosened the ties on her cape, revealing the rich blue dress beneath and the swells of her breasts. Browser felt suddenly starved for air. He could feel the warmth of her body and smell the sweet scent of blazing star petals that clung to her clothing.

"Talk about what, Obsidian?"

Her elegant brows lifted. "You're not afraid of me, are you, War Chief? What have I done to make you feel that way?"

Browser's stomach muscles tightened. There were times, like now, when he swore she was not the same woman he'd spoken to earlier. Her voice had turned deep and husky. Her eyes had a feral glint. "What do you *want,* Obsidian?"

A flock of ravens soared over the treetops, cawing and diving.

Obsidian lowered her eyes to his chest, and her gaze traced the muscles, then moved to his arms and legs, as if seeing beneath his red war shirt.

Browser was burningly aware of her. He clenched his fists. "If you came to speak with me, then speak."

Her eyes returned to his, faintly amused. "Where is it?"

"What?"

"I think you know."

His blood pulsed through his body. He'd left his buckskin cape in his chamber draped over his bedding hides. She couldn't know. Could she?

"What are you talking about?"

Obsidian moved to less than a hand's breadth from him. Her swaying cape patted his legs as she examined Browser's face in minute detail, and the aching need in her eyes made his breathing go shallow. Her lips parted invitingly.

"I have something I would like to show you, War Chief," she whispered, and toyed with the fringes on his shirt. "Will you accompany me back to my chamber?"

"I have duties, Obsidian."

"Later, then?"

As Wind Baby gusted through the trees, she caught the dark cloud of her flying hair and held it until the gust passed, then she released the hair and let it fall freely over her shoulders.

Browser propped his hands on his hips. Curious, he asked, "Who are you, Obsidian? Where do you come from?"

"I am from here, War Chief. Longtail Clan."

"You were born here?"

She touched Browser's hand, and her fingers felt cool and soft. His skin tingled. "Perhaps we could meet tonight when you return to the village?"

He pulled his hand away. "Perhaps you could answer my question."

"Why do you care where I was born, War Chief?"

"I care because I have never heard you speak about it, and generally if someone does not speak of their home it is because they are hiding something."

"Hmm," she said, and laughed softly. "I never heard your Matron speak of her home. Is that what you really mean? You think she was hiding something?"

The words left Browser floundering. Was that what he'd meant? Perhaps his souls had started down the twists and turns of the maze left by Flame Carrier's death, and he was just taking his anger out on Obsidian? He looked into her eyes and felt a deep swallowing nothingness.

Browser pulled his ritual cape from the branch. "Good day, Obsidian."

He walked past her.

Obsidian laughed and called after him, "I will see you later!"

~

Dusty stared down into his coffee, feeling oddly self-conscious. He tapped the table with his fingers and glanced away at the soft pastel colors of the Holiday Inn dining room in Farmington. He and Maureen had spent the morning shopping for the camp and doing their laundry. It had been pleasant. He glanced at her sitting across from him, then looked around the room. The place, like so many in the Southwest, had been decorated in pseudo-adobe with patterned upholstery that echoed indigenous designs.

The Navajo waitress was polishing the brass railing on the low adobe wall that separated the buffet from the dining room.

"Boy, I needed this." Maureen cupped the white ceramic cup in her cold fingers and sipped at the hot coffee. Her long black braid fell over her left shoulder. She wore a cream-colored wool sweater over a black turtleneck, with black jeans. "That wind has a bit of a bite, eh?"

Dusty smiled. "The wind doesn't blow in Ontario?"

"On occasion, but not like this."

He settled back in the chair and stared out the window at the parking lot where grimy pickups had nosed into the spaces.

Dusty lifted a hand. "You get used to the wind after a while. You only get worried when the branches start cracking off the trees."

Maureen laughed. "You know, I've been listening to you all morning, talking about the Anasazi and the modern Puebloan peoples. You speak very passionately for a White guy."

"The Southwest has been the centerpiece of my life. I have a tie to the Pueblos that not even I understand fully."

She set her coffee cup down and peered across the table at him, studying him with that scientist's eye that he both loved and despised. "You mean because you were initiated into a kiva?"

"Partly, yes. But my fascination goes deeper." How on earth did he tell her about things that lived so quietly in his heart? "I guess it started when I was a kid on Dad's digs. I was always too curious, in trouble a lot, but I learned early that you didn't trip over the grid strings, didn't fool around on the pit walls. Believe me, you don't want to deal with the consequences of collapsing one. Not on Dad's digs—or even worse on one of Dale's. And never ever touch the pottery, let alone pick it up. We still found a lot of whole pots back in those days."

Maureen nodded, as though encouraging him to continue. "So what did you play with when you were out in the field? You were a kid, after all."

"Mostly I wandered around playing with things like grinding stones and flakes. I couldn't break them. I'd pretend I was grinding corn in the mealing bins. I'd build my own little pueblos out of the stones. At least until the walls collapsed. Those Anasazi masons were a lot better builders than I was. Sometimes I'd go into excavated rooms and just sit there in the silence. I'd listen, trying hard to hear them."

He slowly shook his head and gave her a hesitant smile. "Maybe it was a kid's imagination, but I could close my eyes and see them. At least they looked like I thought they should. Like the Indians I knew from the pueblos, but wearing different clothes, with different hairstyles."

Maureen's brows lifted. "Really? Did they talk to you?"

"Sometimes."

She frowned down into her coffee. "I thought I heard voices the first time I went to Sainte Marie Among the Huron. They've reconstructed a longhouse at one of the original Jesuit Missions in Ontario. It's magnificent. I swear I could hear them speaking Iroquois, but with a strange accent. I suppose you'd say it was like coming home."

For a moment they were silent, watching each other, measuring each other's responses.

Finally, Dusty said, "That's a curious admission, Doctor. I thought you didn't believe in spooks?" He said it teasingly, but she obviously took it seriously. Her expression tensed.

Maureen smoothed her fingers over the tabletop, as if buying time while she tried to figure out how to answer him. "I don't. But I wonder if some places don't absorb memories in the same way we do. I—"

"You don't have to explain." He lifted a hand to halt her. "The walls in Chaco Canyon often speak to me. I may be a White guy, but my soul is tied to the people here, the old ones. I've tried to explain that I can sense them, but few people believe me."

"Oh, I'll bet that goes over big with the Native folk."

"It depends. Some, like Maggie Walking Hawk Taylor, understand. Others, all they see is the skin on the outside and forget that we're all human beings inside. That you can really care who people were five or six hundred, or a thousand years ago. Just because you don't happen to be a direct descendant doesn't mean that they can't talk to you. It's, well..."

He gave her a probing look. "When I stand over something like that bone bed, I don't see science, Doctor. I see people, and I wonder at their pain and their desperation. I care what happened to them."

The wind hurled itself against the window, and the pane rattled. The trucks in the parking lot seemed to ripple, as though not quite real.

Maureen said, "Do you feel the same way about your European ancestors?"

Dusty thought about that. "I went to a conference

in Paris a few years ago. I wandered into Notre-Dame, and I felt nothing. It was sterile. Dead. Sure, it was a beautiful building, and the rose window was stunning, but it wasn't mine. In Brussels, they have this really neat site under the street in front of St. Michael's Church. The bones of the monks are still sticking out of the excavation units. I looked at them and felt nothing. That connection to those people just isn't there for me. They're strangers. Their spirits don't talk the language of my soul." He paused. "Am I sounding hokey yet?"

"Not yet." She sipped her coffee, and he found himself wishing that they could both let down their guards for just a little while. But he couldn't do it first.

Maureen slipped two fingers through the handle of her coffee cup and pulled it closer. "Maybe it's because half of me is Seneca, but if there really is a Spirit World, the Spirits should be able to talk to whomever they wish. No matter what your racial or ethnic heritage." Her lips tightened, then she said, "Not everybody agrees with me, of course."

"How's that?"

"Oh, two years ago I got hate mail from some Mohawks. They told me in no uncertain terms that they didn't want any 'science' done on their ancestors' bones." Her fingers traced a pattern on the tabletop. "The thing is those skeletal 'people' in my lab are important to me. Sure, I measured, analyzed, and took samples. But I had the feeling that they really wanted to teach me about who they were and tell me what had happened to them. Isn't that what elders do? Teach? I think we should use science as a means of understanding the world. I really believe, unlike a lot of my colleagues in the First Nations, that science is another way of knowing. The best way."

"How Western of you."

"How Indian of you to argue in opposition."

He raised his hands. "Whoa! Remember me? I'm on your side."

"Really?" Her brows quirked as though amazed to hear that. "If you'll recall, you sided with Indian religious fundamentalists and left most of the bodies in the ground at 10K3."

"No, I didn't, Doctor. I sided with Elder Hail Walking Hawk. There's a big difference. If it had been a bunch of angry kids with placards, I would have known they weren't for real and probably would have finished the excavation. Or if they were rabid activists pulling a power play for political reasons. Hail Walking Hawk saw something there that I didn't, and I respected her *knowledge*." He lowered his voice. "Even if it wasn't scientific knowledge."

Maureen's fingers tightened into a fist on the table-top. "Science isn't the only way of knowing. I've never said that."

He took a breath and wadded up his paper napkin. "No, but sometimes I think you mean it anyway. I grew up between two worlds, Maureen: mine and yours. When I was kid, this old Hopi—"

"The one who initiated you into the kiva?"

"That's him."

"What happened?"

"In the kiva?"

"Yes. I'd really like to know."

He felt his brow tighten and forced himself to relax. "This may sound funny, but it was a very private, very personal experience. The journey that I went on can't be related to anyone. The rituals that I underwent aren't for the uninitiated. In short, it's not mine to tell. Not only did I take a solemn vow, but it's my compact with the beings who shared their time with me. Have you had an experience like that? A supernatural visitation?"

Maureen touched the crucifix around her throat. Tugged at it, then said, "Four years ago, after the death of my husband, I had terrifying nightmares about the *Gaasyendietha,* the meteor fire dragons of Seneca mythology. The dragons traveled behind me in my dreams, walking as torches of light. Father Gaha, himself a Seneca, but also a Catholic, helped me to decipher the dream, to understand that the *Gaasyendi-etha* were not chasing me but trying to befriend me, to light my way through the darkness of losing John." She released her crucifix and smoothed her fingers over her cup. "Yes, I think I understand."

A flock of pinyon jaws landed outside the window, cawing and trilling in beautiful voices as they strutted over the dead grass that framed the parking lot.

Dusty fiddled with the napkin on the table, shoving it around. "Do you recall when Hail Walking Hawk told you that she saw a man behind you? A man with light brown hair and green eyes?"

Maureen nodded. "I'll never forget it. She described John perfectly."

"I spoke with Hail about it after you walked out to look at the site. She said that he had loved you very much. Maggie later told me that Hail had seen John moving in a blue glow."

Maureen smiled down into her cup, as though the words comforted her.

Dusty wouldn't tell Maureen the rest. Hail had also said that these things were very hard, but it was too bad John was still in this world. *"His soul ought to be in the Land of the Dead by now."*

Dusty sipped his coffee. "Do you think he's still there, behind you?"

Maureen looked up. "Grief makes you think strange things. At night just before I fall asleep, I often hear his voice. It's so loud it wakes me." She paused. "I feel him there, too. Watching over me. I can't explain it, but it's a very intimate experience, as though our souls actually touch." Warmth filled her eyes.

"I was once told that death is the most personal experience you will ever have. It's about the only thing in Western culture that isn't shared with other people. It can't be shared. When you die, even if it's in a multitude like a plane crash or a gas chamber at Auschwitz, you're still alone at that final instant." He made a smoothing motion with his hand. "My initiation into the kiva was that way. The most intimate experience I've ever had."

She seemed to absorb that without the skepticism he usually saw in women's eyes. Not that he'd told that many, but the few that he had always wanted to pry away at it. As if he were keeping some secret from them. That true intimacy meant spilling the whole story, betraying the trust of his Spirit Helpers.

"Do you go to your kiva often?"

He tilted his head. "My clan is dead, Doctor."

Her open mouth asked the question.

"My mentor and his uncle were the last of their

clan." Dusty took a swig of his coffee. "You have to understand, in this country, among the peoples here, a clan owns certain rituals. Well, 'owns' isn't the right word. Let's say, 'were given certain rituals,' since it was a two-way relationship. Sometimes, because of disease, accidents, infertility, or whatever cause, clans die out. When they do, the rituals, the kivas, the sacred knowledge, die with them."

"That happened when your mentor died?"

He nodded. "There are three of us left. One is in the penitentiary outside of Buckeye, Arizona. He stuck a knife into the man who was living with his wife. The other is sober on those rare occasions when he can't find anything to hock or any White tourists to buy him a drink."

"So, the clan's not dead. There are three of you left."

Dusty gave her a pained smile. God, how he wished that were true. "I was initiated into the kiva, Maureen, not adopted into the clan. Even if I had been adopted, it wouldn't matter. The clan effectively 'died' when the last female died. In this case, my mentor's sister. Hopi are matrilineal."

"Right." Her slim fingers danced on the cup handle. "But you still have the rituals inside you, Dusty."

"I was initiated, Doctor, not trained. I didn't earn the knowledge or permission to conduct the rituals. Neither did the other guys. In fact, I think they were initiated because it was the thing to do. Kind of like a lot of White kids go through confirmation even if they don't believe Jesus is their personal savior."

Her hand returned to her crucifix. She touched the silver body of Jesus in the same way that Dusty would have touched a kachina mask—as though she could feel the Power there and was grateful. "I understand. In fact, I wish I'd listened more to my mother. Attended more of the dances and prayer meetings. But trying to make time, first as a student, then in the struggle from assistant professor to full professor, not to mention all the other crap you have to do." She shook her head. "Modern life ain't all that it's cracked up to be, Stewart."

"Oh, yes, it is," he told her. "At least for this one golden moment between world wars. You go to bed every night knowing that you'll probably be alive in the morning. You don't spend every day with the knowledge that someone out there is trying to kill you, that your world is about to end in fire, death, or terror. You have health, security, safety, and hope. You know that your stomach will be full tomorrow, and the day after that, and the day after that for as far as you can see. You know that you'll have a roof over your head, that you'll be warm and have plenty to drink. If you break your leg tomorrow, even with a compound fracture, you're not going to die after a month's prolonged agony like you would have even one hundred and fifty years ago. An abscessed tooth won't leave pus dripping into your mouth for six months until it falls out. You can step onto a jet tomorrow that will allow you to attend a seminar halfway across the globe. In short, Doctor, it's a wonderful time to be alive." He took a long drink of coffee. "Or would you rather live here in the thirteenth century, when a world was falling into an apocalypse that it would never recover from?"

"You're right, Stewart. Sometimes we lose sight of how good life is. We just can't imagine that anything could be worse than our petty little problems, troubled love lives, and financial worries."

"Yeah. If you could ask any one of those kids you've been digging out of Pueblo Animas, I think they'd take McDonald's over starvation and mass murder any day of the week."

"I'm sure that's true."

The slant of the sunlight changed; it streamed through the window and gave a golden gleam to her complexion.

Maureen let out a breath and looked around the restaurant. Two other couples huddled over tables, smiling at each other and talking in low voices. "What a wonderful day this has been. We got ice, washed our clothes, filled up the water jugs—and here I am, having the time of my life talking to you about serious things. You, Stewart, of all people."

"What do you mean by that?" He couldn't stop the surprise in his voice.

She laughed again, infectious, overcoming any censure in her words. "Well, you have to admit, we do have a history of despising each other."

He turned his nearly empty cup in his hands. "I was kind of hoping that was over."

Her smile warmed him. "I want to thank you for calling me, even if I spent most of the phone conversation talking to Sylvia. I get lonely at home. After John died, I guess I should have sold the house."

"Maybe, but Dale tells me it's a nice house."

She nodded. "It is. It overlooks the lake. But there are so many memories there."

She had a faraway look in her eyes. He waited to

see if she wanted to say more, then said, "Memories are good things."

"Yes. Usually."

"But not always?"

"Of course not," she said, and gave him a skeptical look. "Memories of freezing your penis to the side of a truck in Wyoming can't be all that great, can they?"

Dusty leaned forward, meeting her halfway across the table, and whispered, "True, but I've never exposed my shortcomings to an arctic environment again."

People crowded around Straighthorn, their colorful capes blazing in the morning sunlight. He did not know most of the people who'd come from Dry Creek village, but many of them wept. Ant Woman, the Dry Creek Clan Matron, sobbed uncontrollably. Two women supported her sticklike old arms as they led her up the trail. He had seen Ant Woman often in the past nine moons. About once a moon, she had come to stay with the Matron of the Katsinas' People. They had laughed and talked well into the night, sharing memories from their childhoods. It must have been very difficult to see a friend of seventy summers die.

Redcrop stepped away from the grave, and Straighthorn lifted his head. Wind Baby sent her long black hair fluttering over her white cape. She looked pale and gaunt, eyes swollen. The village elders surrounded her, speaking softly. Cloudblower gently touched Redcrop's shoulder.

"Warrior?" someone called from behind him.

Straighthorn turned to see the War Chief coming up the trail. He wore a red knee-length shirt and carried his ritual cape over his arm. Despite the chill in the air, sweat glued his short black hair to his cheeks. His thick brows had pulled together into a single line over his flat nose.

"Yes, War Chief?"

Browser stopped at Straighthorn's side. "Where is Jackrabbit?"

"He stayed for the final Songs, then went back to his chamber to sleep. It was a long, cold night, War Chief. We grabbed for our clubs at every sound."

"You were not alone. People sleeping in the village did the same thing. I don't think any of us will have a peaceful night until we've captured the murderers."

"Captured? Are you going to send out another search party? If so, I would like to volunteer."

"I wish to speak of something else," Browser said in a low voice and spread his legs as if preparing for a long conversation.

"Yes?"

"Tell me about Obsidian? Was she born to Longtail Clan?"

Straighthorn frowned. Browser had never shown any interest in Obsidian, though she had placed herself within his reach many times. "No, her mother married a Longtail Clan man twenty-five summers ago. His name was Shell Ring. Obsidian was seven at the time. I recall Matron Crossbill saying she was tall for her age and used her height to threaten the other children."

"But she calls herself Longtail Clan. How did that happen?"

Straighthorn shrugged. "Nothing mysterious. Shell

Ring died a few moons after the marriage. Crossbill adopted Obsidian and her mother into the clan."

Browser smoothed his fingers over the war club on his belt, and his gaze drifted over the dispersing crowd.

"Why do you ask, War Chief?"

"What happened to Obsidian's mother?"

"I heard that she was killed, struck in the head by someone, but it happened before I was born. I know little about it. You may wish to speak with Crossbill. She can tell you more."

"Since you have known Obsidian, has she been married, had children?"

"She was married to a man named Ten Hawks for one or two summers as I remember. I was very young. They had no children, though. I remember waking one day and finding the entire village gathered around their chamber. Obsidian had moved his belongings out into the plaza and told him to leave. After their divorce, she never married again."

Straighthorn still went cold at the memory. It was the first divorce he'd ever seen. Among their people, a woman had the right to move a man's few belongings out of her house whenever she tired of him. On the other hand, a man owned almost nothing, not the house, the children, not even his own clothing. He could keep his weapons and whatever else his wife gave him. For a man, divorce meant losing everything.

"Where did Ten Hawks go?"

"I can't say. Why? Do you wish to find him?"

Browser shook his head. "Just curious."

"No one ever spoke of him after he left. Or if they did, I never heard them. It was as though he had never existed." Straighthorn frowned. "That is odd, though, isn't it? Usually after a divorce people whisper about the cause for many moons."

"Unless the cause was so terrible no one dares to."

Straighthorn blinked at the ground, wondering. "What could it have been?"

"Incest. Witchery. Something like that."

Redcrop left the grave and came toward them. She looked up at Straighthorn with tired eyes.

Browser said, "One last question. Has Obsidian been gone over the past ten days?"

"No." He shook his head. "No, she was here in the village every day. I would swear to it."

"I see." Browser let out a breath. "Thank you, warrior."

Redcrop walked into their circle and Straighthorn reached out to take her cold hand. "The Matron is on her way now, Redcrop. We have done everything we can for her."

"I know. I just—I can't believe she's gone."

Straighthorn lifted her fingers and held them to his cheek while he gazed into her hurt eyes. "It is time you ate something. I was hoping you would share breakfast with me. I thought I would bring out my last venison steaks and cook them over the plaza fire."

Redcrop glanced at Browser, then lowered her gaze. "I wish to be alone for a time, Straighthorn. Please do not be upset with me. I promise I will meet you later this afternoon, if that is all right?"

"Of course," he said, but couldn't hide his disappointment. "When you are ready for company, I'll be waiting."

Redcrop squeezed his hand. "Thank you." She

stood awkwardly for a time, then turned and walked toward the knoll to the west.

Straighthorn watched her climb the hillside. As Father Sun rose higher into the sky, every rock on the knoll glimmered and sparkled.

"Strange," Straighthorn whispered. "She usually wishes company when she is sad."

"Many people wish to be alone after burying a loved one, Straighthorn. Give her time to grieve."

He hesitated. "But she shouldn't be going out there, War Chief. Not that direction. It's not safe." He started after Redcrop.

Browser grabbed his sleeve. "Let her go, Straighthorn."

"War Chief, she is not thinking well. She can mourn near the village. That knoll creates a blind spot. None of our guards will be able to see her."

Browser tightened his grip on Straighthorn's sleeve. "I said, Let her go."

Straighthorn tugged away from Browser's hand and turned . "Why?"

Browser opened his mouth to answer, then squinted out at the horizon as if thinking better of it. Cloud People sailed through the blue, their edges gleaming like polished copper.

Straighthorn figured the War Chief wasn't just enjoying the view. And then it came to him. "As I climbed down from the tower kiva last night, I heard you speaking with Redcrop. Is she a part of some plan? What are you doing?"

"Please, I can only tell you that she *is* being watched."

"By whom? I see no guards."

Browser did not answer for a time. Finally, he said, "I hope not, warrior. If you could see guards, they could, too."

Browser put a hand on Straighthorn's shoulder and guided him toward the river trail that ran south, away from the village. "Come. Let us speak of this in private."

R edcrop walked straight up the hill, knowing
full well that the farther she went from the
village and the safety of other people, the
more danger she would be in. It gave wings to her feet.

She had lain awake in the tower kiva most of the
night, watching Cloudblower stoke the ritual fire and
thinking about what the War Chief had told her. He
had stressed the danger, whispered over and over that
she might not live through it. Their enemy was canny.
No one had ever come close to capturing him before.
But if they succeeded, the string of mad killings would
end. By risking her life, Redcrop might be saving the
lives of who knew how many people?

As she neared the crest of the hill, she crossed a
deer trail covered with heart-shaped prints. She stopped
for a moment to study them. Four deer. Two of them
larger. Probably two does and last summer's fawns.

Redcrop followed the trail around a spindly clump
of rabbitbrush. To her right, a cloud of woodsmoke rose
over Longtail village. The fragrance of burning cotton-

wood drifted on the wind. Redcrop took it into her lungs and held it. It made her feel closer to her dead grandmother. Flame Carrier had always favored cottonwoods. She could sit for hours watching the trembling interplay of sunlight and shadow in the windblown leaves, her wrinkled lips curled into a smile.

Redcrop continued her climb to the top of the rocky hill,. There, she eased down on a crumbling sandstone slab and watched the molten streamers that wavered around Father Sun's golden face. A rumpled tan-and-gray world spread before her, dotted here and there with bright splashes of autumn trees. To her left, the snow-covered peaks of the Great Bear Mountains formed a jagged blue line.

She heaved a sigh and watched a flock of pinyon jays flap over her head. Their slender blue-gray bodies sparkled in the sun, and their raucous cries mocked the sound of laughter.

She wondered where her grandmother would be now.

Once a soul passed the traps and monsters that dogged the road to the Underworlds, the trail split. The Sun Trail on the left was a broad shining path of corn pollen. Good people took it. But bad people—people who had caused much pain in their lives—saw a coil of smoke rising down the right-hand trail, the Trail of Sorrows, and thought it was a village. Since they loved people and got pleasure from the harm they caused others, they hurried down the right-hand trail. At the end of the Trail of Sorrows, Spider Woman waited where she kept her sacred pinyon pine fire blazing. Spider Woman listened to the travelers' tales of woe. Some she cleansed in pinyon smoke and sent back to the Sun Trail. Others were cast into the fire and burned to ashes. As the ashes fell upon the ground, Spider Woman tramped them down into the ground, where they stayed forever. Dirt under the feet of the gods.

Redcrop hunched forward, braced her elbows on her knees, and rocked back and forth to ease the pain in her belly. Wind Baby taunted her, gentle one instant, snatching at her long hair the next.

"You must be strong, girl."

The clarity of Grandmother's voice startled her. Redcrop spun around and stared for a long moment at the sunlit slope, expecting to see her. Only the fresh dirt of the grave met her eyes.

Those were the first words she remembered hearing Flame Carrier say. Redcrop had seen barely three summers. The Matron had found Redcrop in the plaza helping the women grind corn, taken her by the hand, and led her to her chamber where she had gently told Redcrop of her mother's death. Her mother had died quarrying stone from a cliff. A boulder had tumbled down and crushed her.

Dust gusted across the desert in the distance. Redcrop focused on it. She had no memory of her mother now, but she remembered screaming her mother's name and had tried to run out of the chamber. Flame Carrier had caught Redcrop, pulled her against her chest, and hugged her tightly, whispering, "You must be strong, girl. Be strong and do your duty. Those things mean survival in our world."

Looking back, she knew that was when her life had truly begun. The person Redcrop was now had been born at that instant, and everything she had known about her own people, even her family, had died.

She'd never looked back, never indulged in resent-
ment or anger, because it drained her strength, and
nothing had seemed too great a price for the happiness
and love Flame Carrier gave her.

The cloud of smoke hovering over Longtail village
billowed as though someone had added more wood to
the plaza fire. Redcrop reached beneath her cape and
pulled her chert knife from her belt. The red blade
glinted as she lowered it to her long hair and began
sawing. She lifted each handful and let Wind Baby
feather it from her fingers and scatter it across the
hilltop.

By now, all of the Matron's closest friends would
have cut their hair in mourning. It was a sign of their
grief, a way of openly acknowledging the loss and
inviting the healing words of others. Those who had not
been as close to the Matron would be filling their bowls
with succulent robins, grass-seed cakes smeared with
roasted bone marrow, boiled beans, and corn on the cob.
After the feasting, Cloudblower would pass around
baskets of pine nuts and toasted squash seeds, and
people would tell wonderful stories of Grandmother's
life and generosity.

Red, white, and yellow capes flashed in the cottonwoods along the river, probably people who needed
time away from the crowd. She saw Obsidian standing
in the cottonwoods. The woman's wind-swept white
cape flapped around her like huge wings. Redcrop
couldn't see her face, but she gazed in Redcrop's direction. Was she looking at her? Or the bluff that rose
behind her to the southwest?

Redcrop turned. On the high bluff, the sandstone
shone golden against the sere blue sky. Eroded terraces

dropped away from the flat top and descended into the river valley like a giant's staircase.

Redcrop frowned and looked back at Obsidian. She hadn't moved, but seemed to see something up there that Redcrop did not.

Redcrop turned away. Jagged locks of hair patted her face. She wished Straighthorn were here. She needed him. But he would be safer in the village than with her.

When she opened her eyes, she noticed strange impressions in the sand below the crest of the hill. At first she couldn't fathom what they might be, then it came to her: a child's arms. The points of the elbows had dimpled the ground, and the forearms had smoothed the sand. Three body lengths down the slope she saw sandal prints.

Rising, she followed them.

In several places the child had tripped over brush and stumbled, leaving overturned pebbles and mashed grass. As Redcrop followed the trail down the hill, the child's stride lengthened into a run.

But why would a child run away from the village?

On an ordinary morning a mother might not know exactly where her child was, but not today. Whenever the village adults were occupied—for example, when someone spotted a war party, and every person who could wield a bow had to take up a position on the walls or in the hills—all of the children under eight were gathered into the tower kiva, the safest place in the village. Redcrop had seen the children go into the kiva with old Black Lace before dawn. Black Lace had a reputation for being fiercely protective of the younger members of the village. None of those children could have escaped her watchful eye.

Redcrop paralleled the child's path down into the drainage bottom and sand oozed up around her sandals. The tracks grew erratic, weaving back and forth across the drainage, running, stopping, running again.

Redcrop's pulse increased when she saw the coyote den in the gully wall. About four hands wide, the opening yawned like a dark toothless mouth. The tracks led straight to it.

Redcrop hurried.

❧

Catkin lurched to her feet when Redcrop disappeared into the drainage. Her long buckskin war shirt snagged on the brush that had been hiding her, and the slender limbs snapped and cracked.

What's she doing? Browser told her to stay on the hilltop!

Catkin waited just long enough to realize that Redcrop was not coming back to her perch on the sandstone slab. What could have lured the girl into the drainage? Had someone called to her? Had she seen something that demanded her attention? Redcrop knew the danger. Browser had explained it to her in excruciating detail. Perhaps grief had taken the girl's senses?

Catkin had lost her own good sense when her husband, Wind Born, died. Every moment had been a nightmare of loneliness. Was that how Redcrop was feeling?

Catkin pulled her war club from her belt and broke into a dead run.

In the brush-clotted drainage near the grave, I move through their burial offerings: bowls of food, bits of colored fabric, small ceramic pots. I sniff the fresh dirt where they stood. One of the females dropped a tear-soaked piece of cloth. I take it into my mouth and chew, tasting her salty taste.

I whirl at the sound of pounding feet and see the warrior Catkin dash by like the wind...and I know they are watching the girl.

I duck back into the shadows, breathing hard.

Redcrop frowned at the coyote den. Had the child been looking for a place to hide, perhaps being chased? Orphans often sneaked up this drainage to get to Longtail village, and the raiders who'd murdered their parents frequently ran right behind them.

Redcrop kneeled before the opening, and the sharp tang of coyote urine stung her nose.

"Hello?"

She glanced over her shoulder, then moved closer, her face inside the opening. A dank coolness coated her skin. "Hello? Don't be afraid. I won't hurt you."

As her eyes adjusted to the darkness, she saw a corn-husk doll lying in the rear, six hands away.

Redcrop stuck her arm into the opening but couldn't reach the doll. She twisted sideways, slipped her arm in first, then tucked her head through the opening. As she grasped the doll, she noticed the scratches that lined the walls and floor.

Redcrop backed out of the den with the corn-husk doll. The painted lips and eyes had faded, but the doll's long black braid hung to the middle of her back. She wore a grimy white deerskin dress.

A little girl's doll.

Redcrop examined the ground. In her haste to peer inside the den, she'd disturbed many of the tracks. The War Chief would not be happy with her carelessness. She looked for the best place to stand, a place away from the sign left by the child and spied a small boulder about two paces away. When she stood on it, her eyes widened. From this vantage she could see many things she had not seen before. Most of the small prints near the den had been covered with larger prints.

She swung around, searching for an intruder. As Father Sun rose higher into the sky, the sand shimmered with a blinding intensity. Redcrop lifted a hand to shield her eyes and squinted back toward the hill that overlooked the grave. Shiny filaments of yellow Cloud People trailed across the sky.

If she was in trouble, why didn't she come down to us? Or call for help?

A Straight Path Nation child would have run down as quickly as her legs could carry her. Perhaps the girl with the cornhusk doll had been born to the Flute Player Believers, or the Fire Dogs?

She looked into the faded brown eyes of the doll. Many of the orphans who wandered into Longtail village carried toys clutched to their chests and would utter inhuman shrieks if you tried to take them away even for an instant. Even if it was just to dress the child, or bathe him or her. It must have broken the little girl's heart to leave her doll behind.

Redcrop slipped the doll into her belt and bent over the large sandal prints. The depressions cast shadows. The man's feet had sunk deeply into the wet sand.

Her gaze followed them down the eroded drainage to the south. Twenty paces ahead, a deer trail cut the bank. The tracks headed toward it, but she no longer saw the child's prints.

Had he carried her?

It was probably just a father who'd come to find his wayward daughter, but it might have been a raider tracking down an escaped child, or...or worse.

The War Chief had told her to stay on top of the hill and within sight of the guards. She'd disobeyed by coming down into the drainage. Could the guards still see her? Would they come if she started to follow the man's trail? She stepped...

"What are you doing?"

Redcrop jerked around so fast that she stumbled and had to catch her balance.

Obsidian stared at her with slitted eyes. The wind had torn locks of long hair loose from their jeweled pins and spilled them down the front of her white cape.

"Obsidian! I didn't hear you. Where did you come from?"

"What are you doing out here?" She walked forward with fists clenched at her sides.

The anger in her voice stunned Redcrop. She stammered, "I—I wished to be alone for a time." She folded her arms across her chest like a shield. "When I reached the hilltop, I found a child's footprints. They led down to this old coyote den."

"A child?" The lines around Obsidian's beautiful

mouth tightened. "What did she look like? How old was she?"

"I didn't see her, Obsidian. Just her tracks." Redcrop gestured to the sand. "It looks like a man came to get her."

Obsidian kneeled and her white cape spread around her in sculpted folds. She stared at the man's sandal prints for a long while, as though thinking. When she rose to her feet, her voice had changed, grown soft and guarded. "Did you see him?"

Redcrop shook her head. "No. I didn't see anyone after I got into the drainage. Why? Did you see him?"

"Don't be a fool. How could I have seen him when I just got here? Why would you think that?"

"Well, I heard fear in your voice, and I thought maybe you—"

"Where do the tracks go?" She glared at Redcrop. "Did you follow them?"

"No. I—I thought it would be wiser to go and tell the War Chief, in case the man was a raider."

Obsidian's mouth curled into a smile. "Yes, that was wise." She reached out and stroked Redcrop's hair in a way that made her shiver. "Go. Tell Browser I'm waiting for him. I'll remain to make sure nothing is disturbed."

Redcrop backed away, her gaze remained locked with Obsidian's. The woman's eyes had a savage glitter. They reminded Redcrop of a weasel she'd seen last summer. He'd trotted by her with a dove in his mouth. Just before he sank his teeth into the dove's skull, his eyes had glittered like that.

"I-I'll return as soon as I can."

Redcrop ran.

Catkin raced toward the hill, panting, her war club clutched in a tight fist. Blood pounded in her ears as she sprinted over the crest and lunged down the slope toward the drainage. Tracks covered the hillside, but she didn't have the luxury of studying them. Every shred of energy went into pushing her legs harder, praying she wasn't too late...

"Redcrop!" she called when the girl climbed up out of the drainage.

"Catkin? Oh, Catkin, thank the gods you saw me! I was going to find the War Chief. I—"

"What's wrong?" Catkin halted in front of Redcrop and gazed down at her, furious. "Why did you leave the hilltop?"

Redcrop's eyes widened. "I'm sorry. I found a little girl's tracks, and I followed them. I know I shouldn't have, but I—"

"You walked out of my sight because of a child's tracks!"

Redcrop jerked a nod. "Yes, I'm sorry, Catkin. Truly. But please"—she gestured down at the drainage —"come and see. I think a little girl was trying to get to us and was captured by a raider."

"Do not do that again!" Catkin ordered through gritted teeth. "Do you understand me?"

"Yes," Redcrop answered in a small voice.

She'd cut her hair and it hung around her chin in irregular black locks. Her eyes were still red-rimmed from crying.

Catkin said, "My duty is to keep you safe."

"I know. I'm sorry."

Catkin relented. "All right. How do you know it was a girl?"

Redcrop shoved her cape aside and pulled a tattered corn-husk doll from her belt. She held it out to Catkin. "I found this in the coyote den where the child was hiding. Don't you think it looks like a girl's doll?"

Catkin stared at the faded eyes and grimy white dress, then handed it back to Redcrop. "Yes, it does. I will go and check the tracks, but I want you to run down to the river trail. There are many people there. You will be safe. Take it back to the village and tell Browser what you found and where I am."

"Yes, Catkin."

She turned to run, but Catkin grabbed her hand and stared hard into her fragile young eyes. "I know you are hurting, Redcrop. But you must listen to me. Grief can take a person's ability to think. I want you to do exactly as I say. Do you understand me?"

"I—I do. I'll run all the way. I promise. I won't even stop if someone calls out to me."

"Good." Catkin released her hand. "Hurry. Remember that while I am in the drainage, no one can see me. I may be in danger."

"You won't be alone, Catkin," Redcrop told her. "Obsidian is down there. She saw me go over the hill, too, and came looking for me. She said she would stay and make sure no one disturbed the tracks while I went to find the War Chief."

A strange floating sensation possessed Catkin, as if her souls hovered high above and could see things that her human body could not. She stared unblinking at Redcrop.

"How long after you climbed down the hill did Obsidian arrive?"

"I can't say. I..." Redcrop shook her head uncertainly. "Less than a hundred heartbeats, maybe? I'm sorry. I guess I've been living in my souls with Grandmother."

Catkin's heart softened. Wind Born had called it "mourning time." Intense pain turned thousands of moments into one single terrible instant. Time had no meaning for the grieving.

More gently, Catkin said, "Thank you for telling me about Obsidian. Now go. Find Browser."

"Yes, Catkin."

Redcrop pulled up her long hem and dashed down the hill toward the river trail.

Catkin waited until she saw Redcrop moving among the people clustered in the trees, then she trotted down the trail to the edge of the drainage.

It surprised her to see Obsidian standing on the opposite bank, not in the drainage at all. Obsidian was leaning over something. Her white hood covered her face.

Catkin worked her way down the trail slowly, studying the tracks. Redcrop's tracks covered many of the child's, but in places she could see the girl's prints clearly. They were small, the size a child seven or eight summers would make.

What would a child this young be doing out here alone?

Redcrop was probably right; another orphan had tried to get to them, and the safety the Katsinas' People promised.

Catkin made her way toward the coyote den, and

Obsidian gracefully walked down the deer trail on the opposite side. Catkin's stomach churned. Just the thought of having to deal with Obsidian made her wish she'd waited for Browser. When Obsidian spoke with a man, she exuded warmth and charm. She treated other women like dung beetles.

Catkin halted three paces in front of the den. Four sets of tracks marred the ground. Redcrop's and Obsidian's, a little girl's, and a man's—a tall man from the length of his stride.

Catkin edged forward and crouched at the side of the den to examine the man's prints more closely. She heard Obsidian coming but did not look up. Her stomach muscles knotted when she saw the distinctive weave. *Blessed gods. He was here, this close, and we didn't know it. But who is the little girl?*

Obsidian stopped and the spicy scent of blazing star petals filled the air. "One over, three under. An unusual weave, wouldn't you agree?"

Calmly, Catkin answered, "Many people might use that weave, Obsidian. Just because we don't doesn't mean it isn't common elsewhere."

"Where? I've never seen it before."

Catkin straddled the tracks and peered inside the den where Redcrop said the girl had been hiding. She waited until her eyes adjusted to the darkness, then frowned at the scratches that covered the walls and floor. A wet splotch darkened the dirt in the rear. Catkin leaned inside. She touched the splotch, smelled its coppery odor, then frowned at the right wall. Footprints marked the wall two hands up from the floor. Her gaze went to the left wall, and she saw tiny handprints.

"What do you see in there?" Obsidian asked.

Catkin backed out of the den and examined the fresh claw marks on the lip of the opening.

Obsidian smiled and in a friendly tone said, "It looks like a coyote was in there this morning, doesn't it?"

"A coyote's claws are sharp and pointed, Obsidian. They leave deep, narrow grooves. These are broad and shallow."

"Well, what else could they be but coyote claws?"

Catkin tightened the grip on her war club. "The work of frantic fingernails. The girl was dragged out of the den by her feet."

"Oh, really?" Obsidian said smugly, "And how can you tell that?"

Catkin paused. Longed to use her war club to beat some respect into Obsidian. It took real effort not to. "She tried to wedge herself on the roof to avoid the man's grasping hands, but he pulled her down hard. There's blood in the back where her chin struck the floor before he dragged her out. That's probably when she dropped the doll. The impact must have knocked it from her hands, and she didn't have time to—"

"What doll?" Obsidian said, as if indignant that no one had told her about it. "There's a doll in there?"

Catkin turned away and followed the man's tracks to the deer trail that cut up the wall of the drainage. Redcrop had disturbed a few of the tracks, but Obsidian had obliterated most of the rest.

Obsidian hurried to catch up. "I noticed there weren't any small prints here."

"He was carrying her, probably afraid she'd try to run away again."

"Do you think it was a raider chasing down an escaped slave?"

Catkin stopped in the deer trail. The steps vanished. She spun around, studying the rocks at the edges of the trail. Had he walked on them? Or...

Catkin turned to Obsidian. "Did you see any tracks here when you first walked up?"

"No. Not even one."

"You're certain you didn't accidentally erase them? I see the places where your cape dragged the ground."

Obsidian blinked as though shocked to hear that. "I suppose I might have. I'm not a warrior, after all. But if they were here, I didn't see them."

Voices rose from the opposite side of the drainage. Catkin looked up and saw Browser coming over the hill with Jackrabbit and Straighthom behind him. He stopped when he saw Catkin and Obsidian, surveyed the drainage, then cupped a hand to his mouth to call, "Are you all right?"

Obsidian shouted, "Yes, War Chief. Come and let me show you what I've found!"

Catkin could see Browser's hesitance. He'd cut his hair in mourning. Ragged tufts covered his head. Browser led the way down, slowly, probably placing his feet on Catkin's tracks so as not to disturb any other sign. Jackrabbit and Straighthom fell in line behind him.

Catkin and Obsidian walked back down the deer trail to the coyote den. Obsidian leaned a shoulder against the drainage wall and watched Browser as a hawk does a juicy mouse.

As he approached, Browser's red war shirt flapped around his tanned legs. A sheen of sweat covered his handsome face. He must have run as hard as he could to get here.

Browser deliberately passed Obsidian without a glance and came to stand beside Catkin. "What did you find, Catkin?"

Obsidian let out a low laugh, and Browser's shoulder muscles bulged through his shirt. He kept his eyes on Catkin.

Catkin said, "He has a little girl, Browser. Seven or eight summers."

"He? Redcrop said a raider—"

"This is no raider."

Catkin dropped and pointed to one of the large sandal prints.

Browser bent over and propped his hands on his knees. It took an instant for understanding to slacken his face. "The child is a captive?"

Catkin met his worried eyes. "I've never heard of Two Hearts taking slaves, Browser. Have you?"

He straightened. "No, but..."

Catkin could see the horror rising behind his eyes, coalescing into a monstrous possibility.

"We can't be sure, Browser, but we must speak with Cloudblower when we return."

"Cloudblower? Why? What could she—"

"Just believe me, she knows."

Browser stared hard into her eyes, silently questioning what she meant.

Obsidian's white cape flashed in the sunlight as she stalked up the hillside trail.

They all watched her, but no one said anything. Straighthorn didn't even seem to notice she'd left. He looked preoccupied, his forehead lined and his gaze distant.

When Obsidian had passed beyond hearing range, Jackrabbit whispered, "Why did she leave?"

Browser said, "The gods must have heard me."

"Or maybe they heard your stomach," Jackrabbit said. "Ever since you crested the hill and saw her, it's sounded like a dog fight in there."

Browser put a hand on his belly and grimaced. "That's what it feels like, too."

Straighthorn said, "The man must have seen Redcrop. Why didn't he come after her?"

"Perhaps he had more pressing considerations," Browser answered. "He clearly wanted to get the little girl away from here."

"Because he feared for her safety?" Straighthorn asked. "Or because she was trying to reach us, and he didn't wish her to?"

"Maybe both. He feared what would happen to her if we found out who she was." Browser crouched in front of the den and examined the claw marks on the lip.

Catkin knelt beside him. "Yes. Fingernails."

"She did not go willingly, that much we can tell. Did anyone hear her scream?"

"I didn't," Catkin answered, "but he may have had a hand clamped over her mouth."

Straighthorn said, "Even if she had managed to scream, with all of the Singing and Dancing surrounding the burial, I doubt anyone would have heard her."

Browser leaned into the den. After thirty heart-beats, he backed out and gazed around the circle. "I doubt that she screamed," he said. "From the way he treated her, I think she knew better."

~

*P*iper lies on her belly, a stuffed girl skin with eyes. Her fingers hurt where the nails are torn. If she does not move, he won't see her.

But she sees him.

Her grandfather's shadow moves on the opposite wall. He walks on knees that slip and slide. His mouth is a dying bird's beak. It opens and closes, opens and closes, but the words are all dead bubbles breaking in the dirt.

From beneath the corner of her blanket, she sees his shadow coming closer, bending down. Piper does not even blink. Firelight lives in his spiderweb hair, shooting about like Meteor People.

His whisper is old blood. "For us it is always daybreak on the second day of the world, child. We live suspended between Father Sun's first and second coming. Remember the daybreak beast. You cannot kill him, but you can tame him and use his Power."

Piper squeezes her eyelids together and her head shakes. The joint-stiffening disease turns her hands into eagle's feet. She tries to find the place inside with arms that hold her, but it is too deep and dark, very dark, and a man's hand clamps over her mouth, crushing her lips, and her lungs are dying.

She's dying.

And somewhere far away a woman cries.

8

Maureen bent over her work. The temperature had dropped to ten degrees Centigrade, but the kiva bottom was warm, barely caressed by the breeze that blew above. Sunlight flecked the red sandstone walls with gold.

She used a sliver of bamboo to pick moist black soil away from the femur and tibia of what looked like a four-year-old child. The bones lay articulated, the epiphyseal caps still in place where the condyles had formed the joint. Above the leg lay a confusing mass of bone, as if several children had been piled atop one another. She had started on the single leg, deciding to remove it in order to have a place to sit while she worked on untangling the mess of intertwined bodies.

The mottled upper leg was dark, stained by the ash-filled soil. The lower limb, however, had been charred, the bone spalled in the characteristic pattern caused by the marrow boiling inside. The distal portions of the fibula, the slim bone in the lower leg, had been completely burned. Tarsals, or ankle bones, were badly calcined from the heat. The foot seemed to be missing.

"Why bamboo?" Sylvia asked as she kneeled beside Maureen with a clipboard in her hands. She had pulled her brown hair back into a short ponytail.

"It doesn't scratch the bone the way a dental pick does." Maureen probed carefully and dug out around the bottom of the bone.

"So, what's the latest?" Sylvia started sketching the bone on the draft paper.

"This child burned whole. That's why the ankle and lower leg are in such bad condition."

Sylvia studied the tangle of bones. "Do you think they were alive when the kiva went up?"

Maureen shrugged. "Hard to say. Without lab analysis, all I can tell you is that they were either alive or hadn't been dead for very long. The meat around the bones still had a lot of water in it."

Sylvia's nose wrinkled. "Gruesome."

"Yes, it is."

"I can't believe it was an accident. I've dug pit houses in Colorado that burned. We were pretty sure in those cases that a spark set the wooden roof on fire, and they couldn't get out through the rooftop entry." Sylvia gestured around. "This is an arid climate. Wood dries out. Sometimes a spark is all it takes, and *whoosh!* The whole thing goes. Air from the ventilator shaft turns the fire into an inferno. Most of the skeletal material is in pretty good shape because when the roof collapsed, the dirt covered everyone and sealed the draft from the ventilator. These kids, though, God. I mean it must have been an awesome fire. Why would forty or fifty children be on the roof of a kiva?"

"Good question." Maureen shook her head. "I don't suppose we can ever prove it, but I'd say someone did this on purpose, set the fire with the intent to burn these children."

Sylvia eyeballed the bone, sketched on her pad for a time longer, then said, "How could anyone do that? Most of these kids were under five."

Maureen took a deep breath and paused to pull back several loose strands of hair that were tickling her nose. "I've seen it before, Sylvia. The massacres in El Salvador, Bosnia, Kosovo, Rwanda. Even the dead from First Nation battlefields in America, like Sand Creek, Bear River, and Wounded Knee. It happens when people hate each other. In Russia, Nazi soldiers herded women and children into barns and churches and burned them alive." She paused. "It's part of who we are as human beings. One of the many images you see in your reflection when you look into a mirror."

"Makes me glad I sleep with my baseball bat."

"Yes, but on the other hand, we're the same species that spends tens of thousands of dollars to rescue beached whales, or to provide food and medicine to people halfway around the globe that we don't know." Maureen cocked her head, and her long black braid fell over her shoulder. "That's the magic of anthropology, Sylvia. We get to study people in all of their many different forms, characteristics, their diverse cultures, languages, and their physical variation. But we're all the same animal."

"Kind of wonderful and horrifying at once, isn't it?"

Maureen smiled. "Sounds like a description of Dusty."

She used her bamboo sliver to pull dirt back as far

as the femur's *linea aspera,* the line of muscle attachment on the back of the bone.

"That's for sure," Sylvia replied, and her green eyes turned thoughtful. "Speaking of which, if you're right that these children were torched on purpose, it would support Dusty's suspicion of holy war."

"Not necessarily. The children could also have been plague victims, or something similar. Sometimes, when illness breaks out, bodies are burned in mass graves. That's also what this might have been."

Sylvia made a face. "Maybe. But if that was the case, why burn the kiva, too? I mean, it's the centerpiece for the entire pueblo."

"Maybe there was an epidemic. They took the children into the kiva and prayed and sang over them, trying to heal them in their holiest place. But it didn't work. One by one, the children died. Heartsick, they carried them all onto the roof and burned the entire kiva. They cremated their children to kill the evil spirits that had caused the illness. Then they abandoned the pueblo."

"In an epidemic, the kids wouldn't have died all at once, though. To prove it was disease, you would have to show that some of the kids had been dead for a while."

Maureen nodded. "That's right. I'll try to discern that in the lab." She resettled where her leg was going to sleep and continued whisking dirt away from the brittle bone.

"We haven't found many grave goods either," Sylvia pointed out. "If they'd died because of warfare or illness, somebody would have prepared them for the journey to the afterlife, left pots of food, new sandals, precious belongings."

"Grave goods would definitely weigh the evidence more toward a funeral than a massacre."

A crow sailed over them, his black wings canted to catch the air currents.

Sylvia chewed her lip for a moment. "If the other sites in the area are any indication, it's going to turn out to be a massacre site."

"You think Dusty's right?"

"I haven't seen him wrong very often, Washais."

Maureen frowned at the tangled bones. "I'm sure that's true."

Sylvia paused, then said, "You know, I don't get you two."

"How's that?"

Sylvia shrugged. "You have a unique relationship, that's all. After you left 10K3, Dusty was glum. I mean, really glum. He spent a lot of time moping. Then, after we packed up, and he went back to Santa Fe, I'd get calls. Maybe about once a week. You know, 'How ya doin'?' sorts of things. Then he'd ask, 'So, you heard from Dr. Cole?' as if it had just slipped into the conversation."

Maureen hesitated, stopped what she was doing, and rocked back on her haunches to get a better look at Sylvia. "He could have called me, you know."

"Not Dusty. It would have been an admission."

"Of what? That he wanted to know how I was doing? My God, I was doing the analysis of those burials we found. It wasn't like he needed an excuse. I thought the reason Dale was always calling for updates on the data was because Stewart wasn't interested.

That, or he'd get what he needed when I wrote the final report."

Sylvia finished her sketch, set her clipboard aside, and sat down cross-legged. "I've never seen him this way over a woman before. I mean, when we cut this bone bed? He was practically phobic about picking up the phone to call you. Then, when he did, you heard him. He said hello, fumbled around sounding like an idiot, and handed the phone to me, for God's sake."

Maureen turned her head when a gust of wind whirled around the kiva. When she turned back, she said, "Dale called him a *Kokwimu* once. I had to look it up to discover it meant a Man-Woman. I don't think Dale meant it, since Stewart certainly has a male body and soul."

"Yeah, he just can't get them together."

"Because of his mother and father?" Maureen raised her face to the sun, thinking.

Sylvia said, "Dale told me that in all the years since Ruth Ann Sullivan left Samuel Stewart, she has never once tried to get in touch with Dusty. I think the fact that old Samuel committed suicide made matters worse for Dusty. I mean, God, talk about traumatic. He was a child." She indicated the delicate bones spread around the kiva room. "Like these kids."

"But he's almost forty now, Sylvia. He should have figured out that not all women are Ruth Ann Sullivan."

"Yeah, and I should have figured out that not all men want to hurt me; but outgrowing your childhood is tougher than normal people think." She shook her head. "Things that happen to you as a kid can really screw up the rest of your life."

"Thinking about Steve?"

"No. Thinking about *him*—my foster father when I was four years old. I still have nightmares about his breath and hair. Isn't that funny? That sight of all that black, curly hair on his chest terrified me." She stared off into nothingness. "Each time I thought I was smothering. And the smell...of his breath...his body."

"That was a long time ago."

"Only to you. I relive every moment every day." Sylvia seemed to come back to this world. She gave Maureen a cautious look. "How about you?"

"What do you mean?"

"I mean you're haunted, too. Do you still have nightmares about your husband?"

"I have one dream. John and I are walking along the beach. It's morning, and the waves are coming in off the lake and splashing. The water is turquoise. Gulls are hanging on the breeze, bobbing, and the sun is slanting in from the east through the clouds. I'm holding John's hand, and dear God, Sylvia, I'm so happy. As if my heart is about to burst through my chest. Then I look into John's face, expecting him to be smiling, happy, as full of life as I am at that moment, but I see his face as he looked lying on the kitchen floor, and I can smell the burning spaghetti sauce."

Sylvia stared at her with kind eyes.

Maureen shrugged. "I wake up and there's a huge gaping hole inside me. The empty feeling is so intense, I just lay there in the dark, in the bed I used to share with him, and ache."

Sylvia's eyes tightened before she turned her attention to the clouds on the southern horizon. "That sounds pretty lonely, Washais."

They were silent for a moment, then Maureen

leaned forward and resumed her excavation of the child's leg. "I just about have this femur ready to be removed."

"Okay. I've sketched the bone to scale. Let me get a photo and a box ready." Sylvia retrieved the camera from the ammo box that sat on the lip of the unit and snapped several shots.

Maureen rocked the small femur back and forth with her fingertips to ensure it was loose, then lifted it free. Sylvia began wrapping it in tissue while Maureen removed the epiphyses and wrapped them.

"You've worked with Dusty for years, right?"

"Sometimes it seems like forever. I was just a sopho-more at UNM. Went to the Pecos Conference that year. It was being held back in Pecos, sort of a reunion kind of thing. I walked around the trucks and there was Dusty, drinking beer with Dale. I can still remember, they were arguing about contamination of a C-14 sample, and Dusty was reaming Dale for letting a big drop of sweat fall from the end of his nose onto this piece of charcoal. The date they got back from Beta Analytic said that their site had been built yesterday."

Sylvia shook her head, smiling. "I couldn't believe I was standing that close to Dale Emerson Robertson! As an anthropology student, I was blown away. I kept wondering who the blond asshole was, and how dare he blame someone like Robertson for screwing up a C-14 date!"

"So you launched into Dusty?"

"God, no. I was just standing there with my eyes bugged out, when Dusty turned. He made this gesture with his hand. Like, 'come here.' I stepped forward and Dusty said, 'Do you promise not to sweat into my charcoal samples?' Well, Jeez, what would a sophomore anthropology student say? I answered, 'Yes, sir.' And Dusty said, All right, Mary, you're hired. We're blowing out of here at noon tomorrow.'

"'Sir,' I said, 'My name is Sylvia.'

"'Okay,' he answered, 'whatever. We're digging a late P-One site that they're running a pipeline through. We've got three weeks. I'll meet you at the old mission at noon tomorrow. You can ride out with me, or Dale, assuming you want to be sweated on.'

"'William,' Dale said in this imperious voice, 'one drop of sweat wouldn't have ruined your sample. They *wash* the material before they run it. I suggest that you see to how you record and package your materials before you send them off to the lab,' and Dale stalked off."

Maureen chuckled. "What an introduction."

"Yeah." Sylvia placed the wrapped bone in the box. "And there I was, hired onto a field crew. I asked Dusty, 'What about my classes?'

"'What about them?' he asked.

"'Well, they're supposed to start in—'

"He cut me off, and said, 'Kid, are you going to be an archaeologist or an academician?'" Slyvia made a face. "It was the way he said 'academician,' as if it was something really foul. Then he added, 'Why didn't you say you were still in school on your *vitae?*'"

Sylvia rubbed her nose. "I was so dumb I didn't know a *vitae* was a resume. So, I shrugged. And Dusty says, 'Where are you going to school?'

"'University of New Mexico.'

"'Don't sweat it,' he says. 'Dale will fix it.' And, of course, he did. I got credits for my fieldwork."

"So you had a job?"

"Right. Doing real archaeology with Dale Emerson Robertson. We'd been working on the project for three days before Dusty figured out he'd hired me by mistake. He thought I was some girl named Mary who had wanted to talk to him about a job. She was supposed to meet him that night. I dug that entire semester, doing archaeology instead of sitting in a classroom learning about it."

Maureen returned her attention to the burned tibia. "So, where did Dusty's reputation as a ladies' man come from?"

Sylvia appraised Maureen. "That's an interesting question. Worried about him?"

"No, just wondering."

"Uh-huh." Sylvia rubbed her chin with the back of her dirty hand. "Women like Dusty's looks, that's where the reputation comes from. The problem is that as soon as they start getting close, he sort of self-destructs. Says and does things that are really bizarre. You ask him about it later, and he doesn't know why he did what he did."

"We all have our little disasters, don't we?"

Sylvia nodded. "It's only when you get to digging something like this site, all these children, and you realize that no matter how screwed up your life seems, it's nothing compared to what these people went through." She stared at the piles of bones. "Imagine how they must have felt. Their children incinerated. How did they survive that?"

"I don't know," Maureen whispered, and chipped away another piece of dirt from the delicate bone.

Browser kept his eyes on Catkin as she shouldered through the crowded plaza on her way to Cloudblower's chamber. She had her right hand propped on her belted war club. She probably wasn't even conscious of it, but Browser knew what it meant.

Danger here.

As Browser passed the great kiva, his uncle, Stone Ghost, called, "What did Catkin tell you, Nephew?" Thin white hair blew around his face as he looked up from the cross-patterned red blanket he sat on.

Browser stepped over, reaching down to pull Stone Ghost to his feet. "Nothing, Uncle, except that Cloudblower knows things about Two Hearts that I do not."

Thin white hair blew around his uncle's wrinkled face as he bent down to retrieve his old blanket, fold it, and drape it over a shoulder. "I'm sure she does. After all, she knew the monster soul that lived inside your wife. Yellow Dove must have told her many things."

Browser ducked his head and looked away as they

passed Springbank and Wading Bird. Acted like he didn't hear their calls as he hurried by. He didn't want to answer any questions before he'd heard what Cloud-blower had to say. "What things, Uncle? Do you know something you haven't told me?"

Stone Ghost stuck a hand through a hole in his ratty turkey feather cape and grasped Browser's elbow. To the people in the plaza it would appear that he was seeking support for his elderly steps, but he squeezed Browser's arm, and Browser realized he was actually offering support, not asking for it.

"Cloudblower told me a few things. That was nine moons ago. Back in Straight Path Canyon, Nephew. That was then....I do not know what she will tell us today."

"Why didn't you tell me, Uncle?"

"The story was not mine to tell. It belongs to her. I discovered long ago that if people wished to tell others the same things they told me, they would."

They veered around a group of mourners, and Browser whispered, "I am War Chief, Uncle. To protect our people, I must know everything."

"Then ask her, Nephew. I think she will answer you."

Catkin stopped in front of Cloudblower's door and turned to watch their approach. Her red shirt clung to every curve of her tall body. Her oval face had flushed, as though she feared what the next hand of time would bring.

Browser could feel his uncle's finger bones through the thin veneer of translucent skin; they felt like knotted twigs.

When they stood before the door curtain, Stone Ghost called, "Healer? We are here."

"Come," Cloudblower said softly. "I think I am ready for you."

Stone Ghost held the leather curtain aside and stepped into the chamber. Catkin and Browser followed.

As the door curtain swung behind them, bright yellow fire light splashed and flickered in the dim interior. The chamber spread three-by-three body lengths. Cloudblower stood to Browser's left. She'd braided her gray-streaked black hair and coiled it on top of her head, then fastened it with bone pins. The style accentuated the triangular shape of her face. Shell beads on her long blue dress shimmered in time with her movements.

Gray pots lined the walls, and the sweet scents of herbs and dried flowers pervaded the air. Katsinas Danced where they had been painted on the white walls; their hands were linked and their masked faces tipped toward the smoke hole in the roof, Singing. In the amber glow cast by the brightly burning hearth, their costumed bodies wavered. The white kirtles seemed to sway as though touched by a wind Browser could not feel. He watched them from the corner of his eye, half expecting them to suddenly look down at him.

"Please, sit," Cloudblower said, and extended a hand to the opposite wall where deer hides covered the floor.

"We thank you, Elder." Browser sat down cross-legged, and Catkin and Stone Ghost settled to his left.

The tension seemed to have sucked the air from the room. Browser had to remind himself to breathe.

Cloudblower touched the pot that hung on the tripod at the edge of the fire, and the beads on her blue sleeve twinkled. "This tea is warm. May I fill cups for you?"

Stone Ghost smiled. "Yes, thank you, Healer. It has been a chilly day. My aching bones could use the warmth."

Cloudblower dipped up the first cup and handed it to Stone Ghost, then she filled cups for Catkin and Browser. Finally, she tipped the pot and poured her own cup full. She did not move. Just clutched her cup and stared blindly at the leaping flames.

Browser said, "Elder, I—"

"Yes," Cloudblower responded and sank back on the floor as though uttering that one word had drained her last bit of strength. Her soft brown eyes filled with sadness.

Catkin said, "He must know the things you told me that day long ago, Cloudblower."

She jerked a nod. "I just did not wish to be the one to tell him." She looked at Browser. "These things will hurt you, War Chief. That is why I haven't told you about them before now. You have had many other burdens to weigh you down."

"Whatever you have to say, Elder, then our lives may depend upon it. I assure you that I can stand it."

Browser twisted his teacup in his hands and prayed that was true. For six moons after he'd killed his wife, no matter where he was, or what he'd been doing, Ash Girl's face had filled his visions. He'd relived the instant before she'd died, how she had gazed up at him with all the love she could muster and tried to warn him that Two Hearts was close. Despite the anger and hatred they had inflicted upon each other over the summers, at the last, even knowing that he had killed her, she had loved him.

"Please, Elder, go on."

Cloudblower nodded, but her voice came out low. "You know about monster souls. How they can take up residence within another person's body. Browser, it was such a monster soul that lived inside your wife. But monster that Yellow Dove was, he still tried to protect her from her father."

Browser said, "Yellow Dove spoke to me the day I killed Ash Girl's body, Elder. I know something of his madness. Please, continue."

He had never told anyone that. Catkin knew because she'd been there. Browser had shot an arrow through the boy's chest, then ripped off the wolf mask he wore, and stood frozen, looking down into Ash Girl's face. The horror of that moment still lived in his heart.

Cloudblower sat down again and laced her fingers in her lap. "Stone Ghost helped me to understand monster souls." She nodded respectfully at the old man. "He told me that murderers are not born but molded as children. He said it takes repeated intolerable pain to chase away a child's souls and make a nest where a monster can be born." Her eyes shifted to Browser. "That's what happened to Ash Girl. Her father chased away her human souls, and in their places a hideous creature was born."

Browser sat quietly, listening.

Stone Ghost shifted. "I have seen only two monster souls in my life, Nephew. Both were born when the frightened children had given up hope, when they could no longer endure the pain alone. Someone stronger was born inside them, a protector who would never leave them, who could stand up to the tormentor and shield the child from the terror. Protecting the child often includes murder."

The popping of the fire seemed to fill the world.

Browser said, "What else?"

Cloudblower bowed her head. "I know it hurt you deeply that your wife fell asleep every time you started loving her. But Browser, she couldn't help it. That's how the monster Yellow Dove shielded Ash Girl from the pain. Her father—he—he started lying with her when she was two."

Browser's grip tightened around his cup. For the first three summers of their marriage, he'd desperately tried to speak with her about it. He could still hear her husky voice shouting, "*I do not know what you're talking about, and it angers me that you would accuse me of such a thing!*"

Browser frowned down into his tea. His reflection stared back with anxious eyes. Jagged black locks fell around his face. He looked like a man who'd been running for summers, scrambling to escape a foe he could not see. That's how he'd felt throughout their marriage, like he was fighting an invisible adversary. Every day he could smell the enemy closing in, but never saw him until the very end when Ash Girl died in his arms.

Cloudblower stared at the snapping fire in the hearth. "If little Ash Girl cried, her father made her play a game he called 'beetle.' He forced her to lie on her back, then push up with her arms and legs until she'd arched her back as far as she could. When she weakened and fell, he beat her in the head with a fire-hardened digging stick. By the time she had seen four summers, she fell asleep every time he walked into their chamber. She went somewhere deep inside to hide. That's when Yellow Dove's soul took possession of her body. He saw what happened. He took the beatings. He endured the agony."

Browser felt as though he were seeing Ash Girl for the first time, and it twisted his insides. "Why didn't my wife tell me these things, Elder? Was she afraid to? Afraid that I would cast her out for being tainted with incest?"

He must have failed her in some way. What had he done? Perhaps he had not shown her enough love or cared enough about her problems. Or maybe she realized that his family would have forced him to leave her if they had known about her father.

Cloudblower said, "Ash Girl didn't speak with you about these things because she didn't remember them. I only know about them because Yellow Dove told me."

Browser kept his voice even. "How could she not know, Elder? These things happened to her."

Stone Ghost put a gentle hand on Browser's wrist. "Tortured children rarely recall what their tormentors do to them. It is the monster soul who keeps those memories."

Cloudblower reached for a stick of wood in the pile to her right and placed it on the fire. Smoke curled up, then delicate yellow flames licked around the fresh fuel. The rich tang of sage filled the chamber.

"Did Ash Girl's mother know?" Browser asked.

Cloudblower nodded. "Ash Girl was five when her mother discovered the truth. Her father ran away to escape being punished for incest. He was a Trader. No one in Green Mesa villages even missed him for two summers. Her mother never told anyone. She loved Ash Girl. She couldn't bear the thought that her daughter might be Outcast from the clan, or even killed to cleanse the village."

"And no one else knew? How could that be?" Browser said in a strained voice. "Children say things without thinking. Ash Girl's strange behavior must have roused someone's suspicions."

Cloudblower shook her head. "Not that I know of. Though I always thought our Matron knew."

The fire crackled and a wreath of sparks spun toward the roof's smoke hole.

Catkin said, "How could our Matron have known? Surely Ash Girl would not have told her."

"Ash Girl *could* not have told her," Stone Ghost reminded her. "She didn't carry the memories, Yellow Dove did. And I doubt that your Matron had the privilege of speaking with Yellow Dove. Monsters are very secretive. They may reveal themselves during times of great stress, but even then it is rare that people recognize them for what they are." He inclined his elderly head toward Cloudblower. "What did the Matron say that made you think she knew?"

The shell beads on Cloudblower's sleeves twinkled as she folded her arms. "About six moons before her death, Ash Girl started acting very strangely, screaming and lashing out at people for no reason. I remember our Matron whispering that it was her father's fault. I didn't understand what she meant and asked her about it. Our Matron just shook her head. She wouldn't tell me anything else."

Browser unconsciously touched the soft hides beside his sandals. For the last seven or eight moons of her life, Ash Girl had awakened swinging her fists and crying from nightmares she would not discuss. Browser had slept with Grass Moon in his arms, just to be certain Ash Girl didn't hurt him.

Stone Ghost's thick white brows pulled together. "Ash Girl's father left the family when she was barely five summers. That's probably what your Matron meant."

"Perhaps," Cloudblower whispered. "But I don't think so."

Stone Ghost's dark eyes glinted. "Why?"

"Our Matron told me once that many summers ago she had spoken with Ash Girl's grandmother. That struck me as odd. Flame Carrier was born in Dry Creek village, not far from here. With the warfare over the past fifty summers, why would she have risked traveling to the far north? Green Mesa is a dangerous place, filled with canyons where raiders ambush travelers."

"Did she say when this trip took place?"

"No. But I thought she meant a long time ago, perhaps fifteen or twenty summers."

Stone Ghost sipped his tea, and steam curled around his wrinkled face. "Perhaps, Healer, your Matron did not do the traveling. Ash Girl's grandmother could have come to Dry Creek village. We should ask Ant Woman."

"Yes," Cloudblower murmured. "She might know."

Catkin's eyes caught the firelight as she leaned forward. "We found something today, Cloudblower. The tracks of a little girl."

"A girl?" Cloudblower frowned. "What girl?"

Browser said, "We don't know, Elder. She had been

lying on the hilltop to the west of the grave, apparently watching us. She—"

"One of our children? Or another war orphan?"

Browser sipped his tea, and the sweet flavor of fire-weed blossoms teased his tongue.

Catkin answered, "Not one of ours, but we're not sure she was an orphan either. Something frightened her. She ran down the hill into the drainage and hid in an old coyote den in the bank. A man found her. The girl tried everything to avoid his grasping hands. She clawed the walls and floor of the den before he dragged her out on her belly and carried her away."

Cloudblower's soft brown eyes widened. "How old was she? Could you tell?"

"Seven or eight summers."

Catkin said, "Redcrop discovered the tracks. She also found a corn-husk doll in the rear of the den."

Cloudblower's gaze lifted to Catkin. "What does this girl have to do with Ash Girl? You don't think she...?" Her lips parted with words she did not speak.

Catkin said, "She may be the same girl whose foot-prints Stone Ghost found at the torture site. The same girl Browser heard at Aspen village. All we know for certain is that the man who found the little girl was wearing the same sandals as the man who helped to murder our Matron."

"Is that why you wished me to hear this?" Browser asked Catkin. "You think the little girl may be suffering the way Ash Girl did?"

Catkin said, "There are three of them, Browser: a man, a woman, and a little girl. I fear it is possible that she is his daughter."

"Blessed gods." Cloudblower bowed her head and closed her eyes for a long moment. "I pray not."

Stone Ghost's deep wrinkles rearranged themselves into sad lines. "We all do, Healer. But we must make plans in case Catkin is right."

"Yes." She stared at Stone Ghost with tear-filled eyes. "I will do whatever you wish me to."

Stone Ghost nodded. "I am grateful, Healer. Where is Redcrop?"

"At the grave, Uncle," Browser said.

Stone Ghost braced a hand on Browser's shoulder and rose unsteadily to his feet. "Please bring her. I want her to be there when we speak with Ant Woman. Your Matron may have told Redcrop things in the past thirteen summers that no one else knows."

∼

I lay on my belly on a sandstone terrace halfway down the side of the eroded bluff. My buckskin clothing blends with the tan rock. Father crouches five hundred body lengths below me. He is invisible to my eyes, like a serpent coiled beneath the sage, but I know he is there, watching. I feel him there.

The girl sits alone by the grave. She rocks back and forth.

The tension in Father's tall body must be unbearable, like a starving cougar with a rabbit in sight, afraid to leap for fear the rabbit will escape.

He has barely slept since he first saw her out there by herself. He wants her badly.

My gaze drifts over the rolling hills. Somewhere, warriors hide, waiting for him to strike.

Father knows this, of course. He must be trembling, his whole body fit to burst from the longing, but he will not give them what they expect. He will bide his time until he can no longer stand it, then he will trick them into turning away, into looking in the opposite direction for one brief instant, and when they do...

"Mother?" *The whisper is barely audible.* "I have been good. Can we go? I want to go."

A man in a red shirt walks the river trail toward the girl below. He is tall, with broad shoulders, and carries a club in his hand. The War Chief, Browser.

"Mother? My legs hurt, please?"

I pull my buckskin hood up to cover my hair and flatten my body against the sandstone ledge. I have not been afraid of being seen before now. The other warriors require only ordinary precautions, but this War Chief scares me. He has eyes like an antelope. No matter how far away I am, or how well hidden, his eyes always find me. I must be some curious color or shape to him. He has not yet realized what he is seeing, but he always takes the time to look more closely. Someday, he will see me, and then one of us will die.

Yes, but first I will play with him as a ferret does a rabbit. We are entwined in the old gods' web. We will Dance together, casting shadows in the moonlight until his is devoured by mine. In the end the only laughter will be the Blue God's—echoing in the empty rooms of abandoned places.

"Mother?"

"Shh. Your grandfather is coming back. I feel him coming."

She seems to turn to stone, her eyes huge.

"Now?" she asks in a trembling voice. "Is he coming now?"

"Yes."

She grabs my hand and tugs with all her strength. "Let's run away! Hurry, let's run!"

I jerk her to the ground. My voice is ice. "He is the only one in the world who loves us. Do you understand?"

Her mouth opens with silent cries. She lies down beside me in the dirt and hides her face in her hands.

I stroke her back. "The *only* one."

Dusty cried out and bolted upright, gasping. He batted the top of his sleeping bag out of the way and gulped air. He was in Dale's camp trailer. On the fold-out bench that made into a bed. "Good God, not again." He bent over in the cold darkness and cradled his head in his hands.

At the creak of the trailer floor, adrenaline shot through him. He tensed, sensing a presence, feeling the faint shift of the springs. His tongue had gone dry in his mouth.

"Dusty?" the voice asked softly from the metal stairs outside.

"I-I'm okay, Maureen. Just a dream."

The latch on the door clicked, and a sliver of light widened across the room. She wore gray sweatshirt and sweatpants and held a flashlight in her hand. Long black hair draped her shoulders, falling to her waist. "You're sure you're okay?"

He shivered. "I said I'm fine. Just a bad dream."

She stood uncertainly in the doorway. The flashlight beam illuminated her face and her black eyes shimmered. "The same one?"

"I wish I'd never seen that little son of a bitch." Maybe it was the hour, the lingering aftereffects of the dream, but he actually wanted company.

"The basilisk?"

He made a gesture and squinted up into the light. "If this is an interrogation, I'm supposed to be in a wooden chair. But I think you've got the light about right."

"Uh, sorry." She lowered the beam. "The basilisk from 10K3?"

He rubbed his bearded face. "I swear it belonged to someone insane."

She stepped into the room and leaned against the stove. The sweatshirt looked two sizes too big, but it must have been warm to sleep in. "That thing really has a handle on your subconscious."

"Yeah, fancy that." He rubbed his face and exhaled. His breath fogged in the cold air.

"It's just an artifact. A piece of stone." She sounded so sure of herself.

"Part of me believes that—the part that went to the university. But the part of me that went down into that kiva when I was twelve thinks you're really naive."

She bowed her head, and her hair fell over her shoulders in thick black waves. "Maybe, but I want you to consider the possibility that the dream is trying to tell you something. Are you struggling with guilt because Elder Walking Hawk wanted that basilisk reburied, or are you torturing yourself over something else?"

He shivered again, mostly from cold this time. "The other explanation is that evil exists, and I touched it.

Somehow or another, it got its hooks into me. Not all the way, but just enough." He rubbed his cold arms. "Remember the cleansing that Elder Walking Hawk did for us?"

She nodded. "Very well."

"I did that again the night I packed the *basilisco*. You know, just to be sure. God knows, if I hadn't, I might have cut your head off or something today."

She crossed her arms against the cold. "You're not the type, Stewart, despite what I originally thought about you."

"How nice of you to keep an open mind."

She tilted her head and smiled. "Tell me about the dream. Was it vivid?"

"Clear and sharp—even the smell."

"The smell?"

"The odor of burned skin and meat. I'm awake and I can still smell it."

"Why don't you start from the beginning."

He swallowed hard. "I was sitting on a bench in the kiva. It was beautiful, the walls painted in white on the top, and bright red on the bottom. Bundles—net bags, I think—hung from the rafters. And really peculiar paintings were on the pilasters. I think they were katchinas; they each had holes gouged in their chests. You could see the stone walls where the plaster had been chopped right out of the paintings, as if they'd cut their hearts out."

"Who did? Did they look like anyone you know in real life?"

"No. I didn't recognize any of the faces. They wore white capes and carried war clubs and axes. Men, all of them. Lots of jewelry. Turquoise and jet bracelets.

Colored feathers. Some wore what looked like necklaces made from bone disks." He shook his head. "They were insane, Maureen. Angry and filled with hatred. I'll never forget those bronzed faces, their black eyes enraged as they grouped around the woman."

"What woman?"

He frowned. "I don't know who she was. Proud, though. Stately. She just seemed to radiate authority and poise. She was someone important. Someone who had lived all of her life respected and obeyed. You could tell by the way she carried herself. And she despised the men around her."

A gust of wind rattled the trailer, and mice scrambled in the walls.

"They weren't her men?"

"No. Anything but. Her face twisted with pain as she watched them set fire to the pile of katchina masks in the middle of the floor. I could feel her fear growing with each beat of my heart."

"What does that mean, burning katchina masks?"

"It's a sacrilege. That's what they were doing. Destroying the katchinas."

Maureen brushed her long hair over her shoulders and braced a hand against the counter. "What happened to the woman?"

"She was dressed in blue, and she had gray hair, long, hanging down like yours. She wore a turquoise and eagle-bone breastplate, a beautiful thing that caught the light. Around her throat, she had a choker covered with beads. And I remember a wolf pendant, hanging down over her chest, but separate from the breastplate."

He exhaled hard and his breath glimmered in the

light. "The men prodded her forward. She turned her head, just far enough to glare at them like they were something she'd scraped off her foot. One of the men shoved her into the fire." Dusty shivered. "That's when the smell came. She pulled up the hem of her skirt and tottered around in that burning mass of katchina masks. I could see the skin on her calves blistering and wrinkling in the flames. When she could no longer stand, she fell and rolled against a big painted olla, a jar. She just lay there, writhing."

Maureen's eyes tightened. "She was dead?"

"No. One of the men leaned forward. It was like he knew the others were losing their will. He jammed his foot down on her burned feet, tramped on them. The burned skin split and peeled back; blood seeped through. Her toes came off, Maureen. I mean, my God, the meat, the muscles, were cooked." He took another breath. "Each time I huddled back on the bench, hoping, praying that they wouldn't see me. That they wouldn't turn and throw me into that fire."

Maureen rested the flashlight on the counter and aimed the beam at the back of the wall. "Did they?"

He shook his head. "They were interested in her. She tried to stand, and...and she fell, because her legs wouldn't hold her. So she tried crawling away, dragging herself. Her skin peeled away on the dirt floor, leaving a smear of blood and fluid."

"That sounds horrible."

He closed his eyes. "That's when the big guy turned and looked right into my eyes."

"Is that when you woke up?"

"No." His tongue felt swollen. "The big guy shouted something. I couldn't understand the words. It wasn't in Hopi, or Zuni, or any of the languages I know. But there he was, looking at me, while the old woman clawed at his legs, and tears ran down her cheeks."

"You're sure you don't know who this man was?" she gently asked.

"No. He was Indian, brown, broad-cheeked, with his hair done up in a bun like in the pictographs."

"Okay. What happened next?"

"I looked back at the old woman. She had wrapped her fingers in her beaded choker and twisted it so that the weight of her arm hung on it." He paused. "She was dead, Maureen. She had strangled herself."

"What did the big guy do?"

Dusty shifted uneasily, crumpling his sleeping bag with his hand. "He laughed, and—and when he looked back at me, it wasn't the big guy."

Maureen shifted and the flashlight beam bobbed around the trailer.

"Who was he?"

His voice cracked. "An old man! A toothless elder. He was wearing *el Basilisco* on his chest."

Maureen cautiously came over and sat down across from him. "You know what I think?"

"What?" He looked up into her dark confident eyes.

"I think you need another cleansing. One performed by an elder who knows what she's doing. Someone like Hail Walking Hawk."

"I thought you didn't believe in such things?"

Maureen leaned toward him and softly replied, "The point is that you do."

Dusty ran a hand through his sweat-drenched blond hair. "You think I've talked myself into this, don't you? I believe the basilisk was evil, and so I'm acting as though I've been witched, right?" He actually wanted her to say yes. It would have made him feel better, like the basilisk really wasn't evil and all of his fears were for nothing.

Instead, she surprised him by reaching out to touch his hand. Her fingers felt cool on his. "No matter what I say, Dusty, you won't believe me. You *believe* you've been witched. The only way you'll know for certain is by talking about this with an elder that you trust."

"Thanks for coming." He squeezed her hand and let it go. "But I feel better now. Why don't you go back to bed and get some sleep. We'll talk more tomorrow, okay?"

"You're sure?"

"I am."

"Okay." She straightened and headed for the door. She looked back just once, before she stepped outside.

Dusty dropped his head in his hands and tried to figure out what the hell was happening to him. Was it just his own mind playing tricks? Could Maureen be right? Or was an ancient witch be tormenting him from beyond the grave?

He flopped back on his blankets and stared at the ceiling.

Wind Baby played on the ridge tops, kicking up dust and whirling it high into the air. In the afternoon sunlight, the tall streamers bobbed across the distances, glistening like powdered amber.

Ant Woman watched the far-off fingers of flying dust for a moment, then let out a breath and turned her attention back to the crowded plaza. Most of the mourners had settled into groups. They huddled around the plaza with food bowls in their hands, whispering, weeping. Some laughed at stories told about Flame Carrier. There had to be more than one hundred adults and perhaps that many children. Colorful blankets lay spread across the ground, topped with food pots, baskets of nuts and breads, steaming bowls of meats, and piles of roasted corn on the cob. Children hovered around them. They knew they shouldn't play today, but it must be difficult, especially for the youngest.

"We're sorry to disturb you, Matron."

The voice jerked Ant Woman from her thoughts. She turned to see old Stone Ghost, Browser, and Flame Carrier's slave, Redcrop, standing before her.

"Yes, what is it?"

Stone Ghost gestured to the logs pulled up around Ant Woman's small fire. "May we sit? We would like to speak with you about our dead Matron."

"That is what this day is all about, old fool. Of course you may sit with me."

Stone Ghost grunted as he sat down by her side. His sparse white hair looked as if it hadn't been combed in moons. It stuck out at odd angles. Through the holes in his mangy turkey feather cape, she could see a threadbare tan shirt. War Chief Browser settled at the old man's side.

"What is it you wish to know?" she asked.

Stone Ghost answered, "We are hoping you can help us find your friend's murderer."

"Me?" she said in surprise. "How can I do that?"

Browser said, "We wish to know things about her early life, Matron. Things that only you may know."

Redcrop knelt to Ant Woman's left, and her white cape draped around her. The girl looked as broken as Ant Woman felt. Though, from the chill, her nose glowed like a ripe chokecherry.

Ant Woman tugged her brown-and-yellow blanket more tightly around her shoulders and gave Redcrop a sympathetic look. The girl didn't notice, but gazed down at her hands as though her entire world lay there now. What had they done? Dragged her away from the grave?

Softly, Ant Woman said, "Are you well, child?"

"Yes, I-I am, Matron. Well enough."

"It's all right to miss her, girl. I miss her, too. She was my friend for seventy summers. I don't know how I will get along without her wisdom."

Redcrop's mouth quivered. She had to swallow before she could say, "She loved you very much, Ant Woman. She told me many times."

"She loved you, too."

Ant Woman placed a bony hand on Redcrop's arm, and tears welled in the girl's eyes. "We'll manage. It will take many lonely nights of wishing and waking to find the wishes unfulfilled, but when the wishes have worn themselves out, we'll both be all right."

Redcrop whispered, "Thank you, Matron."

Ant Woman squeezed her arm and released it, then reached for the bowl of corn bread sprinkled with giant wild rye seeds that sat on the hearthstones before her. She had been picking at the bread for over a hand of time. It was delicious, but she felt sick without Flame Carrier. Sick and lost. Even when they'd been separated by great distances, Ant Woman had relied on Flame Carrier's memory to carry her through. She'd had imaginary conversations with the Matron, asking her what she would do in her position, or what she thought about this problem or that person. All of her strength had come from her friend.

But she's gone. My Flame Carrier is gone.

Ant Woman broke off a chunk of corn bread and put it in her toothless mouth. While she gummed it, she watched Stone Ghost and War Chief Browser. They whispered to each other. Stone Ghost nodded, and his mouth tightened. His long hooked nose had a slight bend to it, as though it had been broken sometime during his long life. Probably from a fist.

Ant Woman squinted one eye at him. Half the world thought he was a powerful witch. The other half thought he was an old fool. She straddled the line. Who ever said a witch and an old fool couldn't be one and the same? There were many stories about his foolishness, and many more about how clever he was. She figured he was probably a clever fool. She glanced down at the holes in the toes of his moccasins. Whatever the truth, his cleverness certainly hadn't gained him much wealth.

"Well?" she said. "What is it?"

The War Chief leaned forward. He had a round face, with a flat nose and thick black eyebrows. Handsome, in a rough-hewn sort of way. "Our Matron rarely spoke about her parents or her childhood."

Ant Woman's souls drifted, seeing faces she had not seen in seventy summers. "Well, I never knew your Matron's father, Ravenfire, but I knew her—"

"I knew Ravenfire, or I should say I met him once." Stone Ghost waved a hand apologetically. "But forgive me. Please go on."

"I was just going to say that I knew her mother well. Spider Silk came to our village eight moons pregnant. She had the child and lived with us for the rest of her life. Spider Silk was running at the time. She never said so, but she must have been."

"Running?" Stone Ghost cocked his head. "From what?"

Ant Woman made a helpless gesture. "I never knew. But only a desperate woman would run away from her people eight moons pregnant, and chance traveling the roads alone. That was back after the Straight Path Nation collapsed. War had just broken out. Villages were being burned."

Stone Ghost stared at her with unnerving intensity. "What of her parents? Did you ever meet them?"

"On occasion Spider Silk's parents came to visit her, and then everyone knew why Spider Silk was strange. Her father, Born-of-Water, had pink eyes and the skin of a corpse, white and shiny. He looked just like a wolf—a human wolf. I swear it. His face was long and pointed, like a muzzle." Ant Woman lifted her hands to her own face and showed them how it was shaped. "Her mother, Golden Fawn, seemed fairly ordinary, but...sad. Even when she smiled, despair lived in her eyes. I remember those two very well. They claimed to have been raised with the Blessed prophets, Cornsilk and Poor Singer. I don't know if that was true, but that's what Born-of-Water told people."

Stone Ghost's white brows drew together, and Ant Woman frowned. "What's wrong?"

Stone Ghost laced his fingers around one knee, and his cape fell back, revealing the threadbare brown shirt he wore. She could see his ribs through holes in the fabric.

Stone Ghost said, "It's just curious. You see, my own grandmother, Orenda, was raised with Cornsilk and Poor Singer. I wonder if she knew Spider Silk or her parents?"

Ant Woman took another drink of tea and wiped her mouth with the back of her hand. "Perhaps Orenda and Spider Silk grew up together?"

Stone Ghost shrugged. "Who can say? Every person alive wishes to be associated with the most important holy people in our history. I often thought that—"

Ant Woman broke in: "Did Orenda ever mention a turquoise cave to you?"

Stone Ghost's eyes went wide. "The Turquoise Cave! Why, yes. After my grandmother left the land of the Mountain Builders and came to the Straight Path Nation, she lived in the Turquoise Cave for a time, before moving to Green Mesa."

Ant Woman broke off another piece of corn bread and ate it. The giant wild rye seeds hurt her gums, but they had a rich earthy flavor that tasted delicious. "Spider Silk said she was born in that cave. Maybe your grandmother, Orenda, was related to Spider Silk."

Stone Ghost relaced the crooked, blue-veined fingers around his knee. "Maybe, but I don't recall my grandmother ever mentioning her name."

Browser said, "If there is a connection between your grandmother and our Matron's mother, could it have something to do with her murder? Perhaps the murderers are hunting down the children of people who knew the Blessed Poor Singer and the Blessed Cornsilk?"

Stone Ghost peered unblinking at the leaping flames before responding, "Everything is connected to everything, Nephew. But that would seem very odd. After all, I've been living alone in the middle of nowhere for most of my life. If someone had wished to kill me, it would have taken little effort."

Ant Woman made a disgusted sound. "You old fool. You're either senile or stupid."

Stone Ghost gave her a genuinely interested look. "Why would you say that?"

"Think of the amount of courage it would have

taken. Most people think you're a witch. No sane human would willingly walk into your lair."

Stone Ghost's white brows lowered. "Well, they wouldn't have had to 'walk into my lair,' Ant Woman. They could have shot me in the back when I was out gathering prickly pear cactus fruit or clubbed me to death while I was dozing in the summer sunshine. And your Matron has been wandering about gathering followers for the Katsinas' People for almost four summers. If someone had wished to kill her, they could have done it easily long ago. Why now?"

Redcrop shifted and toyed with the hands in her lap.

"What is it, child?" Ant Woman asked.

"I was wondering if maybe the murderers just discovered something they did not know before."

"What?"

Redcrop shook her head and raggedly chopped locks of hair fell over her face. "I don't know, Matron. I'm sorry I'm not more help."

"You're grieving, child," Ant Woman said and touched Redcrop's knee. "I'm surprised you can think at all."

Browser lifted his gaze to Ant Woman. "Perhaps our murderers are simply patient. They may have waited many sun cycles for the right moment to strike."

Ant Woman pointed a knobby finger at Stone Ghost. "If that is the case, you had better start walking backwards so you can see who's sneaking up on you."

Stone Ghost smiled. "Don't you think it would be easier if I just borrowed the eyes of a big cat and used pine pitch to glue them to the back of my skull?"

Ant Woman stared at him. On night excursions,

witches often used an animal's eyes to see better, then they left the eyes to spy on people. Ant Woman had known a young man who woke up one morning to see a bobcat's eyes watching him from his ceiling rafters. They'd been there for quite a while because nests of maggots had hatched in them. That's what had awakened the man, maggots dropping onto his face.

Ant Woman said, "I wouldn't joke about such doings if I were you, Stone Ghost. You might find yourself dead at the hand of a friend, rather than one of your many enemies."

Stone Ghost chuckled but didn't respond.

"Matron," Browser said, "I must ask you about something that happened long ago. Do you recall a woman from the Green Mesa clans coming to see our Matron when she lived in your village?"

Ant Woman ate another mouthful of bread and reached for her teacup to wash it down. "When would that have been?"

"I can't say for certain, perhaps fifteen or twenty summers ago?"

"Twenty summers ago," Ant Woman whispered, trying to remember. She sipped her tea. The flavors of dried mint and shooting star petals mixed deliciously. "I would have seen forty or fifty summers. During that time, many people came to see both your Matron and her mother. Spider Silk was getting old, but she had a reputation as a Powerful Healer. Your Matron helped her mother with surgeries and applying poultices, mixing herbs. Those two saved many lives. People genuinely loved them."

She gestured lightly. "They also feared them, of

course. Anyone who is skilled with plants is a little frightening, because she can kill as well as cure."

Redcrop said, "Grandmother knew a great deal about plants. She taught me."

Ant Woman nodded. "She got that from her mother, who claimed she got it from her mother, and she said she got it from her mother, and on back forever, I suppose."

Browser touched Stone Ghost's hand. "Uncle? Who was Orenda's mother? What was her name?"

Stone Ghost shook his head, but Ant Woman could see his hesitation. He said, "She never spoke about her real mother, but a woman of the Hollow Hoof Clan, named Nightshade, raised my grandmother."

Browser looked back at Ant Woman. "Do you recall the name of Born-of-Water's mother, or Golden Fawn's? Was it Nightshade?"

"I don't think I ever heard their names. If I did, I've forgotten."

Redcrop murmured, "Grandmother talked about Badgertail and Nightshade."

Everyone turned in her direction.

Firelight glazed Redcrop's wide eyes.

Ant Woman gently said, "Go on, child. What do you remember?"

"Not very much, Matron. I recall that she said Badgertail had been a great War Chief somewhere far to the east near a huge river. Nightshade was supposed to have been a very Powerful Dreamer."

Browser said, "Then our Matron had at least heard stories of the woman who raised Orenda. Did she say anything else, Redcrop?"

Redcrop touched her temple, as though her head

ached. "I remember that Grandmother had an older brother—"

"Yes." Ant Woman nodded. "Bear Dancer. I remember him. He was an odd one. Many summers ago I heard he was killed in a raid. I recall hearing that she had a half-brother, too, but I don't think she ever knew him."

Stone Ghost tilted his head and frowned at the fire. "Bear Dancer, gods, I have not thought about him in many summers. He was a violent man, always provoking fights just so he could hurt someone—much like his father."

"What about his father?" Browser said. "Did you ever hear our Matron talk about him?"

"No," Stone Ghost answered. "I heard many rumors from other people, but—"

Redcrop said, "I asked Grandmother about him once, and she just smiled and said that she did not wish to remember him. I don't think she liked him very much."

Ant Woman brushed cornbread crumbs from her crooked fingers onto her yellow cape and tried to see through the hazy veil between the present and the past. Contemplatively, she said, "A woman from the Green Mesa villages. Twenty summers ago. I don't recall anyone coming down from Green Mesa, except Traders, of course. But there weren't any women Traders from Green Mesa at that time."

Stone Ghost said, "Perhaps a man from Green Mesa, then. He may have been carrying a message for the woman."

Ant Woman rubbed her wrinkled jaw. "Old Pigeontail was from somewhere near Green Mesa. He frequented our village. He's still around, charging outrageous prices for his trinkets. He may know. And your Matron was married to him for a few summers. He—"

"What?" Redcrop said, stunned. "Grandmother was married to Old Pigeontail? I never knew that!"

Browser added, "Great Ancestors, that's like corralling a buffalo bull with a wolf! What battles they must have waged against each other."

Ant Woman grinned. "That's why the marriage did not last long. She was always chewing at his throat, and he was always trying to kick her senseless—but Spider Silk ordered her to marry him. I never knew why."

Redcrop laughed. She had tears in her eyes, but a smile turned her lips. "When was that, Elder? How old was Grandmother?"

"Oh, let me see." Ant Woman rubbed her wrinkled throat. "It seems like that was forty summers ago. Maybe a little longer. Pigeontail was younger than your Matron. That was part of the problem. She'd seen a lot more of life than he had, but he didn't like it when she pointed that out."

"How strange," Browser said. "Old Pigeontail has often visited our villages, but our Matron always went out of her way to avoid him. I used to wonder why."

Ant Woman could feel Stone Ghost's gaze. She turned and found him staring at her with unwavering eyes. White wisps of hair had glued themselves to his wrinkled cheeks.

"What are you staring at?"

Stone Ghost lowered his voice. "I was remembering a tragedy that happened twenty summers ago in the Green Mesa villages. Four old women were murdered."

He rubbed his thumb over the black-on-white geometric paintings on the side of his teacup. "One of them was my sister."

Browser said, "That would be about the time the woman from Green Mesa supposedly came to see our Matron."

Ant Woman nodded. "I remember those murders. Your reputation soared after you found your sister's killer. Everyone wanted you to come and solve crimes in their village."

Stone Ghost answered, "That is exactly why I've spent the last twenty summers living alone in the middle of nowhere."

"But you have helped many villages."

"Yes. The ones I could."

Ant Woman brought up her aching right knee and rubbed it. On cold damp days like this, a fire built in the joint. She'd have to brew up a cup of willow bark tea before she'd be able to sleep tonight. "Whatever happened to your house down at Smoking Mirror Butte?" She used her chin to point southward. "Is it still there?"

Stone Ghost turned to the south and longing filled his old eyes. His white hair fluttered in the wind. "I hope so. I plan on going back."

"Not until after you've found the people who murdered my friend, I hope."

"That is my first duty, Matron."

Flame Carrier's smiling face appeared on the fabric of Ant Woman's souls and the pain in her heart expanded to fill her whole chest.

"Well," she said, "if you have no more questions for

me, I would like to go to my camp where I can be with my family."

"I understand," Stone Ghost said. "Thank you for speaking with us, Ant Woman. How long will you be staying in Longtail Village?"

"Perhaps another day. I need to speak with Crossbill about trading some of our pots for her pretty red blankets. Then we'll be going."

Stone Ghost rose unsteadily to his feet, and Browser grabbed his elbow to help support him.

Stone Ghost said, "If we have more questions, I hope you will speak with us again?"

"I will do whatever I can to help. Just don't interrupt me when I'm haggling for blankets."

"I promise not to." Stone Ghost smiled and bowed to her. "A pleasant evening to you, Matron."

"And to you, Stone Ghost."

The old man hobbled away with Browser and Redcrop behind him.

Ant Woman watched them with narrowed eyes as they walked through the crowd. Stone Ghost knew something he wasn't telling. She could feel it in her squirming belly. What was he hiding? The reason for Flame Carrier's murder? Maybe the reason for a number of murders that had happened in the past twenty summers?

Ant Woman shook her head, finished her tea, and struggled to her feet. As she walked across the plaza, she saw the pain on the faces of others, and it made her own grief worse.

Could Browser be right? The murderers were hunting down those who'd known the Blessed prophets. Why would someone do that? Cornsilk and Poor Singer had never harmed anyone. Legends said they'd spent their lives teaching and Healing, moving from village to village. They had claimed to have no clans, or families, which made them members of all clans and all families. That was their greatest strength.

Ant Woman sighed, too tired and grief-stricken to think more about it. As she rounded the southeastern corner of Longtail village and looked down at Dry Creek village's camp, a sea of yellow capes flashed. Her people drifted from one fire to the next, speaking in hushed tones. Her daughter, Rock Dove, knelt before her own fire, nursing her baby. The beautiful boy had been born less than four moons ago. Rock Dove waved at Ant Woman.

Ant Woman lifted a hand and smiled. If she could just lie down for a time before the evening Dances, she might be able to stand it.

She forced her aching knees to walk.

The sound of rain drumming on her tent roof woke Maureen. She opened her eyes and stared at the darkness until she realized that the bottom of her sleeping bag was soaked clear through, as were her favorite pair of wool socks.

"No wonder I froze all night."

She shoved out of her bag and looked around. Even in the storm light, she could see pools of water glistening on the tent floor around her.

She tugged off her drenched socks and reached into her suitcase for a clean pair. She had to be a magician to dress beneath the bowed, waterlogged tent walls, but she managed. The aroma of coffee perking and breakfast cooking drifted from the trailer encouraged her. Dusty must be up.

Maureen shrugged on her black down coat and ducked out of her tent. In the light from the trailer windows, she could see the water puddles. While the supply tent, Steve's, and Sylvia's, stood resolute against the storm, Maureen's had become a pathetic pond. The sides sloped inward as though ready to collapse. It took an act of will not to pull the stakes and let the rest of it collapse.

Maureen shoved her hands into her pockets and hurried for the trailer. As she stamped the mud off her boots on the stairs, Dusty called, "Come on in. Coffee's on!"

Maureen pulled the door open and stepped into the warmth. "Oh, this feels good. My tent leaked last night."

At the stove, Dusty turned from the frying pan to give her a knowing look. The white light of the lantern pulsed, giving his blond hair and beard a silver sheen. "I noticed. Sylvia bet me ten bucks that it would collapse on top of you before you got up."

"How nice. You win." Maureen took off her coat and hung it on the peg by the door. Wet splotches darkened her jeans. There must have been more water on her sleeping bag than she'd realized. "You're ten dollars richer. Speaking of Sylvia, where is she?"

Dusty handed her a note with rain-smeared ink:

Boss Man! The skies opened. Since it doesn't look like this is going to quit, we're making a town run. We promise to do the shopping before we find a couple of cold brews. See you late tonight or first thing tomorrow depending on how fuzzed up we get.

Love and Kisses,

S²

Dusty's version of *huevos rancheros* simmered on the stove, made with a local brand of salsa, fresh jalapenos, canned beans, and tortillas; it smelled wonderful. They'd eaten it three days in a row; she hadn't grown tired of it, yet.

"This is going to take a while," he said. "Why don't you sit down, and I'll pour you a cup of coffee."

"Thanks."

Maureen shivered and walked over to the table piled high with specimen boxes. Dusty's neatly piled stacks of papers sat on the opposite side of the table.

"Sometime," he said, gesturing at her with the spatula, "you ought to have my specialty. I make my own refritos. Two parts black beans to three parts Anasazi beans."

"Anasazi beans?"

"Yeah. The same kind the Anasazi grew here eight hundred years ago. It's the single biggest industry up in Dove Creek, Colorado."

"This is a joke, right?"

"No. Fact. If we have time, we can drive up to Dove Creek and look at their bean elevator. That, and the cafe and gas station, *are* Dove Creek. See that and you've seen it all. Unless, of course, you've got a thing for tractors."

Last night after dinner, she'd spread her first collection of bone—a child's femur, a skull fragment, and what looked like an adult's tibia—out onto the little square table and set up her microscope. She started rearranging things so she would have a place to put her elbows. She slid her microscope to the right and blew dust from the table.

"You don't think Sylvia will get her Jeep stuck in the mud getting back in here, do you?"

"No, I know those two. They'll get a hotel room and

watch the weather report. They'll linger, enjoying town life until this lifts."

Dusty set a steaming cup of coffee in front of her, and Maureen cradled it in her cold hands. "Oh, that smells great." She took a swallow and said, "My tent and sleeping bag look grim. Maybe I'd better go in and get a motel room tonight, too."

Dusty leaned against the counter and picked up his own coffee cup, one of those insulated travel mugs. "Dale keeps extra blankets in the cabinet over the couch. It's mouse proof up there. Why don't I move to the rear of the trailer, and you can have the front. That'll save me a trip into town tonight and another one to go get you in the morning."

She hesitated. "I guess you won't come crawling into my bed in the middle of the night."

Amusement twisted his lips. "No, probably not. Not that it would be such a bad bed to crawl into."

Maureen gave him a skeptical look. "You're such a sweet talker, Stewart."

He smiled and took another drink of coffee. "I was thinking I'd go back to work while I waited for the *huevos* to cook. Will you mind?"

"No. I'll just do the same."

"Okay."

Dusty slid into the booth opposite her and huddled behind piles of photo logs, feature records, artifact lists, field specimen forms, and the other minutiae of a well-run archaeological dig.

Maureen had begun her cataloging with the partially burned child's femur she and Sylvia had recovered. It lay before her on the table, next to her notebook.

Dusty didn't seem much inclined to talk this morning, which was unusual. Dark circles filled the hollows beneath his blue eyes. More bad dreams?

She glanced at him, set her coffee down, and picked up her hand lens and pen. As she examined the bone, she wrote in her notebook, remarking on the scalloping and charring, the overall preservation, the fact that the epiphyseal lines were unossified—meaning it was a young child's leg bone.

"Uh, Doctor?"

She glanced up from measuring the mid-diaphyseal diameter—the middle of the long bone—and hesitated, calipers in one hand.

He was watching her with uncertain eyes.

"What?"

"About my nightmare." Dusty seemed to be fighting the urge to cringe. "I just wanted you to know that... Well..."

"You're not a raving lunatic?"

"That, too. But, no, I was just going to say thanks for listening to me. I appreciated it."

"No problem."

She bent back to her work. After several minutes, she could feel his unrelenting blue-eyed stare boring into her. She looked up.

Dusty said, "You don't think I'm on the verge of a mental breakdown of catastrophic proportions, do you?"

Maureen could read the rest in his eyes—*like my father?* "No. I think you're stronger than that."

He fiddled with his pen. "I've been trying to figure out who the old woman is in the dream. The brain cooks up strange things. Maybe it was something I saw in a movie, or on TV. Something that clicked, got a reaction, and stayed buried until the *basilisco* called it up."

She reached for her coffee cup where it steamed next to a dirt-encrusted child's skull. She took a sip and ran a finger over the curve of the frontal bone. "Do basilisks have a reputation for doing that? Calling things up?"

He frowned down at a field specimen list. "Frankly, Doctor, I don't know. They had a lot of trouble over in the Valley early in the last century. *Basiliscos* didn't show up much after World War II." He shook his head. "I keep telling myself I don't believe in them."

"We could call Maggie. Find out how to destroy the evil."

"No," he said, and ran a hand through his blond hair. "She has enough problems herding tourists for the Park Service without us exposing her to some sort of ancient Anasazi evil. Let's leave Maggie out of this. Besides, I know how to deal with the little son of a bitch. You're supposed to force the basilisk to look into a mirror. It creates a sort of feedback loop that makes the evil feed on itself and kills the wicked creature."

Dusty leaned over his specimen list again, his brow furrowed.

Maureen went back to her bones. She studied the curved length of the femur, puzzled for a moment, and then lifted it, hefting the light tube of bone and sighting down the shaft. "Stewart, I think this child had rickets."

"Huh?"

"Vitamin deficiency. I can't prove that here, in the field, but I probably can in the lab. That, or some soil pressure has caused deformation of the diaphysis."

"In English, please, Doctor."

"Vitamin D fixes calcium in the bones. Without it, bones go soft. This bone curves. See it?"

"Yeah, I do."

Having completed her measurements, taken notes, and made a preliminary description, she rewrapped the bone in tissue and newspaper and replaced it in the box. Then she turned to the skull. The fragment consisted of a child's frontal bone, both orbits—eye sockets—and the maxillary bones. She carefully studied the heat-damaged incisors, cracked and broken by the fire. The alveolar area, the part of the upper jaw just under the nose, had been calcined where the lip had pulled back in response to extreme heat. This, she noted, and then used a bamboo pick to break soil loose from the inside of the orbits.

"It was just so real," Dusty said absently. He was staring off into space, and she could almost see the dream playing behind his eyes. Dusty shook his head. "They must have ritually killed the katchinas, that's why they chopped the hearts out of the paintings and burned the masks."

Throwing caution to the winds, Maureen said, "Maybe the woman was a witch and that's why they burned her in the fire with the masks."

"Possibly. That's a universal way of handling evil."

Maureen paused when she noticed the roughness inside the child's orbits. She turned the thin fragment of skull and squinted at it in the gray light. Reaching for her brush, she carefully whisked dirt out of what should have been the smooth top of the orbit. "I'll be—"

"Be what?"

"I've got *cribra orbitalia* here."

"Why is it that every time I talk to you, I have to keep mentioning that the language of the realm is English, not Latin?"

"Science uses its own language, Stewart." She lifted her hand lens as Dusty rose and crossed to watch her. She smiled at the frothy look of the bone; little holes visible across the concave top of the orbit. She pointed as he leaned over. "Look here. See, this is just above where the eyeball is set. This porosity and irregular bone. That's *cribra orbitalia*."

"Okay, so it looks like someone boiled the top of the kid's eyeballs. Was that from the fire?"

"No." She cocked her head, glanced at him, and then turned her attention back to the broken piece of skull. "Remember the hypoplasia, the ripples, I saw in the teeth that first day?"

"Yes, the burned mandible."

"That's the one." She indicated the wrapped femur. "Then I see rickets in that femur, and now *cribra* in this skull."

"Which means?"

"These children were really sick. We're seeing nutritional deficiencies everywhere. A lack of vitamin D causes rickets. Iron deficiency is one of the suspected causes of *cribra orbitalia,* and I'm betting I'll get thickening of the cranial vault, uh—the skull bones—as well as *cribra cranii:* holes in the inner table of the braincase. This whole population was under stress."

He braced a hand on the tabletop. "That fits. If my pottery is correct, if these are like the same people we found at 10K3—" He seemed suddenly stunned.

"What is it?"

For a moment, he was silent. "At 10K3, you found tuberculosis among some of those women. Remember? You told me that for there to be that many cases of tuberculosis in the bones, the disease's attack rate had to be through the roof."

She nodded. "That's right."

"Okay," he said, excitement growing. "Then, like 10K3, this site dates to the period about one hundred years after the fall of Chaco. These folks are making Mesa Verdean-style pottery, they're sick, and running, moving from place to place in search of a sanctuary. They're rebuilding the kivas, right? And I'm willing to bet that once we get through the bone bed and the kiva roof, we're going to find that they remodeled this tower kiva, too."

"Okay. So?"

"Of course they're malnourished. Entire sections of the Southwest were being abandoned at that time. People were fleeing the warfare and crowding into the remaining villages, swelling the population. There had to be a lot of hungry people. Agriculture depends on a predictable workforce."

Dusty picked up the bit of skull and looked into the empty orbits, as if seeing the bright brown eyes that might have once stared back at him. "The poor little guy never had a chance. His whole world was plunging itself into a holocaust."

Maureen unwrapped the fragment of adult femur Sylvia had found. The specimen consisted of the upper, proximal portion, the head, neck, trochanters, and perhaps fifteen centimeters of shaft that ended in a badly calcined end. She couldn't tell if it had been broken or just burned so badly that the bone had crumbled.

Stewart was still studying the child's face when Maureen bent and took a close look at the femoral neck. Using her hand lens, she squinted in the poor light, studying the bone's exterior, then stopped short. "My, my, look at this."

"What?" He put the skull fragment down and dropped one knee onto the booth's padded seat beside her.

She used her bamboo pick to indicate the irregular grooves that incised the bone just under the femoral neck and above the trochanters. "That's where you cut to sever the ligaments." She turned the bone, exposing the round ball of the femoral head to the light. At the top, where the tendon inserted, the bone was marred, as if it had been sawed at. "I'd say they cut the teres tendon." She looked up. "My first guess, based on the diameter of the shaft, and the smooth surface of the *linea aspera,* is that this is a woman. From the light weight, compared to bone size, I'd say an old woman."

She paused to get his full attention. "Dusty, someone cut this woman apart *before* the kiva burned. An adult femur, surrounded by thick muscle, would not have burned away in mid-shaft."

He looked at her intently. "What does that mean?"

"I'm saying that someone threw those bones on the kiva roof before it burned. She was disarticulated—cut apart—and then her bones were scattered over the roof. The only reason we have this section of bone is that a child's body was lying on top of it, protecting it from the heat."

Dusty slid into the booth beside her, forcing her to

move over, and took the femur from her hand. "So the children were marched to the roof and forced to stand in the middle of the bloody bones of one of their elders?"

Maureen sank back against the seat. "That's what it looks like."

The ritual jewelry on the people in the plaza winked as they turned to watch Browser pass. He refused to meet their eyes and walked purposefully, hoping no one would stop him to offer condolences, or to question him about the murder. He was dead tired and needed to be alone.

Ant Woman's words had stirred his souls. Flame Carrier's marriage to Pigeontail disturbed him. If Ant Woman was right, then by the time of the marriage, Flame Carrier must have been greatly revered by her people. She could have had her choice of powerful and esteemed men. Why would Spider Silk order her to marry a young lowly Trader?

A man in a yellow cape took a step toward Browser with his mouth open, and Browser held up a hand and shook his head.

The man called, "Perhaps later, War Chief?"

"Yes. Thank you for your understanding."

The unknown man turned back to his friends.

Browser watched his feet. Stone Ghost and

Redcrop spoke softly behind him, but he ignored their words. His own mother had ordered him to marry Ash Girl, but he had understood her reasons. Spider Silk's order made no sense.

Children sat with their backs to the western wall, plucking food from the array of baskets, stew pots hanging from tripods, and platters of fried breads. Most of the village elders had gathered on the roof of the great kiva. The drying ears of corn had been stacked around the rim of the roof, creating a speckled, many-colored circle four hands high. Wading Bird's scratchy old voice carried, then he laughed.

Springbank shoved through the crowd, his age-spotted face taut, his toothless mouth sucked in as though he was upset. He wore a beautiful white ritual cape covered with glistening circlets of seashells. He called, "War Chief?"

Browser stopped. This one, he could not refuse. "Yes, Elder?"

"Have you seen Obsidian?"

"No, Elder. Why?"

Anger strained his ancient face. "Ant Woman asked me to make certain that Obsidian remembers she is bringing food to the tower kiva for the children tonight, but I haven't seen her since midday. Nor has anyone else. Where can she be?"

Browser shrugged. Fatigue made him less cautious than he would ordinarily have been. He said: "She tells me nothing, Elder. She turns even simple questions like 'Where were you born?' into a game. Perhaps that's what she's doing today. Playing a game of hide-and-seek."

Springbank balled his fists and drew them beneath

his cape. "As for where she was born, she once told me she was born here. As for whether or not she's playing a game, I promise to find out. If you see her, tell her we have things to discuss, and I want her to come to me immediately."

"Yes, Elder."

Springbank dipped his head to Stone Ghost, then marched across the plaza like a warrior on a mission.

"War Chief?" Redcrop called.

Browser turned. "Yes?"

"If you are finished with me, I think I will start sorting through the Matron's things, trying to decide what she would wish people to have."

"You are free to go, Redcrop. Thank you for accompanying us to speak with Ant Woman."

Stone Ghost reached out and lightly placed a hand on her shoulder. "Come for me if you need help. I did not know her as you did, but I can carry things and place them where you tell me to."

Her pretty face looked pale and gaunt. "Thank you, Elder, but you must have many more important things to do. Straighthorn told me he would help me tonight."

Browser said, "I saw him go into his chamber just before I went to fetch you from the burial. I think he's still there."

Redcrop turned toward the ground-floor room where Straighthorn lived at the base of the tower kiva. Water Snake stood guard on the kiva roof. He held his war club in his hand.

She hesitated. "I do not wish to disturb Straighthorn if he is sleeping. He has to stand guard from midnight to dawn."

Browser said, "He's spent most of the day in his

chamber, Redcrop. I suspect he's slept for several hands of time. Why don't you go and see?"

She smiled. "Yes, thank you. I will. I wish you both a pleasant burial feast."

"And you, also," Stone Ghost said.

They watched Redcrop make her way through the crowd toward Straighthorn's chamber. Several people stopped her to speak with her.

Stone Ghost studied Browser from the corner of his eye. Wind Baby's voice had eased to a whisper, fluttering people's capes and tousling their hair. Stone Ghost kept his voice down. "Pigeontail seems an odd choice, doesn't he, Nephew? Is that what you were thinking?"

Browser nodded. "Yes, Uncle."

As the afternoon light swelled, slow and golden over the village, the walls took on a mellow glow.

Stone Ghost said, "You should try to rest for as long as you can. People will be clamoring to speak with you when the nightly Dances begin."

"I know, Uncle."

Every bit of his strength had been focused upon organizing their guards to best protect the surviving villagers and guests, while at the same time struggling to understand why their Matron had been murdered, and by whom. All the while, the mystery of Aspen village lay buried in his souls. Weariness had numbed his wits as well as his body. He needed rest.

"I will speak with you later, Nephew," Stone Ghost said, and he hobbled across the plaza for the great kiva.

Wading Bird, Cloudblower, and the other elders sat in the center with blankets clutched about their shoulders. Another thirty people crouched around them, listening to the tales they told. In the sky above the elders, flocks of Cloud People billowed, glowing the purest white Browser had ever seen.

He glanced over his shoulder toward Catkin's chamber. She would be sound asleep by now. He wished she'd heard the conversation with Ant Woman, but he would tell her every detail later. With everything that had been happening, he'd had little time to really sit and talk with her. He missed the soft sound of her voice.

Browser walked toward his chamber. As he slipped beneath his door curtain, the sweetness of blazing star petals struck him. He glanced around at the darkness. Had she been here?

"Obsidian?"

A shadow moved on his bedding hides, and in the light that streamed around his door curtain, he caught a glimmer of blue dress. A hundred tiny jeweled pins winked through her hair as she lazily rolled to her back.

Browser stiffened. For an instant he thought she was Ash Girl, his dead wife—and it wasn't the first time that had happened. Three or four times in the past nine moons he'd caught himself replacing Obsidian's face with Ash Girl's. He shook himself and clenched his fists. "What are you doing here?"

"Waiting for you, War Chief."

"Why?"

She stretched like a bobcat in warm sunlight, her arms over her head, her back arching, forcing her full breasts to strain against the fabric of her dress. "You know why."

Browser hesitated, under that dark and penetrating gaze, he removed his cape and hung it on the peg by the door. "You have been dogging my steps for moons, Obsidian. No matter where I am, I expect to see you watching me. Do I entertain you that much?"

"Let us speak for a time, Browser. Perhaps we can overcome this—this unpleasantness."

"I don't think so. And if I were you, I would rush outside. Elder Springbank is searching for you, and he isn't happy. He told me to tell you he has things to discuss with you and wishes to see you immediately."

She waved a hand. "He is never happy with me. He spends half his days watching me like a hawk, and the other half ordering me about as though I were his daughter, or worse, his slave. The old man can wait."

She tipped her chin and gazed at him with those gleaming black eyes, and Browser had to fight to control his emotions. He genuinely disliked her, but that meant nothing to his body. His manhood responded to her beauty whether he wished it to or not.

"All right," he said, exhaling hard. "I grant you one finger of time. But speak quickly."

Browser walked to his warming bowl in the middle of the room and pulled a twig from the woodpile. As he laid it on the coals, smoke drifted up. He blew on the fresh tinder. It took a few moments for the twig to catch, then a pale wavering light flickered over the white walls and danced in her black eyes.

She said, "I heard that you asked Straighthorn about me."

Browser didn't look up. He doubted Straighthorn had told her about their conversation. Calmly, he answered, "You have a mysterious background, Obsidian."

"Is that what Straighthorn told you?"

"He told me that twenty-five summers ago your mother married a Longtail man named Shell Ring. After his death, Crossbill adopted you and your mother into the clan. You were seven at the time."

She propped herself up on one elbow, and a wealth of thick hair tumbled around her shoulders. "Straighthorn had not even been born yet. How would he know?"

Sparks crackled and whirled through the air that separated them.

Browser replied, "People hear stories, Obsidian. He's lived in the same village as you for sixteen summers."

"Few people speak about those days. I'm surprised he knows that much."

"Why does no one speak of it? How long were you married to Ten Hawks?"

Her graceful brows lifted. "How long were you married to Ash Girl?"

"That's not an answer."

"But 'people hear stories,' War Chief. I would like to know. How long?"

Grudgingly, he said, "Five summers. We—"

"You lived with her for five summers and did not know she had a monster soul inside her?" Her eyes gleamed at his expression. The words affected him like the blows of a war club. She'd done it deliberately, taking control of the conversation. "You must have seen it peeking out at you when you fought with her."

Browser toyed with the woodpile, rearranging the twigs. "I suppose, but I did not realize what I was seeing, Obsidian."

With mock compassion, she said, "Poor Browser.

He didn't have the courage to gaze into the murderous eyes of the woman he loved."

Browser gave her a thin smile. "Feel better?"

"A bit."

"Good. I've answered some questions for you. Now do me the same honor. I am confused by the stories your people tell about you. When we first arrived, Crossbill told me that you were not human, that you had flown down from the skyworld as a meteorite. She said that your mother had caught you, and when she opened her hands, she found a baby girl there."

Obsidian rolled to her side to face him. "Yes, my mother told me the same ridiculous story."

Browser tilted his head. "Did you ask her about your father?"

She toyed with the hide. "Of course I asked. Many times. She would tell me nothing, and I could see the pain in her eyes when she spoke of him."

"Do you recall him at all?"

Obsidian ran a jeweled hand through her long hair and her voice turned soft. "Sometimes. But I'm not sure if they are real memories or the longings of a lonely child for a father."

Browser added another twig to the fire. "What do you recall?"

"In my dreams, I often feel hands upon me, smoothing my skin like warm fur. I think they are his hands."

Browser looked up sharply. "I don't understand."

She rose to her knees, tipped her chin up, and closed her eyes. "Like this," she whispered.

She ran her hands over her arms and throat, as though showing him her dreams, then her hands moved lower. She caressed her breasts and let her fingers slowly glide down her narrow waist to her groin. It was the most sensual display Browser had ever seen. Even if he had wished to, he could not have taken his eyes from her.

"Obsidian—"

She opened her eyes. "You asked if I recalled anything about him. That is what I remember."

He paused, not certain if he should make the accusation. "...Incest?"

"No, I don't think so. I only recall his hands. If he'd taken me, I think I would recall much more. Wouldn't you?"

Browser inclined his head. "I don't know. I've heard that children often don't recall such violations."

She lay back down and curled on her side on his buffalo hide, watching him. The way firelight reflected from her eyes, they might have been polished onyx. "Because your wife didn't?"

Browser clenched his fists. "Yes. That is one reason."

Her gaze moved leisurely, tracing the line of his broad shoulders, then his chest, and finally dropping to his manhood. She moaned softly. Without taking her gaze from him, the slow way she rose to her feet and walked around the fire toward him mesmerized. Every movement provocative and alluring.

He lurched to his feet.

As though reaching for a frightened child, Obsidian extended her hands until her fingers almost touched his knotted stomach muscles. The firelight glimmered through her magnificent hair. "Take my hands. It is not as difficult as you imagine, War Chief."

"I don't wish this, Obsidian."

"You do. You know you do."

She placed her hands on his sides and smoothed them down over his hips.

He grabbed her hands and held them. He could imagine himself gently removing each turquoise pin that adorned her hair, slipping her blue dress over her head, pulling her naked body against his.

"What was his name, Obsidian? Your father's name? Did your mother ever tell you?"

Her mouth twisted into a pout again. "What difference does it make?"

"If you came here twenty-five summers ago, do you remember hearing stories about Two Hearts?"

"The legendary witch?"

Browser nodded. "Crossbill's grandmother and many other clan matrons had dispatched war parties to hunt him down for his crimes."

"I had seen seven summers, Browser. I may have heard about it, but I do not recall—"

"What about the stories of the cursed little girl who lived in this village thirty summers ago? You must have heard about that."

She leaned forward until her breasts pressed against his hands. The sensation was akin to being struck by lightning. His whole body throbbed.

"That wasn't me, Browser. Is that what you fear? That I have been tainted by incest? Like your wife? Is that why you won't touch me?"

"I won't touch you because I don't wish to, Obsidian. I..."

She bent to kiss his hands, and he abruptly released her and backed into the wall. Before he could avoid it,

Obsidian stepped forward, slipped one arm around his waist pulled herself against him. She pressed her free hand against his straining manhood, and whispered, "Ah!"

He tore roughly away and shoved her toward the door. "Enough. Leave!"

She stumbled, grasped the leather curtain to steady herself, and turned. Her smile mocked him.

"You were close, War Chief. A hair's breadth. The next time, this will end differently. You know that, don't you?"

"There won't be a next time."

She laughed and ducked under the curtain into the afternoon sunlight.

Browser stood for a moment, breathing hard, then he pulled his red war shirt over his head and threw it on the floor.

He paced his chamber like a caged lion, wondering what she wanted, what game she played. She apparently needed Browser to win. But how could that be? What did he have that she...

His gaze went to his buckskin cape hanging on the peg by the door.

That morning she'd asked him where "it" was.

The turquoise wolf would be a prize for anyone, but how could she know he possessed it? No one knew, except Uncle Stone Ghost and Catkin.

And the man who lost it.

Redcrop's white cape whipped around her legs as she climbed the ladder to the tower kiva and stepped onto the plastered roof. The top row of third-story rooms stretched off to either side of the kiva. Straighthorn's chamber was to her left, sandwiched between Elder Springbank's chamber and Obsidian's. Her feet scuffed hollowly as she walked from the kiva roof, onto the elder's roof, and toward the ladder that stood in Straighthorn's roof entry.

People in the plaza turned to watch. The kind looks, the tears, went straight to her heart. The din of conversations died down, then picked up again.

Straighthorn called, "Redcrop? Is that you?"

"Yes. Were you sleeping? I don't wish to disturb you. I know you have to stand guard—"

"I'm coming up," he said, and his steps patted the ladder.

As he emerged onto the roof, he gave her a desperate look. He'd changed into his ritual clothing, a pale-green knee-length shirt studded with circlets of polished buffalo horn, black leather leggings, and sandals. When Wind Baby pressed the fabric against his body, she could see his muscles.

"Come with me."

The urgency in his voice made her stutter, "W-why? What is it?"

He took her by the arm. "We must find a place to speak alone."

"But I was going to sort through Grandmother's belongings—"

"I'll help you later. This can't wait."

"What's wrong, Straighthorn?"

He guided her toward the ladder propped against the village's long northern wall. Behind the village, a grove of junipers covered the hillside. The villagers hadn't cut them down for firewood because they collected the juniper berries to make teas and to season meats. If they stayed here long enough, however, the junipers would go. It always happened. A bad winter would come along, and the people would need the wood more than they needed next year's berry crop.

"You go first," Straighthorn said, and steadied the ladder for her.

Redcrop climbed down into the lacy shade of the trees. Sunlight gleamed from the brown bed of dried juniper needles. "Please tell me? What is it?"

Straighthorn jumped to the ground. "Let's sit in the shade over there."

Redcrop followed him to the fragrant spot between the trees and sat down at his side. Sweat gleamed on his long-hooked nose and above his full lips. His shoulder-length hair had been freshly washed, and blue glints danced through the strands.

"Straighthorn?"

He knotted his fists. "The War Chief told me why you insisted on being alone this morning. I want to know why you agreed to it?"

Redcrop felt the blood rise into her cheeks. "I-I wish to help catch them."

Straighthorn massaged his forehead. "I accompanied the War Chief down into the drainage to look at the little girl's tracks. Redcrop, the man who helped murder your grandmother was there. I saw his tracks! I know—"

"I know, too, Straighthorn. The War Chief told me."

He stared at her. "You know that the murderer was that close, and you don't care?"

"That's why I was out there. To be seen."

His mouth fell open. He looked as though he wished to shout at her, but his voice came out unnaturally quiet: "Blessed gods, do you realize what might happen? If he captures you—"

"I'm being closely guarded, Straighthorn. Catkin was watching me the whole time. When I went over the crest of the hill into the drainage, she came running as fast as she could."

"How long did it take her to get there?"

Redcrop shrugged. "Less than five hundred heartbeats."

"Do you know what can happen in five hundred heartbeats? He could have killed you and left you for Catkin to find. He could have clubbed you and carried you off somewhere to torment for days."

Redcrop squirmed. "I know I shouldn't have followed the tracks. Catkin already scolded at me and made me promise never to leave her sight again, and I won't, Straighthorn. I'll stay just where the War Chief tells me to. But I—"

"I don't want you out there at all!"

"But Straighthorn, please, I—"

He took her by the shoulders in a move that startled her. "Listen to me. I have been too worried to sleep or eat. I could barely contain myself long enough to dress for the sunset Dances. The War Chief is using you! Why can't he use someone else? A woman warrior would work just as well, and she would be able to—"

"I asked to do it, Straighthorn."

In a soft, agonized voice, he said, "Blessed gods. Why?"

"I want to help the War Chief catch him."

"There are other ways for you to help, Redcrop. You could—"

"Straighthorn, nine moons ago we often heard that a woman or girl was missing. We assumed raiders had caught them and taken them as slaves, but later we found their bodies. Most of them still wore the jewelry they'd had on the day they disappeared. Grandmother sent word to the nearby villages, and people came to see if they could find their missing loved ones. Some did." Her voice fell to a whisper. "It was terrible. If the same man killed my grandmother, I have to help the War Chief stop him."

"If he catches you—"

"He won't. After today, the War Chief said he's going to put even more guards on me. All I have to do is sit alone and wait for him to try to take me, Straighthorn. Then, when he does, we'll capture him." Redcrop gazed down at the towering walls of the village. As Father Sun sank below the western mountains, shadows crawled over Longtail village, turning the plastered walls a deep gray.

Straighthorn took her hands in a hard grip. "I know you wish to help, but this is madness. If this witch is the famed Two Hearts, he has escaped every trap ever laid for him. Twenty-five summers ago, dozens of villages banded together to hunt him down. They sent their best warriors, burned every hole he might be hiding in, questioned every person who might have spoken to him or known him before he became a witch. None of it worked. He's still killing!"

Wind gusted over the hill and whipped Redcrop's shorn hair into her eyes. She shivered. "It's not just us. I'm afraid for the little girl. I was stolen from my people. I know how it feels."

"She may not be a slave, Redcrop."

"If she is his daughter, she needs my help even more."

Straighthorn suddenly wrapped his arms around Redcrop and hugged her. "Gods...I'm afraid you'll be hurt."

He smelled of yucca soap and woodsmoke, things she found comforting. The first tendril of relief crept through her. It felt like cool salve on a fevered wound. "I'll be careful, Straighthorn. I will."

"Tomorrow, I'm going to the War Chief, Redcrop. I want to guard you myself. That's the only way I'll be able to carry out my duties. If you are out of my sight, I'll think of nothing else."

Redcrop lifted her head to look into his concerned eyes. "Thank you. I won't be afraid if I know you are watching me."

He gave her a pained smile. "When are you supposed to go back out?"

"He wants me on the hill, overlooking the grave at dusk."

Straighthorn shook his head. "I am supposed to be standing guard east of the village tonight. Perhaps I can switch with someone..."

"Speak with the War Chief tomorrow, Straighthorn. That will be soon enough. I don't think anything will happen tonight, not with the Death Dances going on."

Straighthorn looked at the eastern horizon. A thin layer of dust blew over the hills and feathered the sky like delicate brush strokes. She could tell he didn't agree with her.

In a worried voice, he said, "I pray you are right," and hugged her so hard his arms shook.

He had never held her like this before. The feel of his arms made the world go away as Redcrop closed her eyes and leaned against him.

"**T**ruck coming," Sylvia said, and lifted her head over the rim of the excavation unit where she worked with Steve. He rose beside her and squinted down the road.

The chatter of a diesel could be heard over the afternoon stillness.

Maureen straightened and stretched her aching back muscles. The bright candy-red truck motored over the hill and down toward the camp.

"'Bout time," Sylvia said. "We've been out of beer for over twenty-four hours."

"A tragedy of biblical proportions," Maureen said caustically. She wiped her dirty face on the sleeve of her black sweatshirt and smoothed sweaty, tangled hair away from her face. "I've been looking forward to this. I haven't seen Dale in over a year."

"Go give him a bear hug," Sylvia said, "and ask him where the hell he and the beer have been."

Maureen followed the planks off the kiva rubble

and walked to the camp trailer. Dusty had already jumped out as the big Dodge pickup parked behind the Bronco. Sweat darkened the armpits and chest of his long-sleeved green T-shirt. He brushed futilely at the grime on his pants as he walked toward where the vehicles were parked.

When Maureen caught up with Dusty, he said, "You think we ought to tell him that while he was gone, we got engaged? You know, just to see what his reaction is?"

Maureen arched a condescending eyebrow. "Not on your life."

"Oh, come on. Then we could both say, 'Trick-or-treat,' and walk off."

"You are a sick man, Stewart."

Dale turned off the engine and opened the door. He put one booted foot on the sculptured running board and then lowered himself to the ground. Dale looked like an archaeologist, wearing khaki pants with a gray flannel shirt and his battered old brown fedora. Wiry steel-colored hair stuck out beneath the brim.

Maureen walked forward. "Hey, Dale! It's been a long time."

"Maureen! You look beautiful."

She stepped into his arms, and he hugged her fiercely. Through his coat, she could feel his bones and stringy old muscles. No matter that he kept himself in good shape, the fact remained that he was seventy-three this year. She patted his back, stepped away, then resettled his fedora.

A happy glow filled his eyes. "How have you been?"

"I'm better, thanks. I really needed this break.

Thanks for easing the way. I'm pretty sure the department would have let me come anyway, but a call from you never hurts a thing."

"My pleasure." He smiled, and the action rearranged the wrinkles that a thousand suns had burned into his face. He glanced suspiciously at Dusty, who stood by the back of the Bronco, his arms crossed. The battered brim of the brown cowboy hat and the mirror sunglasses hid any expression above his grim mouth. "And William? Has he been treating you well?"

"Sticking me with dental picks and roasting me at every opportunity. 'Doctor' this, 'Doctor' that."

Dale sighed. "Well, what can I say?"

"Actually, I'm joking," she whispered. "Miracles do happen. We've done fine. Although on my off moments I contemplate dousing his truck with gasoline and setting fire to it and all of its little four-footed inhabitants."

Dale frowned. "I don't follow you."

"It's a long story. Just trust me. Don't turn on the heater."

"Oh," he said with an exaggerated nod. "I *do* follow you."

He smiled, took Maureen's arm, and started toward Dusty. "Hello, William. I don't suppose that you have any coffee in there? I left Zuni before the crows cawed. I thought about stopping at Farmington, and then again at Aztec, but I wanted to get here."

Dusty cocked his head. "I'll trade you a cup of coffee for what they told you in Tucson."

Dale smiled. "According to the dendrochronology, Sample One, taken from the big log, had a cut date of

A.D. 1108. Sample Two, from the little log, was cut on A.D. 1258."

Dusty smacked a fist into his hand. "Am I good, or what? I knew the pottery matched."

"Matched what?" Dale asked on the way to the trailer door.

"A hunch the good doctor and I will let you in on once we get caught up." Dusty held the door while Dale stepped inside. The trailer rocked and squeaked as they followed him in. Dale stopped short when he saw Maureen's sleeping bag on the foldout couch in the front.

"My tent blew down in the storm, Dale," Maureen told him. "Dusty let me sleep on the couch."

Dale's bristly mustache twitched. "What did you do, Doctor, slip him a little Prozac when he wasn't contemplating his beer bottle?"

Dusty answered for her: "Given the nightmares I've been having, a little Prozac sounds really good."

"What nightmares?" Dale asked as he slid into the booth behind the table. His khaki pants and gray shirt matched the colors of the dirt on the table.

Maureen slid into the booth opposite and looked at Dusty, wondering if he'd actually tell Dale.

"Nothing. Just kidding," Dusty said. He rolled up the long sleeves of his green T-shirt, reached for the water jug, and went about fixing a pot of coffee.

Dale turned to Maureen, and his thick gray brows lifted questioningly. She shook her head. It was Dusty's place to share that information, not hers. She figured Dusty would tell Dale when he couldn't stand it any longer.

As he poured grounds into the basket, Dusty said,

"I'm surprised they let you run the samples that quickly."

Dale cleaned off a small spot and propped his elbows on the table. "Oh, of course, William. When I was a kid I used to core samples. Half of the tree-ring reference specimens in the lab are there because I provided them. All those years of sending them little cylinders of wood ought to be worth something." He gave Dusty a curious look. "But, outside of the rain, which is why I assume you shut down, what have you found?"

"We have a kiva filled with burned children and at least one adult. We found another old woman's skull."

"The one with the hole in it?" Dale asked, as he smoothed his fingers over his mustache.

"No, this one had burned in the kiva fire. So that makes two adult female skulls—one burned, one not. Then, yesterday, Maureen identified an adult femur. Probably female. She was cut up, her flesh stripped, and the bone tossed onto the roof before it burned."

Dale grunted to himself, then glanced at Maureen. "What do you think?"

"I'll know more when I get the specimens to the lab. You don't have any more Butvar, do you? Or polyvinyl acetate, to stabilize the bone for transport? I've used all of mine. Some of the bone is very fragile. The calcined stuff is like dust. Touch it and it falls apart."

"I got Dusty's message to bring you some. It's in the truck." He smiled at her. Then his expression turned dour. "I'm going to tell you immediately so we can get this out of the way. I've been in touch with the Wirths. I must say, I gave them the preliminary report that we had a great number of bodies coming out of the kiva. My impression was that they were a little stunned."

"So am I," Maureen said. "What's the—"

"Wait a minute." Dusty cried as he set the coffeepot on the burner and turned from the stove. "I've heard that tone in your voice before, Dale. It usually spells disaster. What's the problem with the Wirths?"

Dale took off his fedora and smoothed a hand over his gray hair. "Well, they want to make a housing development here. A subdivision based on an Anasazi theme. You know, touch the past, take a moonlight stroll through the ruins. Own your own little piece of prehistory. That was the marketing plan."

"Yeah, so?"

Dale sighed. "It would seem they're having problems with the data, William. What we are finding here isn't what they had expected. They wanted a clean kiva, maybe with some intact murals. They're nice people, but they're modern Americans. They purchased this land with the notion of selling romantic home sites. The romance of the Anasazi, William."

"The truth isn't quite so romantic? Is that what you mean?"

"Well, yes. I mean, we're not playing according to the American myth. This is a new age of hope and sensitivity. The baby boomers, who don't believe in war, who believe that Indians were saints before the coming of Columbus, are filling this country. That's what the Wirths were banking on. How do you sell a seven-hundred-and-fifty-year-old mass grave? How do you convince buyers to come and build million-dollar houses on land where someone incinerated a helpless group of little children?"

Dusty slumped against the counter and hung his head. "Okay, give me the bottom line. Are they going to shut down the excavation?"

Dale spread his hands. "We'll know in a few days. They're getting on a plane tomorrow morning."

Dusty paled. He glanced at Maureen, and she could see his fear. "Great. That's just great."

Billowing cloud people drifted through the lavender sky; their hearts blazed as though aflame, while their edges glowed like eiderdown.

Stone Ghost stopped to look at them and inhaled the mingled fragrances of roasted pumpkin seeds and cedar smoke that filled the village.

Dusk seemed to magnify sounds. He could hear turkeys gobbling and macaws squawking. Dogs snarled at each other as they trotted around in search of dropped bits of food. Hungry infants wailed on the northern side of the plaza where mothers had retreated to talk and nurse their babies, and a general hum came from the crowded plaza.

A little while ago, Ant Woman had taken fifty or sixty children into the tower kiva to tell them stories. Death Dances often lasted all night. If the children listened to the Creation stories and napped for a time before the Dances began, they did not complain as much.

Stone Ghost propped his walking stick and searched the gathering.

Three young women moved around the village, lighting shredded yucca bark torches. With each new torch, more faces were illuminated in the plaza, but he did not see Obsidian. The shining white heads of the elders sitting along the western wall reflected the yellow light.

Warriors seemed to be everywhere: on the roofs, around the perimeter of the plaza; several stood guard on the high points around the village. A group of ten men huddled outside the great kiva in front of Stone Ghost, whispering with another twenty or so people from Dry Creek village. The Dry Creek villagers could be easily identified because most wore yellow ritual capes. Bows and quivers hung from every warrior's shoulder.

Obsidian emerged from her chamber on the western side of the plaza, and Stone Ghost nodded to himself. She saw him, glared, and looked away.

He cupped a hand to his mouth and called, "Obsidian?" then waved to get her attention. "May I speak with you?"

Everyone in the village turned to gaze at him, including Obsidian. He gestured for her to come over, and throughout the crowd people whispered and shook their heads.

Obsidian glanced around. She couldn't refuse such a request from one of the village elders, but she clearly did not wish to comply. Gathering her long blue skirt in her hands, she swept across the plaza with the grace of a dancer. She'd tied her long white ritual cape at the throat, but through the front opening he could see the intricately decorated bodice of her blue dress; it glittered with red-and-white beads. Every man in the village watched as she passed, as did several of the women.

"Ah, Obsidian," Stone Ghost said when she stopped before him. "You look especially lovely tonight. I hope that you—"

"Tell me what you want, old man. Water Snake said you questioned him. Is that why you waved me over? You wish to blister me with your tongue?"

Stone Ghost pointed to the shining coral beads that netted her hair and flickered like sparks when she moved. "That is a very old and beautiful style, beads in a woman's hair. I haven't seen a woman wear her hair that way in sixty summers or more. Did your mother wear her hair that way?"

"Yes," she said suspiciously, as though fearing ulterior motives behind the question. "But I doubt that you called me over to discuss beads. *What do you want?*"

Stone Ghost moved the point of his walking stick and shifted his weight to his left hip. It didn't hurt as badly on cold nights like this. "Forgive me for disturbing you. I realize this is a difficult time for you. You must be grieving." She did not appear to be. "I promise my questions will be short."

"Then begin."

Stone Ghost rocked against his walking stick. "I wished to speak with you because Water Snake's story confused me. He said—"

"He confuses everyone," she replied as if bored by the thought of Water Snake. "It is his way."

"Really? Well, he told me he did not hear the Matron's screams, and I—"

"Of course he didn't. He heard nothing but his own squealing."

As her implications seeped in, his brows arched. "I've never known a man who could 'squeal' loud enough to cover death screams, Obsidian. Surely there must be more."

Obsidian folded her arms beneath her full breasts and studied Stone Ghost with cold eyes. "Do you wish me to tell you straightly, or shall I smooth the edges for your elderly ears?"

"Straightly, please. At my age, time is too valuable for smooth edges."

"Very well. Water Snake is a fool. He did not wish to couple on the roof where anyone might see us. He insisted we go inside. I didn't wish to. I like to feel the fresh night air on my skin."

"I see. Where did you go? To your chamber? To his?"

She laughed as though he'd said something ludicrous. "I would *never* invite Water Snake to my chamber. He's a slug." She gave him a sly smile. "I would, however, be very pleased to entertain your nephew in my room."

She obviously expected Stone Ghost to deliver that message, which, of course, meant he would go out of his way not to.

Stone Ghost pressed, "Where did you and Water Snake go to couple, Obsidian?"

She smoothed her jeweled hands down over her cape and said, "Inside the tower kiva."

She smiled, apparently pleased with herself. Not only had she lured Water Snake from his guard duties, she had desecrated the kiva.

"Ah, well, that makes everything clearer. How long were you in the kiva?"

"Less than a finger of time. Water Snake couples like a mouse. He squirts, squeals, and runs away."

Singing rose from the great kiva, accompanied by the faint heartbeat of a drum. Soon the drummer would emerge. The flute players would follow, then the katsinas would rise up from the underworlds and spread out across the plaza. He didn't have much time.

Stone Ghost said, "I would like to know why you did not marry again after you divorced Ten Hawks."

Obsidian frowned at the sudden change of topic. "Why do you care? I didn't marry again because I didn't wish to."

"But you are a striking woman. Surely you could have married any man you wished. A war chief, a wealthy Trader, perhaps a powerful—"

"Yes. I could have."

Stone Ghost held her hot gaze. "I spoke with Cross-bill today. She said you were plagued by suitors after Ten Hawks left, but you rejected them all without even speaking with them."

"My life is none of your concern, old man! If you wish to question me about the night of the Matron's murder, well enough, but I have duties. I am supposed to deliver sweet corn cakes to the tower kiva—"

"Yes, I know I'm delaying you, and ordinarily I wouldn't. But, you see, I started wondering about you after Matron Crossbill said that you had a sister. Since then, I have been quietly asking around. How old are you?"

Her glare turned icy. "I have seen thirty-two summers."

"Are you certain? Is that what your mother told you?"

"Of course I'm sure! Why would my mother lie to me about my age?"

Stone Ghost smiled in a harmless elderly way. "I doubt that she would, I was just curious. How did your father die?"

"Great Ancestors, these are silly questions! There is no secret about that! He was standing guard one night and someone shot an arrow through his heart."

Many eyes turned to them when Obsidian raised her voice, but they stood far enough from the other mourners that Stone Ghost did not think they could be overheard. He kept his voice low anyway. "What about your mother? How long after Shell Ring's death was she killed?"

Obsidian searched his face, trying to ferret out his real meaning. "Six or seven moons. You may ask anyone. They will tell you the same thing. Why do you care?"

"Oh," he answered mildly, "it is just a problem I have been considering. What clan was your mother?"

Obsidian tightened her arms beneath her breasts, and the flesh swelled against the blue fabric. "She was Ant Clan, why?"

"And Shell Ring?"

"I think he was Buffalo Clan. What difference does it make?"

"None really. Old people like me are just curious about family. Perhaps because family is all we have left, and we cherish it so much. That's why I'm happy you like my nephew. He and I are the last living members of our family."

The Cloud People had turned a fine gossamer shade of purple. As Wind Baby pushed them, thin threads stretched across the southern horizon.

Stone Ghost said, "My grandmother Orenda once told me that the Blessed Cornsilk was Ant Clan. Perhaps you are related to her. That would be a great honor, wouldn't it? Everyone wishes to be—"

"If you have nothing of importance to say, I have duties, Elder."

"Yes, I'm sure you do. Forgive me. There is just one other thing that has been troubling me. Crossbill told me that you had seen seven summers when you and your mother joined the Longtail Clan."

"Yes. What of it?"

"That would have been twenty-five summers ago, yes?"

"Yes," she answered irritably.

Stone Ghost scratched at his wrinkled chin. "Well, I'm confused. You see, Longtail Clan has only lived here for about ten summers, but Elder Springbank told my nephew he had heard you say that you were born here, in this village. That leads me to wonder how old you were when you and your mother left here and headed south to find the Longtail Clan? Five, perhaps? Six?"

Obsidian went still. Her gaze fixed on his chin as though seeing it for the first time. She didn't seem to be breathing, as though his words had knocked the air out of her lungs.

"Did I say something wrong?" he asked.

She spun around and ran across the plaza with her white cape flapping.

Stone Ghost touched his chin. Few people these

days knew what the spirals meant, thank the gods. His mother had been the last person who dared to identify her children, and she had lived to regret it. All of Stone Ghost's sisters had been murdered. He did not know why he had been spared.

Yes, few people knew what the spirals meant, but at least two did. He and Obsidian.

Stone Ghost blinked suddenly. "Oh, Blessed gods, that's why her mother was killed. And—and that's why Obsidian did not remarry!"

A cold shiver went through him.

Could it be true?

Stone Ghost glanced around the plaza. Over the heads of two shorter men, he saw Skink watching him. When Stone Ghost looked directly the warrior, his gaze immediately dropped, and he spoke to one of the men in his circle. He couldn't have overheard the discussion with Obsidian, could he? Though Obsidian had raised her voice often enough that a careful listener might have been able to piece together some of the conversation. Even so, very few people would have grasped its dire significance.

Stone Ghost turned away.

Cornsilk and Poor Singer had escaped the wrath of the Made People because they were raised by Made People and adopted into Made People clans— though they later disowned those clans. Stone Ghost's great-grandmother, Night Sun, had not been that lucky. As the last great Matron of Talon Town, the most magnificent and powerful town in the Straight Path Nation, she had been quite a prize. Made People had captured her and tortured her to death in front of her husband, Ironwood. Legends said that she had never cried out, not even once, because she couldn't bear his tears.

Like Night Sun, Obsidian's mother had married one of the Made People, and thereby violated a sacred trust: *First People only marry other First People.*

Stone Ghost propped his walking stick and rubbed his forehead.

"Is it possible?"

Was someone tracking down the last of the First People, studying their lives, and meting out punishment for their transgressions?

The thought made him sick.

Before Obsidian made it to her chamber, Springbank cut her off. The old man lifted a fist and shook it in the woman's face. Stone Ghost couldn't hear the words, but he could tell from Springbank's expression that they were not kind. Obsidian stood like an indignant clan Matron, her breast heaving.

Though Stone Ghost had been looking forward to the Dances, he walked in the opposite direction, away from the village plaza, and out into the growing darkness to be alone with his fears.

The lantern hissed, its white light illuminating the inside of the trailer. Maureen fought a yawn as she removed her calipers and tape measure from her field kit and spread newspaper across the table.

Dusty stood with his back to her, his hands in the dishwater, scrubbing the pot they'd used to make chili. Dale sat to her right, one elbow propped on the booth's backrest, his pipe clenched between his teeth as he puffed. His soft dark eyes were focused somewhere in the distance, perhaps on a memory of another long-ago field camp.

Dusty shook the silverware off and set it in the drainer. Then he pulled a dish towel from the oven door and used it to dry the big aluminum pot. "You know, you can't leave chili in an aluminum pot."

"Why's that?" Dale asked absently.

"I made a batch of chili once back when they used to hold the Little Snake Rendezvous in Wyoming. Won the chili cook-off, but I didn't clean the pot. Left it in the back of the Bronco. By the time I got back to Craig, Colorado—I was working up there that year, doing Fremont stuff—the chili had eaten a thousand pinholes in the aluminum. You could hold it up and see light through it."

Dale grunted in assent, one hand cupping the bowl of his pipe.

"So, what's in chili that dissolves aluminum?" Maureen looked up. "And doesn't the same thing also eat the human stomach?"

"Relax," Dusty said. "Have you ever known a hard-core Mexican to have an ulcer?"

"We don't have a whole lot of hard-core Mexicans in Ontario, Stewart."

"Well, believe me. It's only the Anglos that get ulcers in New Mexico. That and the coconuts."

Maureen arched an eyebrow. Forget it. She didn't want to know. Instead, she opened the cardboard box that contained the old woman's skull. Unwrapping it from the bubblewrap, Maureen withdrew a fabric donut from her kit and rested the skull carefully on it.

The donut shape not only cushioned the delicate bone, it kept it from rolling.

"How is the room beside the kiva coming?" Dale asked, glancing Dusty's way. "Have you and Steve finished removing the rubble?"

Dusty stuffed the pan into a drawer and dried his hands on the dish towel. His muscles bunched and corded under his tanned forearms. She watched his fingers twining with the fabric as they worked the towel.

"We ran two screenloads," Dusty said. "We'll be down to floor fill by noon, I'd say. If there's anything there, we ought to be into it."

"And then?" Dale puffed out a blue cloud. The tobacco had a sweet aroma, one that—if Maureen *had* to suffer through—could at least be tolerated.

"Open another room, I guess." Dusty tilted his head questioningly.

"I'd say it would be best to move into the kiva with Maureen and Sylvia." Dale pointed at Dusty with his pipe stem. "Call it a hunch. Recover the osteological remains, pull that floor, and get a handle on the architectural history of the kiva."

"I can already write that report." Dusty bent, flipped open the battered blue-and-white cooler and fished out a Guinness. He used a foot to push the lid closed and dug a bottle opener from the drawer. Popping the top, he sucked off the oozing brown foam, eyes on Dale's.

"Fascinating. Most archaeologists I know have to excavate. Something about recovering the data before they describe it. I don't know why we have to pay you to excavate, if you can just do it off the top of your head."

Dusty ran fingers through his dirty blond hair. "Okay, let me ask it this way. Do you want us to stop with the Mesa Verdean renovation, or go through it to expose the Chacoan architecture underneath?"

"I'll be happy with the Mesa Verdean occupation." Dale levered himself up and grunted as he picked his way to the door.

"Need a steadying hand?" Maureen asked, starting to rise. "It's dark out there."

Dale gave her a chastising look. "Maureen, I've been relieving myself outside for almost *two* of your lifetimes. I can find my way to the latrine."

"Right. Sorry." Maureen lowered herself back into the bench.

Dale winked at her and stepped out into the darkness. The metal steps complained under his weight. Maureen turned her head. Through the window, she could see Sylvia and Steve sitting in lawn chairs around a low fire. The flickering light shone off their faces. Sylvia held a Coors can, Steve had a Guinness. They seemed to be deadly serious, apparently happy to be left alone to talk their way through their shaky relationship.

"Is Dale going to be all right?" Maureen turned back to Dusty. "Should you go check on him?"

Dusty slid onto the bench beside her. "I cannot tell you how much trouble I'd be in if I did. If he falls down and breaks a leg, we'll deal with it. The other way would subject me to days of cutting comments...the total brunt of his acid ire, if you will."

"I get the point."

Dusty smoothed his fingers over the tabletop. "On the other hand, you could probably get away with it. He thinks you walk on water. Enjoy your sainthood while it lasts, Doctor. Eventually, he's going to figure out that you're just as human as the next person, and then —*whoosh,* you'll drop to my level in the Robertson cosmology."

She smiled and stared at the old woman's skull. "Oh, I don't know. It's different between the two of you. You're his son, Dusty. Face it, fathers and sons have a different relationship than anyone else in the world."

"I suppose." After a pause, he indicated the skull. "What can you tell me about her?"

Maureen turned her attention to the brown globe of bone. "Well, to start with, she's definitely female. At least, we can be about ninety percent sure, based on the bossing of the frontal bone, the small mastoid processes, and the almost knife-like sharpness of the superior borders of the orbits. She had a shallow palate even before her teeth fell out." She lifted the skull, holding it between her and the lantern. "Looking through the foramen magnum—that's the hole the spinal cord passes through—I can see a series of defects in the endocranial vault. In short, she also has *cribra cranii.*"

"So she was stressed like the rest of them?"

Maureen nodded. "The cranial deformation of the skull is interesting. It reminds me a lot of the women at 10K3."

He pointed to the back of her head. "That flatness back there is caused by the baby's head being bound against a cradle board to flatten it."

"Right. This woman has more than her share of it. This goes beyond the usual flattening. This is more severe. Falls into the category that we call lambdoidal deformation; it's higher on the skull. You can see that the back of her head is almost concave."

Dusty smoothed his beard with one hand, while the other clutched the Guinness bottle. "Yeah, we really don't know what that means. Cradle-board deformation shows up in the seven hundreds, at the transition from Basketmaker Three to Pueblo One. This is also the time they start making pottery and building free-standing pueblos. From there on out, we see a lot of cranial deformation."

Maureen turned the skull to the light, exposing the hole that had been cut into the woman's head just back of the coronal suture. She took her hand lens and looked closely at it. "Drilled and scribed," she said softly.

"Huh?"

Maureen held the lens close to the curve of the skull. "Fascinating."

"Yes, Dr. Spock?"

"If you look closely, you can see the initial incision on the outer table. Well, that pretty much answers that. The trephination was done perimortally. From the look of the incision, the scalp was cut when it was soft and pliable."

"I'm not following you."

For a moment, she just stared into Dusty's blue eyes. They seemed to look right inside her soul, and oddly, that knowledge bothered her. She took a breath. "Well, if the scalp was dry, say several days after death, it would take sawing to cut through it with stone tools. We'd see deeper incisions into the bone where the scalp was peeled back. Now, if the incision were made ante-mortally, before she died, we'd know it."

"Why?"

"Because bone is living tissue. When it's damaged,

it immediately begins to heal itself. Looking closely with the hand lens, I can see no evidence that any remodeling took place. I be able to clarify that with electron microscopy in the lab. The same with the incisions."

He frowned. "Any evidence of a wound? Any reason they'd trephine her? Maybe a brain tumor?"

Maureen did a careful inspection. "Not that I can see from the gross morphology. But a brain tumor, stroke, or anything similar wouldn't leave its signature in the bone. That's a soft tissue defect that...whoa."

"What have you got?"

She bent closer, slowly turning the skull so that the lantern light cast shadows along the outside of the skull. "Someone scraped this, Stewart."

"Huh?"

"This isn't scalping; this is scraping, like cleaning off the tissue that was stuck to the bone." She turned the skull so that the toothless upper jaw faced the light and focused her hand lens on the alveolar bone. "My God."

"What?" Dusty was glancing back and forth between her and the skull.

"Polish, Stewart." She cocked her head. "I've seen this before. In the micrographs that both Christy Turner and Tim White documented in their works on cannibalism. 'Pot polish.' They boiled her skull. As they stirred, the bone rubbed the side of the ceramic pot and was 'polished.'" She held the lens for him. "Here, look."

Steward took the lens and leaned over her. She could feel the heat from his body, and her nostrils caught the subtle musk of his sweat. He shifted slightly, and her arm tingled as he brushed it.

"That shiny stuff?" he asked, peering through the lens.

It took her a moment before she could refocus and answer. "That's it. At least I think it is. In all honesty, we're going to need to put it under the microscope." She took the lens back, experiencing a tinge of anxiety as he resettled himself and stared thoughtfully at the skull. He resumed that pensive stroking of his beard.

"How do you know that's pot polish? I mean, what if someone carried her head around in a leather sack? What if there was fine sand in it? Wouldn't that leave the same kind of microscopic surface abrasion?"

She shook her head. "No. If that is indeed the case, the micrograph will show a random scratching of the bone surface. Pot polish resembles microscopic rasping. Lots of parallel striations in the bone. And we should see it all around the skull, places where it was scraped against the inside of the pot."

"You can tell this?"

She nodded, squinting at the facial bones as Dusty turned the skull.

Maureen took the skull and positioned it so that the light struck the left malar, or cheekbone. "Look at this." She used her pen to indicate a shallow cut across the bone. "And here." She slowly turned the skull, the light accenting additional cut marks. Maureen held her hand lens up, studying the V-shaped groove. "My God, what did they do to her?"

Dusty was frowning. "What are you seeing, Doctor?"

She turned the skull upside down, following the hollow bridge of the zygomatic arch from the cheek to the temporal bone. "Someone cut the masseter muscle

—that's the big one in your cheek that bunches when you tighten your jaw—right off the bone."

She turned the skull back to where the lantern light shone into the big hole cut into the side of the cranial vault. The lightning bolts incised into the bone caught the light.

"Okay, so put this together for me." Dusty sipped his stout, eyes on the skull.

"Well, remember that what I'm about to say is a shot in the dark that I'll have to prove or disprove in the lab, but I think someone cut the hole in her skull when she was alive or just freshly dead. Then they skinned and defleshed the skull and finally boiled it. Probably to completely clean the bone."

"How do you know they didn't boil it and then deflesh it?"

She frowned. "Well, I won't really know until I put it under a scanning electron microscope, but I don't think so. For one thing, you wouldn't have pot polish on the alveolar bone. The lips would cushion the skull from abrasion. And you wouldn't have these cut marks." She indicated the nicks in the bone. "Cooked meat would simply peel away in these areas."

He folded his arms. "Cannibalism?"

"Maybe." She pushed herself back and took a deep breath. "Do you think this skull is related to the stripped femur we were looking at the other night? Both specimens are elderly, female, and found in the kiva."

As he considered that, the lantern shot light through his beard and hair. "If it's the same person, the leg was burned in the fire, and the skull was placed in the kiva after the fire. That would be curious." He gave her that careful inspection again and asked: "Can you test the bone? Determine if it's the same individual?"

She shrugged. "I *might* get a blood type out of the skull. It was boiled, Stewart. Heat denatures protein and DNA. The only thing we can do is an exclusionary test."

"What's that?"

"If we test both bones for blood type, and one comes out type A and the other type B, then you can postulate with some confidence that you've got two individuals. If both come out type A, then you can postulate that it *might* be one individual."

"Or two individuals that just happen to have type A," he supplied.

"Right. It all becomes a matter of probabilities and potential contamination."

"Sorry, Grandmother," Dusty said respectfully. "Whatever happened to you, it must have been terrible."

Maureen considered the sadness in Dusty's eyes, then asked: "The woman in your dreams?"

His face turned stony. "I don't believe in astral archaeology, Doctor. I have to tell myself that was only a dream. I'm hardly going to write an article for publication proclaiming..."

Dale's heavy step sounded on the trailer stairs. He entered and nodded to them, shooting a glance at the skull. "Finding anything interesting?"

"Just the enigmatic and magical lure of archaeology," Dusty replied. "She was skinned, drilled, scraped, and boiled."

Dale paused. "Well, tell me the details in the morning. I'm off to bed." He raised an eyebrow. "I take it that you'll want me to pull the overhead bunk down in the back, William?"

Dusty nodded, eyes still on the skull. "Given the wreckage of the good doctor's tent, I think that's a good idea. Besides, it's going to be cold out there tonight."

"Good night, Dale," Maureen called as he stepped back, opened the flimsy door, and entered the cramped little bedroom.

"There's a bed that folds out from the roof over mine," Dusty explained. "I'm used to Dale's snoring. I hope you survive it."

She smiled and rubbed her face, feeling tired as well. "I think Dale's right. We ought to call it a night."

For a moment he didn't move, attention still on the skull. In a voice barely above a whisper, he said, "It's not her. I can feel it. She's—someone different. She doesn't call out to me."

Maureen watched him, and a sudden shiver played along her spine.

Dusty tossed off the last of his beer and got to his feet. "I'll be back."

He opened the door, and the stairs rattled and creaked as he stepped to the ground.

For a long moment she sat, staring at the skull. "Who were you, Grandmother? Why did someone do this to you?"

Flute music rose from the depths of the great
kiva and streamed over Longtail village like
colorful ribbons. Redcrop listened to it as she
walked by the kiva and took the trail down to the river.
The plaza bonfire had been stoked to a blaze. Waves of
orange light washed the plastered walls and illuminated
the faces in the crowd.

The farther she walked from the village, the lighter
her steps became. She would not have to stand bravely
while people patted her arms or took her hands to share
their misery. She would be spared the torment.

Redcrop trotted down the leaf-choked trail. As the
cold deepened, mist curled from the river and twined
through the cottonwood branches. Her long white cape
rustled as it trailed over the glistening bed of leaves.

She did not look across the river at the place where
her grandmother had been tortured and killed. She
paused only a moment at the spot where the murderer
had attacked the Matron, then hurried on toward the
grave. Somewhere out there in the growing darkness,

Browser and Catkin watched her. She trusted them to keep her safe.

When the trail turned damp and slick, she slowed down and placed her knee-length white moccasins with care, bracing her hands on tree trunks to steady herself.

She felt no fear. In the past two days, she had eaten her own heart, leaving her chest hollow and numb. Tomorrow, when Straighthorn came to watch her, perhaps she would feel something. She would be able to look out across the rolling hills and imagine that she saw him standing tall and straight, his bow and quiver slung over his shoulder.

She would not actually see him, of course. He was much too fine a warrior to let anyone observe where he was watching from. But she would dream, and inside, he would be with her.

The thought comforted her.

Redcrop gathered up her cape to step over a log that lay in the path. The beautiful curving trails of worms decorated the bark. As she stepped across, she saw the heart-shaped prints that sank into the mud at the river's edge. The doe had come down to drink, then bounded away into the brush. The tracks were fresh. Redcrop's movements had probably spooked her.

A drum boomed, and Redcrop turned to look back at the village. She could picture the drummer emerging from the kiva and trotting into the plaza. He would be wearing a buffalo-hide cape painted with red wolves, coyotes, eagles, and ravens, the special Spirit Helpers of the Katsinas' People. Two flutes joined the drumbeat, and a wave of coughing went through the crowd as people readied themselves to greet the sacred beings.

Redcrop turned back to the trail. Sister Moon

perched on the eastern horizon. Huge and perfectly round, her pale gold face floated in a gauzy layer of clouds.

She rounded the final bend in the trail and noticed the fresh pile of dirt, darker than the other soil. But it wasn't over the grave; it formed a hump to the right.

Redcrop stood motionless, listening to the gurgling of the water running over the river rocks, and Wind Baby rustling the trees. Tendrils of mist trailed across the fresh dirt like ghostly iridescent fingers.

"What happened?" she whispered.

Had wolves dug up the grave?

In the distance, a dog barked. A frightened bark, as though the katsina Dancers had climbed out of the kiva and begun to whirl, their sacred feet pounding out the heartbeat of the world. Then all the dogs started barking, and an enormous roar filled the night. From the corner of her eye, she could see a bubble of light swelling over Longtail village. Light filled with gouts of black smoke. Someone must have heaped wood on the...

Panting. Very close.

Redcrop jerked to her right and stared wide-eyed at the brush. Something moved in there, parting the brush as it came. A low growl rumbled.

"Hello?"

She backed away a step at a time: *one, two, three, four...*

She saw the long ears first, shining in the moonlight. Then eyes rose above the brush and a painted muzzle. The jaws opened slowly, and rows of sharp teeth gleamed.

Redcrop's knees went weak.

"What's she doing?" Browser asked, squinting across the river into the gathering dusk.

He lay on his belly next to Catkin in a thicket of rabbitbrush three hundred body lengths to the west of the grave. They'd chosen this hill because it was covered with brush, but they could not see the village, or much of the surrounding country, unless they stood up. Through the brush, they had one good view: Redcrop. Her white cape blazed in the moonlight. She had stopped abruptly a few moments ago and hadn't moved since.

"I don't know," Catkin answered.

Browser brought his club up and turned it in his hands. He wore his bow and quiver over his left shoulder. He might have enough light to shoot tonight, but a war club would prove better in a close fight. He glanced at Catkin. She had rubbed soot over her oval face to keep it from shining in the moonlight. Her eyes resembled two black holes cut into a gray blanket.

"What's she looking at?" he whispered.

"She's probably praying or speaking with her dead grandmother."

"Maybe, but she turned toward Longtail village."

"Or away from the grave," Catkin pointed out, her voice sympathetic.

Browser silently pulled himself forward on his elbows.

Catkin whispered, "Where are you going?"

"Closer. I want to—"

"The brush thins out down there, Browser. If we go any closer, we will be visible."

He stopped, turned, twisted his club in his hands. "All right. I will give her a few more instants."

He had enough guards posted in the village, around the village, and along the trails that led to the village that nothing could possibly happen without an alarm going up. But something about Redcrop's stiff posture ate at him. He'd been studying her for four summers. It wasn't like her...

Redcrop collapsed to the ground and put her hands over her face.

Catkin whispered, "See. She's grieving, Browser. That's all."

Browser released his stranglehold on his club and sank to his belly in the grass. As the cold intensified, the mist along the river crawled across the ground like shiny white fingers.

Catkin pulled herself forward until she could look Browser in the eyes. Her plain buckskin coat and pants blended with the darkness. She whispered, "Why are you so anxious tonight?"

He lifted a shoulder. A strange, terrible sense of dread had entered his bones and would not leave. "It's the mist. If it keeps moving like this, in less than a finger of time, we won't be able to see Redcrop. Perhaps we should go and escort her back to the village now."

"Give her a little while longer, Browser. There are four guards watching—"

"How much longer?"

She rolled to her side to face him, and her long braid dragged the ground like a glistening black serpent. "Are you sorry she's out there, Browser? Is that why you're so jumpy? You think that you—"

"I know what I'm doing," he answered sharply and started to slide forward again, away from her.

Catkin caught his hand, and he stopped and looked back at her.

"This wasn't your idea, was it?" she said.

He hesitated for a long time before answering. "It doesn't matter. Two Hearts must be stopped, Catkin. I just—" His stomach twisted. He struggled with himself, trying to shove away the guilt. "She is just so young. I wish we did not have to do this."

Browser anxiously started to move again, but Catkin entwined her fingers with his to keep him still.

"She may be young, but Redcrop understands what she is doing, Browser. No one ordered her to do this. She is out there because she wants the killing to stop, too. And Redcrop is not the only one risking her life tonight. Every warrior on guard is a target."

Browser gazed down at her fingers. They looked small and frail against his big hand. He tightened his grip and could feel the slender bones of her hand and the steady rhythm of her pulse where her wrist touched his arm. For just a moment—just a few heartbeats—he closed his eyes and allowed himself the comfort of her closeness.

"Browser, I have wanted to...to tell you..."

He heard the longing in her voice and opened his eyes. She looked vulnerable and frightened, her love for him very plain. Tenderly, he brushed a lock of black hair from her cheek, and they stared at each other for a long time, listening to the sounds of the night, the wind in the brush, the river splashing over rocks below.

Through a taut exhalation, Browser said, "That tone in your voice scared me, Catkin. Are you certain that you wish to tell me things that you may not be able to take back?"

She suddenly went rigid, and Browser instinctively gripped his war club. Catkin was staring over his head in the direction of the village.

Browser flipped over to follow her gaze.

A strange haunting shimmer lit the sky above Long-tail village. He stared at it, trying to decide what it was.

"What is that?" Catkin asked.

He shook his head. "Even if they piled the entire wood supply onto the ritual bonfire, the glow wouldn't rise that high into the sky."

"A lightning strike? Maybe a grass fire?"

"Maybe." Browser propped himself on his elbows and eased up to get a better look.

Before his head cleared the tufts of rabbitbrush, he heard a thin, high-pitched sound. It rose and slipped away, like someone playing a wooden comb with a juniper stick. He got on his hands and knees—and gaped at the halo of red sparks that swelled in the sky.

"Catkin, there's a fire in the village!"

He leaped to his feet and ran to the crest of the hill. The ground seemed to drop away from beneath his feet. "Oh, gods."

"What is it?" she demanded as she ran up beside him.

A billowing pillar of flame and smoke rose above Longtail Village. When the smoke shifted, Browser saw dozens of children huddled together on the roof of the tower kiva, apparently trapped by the flames. In the plaza below, people raced through the smoke with bowls of water, threw them on the fire, then ran back toward the river.

Catkin cried, "Was it an attack? Do you see enemy warriors?"

"No."

Browser lunged down the hill, his legs pumping as hard as they could.

Catkin shouted, "Maybe the ritual fire burned out of control?"

"Or sparks landed on the exposed roof timbers and caught before anyone knew it!"

Breathless squeals pierced the night.

The children! Gods, not the children!

He jumped a rock and stumbled out of control, his arms flailing until he reached the base of the hill, then he ran flat out, leaving Catkin behind.

"Browser?" she shouted. *"Redcrop!* I'm going after Redcrop!"

"Go!"

Ant Woman appeared out of the smoke and started throwing children off the kiva roof into the arms of people below. They had to fall through a wall of flames, and their terrified screams split the night. A crowd of men and women jostled on the ground, shouting, crying, and leaping to catch each child that fell. Several of the older children ran to the edge of the roof and bravely leaped off by themselves. Ant Woman pulled a blanket-wrapped infant from the arms of a little girl and threw the baby over the edge. The child seemed to hover in the air for a moment, then came tumbling down end-over-end. A woman snatched the shrieking bundle out of the air and ran through the firelit darkness toward the river.

As Browser neared the river, he saw Ant Woman grab the arm of a little girl with long shining hair. The terrified girl struggled to break free, throwing all her weight against Ant Woman's grip. Ant Woman's mouth opened in what must have been a shout of rage, then she jerked the child forward so hard Ant Woman almost toppled over the edge herself. She pulled the screaming girl into her arms and heaved her over the edge. As the girl fell through the fire, her hair caught and burst into flame. In less than two heartbeats, the girl's head blazed like a torch.

A man on the ground caught her, threw her to the dirt, and began beating the fire out with his bare hands while the panicked little girl shrieked and clawed at his face and arms.

Browser hit the river running. Injured people filled the water; many sat soaking burns, others nursed broken arms or legs. Some just appeared to be sitting in the water, weeping.

As he splashed across, Browser shouted, "What happened? Did anyone see what happened? How did the fire start?"

Wading Bird, twenty paces downstream, cupped a hand to his mouth and half-sobbing, half-yelling, called, "We were Dancing when the entire village seemed to go up at once! There were flames everywhere! The entire back wall blazed!"

"Are you all right, Elder?"

Wading Bird dipped his head in a weary nod. "I will live. Go and help those who are still in danger!"

Browser splashed out onto the bank and ran.

Just as he reached the plaza, the kiva roof collapsed, and a thunderous explosion of cracking timbers and roaring flames shook the world. Ant Woman's arms flew up, and she staggered backward into the flames. Several children leaped off the roof. Others clung to the edge as long as they could, but when their clothes caught fire, they let go and fell into the inferno.

"No!" Browser cried as the blast of heat hit him.

Burning splinters flew through the air and wheeled across the ground around him.

The screams died. For a single terrible instant, no one made a sound. People stood like carved wooden statues, their eyes fixed on the flames that flared across the sky like blazing wings.

Then a deep-throated groan began, low and anguished, and swiftly built to a deafening crescendo of shrieks and cries. The crowd surged forward, shouting and shoving each other to get to the children who'd been thrown from the roof.

Straighthorn dashed around the southeastern corner of the village with his bow up, an arrow nocked, his gaze searching for a target. "War Chief!" he shouted when he spied Browser. "Blessed Katsinas, was it a raid? What happened?"

Browser came to his senses. He yelled, "Straighthorn, help me clear the plaza. We have to get people away from here!"

Browser ran forward like a madman, waving his arms, crying, "Get out of the village! Move! Let it burn! There's nothing more we can do. Go on, get out! *Get out now!*"

Straighthorn raced along the eastern side of the plaza, shouting, "Hurry! Run! There's no time! Move!"

Retreating people flooded around Browser, weeping, carrying injured children in their arms.

Browser and Straighthorn, caught up in the rush, were carried down to the river. People waded in and sat down in the water with their children in their laps, washing soot-coated faces, dripping cold water over burns while children sobbed.

Twenty paces away, Cloudblower splashed into water up to her waist and raced about, examining wounds, touching people gently. Locks of graying-black hair had torn loose from her bun and straggled around her triangular face. From the thick layer of white face powder she wore, he guessed she must have played the role of White Shell Woman tonight, grandmother of Father Sun, the creator of light and warmth. Raven feathers and seed beads dotted the fringes on the sleeves of her red dress.

Straighthorn stopped in front of Browser and looked up with terrified eyes. "War Chief? Redcrop. Where is she? Did she return with you or—"

"Catkin went to get her, Straighthorn. I suspect that Redcrop saw the fire just as we did and rushed back on her own. She's probably here in the crowd somewhere."

Straighthorn exhaled hard in relief and said, "Thank the gods."

Browser's gaze darted through the crowd, and for a long moment he couldn't speak. Then he spun around in the water, and shouted, "Uncle Stone Ghost? Uncle? Uncle, where are you? *Has anyone seen my uncle?*"

Ash fell around Stone Ghost, coating his white hair and tattered turkey-feather cape like perverted snow. In the firelit darkness below, he saw Browser running, calling out to someone, but Stone Ghost couldn't hear over the dwindling roar of the flames.

He'd just seated himself on this small hilltop one hundred body lengths from the village when the first tongues of flame crackled to life. Before he realized what was happening, the fire had turned into an inferno.

Stone Ghost cupped a hand to his mouth and shouted, "Nephew? Up here!"

Browser did not seem to hear. He ran along the trail behind the village.

Didn't matter. If Browser was looking for Stone Ghost, he would wind up here eventually. He came here frequently to rest and think.

Everyone knew that.

Stone Ghost turned to the new painting that

adorned the sandstone boulder to his left. Someone had painted a white spiral. Two people, a man and woman, stood at the entry to the spiral with their arms extended toward Longtail village.

"Gods," Stone Ghost whispered in agony. "They have lost their souls."

He clutched his shaking fists in his lap and hunched forward to ease the pain in his heart.

Browser trotted up the trail toward Stone Ghost. Dirt coated the front of his knee-length buckskin war shirt, and ash sprinkled his short black hair.

"Uncle, thank the Spirits! I was worried you had been caught in the fire." Breathing hard, Browser dropped to one knee at Stone Ghost's feet. "Are you well?"

Stone Ghost reached out to touch Browser's arm and his gaze traced the line of his nephew's square jaw and lingered on Browser's worried eyes. Stone Ghost had always planned on telling Browser the truth, but the moment had never seemed right.

"I'm well, Nephew. How is everyone else?"

Browser shook his head. "In shock. No one seems to know how the fire started. Cloudblower told me the Dancers had just emerged from the kiva when the first flames licked into the air. She said the fire grew so rapidly they had no chance to get the children out of the tower kiva. It seems impossible to me, but—"

"That's the way it happened, Nephew. I've never seen an accidental fire roar to life as this one did."

Browser stopped breathing. "What are you saying? That—that it was not accidental?"

Stone Ghost lifted his beaked nose and sniffed the

air. Browser, taking the cue, did the same. His nostrils flared several times, as if to make certain.

His voice came out strained. "Pine pitch, Uncle? Someone threw pine pitch around the village and set it on fire? But I-I," he stammered. "I looked for raiders, Uncle. Most of my guards have come in, and they saw no one!"

Stone Ghost nodded. "They weren't raiders. At least, not in the way you mean."

"Tell me. Quickly."

Stone Ghost gestured to the boulder immediately to his right. The white spiral gleamed golden in the firelight. "I found this tonight."

Browser tilted his head and examined the painting with care. "What is it, Uncle? We found a similar painting on a boulder outside Aspen village, except it was a black spiral. We thought the injured woman had left it for us, to tell us we were walking a path into darkness."

Stone Ghost traced the four rings of the spiral with his crooked index finger and tapped the two white figures who stood on the right side. "Each ring represents one of the underworlds, Nephew."

"But"—Browser shook his head—"there are only three underworlds, Uncle. There should be three rings."

Stone Ghost smiled weakly. "The Katsinas' People believe there are three underworlds, Nephew. The First People speak of four. To them, this world of light is the Fifth World."

"*Is?*" Browser leaned forward as though he had not heard right. But Stone Ghost could see him putting the pieces together. The vein in his nephew's temple started to pulse.

Stone Ghost gestured to the spiral again. "Our enemies are too bold for their own good. They do not think that anyone among the Made People will know this symbol. They left the spiral here to identify themselves to a select few."

Browser's gaze flicked to the spiral and back to Stone Ghost's wrinkled face. "What does it mean?"

"The two people you see on the right side are just emerging from the underworlds. They are First People. *The* First People."

Browser stared at Stone Ghost unblinking. "But the First People died out long ago, Uncle."

Stone Ghost took a deep breath. The fire had died down enough that he could see the people along the river and hear the faint cries of children. A determined group of men stood a short distance from the tower kiva, probably waiting for the flames to die before beginning the grisly work of sorting through the dead.

Stone Ghost closed his eyes to block the view. "You will not understand unless I start at the beginning, Nephew, so please forgive me if I seem to be speaking about things that have no relevance to tonight. Trust me. They do."

"I trust you," Browser said softly.

Stone Ghost opened his eyes and tried to smile. Love for his nephew swelled in his breast. "Over one hundred and ten sun cycles ago, the Blessed Matron of Talon Town, Night Sun, abandoned her people and married one of the Made People, her former War Chief, Ironwood. Night Sun and Ironwood fled the Straight

Path Nation with her daughter, Cornsilk, and the man who would become Cornsilk's husband."

"The Blessed Poor Singer."

"Yes." Stone Ghost bent forward to hold his great-nephew's gaze.

Browser searched his face as though fearing the world might end. "And after they left?"

"You must understand that we are talking about the final scramble for power in a dying civilization, Nephew. The First People were desperate and terrified of each other. They started hiring assassins to take each other's lives. They called them the White Moccasins and considered them to be sacred warriors. My grand-mother, Orenda, told me about it many times. She said that the surviving rulers selected their best warriors, groups of no more than ten, and sent them out to destroy anyone who might threaten them. They paid these assassins handsomely, with baskets of turquoise, coral pendants, rare shells from the distant oceans. The fools did not realize what would happen next. When you give men such unrestrained power and wealth, it is like a Spirit plant in their veins. The assassins quickly amassed enough power and influence that they could adopt their own rules for who should live and who should die. Night Sun had been wise enough to flee before the White Moccasins got to her, but they domi-nated people like the Blessed Sun, Webworm, and murdered Matrons Weedblossom and Moon Bright. Few escaped."

Was it possible that groups of White Moccasins still existed?

Browser sat back. "Are you telling me that you

believe this spiral was painted by one of these White Moccasins?"

Stone Ghost nodded. "I fear that may be the case, and if it is, we are in grave danger."

"We? You mean—"

"I mean you and me, Nephew."

"I don't understand."

Stone Ghost held Browser's gaze as he whispered, "My grandmother, Orenda, married..."

Stone Ghost hesitated when he saw Catkin sprinting up the trail with Straighthorn at her side. Their faces appeared stark in the firelight.

Browser lurched to his feet, posture going stiff, as though he saw more in Catkin's expression than Stone Ghost did.

"Catkin?" Browser shouted. "What is it?"

Catkin clenched her fists at her sides. "We've searched everywhere," she said. "Redcrop is gone."

"What?" Browser blurted. "Are you certain? Did you look—"

"That's not all," Catkin interrupted in a stern voice. "Our Matron's grave was dug up, Browser. Someone took her body."

Browser stood unmoving for several heartbeats, then shot a panicked glance at Stone Ghost. The fear in his nephew's eyes twisted Stone Ghost's belly.

"Go, Nephew. Hurry!"

Piper is down on her hands and knees, throwing up in the sand. Each convulsion of her stomach leaves her aching and gasping for breath. Through blurry eyes, she sees Mother add more wood to the fire. The big pot hanging from the tripod steams. The boiling has been going on for a long time. Another spasm shakes Piper, and she rocks forward and retches up the last of her supper. Her nose burns and runs.

"Piper," Mother says sharply. "Go away."

"I can't...stop." The smell from the pot blows to her on the night wind, and she retches again.

"Go on! Get away from here!"

Piper drags herself to her feet and trots away from the rock shelter out into the darkness. Her knees are wobbly, and she trips many times in the soft sand before she sits down fifty paces from Mother. The smell from the boiling pot is fainter, the damp scent of the creek bottom stronger.

She does not know where Grandfather is. He carried the hurt girl into camp, tied her up, then left without a word. The girl still sleeps near Mother. Grandfather must have gone away to pray and prepare himself for the sacred bowl of life, which they will eat at dawn. He has told Piper many times that the Katsina Believers must be bathed in blood to be saved.

Piper breathes deeply and is grateful when her belly does not heave. She wipes her cheeks on her coat sleeve and in her mind's eye can picture the skull bobbing in Mother's pot. One cooked eye stares at Piper. Gray foam bubbles around it.

Piper can't help it. She flops onto her hands and knees and throws up until she can't breathe.

"Piper!" Mother's voice warns. "For the sake of the gods!"

Piper hangs her head and cries, but the sound is locked behind her teeth.

She stretches out on her stomach and places her hot cheek against the cool sand. The boiling smell almost goes away. Piper wishes she had a cold drink of water to wash the sour taste from her mouth, but the water pots are back in camp.

Evening People sparkle above her, and Piper wonders which of her ancestors might be watching tonight. Only the greatest of the First People get to climb into the sky and become stars. She looks at the biggest brightest one and wonders if it is her grandfather's grandmother, the Blessed Comsilk. She was a great Healer.

Piper hugs herself and whispers, "Comsilk, can you Heal me?"

Piper feels herself splitting inside, rotting, like fabric that's been left out in the sunshine too long.

Mother grunts and Piper turns.

Mother uses a long stick to lift the steaming pot from the fire, then sets it on the ground and kicks it over. Boiling water splashes out. The skull rolls and rocks in the firelight. Mother upends the pot, and when the last trickle drains out, she hangs the pot back on the tripod and lets the heat dry it. The steam Spirits will carry the message to their ancestors in the sky: Another lost soul has been freed. Soon the Cloud People will come, and the dead Matron will be able to use them as stepping stones to get to the skyworlds.

Piper searches the darkness. Two Cloud People sail far to the south. Are they coming for the dead Matron? She hopes so.

Mother takes a hafted chert scraper from her pack and goes to work on the wet skull, carving out the boiled eyes, peeling off the last bits of cooked meat.

Piper gasps and chokes, but nothing comes up.

She closes her eyes and watches the lights flash behind her lids. They flit like the spark flies she saw four summers ago on a journey with her grandfather to the lands of the Swamp People. At sunset the spark flies started to wink and glow, and before she knew it, flocks were Dancing together in the trees. Happiness had left Piper weak. She'd chased the spark flies through the tall grass for half the night.

Mother has finished scraping off the meat. Piper knows because the sound has changed. Mother's scraper makes the rattle of chert on bare bone.

Piper opens her eyes. Mother puts her scraper on the ground and studies the gleaming skull.

Piper's gaze slides to the girl, wondering what her name is. She usually finds out, but not until after the bowl of life.

Wind Baby gusts up the sandy wash, thin and cold, and Piper's teeth chatter. Only a moment ago, when she'd been throwing up, she'd felt too hot to touch. Now she is afraid she might be freezing solid.

She glances at Mother and tries to decide if she wants to go back and crawl into her bedding hides or stay here. Her hides lay rolled up near the girl. Grandfather makes her sleep close to them. He says it calms the girls to see Piper when they wake up. Often Mother and Grandfather leave so that the only person the girls see is Piper.

Piper's souls always die when they first look at her.

Piper quickly pulls sand over her legs, then lies down and covers her stomach and chest.

"Piper?" Mother calls.

Piper's fingers curl into the sand and shake.

"Piper? Where are you?"

Mother stands up and lifts an arm to block the firelight. "Piper?"

Piper pulls more sand up around her face and neck, covering everything but her eyes.

"Piper! If you do not tell me where you are, I will send your grandfather to find you!"

A burning flood shoots up Piper's throat. She bursts from her bed of sand and runs back to camp, throwing up on her moccasins, her pants, her hands.

Mother stands by the fire, holding the skull.

Piper flies past her, crawls into her hides, and covers her head.

She can feel pieces of her souls breaking off and flying away, like autumn leaves in a strong wind.

Soon her body will be empty and dead.

When she gathers the courage, Piper pulls her hides

*down and peeks out, searching the starry sky for Cloud
People, afraid they are coming to take her away.*

Praying they are coming.

S traighthorn picked up a leaf from the river's edge
and turned it in his hands as he listened to the
heated words coming from the crowd ten paces away.
Worry for Redcrop had him half frantic. Desperate to
do something. Anything.

"Who were they, War Chief?" Crossbill demanded
to know. "Who did this?"

The Longtail Matron sat on the ground near
Browser with her bandaged hands in her lap. She had
dragged a little boy from beneath a burning pile of
timbers. Singed white hair matted her freckled scalp
and blisters bubbled over her wrinkled face. A red
blanket draped her shoulders. "Was it raiders? A war
party?"

Browser crouched beside Crossbill. Dirt and ash
coated his buckskin cape and streaked his round face.
He quietly answered, "We know that someone poured
pine pitch over the roof of the tower kiva and splashed
it on the rear wall of the village. They also piled brush
along the rear wall, then set it on fire. That's why the
village burned so quickly."

"But who did it?" Crossbill stabbed one of her
bandaged hands at him. "Flute Player Believers? Fire
Dogs?"

Browser hesitated. He glanced at Stone Ghost, who
stood alone at the edge of the crowd, then looked at the

ground. "It may have been enemy raiders, or even a war party, but both seem unlikely."

The crowd murmured and clothing rustled as they shifted. Several people turned to Stone Ghost, but the old man said nothing. He just watched his nephew with tight eyes.

Crossbill sobbed, "Why do you say that? Surely this was an enemy attack!"

"Matron, we had guards posted on every trail and on the high points around the village. Many more stood guard in the village itself. None of them saw anything unusual. They saw no dust from approaching warriors or other strangers. Straighthorn saw Old Pigeontail running the Great North Road in the distance, but that's all." Browser ran a hand through his shorn black hair and shook his head. "In the morning, when we can see better, I promise you we will know more."

Windblown ash swirled around Straighthorn's feet. He glared at it. Let the leaf he toyed with slip through his fingers, and stood up. Worry for Redcrop might have been a beating heart the way it contracted inside him.

Up the hill, the gutted black walls of Longtail village smoldered. When the wind gusted, the charred roof beams glowed like a thousand red eyes. Now that the fire was out, the panic had turned to shock. Sobbing people filtered through the plaza, kicking over burned debris in search of belongings, calling out to lost loved ones.

They had laid the dead and dying on the roof of the great kiva. Seven sick people had suffocated in their beds from breathing the smoke. Three women and one man had been crushed by falling walls. Five more had mortal burns. Their moans filled the night. Occasion-ally, a terrible cry escaped someone's lips.

Ant Woman's daughter, Rock Dove, walked among the dying, holding cups of water to their lips, or gently smoothing hair from a burned brow. Her yellow cape flashed as she moved. She had accepted the duties of village Matron in a way that would have made her mother proud. As soon as her people had acknowledged Ant Woman's death and cast their voices in her favor, she had begun giving orders, softly, clearly, with no hesitation. Every Dry Creek villager had a duty, carrying water, gathering wood, cooking food, standing guard—it gave them something more important to worry about than their own lives.

Crossbill had performed the same function for the Longtail villagers. She had ordered the injured people to be carried into the undamaged great kiva and then built up the fire to keep them warm while Cloudblower tended their wounds. But several hurt adults stood in the crowd, people with blistered bodies; others had broken arms and legs, injuries received when they jumped from the upper story. Three men supported themselves on makeshift cottonwood-branch crutches.

The acrid scents of burned pitch and scorched hair were so strong they almost gagged Straighthorn.

No one knew the whereabouts of Springbank, and Straighthorn feared the worst.

Browser said, "Matron Crossbill, I have ordered twenty warriors to stay here to guard the village and assigned ten more to the high points around the village. Matron Rock Dove assigned ten of her own warriors to guard the roads. What more do you wish me to do?"

Crossbill closed her eyes and lowered her forehead

to her bandaged hand. She didn't say anything for a long time. Finally, she murmured, "I want you to lead the party that goes to search for Springbank."

"Yes, Matron."

"That is all I can think of. I will organize people to start packing our few belongings so that we can leave this forsaken place. The ghosts of those who died will be wandering about all night, tormenting the dreams of the survivors, trying to drag them away to the Land of the Dead. We must leave."

Browser nodded and asked, "Where will we go?"

"Rock Dove has asked us to come to Dry Creek village. She says they will feel safer with us there. I think we should go, but I will place the decision before the village tomorrow morning." Crossbill looked up and her wrinkled mouth trembled. "I wish all of you to be thinking about her offer. It is a good offer."

Someone down by the river shouted, "Springbank told me that the katsinas had abandoned us, but I did not believe him! Now look! We have nothing! Our families are dead. Our homes are gone. I hate the katsinas!" Several people nodded. Most appeared too stunned to think.

Browser called out, "I will cast my vote with Matron Crossbill. I think Dry Creek village will be a fine home for us. Now, please help me. I must decide what to do about Redcrop. I wish to form a search party—"

"A search party? For her?" Water Snake gazed defiantly at Browser. A thick black bar of soot coated the left side of his weasel's face. "We will find nothing in the darkness!"

Straighthorn ground his teeth and tightened his grip

on his warclub. Took a step forward, blood hot in his veins.

Browser, however, raised a hand and gave the man a lethal glare, silently daring Water Snake to challenge his authority.

Skink stepped forward and calmly said, "I think we should search around the village for missing people and wait until morning to search elsewhere."

Straighthorn, unable to stop himself, exploded, "By morning, Redcrop could be dead!"

Water Snake thundered, "By morning, Springbank could be dead! Who do you think is more important? One of our elders, or a slave girl?"

Straighthorn drew himself up and glared at Water Snake. In a trembling voice, he said, "She is not a slave, Water Snake. She is free."

"It makes little difference," Skink replied tiredly. "I think it would be better for everyone if we used all of our resources to protect the village tonight and care for the injured and dying. I, for one, do not wish to go out into the darkness with search torches. If there are enemy warriors out there, they will be able to shoot us down like dogs."

Matron Crossbill lifted a hand, and the gathering went silent. "People have too many concerns tonight. Let us call for volunteers for both search parties, War Chief."

"Yes, Matron." Browser dipped his head respectfully, then looked around the gathering. "Who will go with me to look for Elder Springbank?"

"I will." Catkin stepped to Browser's side. In the firelight, her hard eyes gazed straight at Skink. She called: "Who else will come with us?"

Skink's mouth puckered as though he'd eaten something bitter. He could not refuse with everyone looking at him. "I will," he said, and grudgingly pulled his war club from his belt.

"So will I," Jackrabbit said, and pushed through the crowd. The ash that filled the lines around his eyes made him look much older than fifteen summers.

"Good enough," Browser said. "And who will search for Redcrop?"

Straighthorn shouldered through the crowd, feeling sick. *"I will."*

People muttered and milled about. Several men waved their hands dismissively and drifted away from the gathering.

When no one else came forward, Straighthorn suddenly hated them. He couldn't even bear to look at them. He walked away, cut down to the river trail, and headed for the Matron's burial site with blood pulsing painfully in his ears.

I'm coming, Redcrop.

He had searched through the Longtail survivors, then raced around the Dry Creek village camp, calling Redcrop's name, looking for her, asking everyone he came across if they'd seen her.

After talking with Catkin, he feared that she might have seen the fire and ran back into the heart of the blaze to help someone. Worry festered in his belly. She could be lying beneath a fallen wall, or trapped under the weight of a collapsed roof, alive, praying he would find her.

His steps faltered, but only for an instant. If she were in the village, eventually someone would hear her, or see her, and pull her out. But if she'd been captured, she had no one but him...

"Straighthorn?"

He looked over his shoulder.

Browser caught up with him and matched his stride. "Straighthorn, wait. There are things I wish to tell you before you go."

Straighthorn kept walking, his head down, eyes on the trail.

Browser clasped his shoulder and forced Straighthorn to stop and look at him. He handed Straighthorn an unlit yucca bark torch. "You may need this."

Straighthorn took it but glowered.

Fear and sympathy tightened the War Chief's eyes. "First, know that as soon as we have finished our search for Springbank, I will be on your trail. Expect me."

Straighthorn swallowed hard and nodded. *You should be, since you got her into this.* "What else, War Chief?"

Browser seemed to read Straighthorn's souls. "Your foes are not merely warriors. You must understand—"

"I don't have to understand them, War Chief. I just have to find them and kill them." He gave his war club an emphatic shake.

Browser pushed Straighthorn's club aside. "Listen to me. I *know* who set the fire tonight, and I know why they did it."

Straighthorn stared at him. "It was the same people who killed her grandmother, wasn't it?"

"Yes, but the important part is that the killers are First People. They are fighting for—"

"*First People?*" Straighthorn laughed out loud. "My

mother used to tell me stories about the great war they fought with the Made People. The last of the First People were killed more than one hundred sun cycles—"

"They are First People, Straighthorn," Browser said and looked around to make sure no one stood nearby. "If you are captured, tell them—"

"How do you know they are First People?"

"Will you listen to me?" Browser searched Straighthorn's face. He seemed to be struggling with himself. "Did you see the symbol painted on the boulder where my uncle Stone Ghost sat tonight?"

"Yes. I thought your uncle had painted it. It was a spiral, wasn't it? A spiral with two people?"

"We found a similar painting at Aspen village. It depicts the First People emerging from the underworlds. Apparently it is the murderers' way of claiming responsibility and sending a message to other First People—"

"*Other* First People?"

"They live in hiding, but they exist."

"Oh...sure they do. And rocks Dance in the moonlight." Straighthorn turned and marched down the trail, his war club over his shoulder.

"Straighthorn?" Browser trotted to catch up. "I told you those things for a reason. If you are captured, tell them that you and Redcrop are not Made People. Tell them you are both Fire Dogs or Tower Builders, or anything else you wish. It may save your lives."

Straighthorn found himself chuckling. "So they only kill Made People? Why? In retribution for a war that ended—"

"The war *hasn't ended*, Straighthorn. Not for them.

And it isn't just against Made People. They hate anyone who believes in the katsinas. I don't care if you believe me. Just remember the things I'm telling you. Remember also that I will not be far behind you. Do not cover your trail too well."

"I am a one-man search party, War Chief. I won't have time to cover it."

Straighthorn couldn't stand it any longer. Angry, feeling betrayed, he broke into a run, his feet pounding the damp leaves.

The War Chief ran after him for several steps, then stopped and called, "I'll find you tomorrow!"

Straighthorn looked back and saw Browser standing in the trail with his fists clenched at his sides.

Redcrop, I'm coming! He ran harder.

20

Browser's buckskin cape flapped around his long legs as he hurried back along the river trail. The crowd had begun to disperse. A line of people headed toward the Dry Creek camp and the shelter it offered. Others curled into borrowed blankets and laid down on the riverbank with weeping children clutched in their arms. Catkin, Jackrabbit, and Skink huddled together a short distance from Crossbill and Rock Dove.

The two matrons knelt before a little boy of perhaps eight summers. The child was from Dry Creek village. Browser did not know him, but the boy must have been hurt in the fire. He wore a splint on his left wrist and his hair and eyebrows had been singed off. As the two matrons conversed, he glanced back and forth.

"War Chief," Crossbill called when she saw him. "You must hear this."

Browser walked into their circle, and the acrid scent of smoke rose from the boy's scorched clothing. "What is it, Matron?"

Crossbill placed a hand on the boy's head and said, "This is Tadpole. He was in the tower kiva tonight."

The boy looked wide-eyed at Browser.

Browser noticed that even his eyelashes had been burned away, and said, "You are a very brave boy, Tadpole."

"I-I cried, though," Tadpole admitted.

"That's all right," Browser replied. "If I'd had to fall through a wall of flame, I would have cried, too."

The hairless boy looked up at Browser with shining eyes and smiled.

Crossbill said, "Tell the War Chief what you saw, Tadpole."

Tadpole took a breath and let it out, then said, "Just before the fire started, we heard things being dropped on the roof of the kiva. They make hard knocks, like someone throwing rocks."

Browser frowned. He had no idea what that meant. "Go on, Tadpole."

Tadpole lifted his good hand and pointed up at the sky. "Then, a little while later, we saw a woman look down at us. She was pretty."

The boy paused, and Rock Dove softly coached, "And what did my mother say?"

"Matron Ant—" Tadpole seemed to realize of a sudden that he wasn't supposed to say her name. "Our former Matron said, 'You are late, Obsidian.' Then we saw fire behind the woman's head, and the woman ran away. We heard her steps go across the roof. Our Matron screamed her name, but she didn't come back. No one came."

The boy shivered, and Browser's souls ached, like

stiletto wounds taken in the heat of battle. He looked up. "Where is Obsidian?"

Rock Dove answered, "In our camp. Her chamber was burned, so she—"

Browser stalked away.

Crossbill called, "War Chief, wait! There is more!"

Browser didn't look back. He seemed to be walking through some nightmare country where time had ceased to exist.

He strode through the center of the Dry Creek camp, then weaved around the hide shelters and cooking fires. Close to two hundred people had taken refuge here. They looked up as he passed, but no one called out to him. They concentrated on feeding the hungry and rocking sobbing children to sleep.

Browser finally spotted Obsidian standing alone under a huge cottonwood at the edge of the camp. A beautiful red blanket with white spirals draped her shoulders. She leaned against the trunk, gazing up at the Evening People.

When she heard Browser's steps, she turned, and fear lit her black eyes. She started to walk away.

"Yes!" he called after her. "Keep walking! Straight up the hill to that boulder with the white painting."

Obsidian's pace quickened. "Leave me alone. I don't wish to speak with you tonight!"

She rushed up the hill, not so much obeying his order as trying to get away from him.

Browser sprinted after her.

When she started to pass the boulder and continue up the hill into the grove of junipers, he lunged for her hand, grabbed it, and dragged her backward.

"Let me go!" she shouted and tried to wrench free. "You're hurting me!"

Browser shoved her against the boulder and placed his hands on either side of her narrow shoulders, trapping her there. "Where were you tonight? Were you looking for me?"

"What are you talking about?"

He reached down with one hand, ripped open the seam in his cape, and held the turquoise wolf up before her eyes.

"Is this what you want? Is this why you destroyed our village?"

She glared at him. "You've lost your senses!"

"Don't lie to me! You as much as asked me about this! You said, 'Where is it?' Don't tell me you didn't mean this wolf!"

Obsidian hissed, "Of course I did! I wanted to see it, you fool!"

"Are you working with the murderer? With Two Hearts? He wants it back, is that it?"

She looked as though he'd struck her in the face. When she could finally manage to close her mouth, she whispered, "I wanted to see it because it proves you are who I thought you were. It proves you are *suitable!*"

Browser threw the wolf at her. "Take it! It has only brought me misery!"

Obsidian gasped and her hand flew to her cheek where the turquoise had drawn blood. She looked at her bloody fingers and snapped, "Why do you think I want it?"

Breathing hard, Browser stooped and picked up the wolf. As he rubbed the dirt away, he said, "I thought you were trying to get it back for him, or—or maybe for yourself. I don't know, I—"

"You fool!" Obsidian jerked the necklace from around her throat and held up her own magnificent turquoise wolf. It swung back and forth in front of his eyes. "Why would I need yours?"

Obsidian slipped her necklace back in place. Twisting away, she started down the trail.

"Wait!" Browser called.

"No!"

He stuffed the wolf into his belt pouch and hurried after her. "Obsidian, wait!"

"Leave me alone!"

He grabbed her arm and whirled her around. She fought, but he refused to let go. The coral beads in her long dark hair glittered like sparks, and he could see her breast heaving beneath her white cape.

"What you were doing on the roof of the tower kiva tonight."

She looked at him as though he were mad. "I had duties! The Dry Creek Matron asked me to bring sweet cakes to the children. I had just walked to the kiva ladder when I heard the flames. I whirled around and saw them racing toward me—"

"You didn't see the pine pitch on the roof?"

She frowned and shook her head. "No. I-I mean there may have been pitch there, but I was so taken aback by the bones scattered over the roof that I hardly noticed anything else, I just—"

"What bones?"

"*I don't know!* There were bloody bones all over the roof! As though someone had just butchered a deer and thrown the bones up there! Except"—she wet her full lips—"they didn't look like animal bones. I didn't have time to really look, but I thought—"

"You thought they were human?" He let her go.

Obsidian nodded.

"Did you know our dead Matron's grave was robbed?"

Obsidian seemed to go weak. She backed up and leaned against a pinyon trunk. "When did that happen?"

Browser shook his head. "I don't know for certain. Before sunset, I think."

Obsidian reached out. When Browser didn't pull away, she touched his arm.

He shivered and her voice turned soft. "I know you are crazy with worry, Browser. So am I. Ever since your uncle questioned me, I've been terrified that someone else may know, and I—"

"My uncle questioned you? Today?"

"Just before the Dances. It was only after speaking with him that I knew for certain you were—"

"What?"

She pulled her hand away. "It is not safe to say it out loud, and you know it."

In the Dry Creek camp, people stood up and shielded their eyes against the glow of the fires to watch Browser and Obsidian. A low hum of concerned voices rose.

"*What? What is not safe to say?*" Browser took a deep breath. "Obsidian, for the sake of the gods, tell me that you know nothing about these murders!"

"I don't!" she shouted. "I do not know how you could even think that I would do something so—"

"Fine!" He strode down the hill.

"Browser?" she called after him. "Let's talk. Please! Perhaps now that we understand each other—"

"No, and *no!*"

He ignored the questioning glances of the onlookers in the Dry Creek camp and trotted to meet Catkin. He could just make out where she stood alone near the river. Behind her, people lay rolled in blankets and hides, trying to sleep. A chorus of whimpers rose.

Browser stopped in front of Catkin. Her soot-blackened face had an eerie sheen in the smoky light. "Where are Jackrabbit and Skink?"

"After hearing the rest of Tadpole's story, I told them to return to their former guard positions in the hills."

Browser knew that tone. "What else did the boy say?"

"Tadpole said that the Dry Creek Matron and Springbank made a deal: she would climb onto the roof and try to figure out how to get the children to safety, while Springbank remained inside and made certain every child got out of the kiva. Tadpole saw Springbank climb up through the entry just before the Dry Creek Matron threw the boy off the roof and into his father's arms." Catkin inhaled and let it out in a rush, "That was moments before the roof collapsed."

"You think he was inside?"

"He must have been."

Browser braced his hand on his belted war club. Another elder lost. What would the Katsinas' People do without Flame Carrier and Springbank? Perhaps when they reached Dry Creek village, Browser could quietly begin moving through the people, suggesting they cast their voices in favor of Cloudblower as their new

Matron. Cloudblower would know what to do, whether they should stay at Dry Creek village or continue moving, searching for the First People's kiva and the tunnel to the Underworlds.

He looked up at the smoldering village, the wind-blown piles of ash heaped against the toppled walls and wondered if, after this, any of them still believed in Poor Singer's prophecy.

Maybe Springbank had been right. They should disband the Katsinas' People and give up the dream.

Catkin asked, "What did you learn from Obsidian? I assume that's who you charged off to find?"

"It turned out that she... Nothing. That's what I learned."

Catkin gave him a measuring look and said, "I filled our canteens." She tapped the two pots tied to her belt. The black-and-red geometric designs gleamed in the flickering light. "Straighthorn can't be too far ahead of us. If you grab your bow and we hurry, we may catch him before he leaves the burial site."

"No, I-I wish you to speak with my uncle first. There are things you must know before we leave, Catkin."

"What things?"

Browser squared his shoulders. "About our enemies."

⁓

Sylvia straightened from where she was bent in her excavation unit. "Whoa, what's this?"

Golden sunshine streamed out of the cool autumn sky—a pleasant companion to the smell of wet earth.

The temperature was in the fifties, forecast for a high of sixty that afternoon, and into the seventies tomorrow. In the protected recesses of the partially excavated kiva, it felt considerably warmer. Slanting sunlight illuminated the reddish tones of the oxidized sandstone the other walls in shadow darker hued.

Dusty looked up from the two-by-two he was digging with Maureen. "What have you got?"

"Maybe a storage cyst, but it looks bigger. Hang on, Steve's taking photos and notes while I excavate around the edges."

Maureen turned to Dusty. She'd pinned her braid up in the back, but strands had worked loose and fluttered around her face when what little wind there was penetrated the kiva depths. She used her sleeve to wipe her sweaty forehead. "How big are these cysts? I mean, they were just used to store corn, beans, and squash, weren't they? How much space can that take?"

"Some of their storage cysts were huge, Doctor." Dusty braced his hands on the lip of the pit and climbed out. "Some as big as you're used to seeing in Iroquois archaeology."

A thin layer of high clouds filtered the afternoon sunlight, turning it a flaxen shade. Where it struck flakes or potsherds, it sparked a blaze.

He brushed his hands off on his jeans as he walked across the kiva floor, and dust clouded the air around him. "Okay, tell me what you've got?" He knelt beside the excavation unit.

Sylvia and Steve backed to the edge of the pit to give him a clear view. "I take it back," Sylvia said. Her freckles had almost merged with her tan. "Now it looks more like a trap door."

Steve used the hem of his blue T-shirt to sop up the sweat on his face, and said, "A kiva tunnel?"

"We'll see." Dusty jumped into the pit and crouched over the floor feature. The three-foot-square opening had a layer of intact, though charred, poles over it. "You've taken all your measurements, photos, written everything down in the log?"

"Of course," Sylvia said. "What do you think we are, government archaeologists?"

Dusty gave her an annoyed look, pulled his trowel from his back pocket, and carefully began excavating around the closest pole. When he'd cleared the edges, he wedged his trowel beneath the tip of the pole and gently levered it out of the ground. Darkness, not dirt, met his gaze. A musty scent rose.

Sylvia said, "I have the feeling you may have just inhaled the same air the Anasazi were breathing seven hundred and fifty years ago."

Dusty said, "Sylvia, you and Steve help me with the other poles. This could also be a burial pit. We need to be very careful removing the lid."

Maureen came over and stood atop the pit wall with her hands on her hips. "How deep is it?"

"Can't tell yet," Dusty answered and worked another pole loose. As he turned it over, he frowned. "Curious."

"What is?" Maureen asked and kneeled.

"The pole is charred on the top but not the bottom."

"Which means?"

Dusty placed the pole to the side and started working on the next one. "Which means that soon after the fire started, the oxygen needed to burn through the poles vanished."

"Snuffed when the roof collapsed?" Steve asked.

Dusty nodded. "I would say so, yes."

Steve eased two poles out and laid them to the side, then helped Sylvia remove the pole she'd been working on.

Dusty got down on his stomach and leaned into the opening. He twisted, looking around at the beautiful masonry-lined walls, and the stairs leading down. "This is classic Chacoan stonework. I'd guess circa A.D. 1090 to A.D. 1100. *Gorgeous.*"

"How deep is it?" Maureen repeated.

Dusty said, "If you will hand me the flashlight from my dig kit—"

"On the way." Maureen contorted as she reached for the green ammo box where Dusty kept his excavation tools. Metal rattled, then she bent back and handed it to him. "Be careful, Stewart. There could be something fragile in the bottom, like a human body."

"That's *why* I asked for the flashlight, Doctor. Feeling my feet slide off skulls unnerves me."

Dusty pressed the switch and a flood of yellow bathed the opening.

In an awed voice, Steve said, "Yes, indeed. That's Chacoan masonry. Look at those stairs. Every stone was rubbed together until it fitted so tightly they didn't even need mortar. I wonder if the Mesa Verdean folks who came here in the mid-twelve-hundreds knew this opening existed?"

"They must have," Sylvia replied. "The poles burned on the top, which means they weren't covered with dirt when the roof fell."

Dusty said, "I'm going in to get a better look. Be

prepared to rescue me if the opening does an Indiana Jones and collapses."

"If it does, and there's a bunch of snakes or rats, I'm outta here and you're on your own, Boss," Sylvia said.

Dusty put his foot on the first stair and tested it to see if it would hold his weight. Then he made his way down, one stair at a time.

"What's down there?" Steve called.

Dusty looked up and could see three heads leaning over the opening. Billowing clouds filled the blue sky above them. "Well," Dusty said as he examined the collapsed wall in front of him. "You were right. This was definitely a tunnel."

"A kiva tunnel!" Steve slapped Sylvia's hand excitedly. "I've never opened one before."

"You have now." Dusty ran his fingers over the cool stones.

Maureen said, "What was the tunnel used for?"

"During the Chacoan period, they were primarily ceremonial. The priests could emerge from the underworlds right before the eyes of the faithful. Later, after all the kiva burnings started, villages began building escape passageways, just in case their enemies attacked during a ritual and caught them inside the kiva."

Maureen called, "Do you think someone tried to escape through the passageway when this kiva caught fire?"

Dusty examined the walls, then knelt and surveyed the floor. A layer of dark-brown earth covered the ground. When the tunnel collapsed, the force had thrown rock and dirt into this part of the passageway, covering up any evidence of usage. He saw no artifacts.

"I doubt that we'll ever know."

Someone prodded a fire with a stick; Redcrop jerked from troubled sleep. Her head was filled with pain., and some second sense told her she was in trouble. What? Yes...a captive. She kept her eyes closed, listening, trying to learn as much as she could before they knew she had awakened.

Moccasins brushed sand. The steps light.

Dried blood matted the back of Redcrop's skull, and she felt like her head might explode. Was that what had happened? She'd been struck in the head? She remembered little about last night. She'd seen the Wolf Katsina rise from the brush, and for an instant, thought it might be one of the sacred Dancers, then the katsina had leaped out with a war club...

The sound of breathing. Close. And the smell of vomit and smoked leather.

Redcrop shivered.

"Are you awake?" a child whispered.

Redcrop opened her eyes, and the little girl jumped

back as though she'd been struck. She squatted five paces away, breathing hard.

Redcrop looked up at the concave stone ceiling of a rock shelter. Dark streaks of soot alternated with lighter patches where the sandstone had spalled off over the years. The firelit roof stretched ten body lengths over her head. Her gaze followed the sloping rear wall down to the rolls of bedding hides five body lengths away. Two rolls. Firelight swirled over the thick buffalo fur. A third roll of hides, smaller, a child's hides, lay near Redcrop.

Where are the adults?

"Who are you?" Redcrop asked.

The girl didn't answer. She wore a filthy grease-stained hide cape, and her long black hair looked as though it had not been combed in moons. Bits of bark and leaves tangled with the snarls.

Redcrop forced herself to sit up and almost collapsed from the pain in her head. Yucca cords wrapped her ankles, and she could sense that her arms had been tied behind her back, but she couldn't feel them. They might have been dead meat.

"Water?" Redcrop croaked. "Could I have some water?"

The girl twisted her dirty hands in her lap.

Water pots sat near the fire hearth, along with nests of cups, bowls, and horn spoons. An enormous soot-blackened pot hung on a tripod at the edge of the flames. Just to the right of the big pot lay a bundle. An object the size of a large gourd had been carefully wrapped in bright yellow cloth.

A sandy wash ran at the base of the rock shelter. The way out?

"Where is this place?"

Redcrop looked up at the juniper-studded canyon rim thirty body lengths away. Humps of tan sandstone stood silhouetted against the pale blue gleam of dawn. Many shallow canyons cut the desert. She might be anywhere, a hand of time from Longtail village or a day's walk.

"How long did I sleep?"

The girl sucked her lower lip.

On the verge of tears, Redcrop choked out, "My name is Redcrop. What's your name?"

The girl cocked her head as though listening to the darkness. Her eyes darted to the junipers and the popping coals. She looked back at Redcrop, then duck-walked closer.

"Are you a witch?" she whispered.

Redcrop stared at her, then shook her aching head. "No. I'm just a girl, like you."

"Grandfather says all of your people are witches."

"The Katsinas' People aren't witches. We just believe in different gods than you do."

The girl peered at her with glassy, inhuman eyes. The feral eyes of a wolf pup.

Redcrop said, "The katsinas—"

"Eat people's souls!" the girl shouted. "That's what happened to her!" She whirled around and pointed to a dark alcove in the rear of the rock shelter. "Katsinas sucked her souls out through her ears."

Redcrop had to squint against the fire's gleam to see the rounded shape hanging on the wall. "What is that?"

"An old husk."

It took Redcrop several heartbeats to realize she was looking at a mummy, a mummy with a rope around her waist. White hair on the desiccated scalp fluttered in the cold breeze.

"Blessed Ancestors," Redcrop whispered.

The girl nodded. "She was the first Matron to believe in the katsinas. She made all of her people believe in them, too. That's why she's a mummy. The katsinas—"

"The katsinas are good gods. They bring rain and game animals, and they watch over us to keep us—"

The girl shouted, "They started the war between the First People and the Made People so they would have food!"

Redcrop felt sick. She sank back to the ground and curled onto her side. When the sickening throb in her head dimmed, she repeated, "What's your name? My name is Redcrop."

The girl chewed her lip for several moments, then answered, "Piper's Song, but my people call me Piper."

"Piper," Redcrop said and smiled. "That's a pretty name."

The girl smiled back, a quick, almost horrifying gesture: an animal pretending to be a little girl.

Piper hissed, "Are you one of the Made People?"

Redcrop's heart thudded against her ribs. "No. I was captured when I was younger than you. My people believe we came to this world as wolves made from gouts of Father Sun's fire. We—"

"Oh. You're a Fire Dog."

"Yes, though I've lived with Made People almost my whole life."

"Made People aren't really human," Piper confided. "The Creator made them look human, but they have animal souls. Under their skins they are really buffaloes, and bears, and ants. That's why they worship the katsinas. Katsinas have animal souls, too."

Redcrop lay there, her head splitting, and forced her lungs to slowly breathe in and out.

Piper pointed a dirty finger at the mummy. "My great-great grandfather was the son of the Blessed Cornsilk and the Blessed Swallowtail."

Redcrop frowned. She'd never heard of Swallowtail. His name had no place in the sacred stories of Cornsilk and Poor Singer. She wondered who he might have been. Perhaps he'd been made an Outcast, and his name deliberately forgotten by his people. Her gaze returned to the mummy.

"What was her name?"

"Hmm?" Piper turned to look. "Oh, she was Matron Night Sun. Grandfather looked for her for many summers."

Night Sun.

The red gleam from the coals danced across Piper's face.

"Where did he find her?"

"In a fallen-down room at Talon Town. Made People captured her and her family and dragged them back there. They kept them as slaves for a while. Then they killed her and walled her up in a room." Piper pounded the air with her fists. "Grandfather had to knock the wall down with a big rock to get to her."

Wind swirled through the shelter, and the fire spluttered. Light danced over the mummy's shriveled face.

"He knocked down a lot of walls before he found her," Piper said. "I've been to Talon Town. It's old and dirty. I don't wish to go back. It scares me."

Night Sun had been the last great ruler of the Straight Path Nation. She'd given up everything to marry one of the Made People. After she was gone, the other First People had made her an Outcast. But rather than ordering that she be forgotten, they had decreed that no one would ever forget her name. It seemed a pathetic irony that Made People had dragged her back to the town she had abandoned and forced her to live there as a slave before they'd killed her.

Flame Carrier had always told Night Sun's story in a reverent but pained voice. Redcrop recalled because she'd never understood that pain. It had verged on guilt, and Redcrop couldn't fathom why her grandmother would feel guilty about Night Sun's decision to abandon her people for the love of a man.

Redcrop said, "I've heard stories of Night Sun."

"You have?" Piper said excitedly. "Tell me!"

Redcrop shook her head. If she was going to have any chance of escape, she had to build up her strength. "I need food and water. I'm very thirsty and I haven't really eaten in days."

Piper turned to look back at the pots near the fire. Her young brow furrowed. "I don't think I'd better. Grandfather didn't say you could drink or eat."

"Where is your family?"

"Mother and Grandfather went away to pray. They'll be back soon."

"Where's your father?"

Piper tilted her head as though she didn't understand the question. "Grandfather will be back soon."

"How soon?"

Piper lifted a shoulder. "They usually come back around dawn."

Redcrop surveyed the slice of pale blue sky visible over the canyon rim. Less than a hand of time away.

"Piper, I'm sure your mother would want me to have water. I'm just a girl, like you. Your mother would give you water if you were thirsty, wouldn't she? And food?"

Piper thought about that for a time, then nodded. "Yes."

"Did your mother or grandfather say I couldn't have food or water?"

"No."

"Then I think it would be all right. I would be very grateful if you would bring me a cup of water and some food."

Piper rose uncertainly, hesitated, then trotted to the fire. She dipped up a cup of water and tucked a brown fabric bag under her chin. As she walked around the fire, carrying the cup in both hands so she wouldn't spill it, Piper tripped over the yellow bundle. The bundle started rolling down the slight incline, peeling off the cloth until a skull tumbled out.

Redcrop saw the toothless mouth and the hole in the bone, and memories of last night came flooding back. Her grandmother's grave had been desecrated, her body stolen...

Oh, gods.

Piper set the cup of water in front of Redcrop and sat down cross-legged at her side. "I can't untie you," the girl said as she placed the brown bag at her feet, "but I can help you."

Piper lifted the cup to Redcrop's lips, and she drank greedily, spilling water down the front of her white cape, but her gaze remained on the skull.

It can't be. Can it?

Redcrop said, "Thank you, Piper. That was good."

Piper nodded and gestured north up the wash. "There's a little pool. It isn't big enough to bathe in, but we fill our water pots there."

Redcrop watched Piper untie the laces on the brown bag and pull out a long strip of jerky. She held it up for Redcrop to take a bite. Redcrop tore off a hunk with her teeth and chewed. Crushed bee weed sprinkled the meat, giving it a delicious peppery taste. Redcrop swallowed and Piper held up the jerky for her to take another bite. As she chewed, her stomach squealed, longing for more.

"Do you live here?" Redcrop asked.

"Sometimes." Piper jerked a nod. "But mostly we live in falling-down villages where Grandfather's people used to live."

"Do you know the names of the villages? Maybe I've been to them."

Piper, too, ate as though she hadn't had food in a moon, chewing swiftly, swallowing, and ripping off more jerky. "We lived in Talon Town for a while, then Center Place, and Sunset Town. Since last spring, we've lived around here. I like it better here than in Straight Path Canyon. Too many bad ghosts live there."

With the food, the pain in Redcrop's head began to ease. She took a deep breath and felt a little better. "Who is your grandfather? What does he do?"

"He's a great Trader. He lives in other villages most of the time." Piper stuffed the last bite of jerky into her own mouth and pulled out another strip. She let Redcrop take a bite and slurred, "This is good meat, isn't it?"

"Yes. I like the bee weed flavor."

"Me too. Mother sprinkles the meat with bee weed and dried phlox blossoms. It's the flowers that give the meat the sweet taste."

"It's really good."

Piper smiled as if proud of her mother. "Yes, Made People have animal souls. That's why we can eat them. They're not really human. They're like buffalo and bear...what's wrong?"

Redcrop choked down the meat she'd already started to swallow and sat trembling.

"Do you need water?" Piper asked, her young voice worried.

The more Redcrop shook, the more stunning the pain in her head became. She tried to calm herself by closing her eyes and taking deep breaths. She choked again and Piper scrambled to her feet.

"I'll get you another cup of water!"

Piper ran to the water pots by the fire, filled the cup, and rushed back. "Here," she said as she tipped the cup to Redcrop's lips.

Redcrop drank, cleaning the taste from her mouth.

When Piper lowered the cup, she leaned close and stared deeply into Redcrop's eyes. "More?"

"No. No, thank you."

Piper sat down in front of Redcrop, drew up her knees, and reached for another stick of jerky. She propped her elbows on her knees as she ate, staring at Redcrop with bright curious eyes.

Piper said, "You're pretty."

"You're pretty, too, Piper. Doesn't your mother ever comb your hair?"

Piper stopped eating and looked at the filthy snarls

that fell over her shoulders. "There have been a lot of Bead Days."

"What's that? A bead day?"

Piper's shoulders hunched, and she went back to her jerky, chewing, swallowing, chewing, as though she hadn't heard the question.

Redcrop couldn't move her numb arms, but she worked at the cords around her ankles, trying to loosen them.

Piper watched her intently for a time, then said, "You can't get away."

Redcrop twisted her ankles and grimaced as the cords sawed into her flesh. Blood seeped from her chafed skin. "Piper, did your family kill my grandmother?"

Piper cocked her head like a surprised bird. She pointed up at the ceiling. "Her bones went to the clouds. Grandfather cleaned them and turned them into smoke so they could fly."

"You mean he burned—"

"Shh! They're coming." Piper used her chin to gesture northward down the sandy wash. "See."

Redcrop glanced out at the darkness, and fear pumped like fire through her veins. "Your family?"

"No." Her voice got very small. Piper sucked in her lower lip and clamped it with her teeth. Her eyes went huge.

Redcrop fell to her side and kicked her feet to stretch the cords. They were going to kill her, just as they had Grandmother. She tried to remember everything Grandmother had taught her about the journey to the afterlife, where the monsters stood, the traps along the trail...

"Closer," Piper whispered. She pulled her knees against her chest and hid everything but her eyes, which stared unblinking at the darkness from a halo of filthy tangles.

"Where?" Redcrop sobbed. "I don't see anything!"

In the barest murmur, Piper said, "There are only two of them. Usually there are ten."

"Who are they?"

Piper's gaze fixed on the darkness. "White Moccasins."

"Who?" Redcrop fought to blink her tears away and see something, anything, but she saw only the junipers rocking in the wind and the tan sandstone walls shimmering in the azure gleam of approaching dawn.

"Piper, please, help me? Cut me loose!"

Piper hissed, "It's Him."

"Him?"

In an awed whisper, she said, "First Man."

Redcrop wanted to scream but kept her voice controlled. "Who?"

"Wolf Slayer," Piper replied, almost too low to hear.

"He eats wolves."

Redcrop curled into a ball and wept. These were gods she did not know, and she feared all the more because of it.

"Who is Wolf Slayer?"

"Your people killed him."

"If he's dead, how can he be coming?"

"He's coming," Piper said and pointed. "Right there."

Two men walked into the rock shelter, their long white capes swaying around their bodies. One of them, the tallest, wore a wolf mask and had long black hair.

The other, a head shorter, wore a raven mask. Redcrop should have scrambled to get away. But she shocked them.

She sat up and started singing in an agonized voice, a voice that resembled a death cry. Flame Carrier had taught her the words as a little girl of barely two or three summers. She had forced Redcrop to learn them:

> "Come the brothers, born of Sun!
> One is slayed.
> Here by the long trail, his corpse is laid.
> You, born of Father Sun,
> laid in the light next to night.
> Choose my people.
> Come the brothers, born of Sun!"

The man in the raven mask turned to his companion and whispered, "That is one of our most sacred Songs. How does *she* know it?"

Redcrop sucked in a breath. His voice sounded familiar.

The tall man walked forward.

When he stood over her, he pulled off his wolf mask and stared at Redcrop, his eyes electrifying in their intensity. He had a triangular face, with a long nose. His black hair came off with the mask, and she could see that a human scalp had been fitted inside the wolf's fur. His real hair, long and white, tumbled around his shoulders. "My sister taught you that, didn't she?"

Redcrop swallowed hard. "Your sister?"

"The one you call Blessed Flame Carrier."

Redcrop paled at the mention of her name. Had he no fear that he would pull her grandmother back from the Land of the Dead? That she might be trapped here on earth and become a wailing ghost?

"My words can't draw her back," he said, startling Redcrop. Could he read her thoughts? "She is already in the skyworlds with our ancestors. She climbed up with the smoke. The greatest of us do not run the road to the underworlds." He gestured expansively to the sky. "We fly."

He stared up at the last of the Evening People, then crouched in front of Redcrop. His eyes gleamed like polished black stones.

"What my foolish sister did not tell you," he said, and smiled at her with broken rotted teeth, "is that coming from your lips, those words were an abomination. You are not one of us, no matter what Songs you know."

He slapped Redcrop across the mouth.

Redcrop cried out and sobbed, "But she told me—"

"She told you the Blessed Ancestors would hear you and save you?"

Redcrop wept. "Yes."

He leaned down very close and whispered, "Only when you have been bathed in blood will you be saved. In less than a hand of time, the Blessed Two Hearts—"

"Bear Dancer!" the man in the raven mask called and furiously waved his war club. "There's someone out there!"

Bear Dancer! Grandmother's older brother?

Bear Dancer stood. "My son?"

"No. I don't think so. I think there's more than one."

"Perhaps my son and my brother. But let us make sure."

Redcrop tried to think. Grandmother had only

spoken of one brother. Could Bear Dancer be talking about Grandmother's half-brother? The brother she'd never known?

Bear Dancer jerked the cotton sash from around his waist and threw it at Piper. "When I am gone, gag her."

He rose and took three long strides to look at where the other man aimed his club. They spoke softly, and both men sprinted away, up the wash into the dark canyon shadows.

Redcrop rolled to her side, and her belly heaved. Burning liquid seared her throat and nose.

Piper scampered across the ground, glanced repeatedly up the sandy wash, and squatted next to Redcrop. "Are you all right?"

Redcrop nodded.

Piper said, "Here," and pulled a turquoise wolf from her pocket. Tiny, and crudely carved, it looked almost identical to the one that Stone Ghost had found in the hole in Grandmother's head. "I was going to give it to you after they killed you, but they may take you away." She tucked it into the top of Redcrop's left legging.

Redcrop stared at her with blurry eyes. "Piper, did you give one of these to my grandmother?"

Piper nodded, but glanced around as though frightened someone might hear. "Yes. No one told me they were going to burn her and send her to the clouds. I thought she was one of the Made People."

"And you wanted her to be able to find her way to the Land of the Dead?"

"If you can't find your way, you get lost, and the monsters eat you."

As if that young voice had painted perfect images

on her souls, Redcrop had a momentary glimpse of a lonely little girl forced to see things no child should—a girl who heard the cries of the victims, watched them die, and could not walk away without making certain their souls were safe. The realization pierced Redcrop's heart.

"Piper, please untie my hands."

She shook her head.

"Do you want to see me dead?"

Piper twisted her hands in her lap.

"Piper, I have a gift for you. Please look beneath my cape."

"What is it?"

"Please, look. I can't hurt you."

Piper crept forward, flipped Redcrop's cape aside, and jumped backward. Her mouth gaped at the cornhusk doll.

"Where did you find her?" She snatched the doll from Redcrop's belt and scuttled backwards with the doll clutched to her chest.

"I found her in the coyote den where you dropped her when your grandfather Bear Dancer came to get you."

Piper sat on the ground and stroked the doll's hair so roughly that Redcrop feared she might rip off the frail cornhusk head.

It took twenty heartbeats before Piper remembered the sash, grabbed for it, and ran forward.

Before she gagged Redcrop, she looked at her with shining eyes and said, "He's not my grandfather."

D ry needles and fallen berries crackled as
Straighthorn crawled through the junipers
overlooking the shallow canyon. The
brightest of the Evening People sparkled above him, but
pale lavender light banded the eastern horizon. He
studied it, gauging how much longer he had before the
darkness failed him.

A hand of time. Maybe a little less.

He blinked the sweat from his eyes, gripped his war
club, and got down on his belly to slide to the edge of
the rim.

One hundred hands below, the firelit rock shelter
gleamed. Redcrop lay on her side with her white cape
spreading around her like a mantle of snow. Dead? A
little girl crouched a few hands away, furiously rocking
a cornhusk doll in her arms, as if trying to get a stubborn
baby to go to sleep. Redcrop lay perfectly still.

Straighthorn pulled himself forward on his elbows
and looked along the rim for a trail down. A dark slash
cut the canyon wall perhaps two hundred body lengths

to the south. It was probably a shadowed crevice, but it might be a trail.

He swiftly backed away from the rim, got to his feet in the thickest junipers, and sprinted headlong toward the slash. His fringed sleeves whipped against the branches as he passed.

It is a trail!

He flopped on his stomach fifty hands away and surveyed the junipers. Dust puffed before his face every time he exhaled, scenting the air. Toppled boulders the height of a man lined the trail down into the canyon. It didn't appear to be guarded, but it must be.

Straighthorn eased forward on his hands and knees.

Just as he rose, he heard a sound and spun around with his club up.

"*Straighthorn?*" a familiar voice called.

"Who's there?" Junipers rustled as the man pushed through.

"It's me, you young fool."

Skink ducked beneath an overhanging limb and trotted toward Straighthorn. Tall and lean, he wore a knee-length buckskin shirt and carried a bow and quiver over his shoulder. His flat, heavily lashed face bore a sheen of sweat, as though he'd run all the way to get there.

"Blessed gods, Skink! What are you doing out here? I thought you stayed to help search for Elder Springbank."

Skink grasped Straighthorn's shoulder in a friendly gesture, and whispered, "Our elder died in the fire, my friend, and there's no time to talk. Have you seen Browser or Catkin?"

"No."

"They should be here soon. We left the village at the same time." He turned to the firelit canyon. "What's your plan?"

Straighthorn let out a breath and gestured helplessly with his club. "I was going to sneak down this trail and dash to the rock shelter and get her."

Skink's mouth tightened. "Oh, very clever. You want to charge out in the open so everyone can shoot at you. That should work."

Straighthorn's face reddened. He flapped his arms. "I thought I was alone. I didn't know what else to do."

"You're not alone." Skink's eyes narrowed as he studied the lay of the canyon. "All right, do you see that trail to the north?"

In the darkness, he'd have run right past the narrow game trail that now could just be discerned. Shamed, he said, "Yes. I see it."

"You start down this trail. I will go up and take the northern trail. I'll hide in those trees at the base of the cliff. You won't see me, but I'll be guarding you the whole time. You understand? If something goes wrong, do not look in my direction. If you do, you'll give away my position, but that is where my shot will come from. Be ready for it."

Straighthorn jerked a nod. "I understand, Skink."

"Good." Skink slapped his shoulder. "Go."

Skink trotted away into the dark junipers, and Straighthorn began the descent into the canyon.

Loose gravel rolled and slipped beneath his feet as he dodged from boulder to boulder.

Redcrop still had not moved, but the little girl skipped around on the charcoal-stained sand. Her shrill singing rang out, magnified by the arched ceiling of the rock shelter.

When Straighthorn reached the sandy wash, he was less than one hundred hands from the rock shelter. He took cover behind a thicket of greasewood and used his sleeve to wipe his forehead. Through the spiky tangle of limbs, he saw Redcrop shift and Straighthorn's heart almost burst through his ribs. She sat up, sobbed, and struggled with the cords around her ankles.

The little girl started running around in circles, faster and faster...then suddenly stopped and looked out into the darkness where Straighthorn hid.

Straighthorn frowned. Could she see him?

The girl whispered something to Redcrop, and Redcrop whirled around to look.

Straighthorn searched the canyon bottom, then slowly rose to his feet. "Redcrop?"

She screamed against her gag, fell onto her belly, and struggled to reach him.

Straighthorn's feet pounded out a muted rhythm in the sand as he sprinted across the wash and up to her side.

"Gods, I'm glad to see you alive," he said as he laid his war club down, ripped his knife from his belt, and began sawing through the bindings on her ankles. If someone came, at least she would be able to run.

She kept moaning, shrieking against her gag. He jumped around to free her wrists next.

"Redcrop, hold still! I don't wish to cut you, and I—"

"You really are a fool."

Straighthorn whirled. For a moment, he did not understand. He watched Skink step into the firelight with his bow drawn, the keen chert-tipped arrow aimed at Straighthorn's heart. Two men in white capes flanked Skink. One wore a black raven mask. The other, the taller man, looked to be around seventy summers. He had long spiderweb-thin white hair.

Straighthorn looked from Skink to the others and whispered, "What's happening?"

Skink shook his head disdainfully. "You are about to die, Straighthorn."

The tall old man with white hair smiled at Skink. "Well done, my son. Did you have any problems?"

"No, Father."

The old man stepped around Skink, knelt, and picked up Straighthorn's club.

Straighthorn glared at Skink, and the tall man ordered, "Throw your knife away, then toss your bow and quiver to the side."

Straighthorn almost trembled with a sick rage. "That's why you ended the search for the murderers after the Matron's death. Why you didn't want to hunt for Redcrop. You've been spying on us, working against us all the time."

Skink laughed, head back, slapping a hand to his thigh.

"Was it you," Straighthorn asked, "who set fire to the village tonight?"

Skink smiled. "Who'd look twice if I was carrying pots of pine resin up to the kiva?"

"No one." Straighthorn whispered.

Skink would have been on guard duty. People expected to see him slipping around. More importantly, Browser had left Skink in charge of the guards. He could have ordered everyone else away while he piled up brush and poured pine pitch—

"Drop your knife!" Skink repeated his father's order.

Straighthorn let his knife fall to the ground and eased his bow and quiver from his shoulder. He tossed them to his right, almost striking the filthy little girl. She let out a shriek and ran to the rear of the rock shelter. There, she huddled with her doll pulled to her chest. She looked more like a wild animal than a child.

Straighthorn wrapped his arms around Redcrop. He could feel her working to pull the last threads apart, to free her hands. He had to fight to keep his voice even. "What do you want from us? We've done nothing to you."

Redcrop leaned against him, shuddering, and he tightened his arms. They were going to die, here, now, and the only thing Straighthorn could think of was his indignation that Skink had fooled them all.

"Did you help to murder our Matron? Did the man's tracks belong to you?" Straighthorn asked. "That must have been a challenge, eh? It takes a great warrior to kill an old woman."

"Shut your mouth!"

Redcrop had worked her hands free. Straighthorn could feel them moving beneath her cape.

Please, tell me you hid a weapon...

To distract the onlookers, Straighthorn said, "Ah, but I forgot about the woman. Perhaps you grew squeamish and had to let her do your killing for you? Yes, the brave Skink. I hope you live long enough that I can beat your guts out with my club."

"I will," Skink replied and pulled his bowstring taut. "But you won't."

"No, wait." The tall man touched Skink's arm. "We must wait for Two Hearts. He said he—"

A hiss.

The white-haired man staggered and stared wide-eyed at the arrow sticking from his chest. The bright red fletching shimmered in the firelight. A hideous scream broke from his lips. The next arrow hit almost simultaneously, striking the short man who wore the raven mask in the throat. He clawed at his neck and tried to run. Made a step, and fell face first to the sand, gurgling and rolling, trying to dislodge the arrow.

Straighthorn roared and leaped for Skink, shouting, "Redcrop, run! *Run!*"

As Straighthorn hit Skink, the man's shot went wild, flying out into the darkness. With his free hand, Skink grabbed a handful of Straighthorn's hair and slammed him in the head with his bow. Straighthorn got his fingers around the bow and screamed, "I'm going to kill you, you traitor!"

Straighthorn jabbed his thumb into Skink's eye, and when Skink shrieked, his grip loosened. Straighthorn ripped the bow from Skink's hand, twisted, and bashed Skink across the face. From the corner of his eye, he saw Redcrop pelting headlong down the wash.

Skink's fist landed squarely in the middle of Straighthorn's chest, knocking the air out of him. He lost his grip on the bow as Skink tried to backheel him. Locked in a death grip the two skidded across the sandy floor of the rock shelter, roaring, kicking, shouting. Then they were on the ground, rolling, striking.

Straighthorn smashed his forehead into Skink's

nose twice before Skink brought his knee up into Straighthorn's groin. Straighthorn cried out and grabbed Skink's hands, but Skink, much heavier than Straighthorn, rolled him over, and glared into Straighthorn's eyes.

"You worm," Skink hissed. Clotted blood bubbled from his broken nose. "I always wanted to kill you with my bare hands."

Skink tore lose from Straighthorn's grip and slammed a fist into the young warrior's throat. Straighthorn choked and gasped for air. He grabbed Skink's hand again, but he could feel Skink working free. Knew it was but a matter of time. Had he given Redcrop enough time to get away?

As a last resort, Straighthorn let loose of Skink's arms,roared, and lunged. Grasping Skink's head in both hands, Straighthorn fastened his teeth onto Skink's broken nose. Skink screamed and beat at Straighthorn's head, but Straighthorn refused to let go. He bit down hard, felt bone and cartilage crushing. Blood spurted hotly, filling his mouth, running down the sides of his chin.

Skink jerked one hand loose, balled his fist, and pounded the side of Straighthorn's head until Straighthorn's teeth tore through Skink's nose. The loose flesh came off in Straighthorn's mouth. Skink bellowed and jerked away. Straighthorn spat the rubbery mess out, locked an arm around Skink's head, and gripped his jaw.

As he twisted, Straighthorn shouted, "You were going to kill me? I'm going to cut your eyes out and feed them to the village dogs, then I'm going to boil your miserable testicles—"

Skink slammed his knee into Straighthorn's groin again. Pain-shocked, Straighthorn's stomach heaved. He vomited in Skink's hair but didn't let go. He kept twisting and roaring. He could feel Skink's fingers groping for his windpipe and panic fired his veins. He groaned as he threw all of his weight into twisting Skink's head off.

A loud crack split the night and Skink turned into a jerking mass of flesh. Straighthorn shoved the body off and crawled across the rock shelter. His war club rested beside Skink's dead father.

Straighthorn grabbed the club, stumbled to his feet, and saw Catkin sprinting down the southern trail, coming hard. The dust she kicked up glimmered in the firelight.

"What took...you...so long?" Straighthorn asked through gasping pants.

"You didn't slide your feet enough." She knelt beside Skink and pressed a fingertip to one of the man's staring eyeballs, then put two fingers on his throat to test for a pulse. After a few heartbeats, she rose and checked the man in the mask. Over her shoulder, she asked, "Are you all right?"

Straighthorn sucked in a breath and staggered after her. "God's...no. I hurt everywhere."

Catkin ripped the raven mask from the man's face.

In shock, Straighthorn gasped. "Water Snake!"

"Of course," Catkin hissed and threw the mask into the dirt. She glowered down at the dead man's bloody face. Her voice filled with rage. "I should have known. Obsidian didn't draw him from his duties on the night of the murder. He took her into the kiva and coupled with her so she wouldn't hear our Matron's screams."

"What?" Straighthorn said in confusion. "I know nothing about—"

Catkin interrupted, "Are you well enough to keep up with me?"

He nodded. "I will keep up. Where is the War Chief?"

"He ran ahead. To the trail that cuts down at the head of this canyon."

Straighthorn struggled to his feet, wiping futilely at Skink's blood where it was drying on his chin. "So you know where we are?"

"We ran up this canyon on the way to Aspen village. Now gather your weapons and follow me. Browser may be in trouble." She sprinted up the wash.

Straighthorn grabbed for his bow and quiver. That's when the little girl caught his eye. She huddled in a dark corner of the rock shelter, petting her doll, humming softly to herself. Her eyes resembled those of a suffocating animal, huge and bulging, ready to burst from her skull.

A helpless sensation went through him. Take her with him? Would she give away his position to his enemies?

They are her people. Of course she will. Straighthorn pulled his gaze away and ran after Catkin.

Redcrop stopped in the middle of the wash. The canyon had grown steep and narrow. Pines fringed the rim five hundred hands above her. Despite the pale blue sky, shadows cloaked the canyon bottom. The screams and shouts had died a finger of time ago, leaving her in eerie silence. She didn't know what lay ahead, but she couldn't risk going back.

"He's coming," she whispered, and tears blurred her eyes. "He'll be here soon."

She didn't want to imagine what she would do if it wasn't Straighthorn who came for her.

Redcrop trotted up the winding canyon, searching for a place to hide. She studied the toppled boulders and brush, but nothing moved. Not even a whisper of wind penetrated this deep. After about one hundred paces, the sand started to grow damp, and she could smell water. Her dry throat constricted, longing for a drink.

Mist crept from around the next bend like ghostly

serpents, slithering out, then retreating, only to slither out again. A spring?

She pulled up the hem of her cape and ran.

When she rounded the curving canyon wall, she stopped dead in her tracks.

A tall old man moved through the mist, arranging what looked like stones around a tiny black-and-white pot. He grunted as he bent, then straightened and sighed, as if pleased by his work. He wore a brown-and-white turkey feather cape that flashed as he walked. Even in the dim light, Redcrop could see his long-hooked nose and white hair.

Something about the way he moved...

Redcrop walked closer and frowned as he placed another object. Red-crop's foot slipped off a slick piece of wood, and the old man gasped, and spun around. His wrinkled lips sunk in over toothless gums.

Redcrop blurted, "Elder Springbank! What are you doing out here?"

His black eyes widened. He rushed toward her with his gnarled old hands out. "Blessed gods, child. What are *you* doing here? You must leave immediately! You are in great danger."

"I know, Elder, I just escaped—"

"What you just escaped from is nothing compared to what's coming! Do you understand me? Run, child!"

Springbank's fingers sank into Redcrop's arms like talons, and he swung her around and shoved her back the way she'd come.

"Elder, wait! I think there are warriors coming up this canyon. If I go back—"

"There *are* warriors coming!"

Redcrop spun around breathlessly. "You know there are?"

"Of course, I do!"

"How—"

"*I know it!*" he said furiously. Then, more quietly, he added, "Please believe me. They are coming to meet me. I've been waiting for them since they dragged me out of the burning kiva last night."

"The burning kiva?" she said, and horror prickled her veins. "At Longtail village?"

"Yes," he said softly. Beads of sweat glistened on his hooked nose. "If we live through the next hand of time, I will tell you all about it. But for now, we must find a place to hide you."

The village burned? How many of my friends are dead? Is that the glow I saw last night just before...?

"Come with me," he said, and guided Redcrop toward a dark wall of junipers that grew in a pile of boulders. "The problem is, they know about this place, too. In fact, I suspect their people have known about it for hundreds of sun cycles. Every time they find a precious object that belonged to one of the First People, they bring it here to hide it. I can't guarantee they won't follow us inside."

Redcrop followed him. "Where are we going?"

"Over there. Climb up on that slab of sandstone."

Springbank shoved her toward it, and she climbed.

A muffled groan escaped his lips as he stepped up behind her. He wobbled, and Redcrop grabbed his sticklike old arm to keep him from falling.

He steadied himself, patted her hand, and said, "Thank you, child."

The stringy muscles in his neck stood out like cords

as he parted the branches and peered into the darkness beyond.

Redcrop cast a glance over her shoulder, but she saw no sign of warriors, not yet.

Springbank stepped through and held the branches aside for her. "Come, child. Hurry."

Redcrop gaped at the cave. The small round opening spread perhaps seven or eight hands wide. She would have to get down on her hands and knees to crawl inside.

"Move, child!"

Redcrop got down and scrambled into the hole. Cool air blew strands of hair around her face.

Springbank crawled through behind her and said, "Stand up. It's all right. The cave is more than twice your height, but it's less than a body's length wide. Extend your hands and you'll feel the walls."

Terror sent shivers through her. Redcrop did not know which was worse, the warriors outside or the impenetrable darkness that lay ahead. She extended her arms, and her fingers touched cold stone. "Where are we going?"

Springbank gave her shoulder a comforting pat. "Don't you feel the wind? There's another way out."

"How far?"

"Just brace your hands on the walls and walk. The tunnel slopes upward and breaks the surface of the ground about a thousand hands from the canyon. I'll accompany you until you can see daylight, then I must go back."

To Redcrop's surprise, the floor of the tunnel was fairly even. They moved swiftly through the musty darkness.

"There's a bend up here," he whispered. "You are going to curve to your right."

Something skittered in the darkness, and for an instant, cold air bathed her face. Cold air and a strange scent that made her quake. Something fetid and old, like the dust of lost civilizations. Where had she smelled that odor before?

Redcrop glanced over her shoulder, and Springbank whispered, "We haven't time to dally, Redcrop. Please, *walk*."

She felt her way around the curve and saw a luminous blur ahead. "I think I see the opening." Relief made her light-headed; she started to run.

"Don't run!" Springbank shouted. "The floor is much more uneven up here. Walk carefully until you can truly see."

"I will, Elder, I just—I'm anxious, I want to—"

The floor dropped away suddenly, and Redcrop cried out and clawed at the walls. Springbank caught her flailing arm and pulled her to her feet. The drop had been little more than two hands deep, but she'd twisted her ankle.

"Are you hurt, child? Can you walk?"

"I don't know!"

Springbank held her arm in a tight grip. "Try it."

Redcrop tested her ankle and had to bite back the cry of pain. "It—it doesn't want to take my weight, Elder."

"Then you must crawl, child. Believe me, crawling is better than staying here. I promise you that I will try to return for you, but I cannot guarantee you that the next footsteps you hear will be mine. Do you understand?"

Redcrop felt sick. "Yes."

She longed to sit down and weep. Springbank supported her arm until she got down on her hands and knees and started feeling her way along the floor.

"I'm all right, Elder."

"You're certain?"

She felt the same way she had as a child when she'd first learned of her mother's death. As if the world had died. "Yes, I can crawl."

"Good. I should go. I don't think they will take kindly if I'm—"

"Go, Elder. Thank you."

He was silent for a moment, then she felt his hand on her back, the touch light. "I pray the Blessed Katsinas keep you safe, child."

"You also, Elder."

She heard his steps going rapidly back down the tunnel.

Redcrop hung her head and fought to regain control. Without him, she felt terrified and alone.

But she crawled.

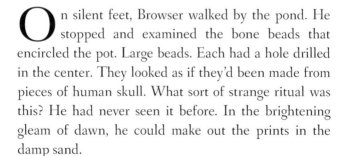

On silent feet, Browser walked by the pond. He stopped and examined the bone beads that encircled the pot. Large beads. Each had a hole drilled in the center. They looked as if they'd been made from pieces of human skull. What sort of strange ritual was this? He had never seen it before. In the brightening gleam of dawn, he could make out the prints in the damp sand.

He scanned the dark gray cliffs, searching for movement, then followed the man's tracks; he had hurried away from the pond, his stride long, almost running. When the man's tracks connected with a woman's, Browser glanced at the junipers and the toppled boulders.

Gods, is it them?

He gripped his war club and continued on. The steps vanished below a sandstone ledge covered with scrubby junipers. A strange musky scent surrounded the junipers.

Browser stepped up onto the ledge and peered through the dark weave of branches. Someone had passed through the trees, snapping twigs. A turkey feather hung from a tuft of needles.

Browser eased through and saw the cave. Most of the prints had been smoothed away by a dragging cape, or the hem of a long dress, but he saw two handprints pressed into the dust near the cave's mouth.

He whispered, "They crawled inside."

Browser bent to examine the interior. Utter darkness met his gaze. He sniffed at the dank odor of packrats and mold, then got down on his hands and knees.

As he stuck his head through, he glimpsed a fringed white moccasin...

The blow came out of nowhere, slammed into his head, and knocked him face-first into the dust. He twisted desperately, trying to look up. A shifting blur of faces swam above him. One face...or ten?

∼

atkin walked carefully around the pond, studying the tracks. The sky had begun to purple overhead, but the cliffs remained a deep dark gray.

"Browser found the man's tracks first," she said to Straighthorn, who stood guard looking down the canyon. "Then he followed the man's tracks until they met up with Redcrop's."

Straighthorn glanced over his shoulder at her. "And then?"

"Let us find out."

Catkin placed her steps to the side of Browser's and followed them back to where they met Redcrop's tracks. "They veer off," she said, and swerved right toward a tangle of junipers that grew in a boulder pile. "All three of them stepped onto this sandstone slab."

Straighthorn eased back to look at the scuffed dust and the mixture of moccasin and sandal prints. "They pushed through the junipers. See the broken twigs?"

Catkin nodded. "I will let you know what I find."

Straighthorn licked his lips and jerked a nod. Sweat coated his bruised and bloodied face. A huge black knot had swollen on the left side of his forehead. Catkin sniffed the air, and the coppery tang ate at her insides.

She shouldered through the junipers and frowned. The mouth of the small cave was splattered with blood. She knelt and ran a finger over dark spots. Fresh blood. It had just begun to dry. Knee and handprints marked the soil. A runny feeling grew in her gut. Browser's blood? Redcrop's? She prayed that Browser had caught Two Hearts and the blood belonged to him.

"But if that were true," she whispered to herself,

"the man would be lying here dead. Unless Browser wounded him—"

"And had to follow him inside?" Straighthorn asked.

He peered at Catkin through the weave of juniper needles.

She nodded. "I'd say that's our best guess. Browser probably struck the man, and the man ran away and crawled into this cave."

Straighthorn looked at her with soft eyes. "But where are Redcrop's tracks? Where was she when Browser attacked her captor?"

Catkin shook her head. "I see a woman's handprint on the left side of the cave, but—"

"Maybe she went in first?" Fear lined his face. "Perhaps the man forced her to crawl inside?"

Catkin wiped the blood from her finger onto her buckskin war shirt. "There's no sign that she was forced in here, Straighthorn. You can look at the tracks yourself. She met the man and walked here with him. She never stumbled or dragged her feet as if being forced. She never tried to run. I think she crawled into this cave willingly."

"But"—he gave her a heartsick look—"how could that be? She would never..."

Straighthorn's eyes flew open, but before he could spin around, Catkin saw the white capes flash. The warriors crept from behind boulders and trees and glided forward in ghostly silence.

"Oh, gods," Straighthorn whispered.

Catkin shouted, *"Get into the cave!"*

Straighthorn dove through the trees for the hole in the cliff.

24

The floor undulated, the dips and protrusions hidden in the darkness. Redcrop crawled on through the black cavern. Every time her injured foot stubbed rock, she wanted to scream.

The strange smell grew in strength: like old bones that had been moldering for sun cycles.

Redcrop's palm struck something small, cold, and round. She lifted it.

It tinkled.

The notes were so pure and beautiful that she rang it again.

"A bell," she whispered to herself. "It's a bell."

She turned it in her palm, smiling, longing to laugh. It had the cold, smooth feel of metal. She touched the bell to her tongue. *A copper bell!*

She tucked it into the top of her moccasin and continued on.

The luminous blur turned into an awl-prick of solid gray light.

Redcrop forced herself to crawl faster. How could

the air be getting more foul as she neared the opening? She should be smelling dew-soaked earth and damp trees.

"Ow!" she cried without thinking when her knee ground over a pebble.

Redcrop reached down and started to throw it away when it clinked.

"What—?"

She turned the object over until she knew for certain that it was another copper bell.

"Gods, how did these get here?"

They must have been left by the First People who had built Longtail village more than a hundred summers ago. Awe prickled in her chest. Perhaps this cave had been one of their secret places? A sacred tunnel...

From her place in the womb of earth, she looked up suddenly and listened.

A faint voice whispered through the darkness.

"Come the brothers...born of Sun..."

The words floated across her souls; she wasn't certain if she actually heard them or was remembering them from the rock shelter. Her grandmother told her that First Woman had spoken those words right after she had emerged from the underworlds.

"One is slayed. Here by the...trail...his corpse is laid."

A man's voice. Breathless, the words more panted than sung. The voice verged on ecstasy. Or an agony too terrible to be borne.

The voice of a dying man.

Scarcely perceptible footfalls echoed.

"You, born of F-Father Sun, laid in the light next to n-night..." Sobs.

Elder Springbank's voice!

She had heard him Sing many times at ceremonials. Usually, he had a deep, ringing voice. She would know it, even when whispered in agony.

On her knees, her eyes blind with tears, she turned and started back down the cavern.

A scream echoed through the cave and froze her blood. In the middle of the scream, she made out the words: *"Come the brothers, born of Sun!..."* The last word ended in a high-pitched wail.

A sudden trembling left her shaking so badly she could barely force herself to breathe. Had they caught him? The warriors he'd been expecting? He said they knew about this tunnel. Perhaps they hadn't found him where they'd anticipated and came looking?

In a fit of frenzy, she turned and scrambled toward the light, toward the foul smell.

Hurry! Hurry!

Behind her, feet scuffed stone. She could hear him staggering, as though the man could not find the strength to put one foot before the other.

Tears trickled down Redcrop's face. She crawled like a madwoman.

The metallic taint of blood carried on the air. She heard a tortured groan but couldn't tell if it had come from behind or ahead.

The tunnel opened into a chamber. A yawning maw.

Redcrop's heart expanded at the sight. Her gaze swept the walls and lifted to the towering ceiling. She might have been kneeling in a womb of dove-colored radiance. Pots, hundreds of them, lined the shelves that had been carved into the stone. Pots of all colors and designs, red-on-tan, black-on-white, red-on-black. Some had lids, others did not. Precious shells and carved fetishes packed the open pots. Redcrop gaped at the wealth. One pot held nothing but jet frogs with turquoise eyes, another had a jumble of malachite wolves and red coral birds.

She heard a body thump onto the stone, and a man moaned, then wept, his desperation beyond pain. Beyond words.

In a quavering voice, Redcrop whispered: "Elder Springbank?"

The dark throat of the tunnel stirred, then fluttered as though filled with black wings—and she realized someone was coming through. Staggering toward her.

The man stepped into the pale gleam.

Crimson splotched Springbank's cape and dotted his white hair. Tears flooded the elder's wrinkled cheeks. He had both fists twined in War Chief Browser's collar, dragging him along behind.

"Help me, child!" he begged. "I found him lying in the cave entrance. He's hurt badly!"

"Oh, gods, what happened?"

How on earth had the fragile elder managed to drag the War Chief? Redcrop scrambled back, clenching her teeth against the pain in her ankle.

Springbank eased Browser down and sank to the floor as if he'd used his last bit of energy. A club hung from Springbank's belt. She hadn't seen it earlier. Had it been hidden by his cape?

Springbank said, "The warriors I was supposed to meet—I think they found him." He held blood-soaked hands out to Redcrop. "Your grandmother was a Healer, child. Do something!"

Redcrop rushed to Browser's side and brushed the hair from his round face. Blood leaked down his forehead in ropy red lines.

"It may not be as bad as it looks." She reached down to tear a length of cloth from her skirt. The sound of ripping fabric echoed in the still chamber. "Scalp wounds always bleed like this."

Springbank used his sleeve to wipe at the blood speckling his wrinkled face. "I've suffered enough of them to know that, but he's unconscious, and that means the blow was severe enough to make his souls flee."

"Yes, but often they return fairly quickly."

Browser's eyelids jerked. That was a good sign.

Springbank suddenly gasped and slid closer. "Gods, do you think he's wounded anywhere else? I'll search while you tend his head wound."

"Thank you, Elder."

Springbank's gnarled fingers untied the laces on Browser's buckskin cape and pulled it away from his muscular body. "I don't see any blood." He continued searching, pulling up the War Chief's sleeves, scrutinizing his chest and belly. He pulled a bone stiletto from the top of Browser's red leggings and tossed it away. Springbank's eyes narrowed when he saw Browser's small belt pouch. He opened it, and a sharp cry came from his lips.

Redcrop blurted, "What's wrong?"

Springbank pulled out a magnificent turquoise wolf and clutched it to his chest. "I searched for twenty-two summers before I found this. I feared it was gone forever."

Redcrop frowned at the wolf, wondering why the

War Chief had been holding something that belonged to Elder Springbank. It resembled the wolf Piper had tucked into the top of her legging. "Twenty-two summers? Where did you find it?"

He peered down at the wolf with blurry eyes. "In a walled-up room in Talon Town. It was hanging around the throat of a hideous mummy."

Redcrop's veins constricted as fear sent its flush through her. The mummy in the rock shelter? With trembling hands, she used the cloth to wipe blood from Browser's forehead. The long gash began at his hairline and extended back across the middle of his skull. Redcrop folded the cloth, placed it over the wound, and pressed hard, but her eyes sought the daylight streaming through the hole less than fifty body lengths away.

Escape. It lay so close.

"The bleeding will stop s-soon, Elder," she stammered.

Springbank put a hand on her hair and stroked it. "I thank you, child. I knew you could help him."

Springbank's hand gently moved down her hair to squeeze her shoulder. "I wish I knew what happened to him. There were no warriors around when I found him."

"He was struck from above, Elder."

Springbank's wrinkled mouth opened. "How do you know?"

"The wound. It's deeper in the front than the back. I think he was on the ground when someone hit him from above."

"You mean Browser may have been crawling away and his attacker straddled him and brought the club down on top of his head?"

Redcrop gave him a sidelong glance. "Yes."

Her hands started to shake. Had the War Chief followed their tracks to the tunnel and been attacked when he got down to crawl inside?

Springbank stroked Redcrop's arm in a way that sent shivers down her spine. "You are very good at helping people."

Redcrop pulled away and stared at him.

Springbank grabbed her hand. His bony fingers closed around her wrist in a viselike grip. "Why did you pull away from me?"

"I'm sorry, Elder. I'm just not accustomed—"

"Don't be frightened," he whispered, and slid closer to her. The sparse white hair that framed his cadaveric face had a blue glint. "I have been watching you for a long time. Unfortunately, you never left the Matron's side. It was impossible to speak with you privately. Now that she is gone, we will have a great deal of time together."

"Run!"

Redcrop saw Browser's fist come up and felt it slam her in the shoulder, knocking her away from Springbank, then he rolled, ripped the war club from Springbank's belt, and brutally slammed the old man in the chest. A sickening thump echoed in the room.

"Go!" Browser shouted at her. "Run! *Now!*"

The blow sent Springbank toppling backward into the cavern wall. In a weak voice, the old man cried, "Why are you attacking me?"

"War Chief!" Redcrop cried, stunned. "What are you doing?"

Browser staggered as though he could barely stand.

His scalp wound had broken open again; blood poured down his face. "Redcrop, *run!*"

"But you struck the elder!" she shouted and crawled toward Spring-bank. "He's hurt badly!"

Browser reached down, gripped a handful of her hair, and flung her across the chamber. When she landed hard, a wrenching cry broke from her lips. She screamed, *"I was trying to help!"*

Browser weaved on his feet. Blood traced web-like patterns down his round face and clotted his hair. "Who are you?" he shouted at Springbank. "I want to know!"

Springbank cradled his ribs and slid back against the cavern wall. As he did, he dislodged several pots that hit the stone floor to break with a hollow popping sound and spill their contents. He winced every time he inhaled. Pain glazed his old eyes. "What you really wish to know is...if I killed your lover, Hophorn."

Browser nearly collapsed, as if his legs were failing him. He locked his knees and stood silently a moment, as though mustering his strength to ask: "Did you?"

A smile curled Springbank's toothless mouth. "She converted to the Katsina faith...as did your wife."

Browser turned to Redcrop again and cried, "For the sake of the gods, girl, leave! I don't know how long I can stay on my feet. Someone must run back to the village and tell our people what happened here!"

Redcrop slid toward the exit, but she cried, "But I don't know what's happening! Why are you speaking to Elder Springbank this way?"

Springbank, cradling his crushed chest, laughed. "Do you really think I would guide her in here without having a guard posted at the exit? The instant she sticks her head outside, it will be lopped off!"

Redcrop hesitated, confusion building.

Browser shouted, "He's lying! If there was a guard out there, he would have already heard our shouts and come!"

Springbank's grin belied the terrible pain in his eyes. "The guard has orders not to enter this chamber until called. I assure you, she's used to hearing screams in here."

Redcrop's exhausted arms and legs would no longer hold her. She slumped to the floor, a soft mewing in her throat.

Browser shook his head, as though he couldn't think, or perhaps his vision had gone dim. He wasn't going to black out, was he?

Browser, as if having trouble finding words, asked, "Are you descended from the Blessed Cornsilk?"

Springbank watched him like a hawk with a wounded mouse in sight, as though waiting for the first sign of weakness to pounce.

Springbank sighed. "Cornsilk is the cause of all this, you young fool. *She should have become the Matron of Talon Town.* When she abandoned her duty, she killed us all. Our nation fell to pieces. My father would have been the Blessed Sun, the ruler of the Straight Path Nation!" He lifted a fist and shook it. "I would be the Blessed Sun this instant!"

Browser put a hand over his left eye, as though to block the light, and squinted through his right eye. The blood streaking his face gave him a fearsome appearance. "Did you kill my grandmother?"

Redcrop gaped at Browser. *His grandmother?*

Springbank chuckled and flinched as he cradled his chest. A shiver went through him. "Ash Girl was two at the time. She must have said something to Painted Turtle at one of the ceremonial gatherings. I never knew what, but Painted Turtle found me, dragged me aside, and told me she knew what I was doing to the girl."

Tears welled in Browser's eyes. "She should have killed you for what you did to her!"

Springbank's black gaze burned into Browser's. "She would have if she'd had a little more proof. She even sent a messenger to Spider Silk to ask her if my father had hurt my half-brother Bear Dancer when he was a boy. She suspected that I was treating my daughter the same way I'd been treated as a boy."

Browser braced his feet, struggling to lift the club. "I curse you, you filthy..."

Browser stumbled and almost dropped the war club. He gripped it so hard his fingers went white. "What about the other old women who died at the same time as my grandmother?"

Springbank studied Browser's eyes, then his gaze lowered to Browser's jerky hands. A knowing gleam replaced the pain in his eyes. "Painted Turtle couldn't keep her jaws closed. I could tell from the way those elders looked at me after the ceremony that she had shared her suspicions. You know what our people do to those who commit incest. It was my life or theirs. What would you have done?"

Incest! Redcrop glanced back and forth between them, struggling to understand.

Browser said, "I wouldn't have abused my children in the first place."

Springbank smiled, as if gleeful. "Only because you don't know what it's like. If you knew the feel of that young flesh, you—"

"Shut up!" Browser staggered back, trying to prop himself with the war club. His other hand went to his head. He'd started breathing raggedly. "Gods, how many people have you killed? How many children have you molested—"

"Ash Girl's mother would have discovered the truth if it hadn't been for Stone Ghost. I was very grateful when he arrived to 'solve' the crime and found the blood-encrusted knife I hid in that young warrior's chamber. Everyone, including Ash Girl's clan, thought he'd found the murderer."

Browser's knees wobbled, and he nearly pitched over. "I had seen eight summers at the time. I must have known you, or at least seen you at the gatherings. What was your name?"

Springbank glanced at Browser's trembling knees, then at the war club propped on the floor like one leg of a tripod.

Patiently, he answered, "I have had many names. As a boy I was known as Silver Shadow, but when I went through the manhood ritual—"

Browser blurted, "And Obsidian?"

Springbank's eyes widened, as if surprised. "Did she tell you, or are you guessing?"

"I think she helped you to kill our Matron. I think—"

Redcrop shouted, *"What?"*

"She didn't help me, you fool!" Springbank broke into a coughing fit and his whole body spasmed. Blood bubbled at his lips. He wiped his mouth with his sleeve and stared at the blood as though he had expected as much. "You may not need your club. It looks like one of my broken ribs punctured a lung, which means I don't have long—"

Faint voices echoed in the tunnel.

Browser looked up, and Springbank smiled.

"I told you they were coming."

Browser backed away unsteadily and staggered toward the tunnel. He stood to one side with his club up, blinking the blood from his eyes, waiting for the first person to come through. He'd be lucky if he didn't fall flat on his face.

Redcrop scrambled for the bone stiletto Springbank had thrown away earlier and crawled to the opposite side of the tunnel. She braced her hands and dragged herself to her feet with the stiletto in her trembling fist. A stab of agony shot up her leg.

Browser gave her a confident nod, but his eyes kept drifting, as though he couldn't keep them focused. He closed them and sucked in deep breaths. It seemed to help. When he opened them, his fingers tightened around his club. He leaned against the cold cavern wall.

The whispers grew louder.

Redcrop had to fight her own hand to keep hold of the stiletto. Silent sobs shook her.

Feet shuffled, then dust puffed from the tunnel and shimmered in the gray light.

A head appeared.

Browser said, *"Catkin! Thank the katsinas,"* and he crumpled to the floor.

Catkin crawled out slowly, her eyes glinting like polished stones.

That look told Browser something Redcrop didn't

understand. He scrambled to get to his feet and lift his war club...

"Put it down, or she dies!"

Redcrop saw the hand twined in Catkin's red collar. A large, powerful hand.

Browser's club clattered to the stone floor.

As the man emerged from the cavern behind Catkin, he ordered, "Sit down and don't move, or we will kill your friends."

"Don't listen to them!" Straighthorn screamed.

Redcrop straightened, her veins on fire, and clutched the stiletto in both hands.

Catkin was forced to her knees just outside the tunnel, facing Browser. The tall, black-haired man who emerged behind her straightened. His strong fist knotted in the fabric, he kept Catkin's body between him and Browser.

Browser's voice shook with anger. "Who are you? What do you want?"

The tall warrior gave him a crooked smile. "Didn't Two Hearts tell you? We came for the ritual feast."

The words hit Redcrop like a blunt fist to the belly. She gaped at Springbank. *Two Hearts?*

Browser said, "I don't know what you're talking about. Who are you?"

Redcrop swallowed hard and gripped the stiletto. If only the man would turn his broad back to her...

Springbank shouted, *"Ten Hawks, you fool, there's one behind you!"*

The man spun around as Redcrop threw herself forward, all of her weight driving the deer-bone stiletto into his chest. *Have to hold him long enough. Hurry, Straighthorn. Hurry!*

The man flung his arm up and knocked her sideways. Pain, like fire, lanced up her leg, but got a grasp on his shirt with one hand as she lunged again, driving the stiletto into his shoulder, stabbing at his chest, shrieking, sobbing. Blood spattered her face and smeared warmly on her hands.

Ten Hawks screamed, twisted away, and his fist slammed into Red-crop's shoulder hard enough to knock her to the floor. Stunned by the brutality, she had barely managed to get her hands under her when he dove headlong onto her. A woofing sound burst from her lips as his weight drove the air from her lungs, and he wrenched the stiletto from her hand.

She looked up in time to see the primal rage in his black eyes. Then he struck her, blasting lights through her vision. Her head made a sickening, hollow thud as it bounced off the floor. Through the ringing in her ears, she heard his bellow. Blinked to clear her swimming vision and saw him loom above her. Like a shimmering mirage, he plunged the stiletto down. Three times, in rapid succession, the white-hot pain pierced her breast. She was gaping, mouth open, when he heaved to his feet.

In the growing river of pain, fear, and shock, she almost didn't see the four white-caped men who crawled through the tunnel.

Redcrop tried to rise, only to collapse onto her side. When she tried to breathe, her lungs gurgled, and she coughed up blood. Panic powered her. She writhed on her side and watched the red pool fill the hollow in the cave floor in front of her. With each labored breath, the red spewed. Blood seemed to explode from her mouth. So much blood!

atkin scrambled to one side on all fours as Redcrop leaped on Ten Hawks. She roared at Browser, "Throw me your club!"

Browser, weaving on his feet, gave her a dumb look, his blood-streaked face oddly pale, his eyes glassy. Gods! How badly was he hurt?

Catkin got her feet under her, leaped, and ripped the club from Browser's hand, tumbling him in the process. She turned just in time to see the four white-caped warriors emerge from the narrow cave. From the corner of her eye, she saw Ten Hawks stand and sway. Blood was bubbling from Redcrop's mouth.

Then Catkin waded into the enemy horde, swinging her club with deadly intent. One man fell immediately, howling and jerking like a clubbed dog.

Browser, down and dazed, but not out, scuttled forward and grabbed the last man out of the tunnel by the ankle. The warrior tried to kick the hand off, then Browser was on him, pummeling him with his fists, kicking, biting. They rolled across the floor.

Inside the tunnel, she could hear Straighthorn's screams and shouts.

Catkin spun in time to parry a blow that would have crushed her skull. Her attacker lifted his club again, triumph in his eyes as he savored the moment of the kill.

His mistake. In that instant before he could kill her, she swung Browser's stone-headed war club into his testicles. She sidestepped as he stumbled forward, his throat bulged from a stifled scream. She caught the barest glimpse of his pained eyes, then twisted, hammering him across the stomach. As he curled around the blow, she ripped the club loose, pirouetted on tiptoe, and crushed the back of his skull.

Springbank's hollow voice shrilled, "For the sake of the true gods, Browser! We shouldn't be fighting! *You are one of us.* Join us and we will let your Made People friends live!"

Catkin whirled, skipped aside as the third warrior's club whistled past her head. Catching a desperate glance, she could see that Browser was losing—driven back against the wall by a much younger man with a body like a stout tree trunk. Browser's hands were pinned, and blood gushed from his wound. His face resembled a shiny red mask.

Catkin blocked another blow, the sting of it transmitted through the seasoned wood of Browser's club.

"Join us!" Springbank shouted. His bloody fingers dug into the sandstone wall as, ledge by ledge, he pulled himself to his feet. He leaned against the wall of pots, coughing. Blood welled from his wounded lungs and poured down his chin. "You don't believe in the katsinas, do you? I know you don't!"

Catkin danced to the side, avoiding another blow by a hair's breadth. Gods, this man was no callow youth, but a seasoned warrior. Her only hope lay in her agility. Ten Hawks? What had happened to Ten Hawks. She couldn't spare the glance.

Think, Catkin! This man is going to kill you!

≈

P anic cleared Browser's foggy mind as he stared into the warrior's hard black eyes. The man had him in a firm grip, was raising his war club for the final blow.

Reactions fed by the years of war, Browser kicked his legs out and let himself fall, tearing free of his opponent's hands. He grabbed the man around the waist and bowled him backward.

Two Hearts words, *You are one of us!* echoed in his Browser's head.

The rage came boiling up from deep within. As they fell, Browser got a hold on the White Moccasin's genitals squeezed as hard as he could and twisted. The man's shriek was deafening. Distracted by pain, the warrior dropped his club, was clawing at Browser's back with both hands.

Seizing the opportunity, gave one last wrench and twist, broke loose, and twined his fingers into the man's hair. He screamed: "Murderers! You think it is heroic to slaughter innocent people? Like in Aspen village!"

He butted his bloody head into the man's face, spattering it into the warrior's eyes. Then Browser got his hands on the man's war club where it lay forgotten on the cavern floor. The White Moccasin recovered enough to block the blow, and they struggled, Browser intent on forcing the handle down across the man's throat.

"Aspen village was full of witches!" Springbank cried. More pots fell from the shelves to break and spill as the old man struggled to remain upright. "You know it! In the name of the gods, Browser, *think!* The coughing sickness comes from the katsinas! Good people everywhere are dying from it. As soon as they start to believe in the katsinas, the sickness nests in their lungs and..."

Browser lost the rest as the warrior twisted sideways, and Browser lost the leverage. They rolled across the floor, screaming, as the White Moccasin got a foot out amidst the broken pottery and spilled beads. As he started to stand, the beads rolled out from underfoot.

As the warrior fell, Browser drove the club down onto the man's throat. Their souls touched as they looked into each other's eyes.

The stiletto flashed out of nowhere. Only Browser's reflexes saved him. He jerked away and the keen point missed his eye by a lash's breadth; the passing fist tore through his hair. Browser bucked, driving his knee into the warrior's groin. With all his weight, he bore down, pressing the war club into the man's windpipe, seeing the throat bulging around the wooden handle.

When the animal scream died in Browser's throat, he was still driving his knee into the man's crotch, still pressing down with all of his weight, glaring into sightless eyes. The man's tongue stuck out between the lips like a bloated worm.

Browser stared at the mangled flesh of his left arm. When had the stiletto found him? He straightened, feeling the pain, and caught sight of Catkin in the rear of the cavern.

Catkin danced back, fear in her eyes, and Browser saw the triumphant look in her opponent's face. As the man skipped, twisted, and raised his club for the deadly strike, Catkin spit in his face. In the split heartbeat it bought her, she hammered the man in the ribs. Spinning, she swung the stone head of the club in a high arc.

The warrior saw, pivoted. The blow caught his shoulder. The collarbone snapped, the sound loud and meaty.

The White Moccasin cried out and dropped to his knees, gasping as his club slipped from nerveless fingers.

The cave, with its pots and piles of wealth, was eerily quiet.

"Join us," Springbank whispered into the silence.

Browser shouted, *"I'll never join you! Never!"*

Springbank coughed and coagulated blood coated his lips. "Yes, you will. It's in your blood...one of us."

Straighthorn pushed his way through the entrance with another man before him. The white-caped warrior was bleeding badly from a belly wound. When Straighthorn saw Redcrop, he cried, "No!"

The youth's reaction was instinctive. He clubbed his captive in the head. A pumpkin made that hollow sound when dropped from a height. The warrior jerked and collapsed in a heap, and Straighthorn dropped at Redcrop's side.

He gathered Redcrop into his arms. *"Redcrop!"* All the pain in the universe might have been in that wounded voice.

Browser got a good look at Redcrop and read her dilated pupils, fixed now in death. She seemed to wilt in Straighthorn's arms.

"Oh, gods, no!" Straighthorn cried.

Filled with futility, Browser slammed his bloody fists into the stone floor. His skull felt as if it might split wide open. His vision was swimming again, and stomach spasmed an instant before he bent double and threw up.

When he could, he wiped a sleeve across his mouth and tried to get his bearings.

Straighthorn still cradled Redcrop in his arms. Then the young man rose and started toward the round hole of daylight on the far side of the cavern, saying, "I have to get you out of here."

Redcrop hung limply, a dead weight. The blood that leaked down her arms splashed onto the floor in crimson stars.

Browser struggled to his feer. Took his war club back from Catkin where she was bent over, arms braced on her knees, gasping for breath. As she straightened, he handed her the one from the dead warrior. Ten Hawks lay to one side, curled into a fetal ball, blood soaking his white cape.

"Redcrop"   —Catkin   panted   for breath—"saved us."

"You're not saved," Springbank wheezed through his blood-clotted windpipe. "Shadow's coming with the rest."

Browser staggered as the room seemed to spin. "The other warriors from Aspen village?"

"Join us, Browser," Springbank said, his voice insidious. "The blood of the First People runs in your veins!"

Browser swallowed hard. Couldn't find the words.

"We *will* destroy the katsinas," Springbank gasped. "That was the *true* vision." The old man's clothing scraped as he slid down the wall. Another pot tumbled and broke on the floor, this one spilling eagle-bone beads.

The old man's eyes seemed to lose focus. "The true vision..."

He coughed weakly. "Think, Browser. When did this begin?"

Without waiting for an answer, he said, "With the coming of the katsinas. They came, and within a generation, the First People were hunted down and killed. Forced to run and hide. All we need to do is destroy the katsinas, and the Straight Path Nation will rise...from the ashes...like gods from Spider Woman's web."

Springbank slumped sideways, his body tumbling like a sack of old bones. He lay there, unmoving, with bloody drool leaking from the corner of his mouth onto the spilled wealth of beads and precious stones.

Catkin blinked at Browser with wonder-filled eyes. "Springbank is one of the First People?"

Browser rubbed his face, sticky with blood. He nodded. "Yes."

They heard voices echoing from the mouth of the tunnel. Browser cocked his head. From the sounds of scuffing feet, and the rustle of clothing, it was a large party.

"Shadow?" Catkin asked. "Those other warriors he was talking about?"

Browser fought to pull his thoughts together. "Come on. Our only chance is to get Straighthorn and run. We'll come back, but with all of our warriors. Then we'll clean out this witch's nest once and for all."

Catkin carefully backed away.

"And"—he blinked against the splitting headache —"I'm not good for another fight. The run is going to be hard enough."

Browser winced at the pain as he bent down and uncurled the old man's hands. He pried the turquoise wolf from his leathery grip. Took two steps toward the opening and turned. The old man's white hair resembled a glistening blur of snowflakes, but his eyes were pits of darkness.

Springbank seemed to be smiling at him, a gloating smile, as if he knew something...

Browser was raising the war club, ready to go back and cave in the old man's head, when laughter could be heard in the tunnel. Close now.

Catkin took his arm. Steadied him as she led the way and ducked out into the light. The daylight seemed to burn right through his eyes and into his brain.

Catkin was shouting, "Straighthorn, let's go! Hurry!"

"No! I won't leave her!"

Catkin let loose of Browser long enough to drag Straighthorn to his feet and shout in his face, "She's *dead!* Leave her or you will be, too!"

She flung Straighthorn into a shambling trot and raced after him, shoving him hard. He kept screaming and batting at her with his fists, but Catkin fended off every blow and drove him ahead of her with the handle of her war club. Browser followed, feeling woozy. All of his concentration went into putting one foot ahead of the other.

Thank you, Catkin. Thank you.

Gods, now, if Browser could just make it back to Longtail village without collapsing. If the White Moccasins didn't chase them down. If...if...

Maureen worked on the next of the carefully pedestaled bones: a child's radius and ulna that ended in a fragile calcined mess. Sylvia had already photographed it, mapped it in, and recorded the provenience.

Maureen uncapped the diluted polyvinyl acetate that Dale had brought her, and carefully painted the mixture onto the bones. The tang of acetone carried on the cool morning breeze. As an undergraduate, before she'd understood the effects of acetone, she'd cooked a lot of brain cells cleaning specimens.

The rattling of the aluminum ladder alerted her to Dale's long body as he climbed down into the kiva. She watched him pick his careful way across the floor to where Maureen recapped the PVA jar. His gray hair and mustache shone as if freshly washed.

He cleared his throat. "Um, Sylvia, would you mind going down to the trailer and making me a pot of coffee? If you could fill my thermos, I would appreciate it."

Sylvia tucked brown hair behind her ears and gave Dale a measuring glance. "Sure, Dale. I'm on it." She stood and knocked the dirt from the knees of her jeans. "Probably take me a while."

"Thank you," Dale told her warmly, and watched as Sylvia clattered up the ladder and disappeared over the kiva rim.

"What's up?" Maureen asked.

Dale sighed and retrieved a big plastic bucket. He turned it over to use as a seat and leaned close to Maureen's ear. "Tell me about these dreams William is having. I almost jumped out of my skin when he yelled last night. You've been staying in the trailer; has this happened before?"

Maureen wiped her hands on her black Levi's. "Dale, you need to ask Dusty, not me."

Dale pushed his fedora back on his head. "So. This is a recurring nightmare?"

"I never said that."

"You didn't have to." Dale frowned. "It's something tied to 10K3, isn't it? That's why he's so sure this site is related?"

"Regardless of the dream, I think he's right."

Dale looked thoughtful. "The dating is correct, the pottery is the same design. We have another trephined skull. But you can't dismiss coincidence. It isn't that unlikely that people in a similar time would have similar pottery motifs. But..."

Maureen stiffened at his hesitation. "This is completely off the record. No matter what you tell me, it's between us."

Dale's gaze held hers. "When you're around the

Native people long enough, you learn to respect their beliefs. And, in my years, I've seen some pretty curious things. Been part of things." He paused. "Even, once upon a time, Puebloan witchcraft."

Dale made a face, as if in pain, and tried to shift his weight.

Maureen pointed and asked, "How are your knees?"

"The damn things hurt," he admitted, eyes widening. "How do you know—ah, William, of course." He shook his head. "I wish I'd never gone up there. Never should have gotten involved with the things I did. But I was young...and White."

"You're still White."

"Not as much as I used to be," he answered and smiled as he shifted on his bucket.

Maureen released his hand and rose.

Dale looked up at her. "Where are you going?"

Maureen gazed up at the crystal blue sky, then propped hands on her hips. "To make a phone call. Dusty needs more than either you or I can give him. He won't make the call himself, so somebody has to do it for him."

As she walked for the ladder, Dale called, "Don't tell me you believe in witchcraft?"

"No. But Dusty does."

She ran up the rungs, a new spring in her steps, and started across the planks. To either side, the ruins of Pueblo Animas lay in mounded desolation, only the round ring of the kiva and Dusty's single rectangular room opened in the rubble.

She waved to Dusty as she passed. He was bent

over a screen, one foot propped in the back dirt as he sorted through bits of rock and root mass for ceramics and other artifacts.

Her route took her directly to the Bronco, where she opened the door and dug the cell phone out of the center console. She flipped the cover open and watched the display come to life. Four bars of power, that ought to be enough. She punched in the number and waited through two rings.

At the voice prompt, she said: "I would like the number for Chaco Culture National Historical Park. Maggie Walking Hawk Taylor, please."

"There's a car coming," Sylvia called. She had Dale's thermos of hot coffee as she stopped at the kiva's edge .

Dusty stretched his back muscles and stood from where he'd been using his trowel to pedestal another tangle of charred bones. He propped his elbows on the lip of the pit. "Who is it?"

Sylvia squinted out at the access road. "Blue Mercedes. I think it's the pygmy."

Dale narrowed one eye disapprovingly where he sat on his bucket. "You mean Mr. Wirth?"

"Yeah. Right."

Dusty climbed out of his pit and walked over to give Dale a hand up from his bucket seat. Steve crawled out behind him, his black face smudged with streaks of tan dirt. They both wore faded jeans, but Dusty's red flannel contrasted sharply with Steve's denim shirt.

By the time all three had climbed out of the kiva, the Mercedes pulled up, trailing a cloud of dust. It rolled to a stop behind Dale's gleaming red pickup.

Sylvia added, "He's got somebody in the car with him."

Steve wiped his forehead on his blue sleeve. "His wife?"

"Hard to tell."

The people inside waited for the dust to clear, then popped the doors and got out.

Sylvia let out a low whistle. "Wow. I'll bet those silk suits cost over a thousand bucks each."

"Fifteen hundred," Dusty guessed. He shoved his battered Resistol hat back on his head, revealing a thin line of mud where sweat had mixed with the dust.

Peter Wirth's pale gray suit was shiny enough to blind through a welder's helmet. The other man, tall, with dark hair, wore a cream-colored suit with a black-and-gray striped tie. They both had on reflective sunglasses.

Dusty brushed the caked dirt off his hands and morosely said, "Time to take a break. Why doesn't everybody grab something cold to drink."

Steve said, "I'll get it. Sylvia, what do you want?"

"A Pepsi, thanks."

"Sure. Dr. Robertson? Dusty? Can I get you something?"

Dale said, "Sylvia just brought me a thermos of fresh coffee, but thank you anyway, Steve."

"Dusty, what about you?"

Dusty shook his head. "Don't worry about me. I'll get my own later."

As Steve headed for the cooler, Dusty studied the two men. Wirth's white hair didn't move an inch despite the fact that the wind had picked up. He must really want to keep that pygmy-mannequin look today. The other guy stopped frequently to pick up a potsherd, or a flake, then lay it down very gently, before continuing on up the hill.

As Wirth closed in, Sylvia leaned over and whispered, "Tell them we're from Earth and mean no harm."

Dusty adjusted his sunglasses. "It's not them I'm worried about."

"What do you mean?"

"Well, check out the guy in back. What do you make of him?"

Sylvia's gaze took him in from head to toe. "For what he paid for those shoes alone, I could cover my entire college education. I wager Italian mob."

Dale scratched his wrinkled chin. "I wager he's another investment banker."

"Yeah, well," Sylvia granted, "same thing."

Dusty crossed his arms, figuring whatever it was, it wasn't going to be good.

As Wirth came up the rubble slope, he called, "Hello, Dr. Robertson, how are you? Mr. Stewart. How is everything coming along?"

Sylvia cupped a hand to her mouth and yelled, "We dug up about forty burned babies, a cannibalized old woman, and just yesterday we found a secret passageway to hell."

Dale sighed as Wirth gave her an irritated glare.

"Good day, Peter," Dale said, and stepped forward to shake Wirth's hand. "Don't mind Sylvia. She attended university in an attempt to develop her wit. Unfortunately, she only made it halfway."

Dusty examined the other man as he came up and stood to Dusty's left. Sadness reflected from the man's eyes, as though he sensed the pain that lingered in the walls of Pueblo Animas. A curious ability for an investment banker.

"Good day, Doctor Robertson," Wirth said, glancing unsurely at where Sylvia had adopted a way too-innocent expression. "Just what did the young lady mean?"

Dusty saw Sylvia's mouth open and shot her a warning glance. Wirth smelled like the perfume department at Penney's. No telling what she might say at a moment like this.

Dusty smiled. "Actually, Sylvia gave you a good description, Mr. Wirth. All except for the part about the passageway to hell. The tunnel is collapsed so we don't know for sure where it leads."

Wirth took off his sunglasses and looked Dusty straight in the eyes. "You've found that many dead children?"

"About forty. Most of them are under the age of five, including several infants, but I can't give you an official minimum or maximum until we've fully analyzed the remains. In kivas like this, we often find a lot more skulls than bodies, or vice versa."

Wirth said something to his companion in a language Dusty didn't understand, then turned back to Dusty. "And you really found an old woman who'd been eaten?"

"Well, we can't say that for certain. She was butchered. That is, the flesh was carved from her bones with stone tools, but whether or not somebody threw a little salt on it..."

Wirth turned to the unknown man again and rattled off something. Dusty assumed the language to be Arabic. Middle Eastern, at least. The guy kept nodding, staring around at the ruins with those sad eyes.

Wirth took his partner by the arm and led him a short distance away to continue the conversation in private.

Steve returned. He handed Sylvia her Pepsi and asked, "What's going on?" Sweat had cut lines in the dust that coated his dark skin. He used his sleeve to wipe his forehead.

Sylvia whispered, "I think the curtain's going up on the great and powerful Oz."

Steve's black bushy brows lowered. He looked around the site. "I didn't see Toto run by. Who's pulling the curtain back?"

"The guy with ten-thousand-dollar shoes," Sylvia replied.

Dale cocked his ear to the bankers' conversation. "Hmm," he said. "Hebrew."

Dusty's gave them a second look. "Really? What are they saying?"

Dale listened for a few seconds. "Well, they're talking very low, and I haven't dug in Israel in forty years, but I think Wirth just said *kesef,* which means money."

Dusty watched the men going back and forth, their voices rising and falling. "You mean they're haggling over the price?"

"I would say so, yes."

"How much are they up to?"

Dale listened, then shook his head. "Bigger numbers than I ever needed to know to buy a falafel and a bottle of Gold Star."

Dusty scuffed a worn boot on the ground and shook his head. The very idea of haggling over the price of forty dead children left him nauseated. Pueblo Animas was a great American tragedy, like the Gettysburg battlefield, or the Sand Creek Massacre site; it should be treated with reverence and used to teach people the horrors of war. A sour taste rose into his mouth, and Sylvia gave him a worried look, as though she knew exactly what he was feeling.

To lessen the tension, he sucked in a deep breath, smiled, and said, "Yeah, well, speaking of big numbers. When I was digging in Mexico, they only taught us to count to twenty. They were afraid that given our lack of mathematical education Americans would get arrested if we had to count to twenty-one."

Sylvia's mouth quirked. "What are we discussing? Imaginary numbers?"

Dusty spread his arms as wide as he could. "Yes, but it's a really *big* imaginary number."

Steve looked around Sylvia with an incredulous expression. "Even after that event with big Bob Deercapture? I thought you left half of your number sticking to the side of his truck."

"Not half," Sylvia replied. "It was more like a circumcision. You know, a little foreskin—"

"Okay, Sylvia," Dusty said. "Nobody needs *that* many details. I can't—"

"Looks like the bargaining is over," Dale interrupted and jerked his head toward the bankers.

Wirth shook hands with his friend, and they both walked forward smiling.

Wirth said, "Dr. Robertson, William Stewart, I'd like you to meet Moshe Alevy."

Dale shook first, then Dusty offered his hand, and Alevy gave it a hearty shake.

To Wirth, Dusty said, "Does he speak English?"

"No, but he'll learn." Wirth put a hand on Alevy's broad shoulder. "He's the new owner of this parcel of land. He will likely be spending a good deal of time in the United States."

Dusty's smile faded. He could feel the crash coming. "What do you mean, the new owner?"

Wirth smiled warmly, as though proud of himself. "Well, we have to sign the papers, of course, but in a week or so, he will be."

Wirth and Alevy shook again, both grinning like cats with freshly killed birds. Alevy's smile, however, died as he turned his thoughtful gaze back to the mounded ruins.

Dusty said, "Uh, Mr. Wirth, could I speak with you for a moment? Alone."

Wirth looked at Dale, and when Dale shrugged, he gestured toward his Mercedes. "If you can do it in five minutes, Stewart. Mr. Alevy and I have a meeting with our attorneys in Farmington later this afternoon."

"I won't take long," Dusty promised and led the way toward the dust-covered blue Mercedes. Behind them, Alevy had taken a position on the edge of the kiva and was staring down into the depths.

When they stood at the bottom of the rubble mound, out of earshot, Dusty said, "Forgive me, but I thought you told me that this pueblo was going to be the centerpiece for the subdivision, like a park."

Wirth leaned against the blue hood and looked up at the sky. His reflective sunglasses were filled with clouds. "Can you pay me a half million dollars for the ten acres where the pueblo sits?"

Dusty felt a little faint. His fists knotted involuntarily. "That's what he's paying?"

"It is, and I'm lucky I could sell it at all after what you found here."

Dusty kicked at a rock and watched it bounce down the hill. "That's archaeology for you. We're always digging up dirt about people's past, and few appreciate it."

Dale, Sylvia, and Steve had turned away to watch Alevy roam his brand-new archaeological site. He was now picking up artifacts, examining them, then almost tenderly placing them in the exact location where he'd found them.

Dusty said, "Is he an archaeologist?"

"No."

"Hmm. He acts like one." Dusty waited a moment, then said, "Okay, so. Let me get this straight. You're going to sell priceless pieces of our American heritage to a foreigner?"

Wirth's mouth curled into what approached a sneer. "They're not 'priceless,' Stewart. Just very expensive. Besides, people have been doing it for centuries. Remember all of the Aztec golden idols the Spaniards plundered to take home to Europe?"

"As I understand it, that was to help fund the next glorious crusade against the infidels. You know, for God and country, not a new Porsche. Uh, excuse me, a Mercedes."

Wirth straightened, and though Dusty couldn't see the threat in the man's eyes, he could feel it in the air. The hair on his arms stood on end.

"Now, you listen to me." Wirth aimed a manicured finger at Dusty's heart. "Mr. Alevy buys holocaust sites, and he takes special care of them. He protects them for future generations, do you understand?"

Dusty felt like he'd just been punched in the stomach. He stuttered, "No, I—I mean, that's great. If true. Tell me how he protects them?"

"You need to ask him that. But, believe me, there is *no one* who will take better care of your precious archaeological site than Moshe Alevy."

"That's a little vague, Mr. Wirth. Does it mean he wants us to backfill it, to keep excavating, or what?"

Wirth smoothed his hands down his shiny silk sleeves and said, "I'm sure Mr. Alevy will be in contact regarding the details."

Wirth strode vigorously up the hill, and Dusty chased after him, calling, "Wait a minute. Please? Let me talk to you. You told me I could have five minutes!"

Twenty paces away, Steve leaned sideways and whispered to Sylvia, "Dusty looks like he's surrendering to the *Federales*. Why does he have his hands up like that?"

Sylvia studied Dusty for a moment, her mind working. "I suspect he thinks it's a lot more dignified than pulling his pants down."

Dale gave them both disgruntled looks and walked toward Alevy, calling out in a language Sylvia didn't understand.

Alevy stopped and smiled.

"Now what's Dale doing?" Steve wondered.

Sylvia brushed a lock of brown hair behind her ear. "Probably trying to figure out just how screwed we really are."

As they walked away, talking, Dale's face tightened.

Peter Wirth stalked back for his Mercedes, and Dusty trudged up the hill toward where Dale and Moshe Alevy stood. Before he got there, Alevy shook hands with Dale and hurried down the hill to catch up with Wirth. Dusty and Alevy nodded politely to each other as they passed.

As Dusty, thumbs in his belt, thoughtfully ambled up, Steve asked, "So? What did you guys talk about?"

Dusty sighed. "Talking with Wirth was what you'd call an irksome experience. The man offered no information and has little interest in the actual archaeology, other than the fat check it is going to bring him. Just the sort of thing we expected when we began this project."

A wall of thunderheads was pushing up from the south, eating the blue sky as it came. Beneath the largest clouds, translucent veils of rain waved like gray silk scarves. By dusk, they'd be hip-deep in mud again.

Sylvia shot a knowing glance at Dale, who'd stopped, and was looking thoughtfully at the partially excavated kiva. "Maybe Dale knows something."

Sylvia took off like a woman with a mission, and Steve saw Maureen get out of the Bronco. Whatever she'd been up to, she'd missed the whole thing.

As he and Dusty got close, he heard Sylvia ask, "So, should we start packing, or wait for the pink slips?"

Dale shoved up his fedora and scratched the wiry gray hair over his right ear. "Keep digging. He'll need as many artifacts as he can get for the museum he plans to build."

At the same time, Steve and Sylvia shouted, "*What?*"

Dusty peered at Dale over the rims of his sunglasses. "He's building a museum?"

"A good one, William. Right here on site." Dale wiped the sweat from his neck with his sleeve. "It's an interesting story, actually, and with my poor Hebrew I'm sure I only caught half of it."

Maureen joined them, carrying an ice-cold bottle of Snapple peach iced tea in her hand. As she unscrewed the top, she said, "What story?"

Dale tipped his head sideways. "Well, it begins almost sixty years ago. His grandparents were Polish Jews. They died in concentration camps, along with almost everyone else in his family—cousins, aunts, uncles. Moshe's mother lived only because her father begged a Catholic family to take his daughter and raise her as their own."

Dale spread his hands wide. "I think he's visited every holocaust site in Europe, as well as several of the killing grounds in Asia, South America, and Africa. Moshe Alevy genuinely believes that 'In remembrance lies redemption."

When Dusty managed to close his gaping mouth, he said, "So. He really does want to protect this site? You believed him?"

"Very much. He told me that in every religious war,

the enemy has three ways of accomplishing its goals: First, they try conversion. If that doesn't work, they use expulsion as a means of getting rid—"

"—Like happened here in the Southwest?" Sylvia's green eyes flared. "I mean, isn't that another way of looking at the mass exodus of the Anasazi during the thirteenth century? The heretics were being forced out?"

Dale studied Sylvia. "Possibly."

Dusty said, "What was Alevy's third way?"

"Annihilation. If you can't convert them, and you can't make them leave, you have to kill them to cleanse the world."

Maureen's dark eyes looked out over Pueblo Animas, taking in the burned roof timbers, the charred walls, the mass grave. "I'd say this kiva, and many others in the region, fall into the last category."

Steve sipped his Pepsi and said, "Good Lord, the things human beings do to each other."

"That," Dale said, and pointed a finger at Steve, "is precisely why Alevy buys and preserves holocaust sites. No matter their location, no matter the culture, race, or religious affiliation, he believes they must be preserved as constant reminders of what we, as human beings, are capable of."

Dusty frowned out at the site. A pair of crows perched on the kiva wall, peering down at the bone bed with bright eyes. "Well, if that's the case, I wish there were more like him. What does it mean for us?"

"For the time being, he wants you to keep digging, William."

Sylvia let out a triumphant whoop and said, "Great!

Let's go make dinner to celebrate, then tip a few until the stars come out."

Maureen brushed her hands off on her jeans to an accompanyment of puffed dust. Curls of damp black hair fringed her forehead. "Good idea. Then Dusty and I need to get some rest. We have an appointment at dawn."

Dale smiled and heaved a sigh of what sounded like relief.

Dusty glanced at Dale and gave Maureen a suspicious look. "What appointment?"

S traighthorn concentrated on his feet as he trotted across the brown sandy soil. Sagebrush, rabbitbrush, and four-wing saltbush kept whipping off his calves as he maintained a trot across the flats above the canyon. Evening was falling, the sky literally burning where the clounds on the western horizon were backlit.

Something had died inside him. In its place, a murderous rage had been kindled. Like a beast, it lay there next to his heart, waiting for the moment it could be loosed in vengeance. Maybe the man who had killed Redcrop was dead, but there were more like him. White Moccasins. The people who had murdered in Aspen village, murdered his Matron, and set fire to Longtail village and burned all those children alive.

He did not know this new man who lived in his hate-filled body.

Thirty warriors, led by Catkin, trotted in front of him. Browser had barely made it back to Longtail village; the last half of the run he had been supported by Catkin and Straighthorn. When they stumbled into the village, Cloudblower had taken charge of the War Chief.

Straighthorn trotted up the ridge, lungs working as his legs pumped and dust puffed from under his yucca sandals. Half wore the yellow color of Dry Creek villagers, the others, the warriors of the Katsinas' People, wore red war shirts.

Straighthorn lagged a few paces behind the last man.

The trail back to the secret cave led over rolling hills and around pine-covered rock outcrops. Yellow-orange, the afternoon sunlight shone on the fallen cones and needles that littered the way. He didn't wish to speak or look at anyone. The sympathy in their eyes affected him like a knife in his belly.

When they crested the hill overlooking the cave opening, Catkin held up her hand and the war party halted and unslung their bows. Whispers passed through the group as they nocked arrows. Catkin had cut her hair in mourning for Redcrop. Jagged locks blew about her beautiful face, but a terrible darkness lay behind that angry gaze.

She pointed with a straight arm. "Those boulders at the foot of the hill mark the opening to the cave. This morning, there were five warriors there. By now, there may be a hundred. If we are attacked and outnumbered, I want you to fall into a defensive formation, and we'll fight our way out. These warriors are tested and tough. Do not let your attention waver even for an instant."

Mutters of assent went through the ranks. Straighthorn numbly pulled an arrow from his quiver and slid it into place in his bow. As they started the run down the hill, his heart thudded against his ribs.

Could he stand it? Seeing her face again?

"It isn't going to end here," he whispered, and his throat constricted.

Upon his return, after retrieving her body, he would be up all night helping Cloudblower prepare Redcrop's body, washing her, dressing her, combing out her hair. She had no family—but him.

The dirt trail, barely four hands wide, curved around a clump of junipers, then dipped. As they rose up the other side, Catkin called, "I want guards on those four high points. The rest of you spread out! Search the area along the rim and in those trees to the east. We don't want to stumble into an ambush. Then come together at the cave entrance."

Straighthorn followed ten other Katsinas' warriors as they fanned to the right and sneaked along the canyon rim. Scrubby pines clung to the edge. Far below, he could see his own tracks in the damp sand and the winding trails cut by other feet. From the looks of it, at least thirty people had crossed that patch of ground.

As the trail veered away from the rim and dipped into a thicket of head-high greasewood, Hummingbird, in the lead, softly called, "Let's split up and go around it. Jackrabbit? Take Straighthorn and Little Firekeeper and go to the east."

"Yes, Hummingbird."

Jackrabbit waved to them, and Straighthorn and Little Firekeeper—a youth of fourteen summers—followed him. Jackrabbit slowed to walk at Straighthorn's side. Voles scampered through the thick grass as they passed, and birds took wing, swooping up into the sky like many-colored arrows.

Jackrabbit said, "I know you and Catkin are supposed to carry the burial ladder back to the village, but I thought that perhaps you might allow me to carry it in your place."

Straighthorn bowed his head and stared at the sand. In the past nine moons, they had become good friends. Jackrabbit was trying to spare Straighthorn the pain of staring into her wide dead eyes all the way back. "Thank you for offering, Jackrabbit, but it is something I must do."

Jackrabbit's brow wrinkled. "I heard Catkin say that after we finish here, she is going to send a small detachment to the rock shelter to find the Matron's skull and retrieve our, um, former friends' bodies. Are you certain you wouldn't rather go with that party?"

Straighthorn looked up and met Jackrabbit's concerned eyes. Dust had settled on Jackrabbit's pug nose and filled in the lines around his wide mouth. "I don't know why Crossbill ordered the traitors to be brought home. I think we should leave our 'former friends', as they are mistakenly called, there to rot. They'll be of more use in the bellies of coyotes and crows."

Jackrabbit nodded. "My heart votes with yours. I still can't believe that they—"

The anger surged, tickled to life. "Believe it! Skink attacked me when I tried to rescue Red...my girl. He told me he was going to kill me." They skirted a gnarled lump of tree roots. "Springbank is the one who shocked me."

"He shocked all of us, my friend. When I first came

to the Katsinas' People, our Matron told me that he was their most faithful member. She said he had joined the quest only a few moons after she revealed Spider Silk's vision. We all thought he was a deeply holy man. When he left for days at a time to pray, no one thought much about it. Holy people need the company of Spirits more than ordinary people do."

"Holy people...and witches, you mean."

As they came around the brush, Straighthorn saw Catkin gently placing Redcrop's body on the burial ladder, and his steps faltered. He was surprised that she'd been so far ahead of him.

Jackrabbit said nothing; he just stopped beside Straighthorn. When Little Firekeeper walked up, Jackrabbit said, "Go on ahead, Firekeeper. We'll be there soon."

Firekeeper glanced at Straighthorn and nodded. "Yes, Jackrabbit."

Dust puffed beneath his feet as he trotted away. Twenty warriors gathered around Catkin and the burial ladder. They warily split their attention between her body and the surrounding countryside, anxious lest there be an ambush.

Straighthorn watched several men break from the group and duck into the cave. He frowned. Catkin would have checked the cave first and turned to Redcrop only after she'd found it empty.

Jackrabbit said, "I hope they leave some for the rest of us."

"What?"

"The wealth!" Jackrabbit replied with a barely masked excitement. "Matron Crossbill told Catkin to clean out everything and bring it all back to Longtail village. Do you know how much food and clothing we—"

"I didn't hear Crossbill say that."

"I think, my friend, that you had other things on your mind. You were helping Elder Cloudblower with the War Chief when this was being discussed. Crossbill is right. After all the murders committed by the White Moccasins, why shouldn't the Katsinas' People benefit from their treasure? The White Moccasins plundered the ruins of the First People to get it. The Katsinas' People need it. It seems just to me."

Straighthorn narrowed his eyes, jaw tightening.

"You think they are tainted with witchcraft?" Jackrabbit asked. "I heard the War Chief whisper that to Cloudblower."

"I think it comes to us on a river of polluted blood. We are going to live to regret this day. Mark my words, Jackrabbit. We will, and so will the White Moccasins." Eddies of rage trembled his souls.

Hummingbird whooped as he ducked out of the cave carrying an enormous basket of turquoise and jet fetishes, coral beads, and shell bracelets. He held up a copper bell and shook it. As the delicate music rose, warriors crowded around him to look, and a low roar of conversation built. More warriors appeared with baskets and began dancing around as if they'd drunk too much fermented juniper berry drink. Yells and shouts of glee rose.

Straighthorn slung his bow and slipped his arrow back into its quiver. "Come, my friend. I have more important things to worry about." He took a deep breath to fortify himself and set his steps for Redcrop's burial ladder.

And the end of a dream.

Catkin stood when she saw him coming.

Straighthorn pushed through the jostling warriors, looked at Redcrop, then his gaze darted, and he spun around, crying, "Where is the witch's body?"

Catkin stepped up to him. She stood tall, her eyes shining in the afternoon gleam. Ugly bruises splotched her face and arms, and one of her eyes had almost swollen shut, but she wore the injuries with a warrior's pride. "Gone. The White Moccasins carried Two Hearts away along with the other dead. Ten Hawks, the rest, all gone. Only their blood is left."

A breathless sensation swept through Straighthorn. "But he *was* dead, wasn't he? You didn't find his tracks, did you?"

Catkin said, "No. But they would have taken him. He was their leader."

Straighthorn's ears filled with a loud hum, like a gale rushing through a pine forest. "The way he was coughing up blood, no one could survive that."

Catkin put a hand on his shoulder and squeezed "Small enough justice for those he's murdered and the atrocities he's committed."

Straighthorn gazed into her confident eyes and felt better. He shoved the fear away and crouched at Redcrop's side. As he took her cold and death-stiff hand in his, the beast inside him cried out. He barely heard the whoops and laughter that surrounded him.

"Cousin Barbara told me she would bring Dusty and Maureen out at sunrise," Maggie Walking Hawk Taylor told her great aunt, Sage. Tall and slender, Maggie had a round face, with short black hair. "They shouldn't be too far behind us."

"Okay," Sage Walking Hawk said weakly.

Sage propped her cane and took another step. The cool predawn breeze fluttered the hood of her yellow coat and blew wispy gray hair around her deeply wrinkled face. She made soft pained sounds as she climbed the trail. She'd had trouble with her balance since a car accident more than ten years ago. Sometimes she walked fine, other times she staggered like a drunk.

Maggie used both hands to steady her great aunt's elbow. With each step, the folding lawn chair she carried over her left elbow patted against her hip. It was a cool autumn morning, the temperature around fifty degrees. The faded blue jeans and denim shirt she wore barely kept the cold at bay.

They walked along the western wall of the ancient

pueblo toward the circular structure at the top of the hill. The glow of dawn poured through the towering cottonwoods, scattering their path with pale blue diamonds.

Sage stopped and blinked her cataract-covered eyes at the ground while she tried to catch her breath. She was trembling.

Maggie's grip tightened on her great-aunt's arm. She had promised herself that when this ordeal was over, she would go sit on a mesa top somewhere and give her grief-free rein. But not today. If she broke down today, it would make this last morning harder for her aunt.

"Does this seem like the place you saw in your dream, Aunt?"

Sage nodded. "Yes."

To their right, a wall of finely fitted tan sandstone blocks rose fifteen feet into the air. A broad band of green stone ran along the base of the wall, but it looked black in the predawn light.

The Chaco Anasazi had abandoned the giant walled town in the twelfth century. Two generations later, a new group of Anasazi had reoccupied it. The later "Mesa Verde" occupants sealed several entryways, converted many living rooms into storage chambers, latrines, and burial rooms. Though the Chaco Anasazi had carried their trash outside, the Mesa Verdeans used interior rooms for trash dumps, packing them floor to ceiling with garbage. The Mesa Verdeans had done everything they could to minimize the need to venture outside the pueblo's protective walls. The warfare was so intense that by about A.D. 1275, the pueblo had been abandoned again.

Sage turned to gaze longingly westward where a few of the brightest stars still sparkled. "I flew over it in my dream." The words came haltingly, puffed more than spoken. "But I think this is it. Where's the Sun Room?"

"The way you described it, it sounded to me like one of the tri-walled structures, Aunt. There's one up the hill."

Only twelve of the mysterious circular structures had been discovered in America, and three were here at Aztec Ruins in New Mexico. They consisted of two rings of rooms around a central chamber.

"Up there?" Sage pointed a crooked finger up the path that led north along the side of the ruin. "It's up there?"

"Yes, Aunt."

Sage nodded and took a deep breath.

"Aunt, do you need to sit down for a while?" Maggie started to slip the lawn chair from her elbow.

"No, child. Thank you." Sage clutched Maggie's arm. "I want to go see if he's there."

Maggie frowned. "He? Who do you mean?"

Maggie supported her aunt as she hobbled up the slight incline past the numbered interpretive markers. An orchard filled the hollow to their left, and a modern farmhouse sat against the hills just beyond the tri-walled structure. The scents of dew-soaked brush and damp stone filled the air.

Sage stumbled, and Maggie gasped, "Aunt? Are you all right?"

Sage patted Maggie's hand. "I'm just clumsy this morning. Your grandmother would have said she tripped on a ghost rock, a rock that was here when the ghosts were alive. But I think maybe I'm just not as light on my feet as I used to be. I never have been able to step into other worlds like she could."

Maggie squeezed her aunt's sticklike arm. The elderly woman resembled a tiny hunchbacked skeleton. In the past year she had shrunk in size, and her skin had turned shiny and translucent, as though the cancer had eaten away her muscles and bones.

Sage said, "The man in my dream, he was calling to me from inside a tower."

"Well, there's nothing left up here but rings of stones on the ground, but it was a tower once. What did the man say?"

Sage shook her gray head. "I couldn't make out his words. It sounded like he was talking with a mouthful of cooked squash."

Sage took three steps, breathed, then took two more steps, forcing herself up the hill. As sunrise neared, a purple halo arced over the eastern horizon, and the rolling hills turned the deep rich shade of thunderheads.

Sage stopped, breathing hard, to survey the opening to the tri-walled structure—now a mere break in the outer ring. Interpretive marker number five stood in front of them. The walls were clearly visible as three concentric rings of stones.

Sage lifted a shaking hand and pointed to the opposite side of the structure. "There. That's where his voice was coming from."

Sage turned right and started to walk around the circumference of the structure. Maggie hurried to grab her arm to help steady her steps. When they had made it almost halfway around, Sage suddenly shivered and leaned on Maggie.

"What is it, Aunt?"

Sage bowed her head. For a few seconds, she didn't speak. "Don't you feel him? The desperation? The sadness?"

Maggie frowned at the tall golden grass that filled the spaces between the stone rings. She tried to open her souls to the "other" world but felt only the cool morning breeze tousling her short black hair. Every elderly woman in Maggie's family could touch the Spirit World. Her grandmother had been known as "She Who Haunts the Dead." Aunt Hail had been called "Ghost Talker," and her aunt Sage was known as "Empty Eyes," because of the way she looked when she was listening to ghost voices.

The talent had apparently missed Maggie's generation. Oh, she'd had a few strange experiences, particularly around ancient ruins, and there were times when she sensed something roaming the darkness, but she couldn't say it was a ghost. It might just as well have been a hungry coyote.

Headlights came up the road in front of the Aztec Ruins Interpretive Center, and Maggie heard the low roar of an engine.

"That must be Barbara with Dusty and Maureen."

Sage looked up. "Hmm? Did you hear something?"

"Yes, Aunt," Maggie half-shouted so she would hear. "A car engine. I saw lights, too."

"They're early," Sage said, and smiled. "Go on. Go meet them. I'll be fine here by myself. I need to do some talking in private."

Maggie unfolded the lawn chair and set it on the

flattest place she could find. "Let me help you sit down first."

She took Sage's arm and guided her to the seat. Sage sank down wearily. Her claw-like fingers curled over the chair arms. "Remind Barbara to bring the cornmeal."

"I will, Aunt." Maggie bent and kissed Sage's forehead, then trotted back down the trail.

When Magpie disappeared behind the giant pueblo, Sage looked down at the stone rings. They had a blurry silver glow, as did the blades of grass that swayed and nodded in the breeze.

"Well," she whispered. "I'm here. Why did you call me?"

Whimpers eddied around her, but it might just have been the wind. She could no longer tell for sure. Each time the doctors gave her chemotherapy, she lost more of herself. The last bout had wounded her souls. She could feel her breath-heart soul—the soul that kept her heart beating and her lungs moving—hanging around her like a ragged old sun-bleached cloth while her afterlife soul huddled somewhere deep inside, eager to go free.

From her right, the place she'd seen the man standing in her dream, the feeling of sadness swelled, as though it upset the ghost that Sage couldn't hear him as well as he'd expected she would.

"You'll just have to speak louder," she said, and smoothed her arthritic hands over her yellow coat.

She hadn't wanted to take the radiation or chemotherapy. She'd been longing to get out of her sick body for over a year, but Magpie had pleaded with her to try the treatments. Sage loved her great-niece with all her heart. She would have walked through a den of rattlesnakes even if it would have made Magpie smile for just a few seconds. Sage had swallowed the poisons and survived much longer than her doctors had predicted. But all the pain and anguish was finally coming to an end. Yesterday, the doctor told her he wanted her in the hospital this afternoon.

Sage gazed out at the orchard. They looked like apple trees, planted in rows. High above them, clouds sailed through the brightening morning sky.

Sage offered a silent prayer of thanks to the *Shiwanna,* the Spirits of the dead who had climbed into the sky to become cloud beings. They watched over the living and brought the blessed rains.

"Are you up there, Slumber? Hail?"

Her sisters, Slumber and Hail, had died a few years ago from the same cancer that was killing Sage. It would give them something to talk about when her sisters came to get her. If Sage could get a word in edgewise. Slumber had been a real talker. Hail had told her once that Slumber could talk a dead rabbit away from a starving weasel.

Sage chuckled, remembering the irritated expression on Slumber's face.

Voices drifted up from the Interpretive Center, and Sage twisted around to look. Barbara and Magpie walked side-by-side, holding on to each other affectionately as they approached Sage.

That brought her joy. Funny how at the end of life, nothing a person had done mattered. Not the things they'd owned or built. The only things Sage counted were the people she loved. Everything else in the past eighty years had been leaves tumbling in the wind.

A child's voice...

Sage turned her good ear toward the tri-walled structure.

"What's wrong?" she asked in concern. "Are you here with the tall man?"

The whispers turned to cries, muted, breathless, as though they strained against tightly closed lips.

"It's all right, child. I'm here. I won't let him hurt you if I can stop him."

Magpie and Barbara stopped in front of the tri-walled structure with a blond man, and a woman with a long black braid. Magpie said, "Aunt Sage, I want you to meet Dusty Stewart and Dr. Maureen Cole."

As they walked around the ring of stones, Sage saw it, glowing like a sickly green light around Dusty Stewart. The woman, however, was surrounded by a beautiful blue glow. It fluttered around her like concerned hands.

"Good morning," Sage said. "I see the ghosts haven't got you."

"Yet," Dusty answered, and glanced around uncomfortably. He knelt in front of Sage and said, "Thank you, Elder, for helping us today."

"I haven't fixed anything yet," she said. "You'd better wait to see what happens."

Dusty nodded and backed away.

Maureen knelt in Dusty's place. "Good morning, Elder." She pulled a necklace over her head and gently placed it in Sage's fingers, then she closed her own fingers around Sage's. "This is a gift from my people, the Seneca. It was blessed by our elders. I hope it brings you luck."

Sage opened her trembling hand and looked at the

beautifully carved tortoise fetish. She smiled and touched Maureen's cheek. "It's beautiful, child. What's your real name? The name your people call you?"

"Washais," Maureen said, and explained, "It's a drawknife that my people use to carve sacred masks."

Sage stroked Maureen's face. "I'm going to free you, child." She gestured to the Sun Room. "I want you and Dusty to take off everything metal and go sit in the middle ring there. No watches, no silver buttons, no change in your pockets. Kind of like being at the airport."

Magpie had warned them, so they'd both worn sweatpants and sweatshirts, but they sat down to remove their coats and boots.

Sage waved a frail hand to Magpie and Barbara. "Keep the metal outside the circles."

"Yes, Aunt Sage," they said almost in unison, picked up the coats and boots, and hauled them a short distance away.

Short and pudgy, with a big nose, Barbara had a round moony face that always seemed to glow with happiness. As she came closer, Sage could make out her red shirt and blue jeans.

Barbara kissed her on top of the head, and said, "Good morning, Aunt Sage."

"Hello, Barbara. Thank you for bringing Dusty and Maureen out to me. Did you remember the bags of cornmeal?"

Barbara pulled four tiny leather bags from her pocket and placed them in Sage's hand. "They're right here, just as you asked."

Sage fingered them, looking down to make sure she could tell the colors apart: blue, red, white, and yellow. Yes, she was going to be able to do this, just like Magpie wanted. The knowledge made her feel better. She couldn't do much of anything anymore. Not even for herself. But she still knew the sacred ways.

Sage sighed and looked at the three stone rings. Faint whimpers echoed, like standing inside a big seashell. Sage cocked her head. After a moment, she asked, "Is that a little boy? Or a little girl?"

Magpie and Barbara exchanged a look, then took up positions on either side of Sage's chair.

Magpie said, "I'm sorry, Aunt, we don't hear anything."

Sage whispered, "It sounds like a girl to me."

Magpie's forehead lined. "I thought it was a man who came to you in your dream, Aunt Sage?"

"Yes, but ghosts don't always come by themselves. The girl might want to be freed today, too."

It took two tries before Sage could shove out of her chair and stagger into the inner ring to stand between Dusty and Maureen. They both looked up at her expectantly.

"I'm almost ready," she said and fumbled open the laces on the white-painted leather bag. The sweet nutty aroma of white corn rose.

Sage waited until the first golden sliver of Father Sun's face crested the dark hills in the distance, then she dipped her fingers into the sacred cornmeal. As she Sang, she walked forward, sprinkling a path of white cornmeal to the east. Then she followed the path back, tugged open the bag of red cornmeal, and poured a path to the south. The yellow road led west, and, finally, Sage poured a blue cornmeal road to the north—sacred roads for the trapped ghosts to follow to the Land of the Dead.

A luminous haze of meal swirled around Dusty and Maureen, coating their clothing and sticking to their hair, purifying them.

A little girl's laughter, sweet and high.

Sage saw the green glow seep out of Dusty and sail away up the blue cornmeal road to the north.

As Father Sun rose higher, the hills cast off the dark capes of night and gleamed like molten gold. Sage lifted her arms to the sky, then carefully bent over and touched earth, sealing the prayers.

When she straightened up, Sage just looked for a time, not thinking of anything, not wanting anything, just being grateful she was alive to see the morning light.

Finally, she braced her wobbly legs and looked down at Dusty and Maureen. "You can go now. The ghost that was squatting inside you is free, gone. She's running the road to the Land of the Dead. I don't know how that old witch managed to lock a sad little girl's soul in that *basilisco* you had, Dusty, but she was glad we set her free."

Dusty's blond hair shimmered with cornmeal. "It was a little girl who was giving me bad dreams?"

Sage nodded. "I think she knew that someday you'd have sense enough to get cleansed. That's why when she touched your soul, she wouldn't let go."

Maureen reached up to lightly take Sage's hand. In a soft voice, she asked, "Elder, what about me?"

Sage squeezed her fingers. "Every person carries within her a life road that is watched over by Spirit beings. Yours are strong. You have fiery creatures who protect you, Washais. Do you know them?"

Maureen's face slackened. "The *Gaasyendietha,* yes. Thank you for telling me, Elder Walking Hawk." She touched her forehead to Sage's fingers, silently asking for her blessing, then smiled.

Sage patted her hand and released it.

As she hobbled back to her chair, she waved a hand. "Now, I want all of you to go away. I need to sit here by myself for a while." She slumped into the lawn chair and heaved a tired breath.

Sage waited until Dusty and Maureen had put on their coats and boots and started down the trail to the ruins with Barbara and Magpie, then turned to the man who stood to her right, near the outer ring. He was tall, with light-brown hair and green eyes.

Sage said, "She's all right now. You've taken good care of her, but you've got to think of yourself. This may be your last chance to get free."

Sage could feel his worry, his love for Washais. She pointed to the north. "That's the way. Go on now. She'll be with you again before you know it."

The blue glow faded, then flared, as if he'd turned to look at Washais one last time.

"Isn't that why you called to me in my dream?" Sage asked gently. "You knew it was time? You were right. It's all right to let her go. Go on. Let her go now. Let her go."

The blue cornmeal at the edge of the ring whirled up in a gust of wind and sailed away with the man's soul, carrying it northward.

Sage smiled and nodded to herself.

Maureen shivered suddenly and gasped, feeling as if she'd just been bludgeoned. She braced a hand against the magnificent sandstone wall of Aztec Ruins.

She heard Dusty say, "Excuse me."

He left Barbara and Magpie watching their aunt and trotted to Maureen. "Are you all right?"

Maureen's throat had constricted; it hurt too much to speak. She shook her head.

Without a word, Dusty put his arms around her and pulled her against his chest. He didn't ask anything, he just held her. Maureen listened to his heartbeat and the steady rhythm of his breathing.

Dusty finally whispered, "Is there something I can do?"

Maureen disentangled herself. Dusty seemed reluctant to let her go, but he did.

She said, "Thank you, but I'm all right. I just felt suddenly empty, like a part of me had been ripped away."

Dusty scrutinized her face, then said, "It's probably hunger. I'm starving, aren't you? These cleansings take a lot of energy."

Maureen gave him a shy smile. "Yes, actually, I am hungry."

"Why don't you let me take you and the Walking Hawks out to breakfast? I know a place nearby with great *huevos rancheros*."

"Sounds good." She tried to understand why she was feeling this hollow sense of loss.

"Great. I'm going to go ask them." But before he

left, he looked her over carefully again. "You're sure you're okay?"

"Yes," she said and waved him away. "Go on. I'm just going to stand here for a minute."

As Dusty hiked up the trail, Maureen sagged against the stone wall. She felt like weeping. She was alone for the first time since John's death, and she knew it. She looked northward and her eyes blurred. A pale blue gleam lit the horizon.

"I'll miss you," she whispered, "but I'm glad you're finally on your way."

28

Stone Ghost stood on the burned kiva wall gazing up at the ash-filled sky. Even so long after the fire, parts of Longtail village still smoldered and smoked where the wooden ceilings had burned through and fallen into the rooms. Buzzards circled high above. They looked like windblown black leaves against the snowy clouds.

Straighthorn breathed, "I pray I can stay here until the end."

Stone Ghost turned to the youth. He stood barely an arm's length away, but the still autumn day seemed to catch his voice and throw it around the burned village. It had the same effect as a shout.

The mourners who had gathered for the burial ceremony turned to look at him, then murmurs broke out.

Stone Ghost put a hand on the young warrior's shoulder. His buckskin cape felt warm and soft. "You can. Just think about the color of the sky and the birdsong."

"I can't think of anything but her face when she

died."

Stone Ghost tightened his grip on the young man's shoulder. Inside him, he had a wall of faces like that, each one caught in that final moment, each one a silent scream. He said, "I hope you will share my supper tonight, Straighthorn. I knew so little about her, I would like to know more."

Straighthorn closed his eyes, and his jaw clamped as though struggling with overwhelming emotions. "Thank you, Elder. I would like to share your supper."

The people standing on the kiva walls whispered as they handed around baskets of dirt. Jackrabbit reached up for each basket and handed it down to Catkin, who silently stepped through the dead, pouring dirt over them.

The pungent scents of burned bodies and scorched walls made it almost impossible to take a deep breath. Coils of smoke continued to rise from the smoldering beams and latillas; they rose to twist away in the wind.

Catkin's small detachment had found Flame Carrier's skull and the bodies of Skink and Water Snake. They had also looked for the little girl. Catkin had tracked the child for a hand of time, then lost her small tracks in the rocks. Catkin had also reported seeing the mummy still hanging in the rear of the rock shelter. Since she had belonged to a powerful witch, no one would touch her. No one would bring her home.

That morning, Crossbill had ordered that Skink and Water Snake be thrown into shallow graves. Everyone had watched as Cloudblower placed sandstone slabs over their heads, sealing their souls in the earth forever. They would wail into the darkness for eternity, never able to join their relatives in the Land of the Dead.

Redcrop had been gently lowered into the tower kiva with the burned children, and Cloudblower had arranged Flame Carrier's skull so that her forehead touched Redcrop's temple—that way they could whisper to each other as they always had.

People had been carrying baskets of dirt for five hands of time now. The bodies and a few small pots of offerings—everything people had left after the fire—were almost covered.

Browser rounded the northeastern corner of the ruined village, and Stone Ghost turned to watch him. He walked as though he had barely enough strength to force his feet to move. Cloudblower had cleansed and wrapped Browser's head wound with tan cloth. The tied ends fluttered over his left ear. Browser's chamber had been completely burned, all of his belongings lost. One of the Dry Creek village warriors had given Browser a clean knee-length yellow shirt to wear. It complemented his red leggings.

Stone Ghost patted Straighthorn's shoulder and said, "I hope to see you at supper." Then he turned for the ladder that leaned against the rear wall. He took the rungs down one at a time, wincing at the pain in his knees. When he stepped to the ground, he sighed and headed toward his nephew.

Browser smiled weakly and lifted a hand at Stone Ghost's approach.

Stone Ghost gave his nephew a weary smile, "How are you feeling, Nephew?"

Browser put a hand to his head. "My left eye is still blurry, but Cloudblower says she thinks it will pass. Is the burial ceremony almost over?"

Stone Ghost looked up at the people standing on

the high kiva wall. "Yes, very close. Catkin has a few more baskets of dirt to pour." He took Browser by the arm. "I would like to show you something, Nephew, if you are well enough."

Browser frowned. "What is it, Uncle?"

Stone Ghost led Browser across the plaza and out into the juniper grove. Ash coated the evergreen branches and lay thick on the ground. It puffed with every step they took, swirling up to coat their hair and clothing. The entire world seemed to have turned gray. Even Father Sun's brilliance had been dimmed by the ash that swirled in the air.

"There," Stone Ghost said, and pointed.

A hundred hands north of the village, a large sandstone boulder lay overturned. Clumps of damp earth clung to the side that had been on the ground.

"What happened to the rock?"

"Someone rolled it aside, Nephew."

"Why?"

Stone Ghost released Browser's arm. "See for yourself. I found it this morning."

Browser plodded up the hill and frowned down at the square pole-framed hole in the ground. The timbers were old and brittle. He swiveled to look back at the village. "What is this?"

Stone Ghost hobbled up and eased down onto the boulder. "A tunnel to the tower kiva. I crawled into it right after I discovered it. It goes all the way to the middle of the kiva floor."

Cold panic filled Browser. His heart started to hammer. "You mean you think this is how Springbank got out? Or should we call him Two Hearts?"

Stone Ghost nodded. "I think he shoved the last

child up onto the roof, so no one would see him leave, then he dug up the door in the kiva floor and ran."

"But how old is this? How could he have known about it?"

Stone Ghost laced his fingers in his lap. "I suspect it was originally constructed over one hundred sun cycles ago, to allow First Man and First Woman to make a grand entrance during ceremonials. Can you imagine them climbing up into the kiva, emerging from the underworlds, as they did in the Beginning Time? The spectators must have been amazed."

Browser reached into the tunnel and pulled out a handful of dirt. "It smells old and dank. I wonder how long it's been since someone used it?"

"Other than two nights ago, you mean? Oh, many summers. Sixty, seventy. Perhaps more."

Browser let the dirt trickle through his fingers. "But Two Hearts knew about it."

"Yes. He probably discovered it when he lived here thirty summers ago. Or maybe he was told about it by relatives who lived here long before that. It's hard to say." Stone Ghost's eyes tightened.

He paused for a long while, then said, "Nephew, there is something I must tell you. Do you recall the story I began that night when we were sitting by the First People's spiral?"

Browser nodded with care, as though the motion hurt. "Yes, Uncle. What of it?"

Stone Ghost reached for his nephew's hand. "I would like to finish that story, if you don't mind."

"Go on."

Stone Ghost took a deep breath and very softly said,

"My grandmother, Orenda, married the second son of Cornsilk and Poor Singer."

Browser's strength seemed to fail. *"What?"* He sank to the ground with his mouth open. "So, what Two Hearts was telling me...?" He swallowed hard. "It's true?"

Stone Ghost held up a hand to halt the flood of questions he knew would be coming. "His name was Snowbird. I don't know much about him, except that he was a very gentle man, much like his father, Poor Singer. But despite his peaceful nature, Snowbird was always at war with his older brother. He—"

"Who was his older brother?"

"The Blessed Ravenfire." At the look on Browser's face, Stone Ghost said, "Yes, your dead Matron's father. He was Cornsilk's firstborn. I don't know how it happened exactly, but Ravenfire was not Poor Singer's son. I heard rumors that Cornsilk had been raped. It may be true. At any rate, Ravenfire grew up to hate everything his parents stood for. He hated the katsinas. It was Ravenfire"—Stone Ghost said through a long exhalation—"who betrayed Night Sun to the Made People."

Stunned, Browser murmured, "When did this happen, Uncle?"

"Oh, she was around sixty summers at the time. The great war had just begun."

Browser blinked at the ground. "You are telling me that I am related to the great Matron of Talon Town? The Blessed Night Sun was—"

"—Your great-great-great-grandmother, yes."

Browser glanced over his shoulder and swallowed

hard, before he whispered, "I am one of the First People?"

"*We* are, Nephew."

Browser shook his head as though refusing to believe it. In a strained voice, he asked, "Gods, why are we alive?"

"Well, you were lucky. Your family forced you to marry Ash Girl. She was one of the First People."

"She was..." He seemed to run out of air. "Why did no one tell me?"

Stone Ghost shrugged. "It would have been dangerous. My sister, Painted Turtle, decided it would be better for everyone concerned if her grandchildren never knew the truth." He touched his chin. "That's why you did not receive this tattoo at your birth, Nephew."

"That's the same tattoo the mummy—"

"Yes," Stone Ghost sighed, and his wrinkles deepened. "I'm afraid I know who the mummy is and why she was hung at Aspen village."

"Who? Why?"

"The Blessed Night Sun."

Browser looked as if he'd been gutted. "That's why our Matron struggled so hard to keep the Katsina religion alive? She was related to Night Sun?"

"Well..." He tilted his head. "Yes, she was. But because she was Ravenfire's daughter. My grandmother told me that he had brought her up to hate everything about the katsinas. That's why Spider Silk divorced him and ran away. Ravenfire kept their son, Bear Dancer, and I heard that Ravenfire remarried a woman from the Green Mesa clans. I think at the end of her life, Spider Silk was trying very hard to..."

"Dear gods," Browser whispered. "That's what Obsidian meant when she said that the turquoise wolf meant I was 'suitable.'" He knotted his scabbed fists. "That's why Two Hearts said it was in the blood!"

Stone Ghost nodded. "That is also why they didn't kill you at Aspen village, Nephew. There are so few of us now that they must be cautious who they put to death."

"What about Catkin, Uncle? Is she—is that why they didn't kill her?"

Stone Ghost shifted on the boulder and his turkey feather cape fell open, leaving his chest vulnerable to the cold wind. He shivered. "I truly don't know, Nephew. Perhaps you should ask her."

"No." Browser shook his head. "I won't do that." He placed a hand on Stone Ghost's shoulder. "Uncle, I know it wasn't easy for you to tell me after all the summers of keeping the truth locked in your heart. I am grateful."

"The burden is yours now, Nephew." Stone Ghost patted his hand. "You must decide whom to tell and when."

"I will tell no one, Uncle. The truth is too dangerous. For all of us."

Browser shakily rose to his feet. Cloudblower had been pouring willow bark tea down him to ease his pain, but Browser seemed to be growing weaker. He squinted against the sunlight. "Is there anything else, Uncle? I came out here to find Obsidian. If I don't do it soon, I'm afraid I won't have the strength to."

"Go, Nephew. I will wait here for you to return."

Browser nodded. "Have you seen her?"

Stone Ghost pointed. "She was on the river trail a little while ago."

Browser started to walk away, and Stone Ghost gripped his yellow sleeve to stop him. "What are you going to say to her, Nephew?"

Browser shook his head. "I don't know."

"Be prudent. She is more than she seems. *Much* more."

Browser squeezed Stone Ghost's hand, nodded, and walked away.

"Be careful, Nephew. More careful than you have ever been."

~

A bow shot away, two eagles played. The huge brown birds floated on the air currents as though weightless, tipping their wings and chasing each other.

Browser watched them dive over the cottonwoods, then soar down to the river. The scent of the water was strong today, a pungent mixture of damp earth and ash. He inhaled a breath and let it out slowly.

He found Obsidian kneeling beside the Witches' Water Pocket, staring down as though she saw something stir far beneath the wavering reflections of autumn leaves. She had the blue hood of her cape up, shielding her face, but long strands of black hair fluttered around the hood. Her heavily ringed hands rested on her knees.

Browser's feet crunched in the old leaves as he walked up behind her. "Do you see them?"

She hesitated. "Who?"

"The witches who are supposed to live beneath the

water."

She expelled an irritated sigh, and answered, "I see only water, War Chief."

He crouched beside her, picked up a golden cotton-wood leaf with green stripes, and twirled it in his fingers.

"You weren't at the burial," he said.

She turned, and sunlight bathed the perfect lines of her tear-streaked face. Her black eyes shone like the darkest of jewels. "Youwish to question me, or you wouldn't be here. What is it?" She wiped her cheeks with her hands.

He tipped his aching head back to look up at the cloud-strewn sky. The sound of the wind in the juniper branches soothed him. "Did you know about the tunnel?"

"Not until this afternoon."

Browser closed his eyes for a moment and let the sun warm his face. He'd drifted through the day like a man without souls, feeling empty. So many things had happened that he could not take them all in. His dreams had been tortured. He kept reliving the fight in the cavern, analyzing each minute detail. Everywhere he looked now, he saw First People; it was the triangular shape of their faces, the way they held their heads and moved their hands. Even the lilt of their voices. Why he hadn't seen these things before?

Obsidian threw back her hood; it was an elegant gesture, filled with superiority. His own mother had moved like that. And his grandmother. Without real-izing it, they had radiated an authority that had vanished long ago.

He squinted down at the trembling heart-shaped

golden leaf he held.

"I'm sorry for the way I treated you," he said.

"It's my fault. There are just so few of us now, I was too eager."

"No. It's mine. Somewhere deep inside I knew I'd seen you before, but I couldn't place where we'd met."

She looked at him from the corner of her eye. "We met nine moons ago when your people came here, Browser."

"Yes. But you look so much like my dead wife that sometimes in my dreams I find myself replacing your face with hers."

She stared at him, then shrugged as if dismissing it. "I am much older than she was."

"That's what fooled me."

"Fooled you?"

"I always thought she looked like her mother until I met you." Tiny lights flashed behind his left eye, and he had to close it to ease the sudden stunning pain. "I don't know what was w-wrong with me. I should have seen your resemblance, and her resemblance, to Springbank before."

"You think *he's* my father?" she asked incredulously.

Browser looked down at the pool. Sunlight sprinkled the water like goldfinch feathers. *"Was* your father. Isn't that why you're crying? You're grieving for him?"

"No, that's not why I'm crying, you fool."

"Then why—"

She whirled around. "My husband died yesterday!"

The wind pulled the leaf from his fingers. It fluttered into the river and bobbed away on the current. "He was the man—"

"Yes, Ten Hawks! The gods know I've heard the story often enough today. The girl killed him! Do you understand now why I could not attend her burial?"

Browser frowned and looked away. "It wasn't just her burial, Obsidian. We were burying over forty children, one old woman, and one girl." He looked back and pinned her with hard eyes. "Besides, I thought you were divorced?"

She smoothed her hands over the fine blue fabric of her cape. "That's *why* I divorced him. When he joined the White Moccasins, I knew he would end up dead. I told him so, but he said Two Hearts was more powerful than I could possibly imagine. He told me Two Hearts would lead all of our people back to glory."

Browser chanced removing his hand from his left eye and opened it. The pain nauseated him. He closed it again. "You didn't believe him?"

"Two Hearts was insane. Everyone knew it." She flexed her jeweled fingers and frowned down at the wealth of jet and shell rings. "Everyone except Ten Hawks."

Browser's thoughts flitted around inside his head like bats, trying to coalesce into a sentence. What was wrong with him? "That's why there was no scandal when you divorced. No one knew what he'd done, but you."

"I couldn't tell anyone, Browser, not without risking my own life."

Browser bowed his head. "Yes, I understand now."

"No, you don't. Not really. The White Moccasins operated silently, in secret—until four summers ago, when your Matron formed the Katsinas' People; it gave them a reason to become more bold. Their numbers have been growing steadily ever since. This is not the end, Browser; it is the beginning."

The ties on his bandage flipped in the wind. He put a hand up to keep them out of his eyes. "Two Hearts is dead. A leader's death often—"

"You think it stops with him?" Obsidian looked at him as though he'd turned into a rabbit. "There is another! And she's the scary one, Browser. His daughter, Shadow Woman, she's the one you should be afraid of. Without Two Hearts to restrain her—"

"But I thought you—"

"Me?" she blurted. "Shadow is the one who helped him to kill your Matron, not me!"

When she raised her voice, his head throbbed sickeningly. He didn't speak for a time, then, in a hushed voice, he asked, "How do you know she helped to kill our Matron?"

"Because Ten Hawks told me at the Matron's burial!"

Browser thought back to that day. She'd walked the trail with a tall man and a woman.

"Was she there, too?" he asked.

Obsidian's full lips pressed into a white line. "She passes where she will."

"So you know what she looks like. Will you help us find her?"

Obsidian laughed softly at the absurdity of it. "Oh, you simple fool. If you value your life, and the lives of those close to you, do not even try! Shadow will cut you into tiny pieces and serve you to your family for supper."

Browser rose to his feet, felt the world spin, and

concentrated on keeping his knees locked. "You won't help us?"

"I don't know who 'us' is, Browser." Her black eyes blazed. She leaned toward him, and the front of her cape fell open. *"Do you?* The one thing I can tell you for certain is that as more and more people convert to the Katsina faith, more will die."

Browser stared at the pendant nestled between her breasts. He swallowed down a dry throat and said, "That's beautiful. Where did you get it?"

Obsidian reached up to clutch the black serpent coiled inside the broken eggshell. Its one red eye glared malignantly at Browser. "My father carved it for me when I was a baby. Why?"

Her father. Shadow Woman's father.

The same man?

Browser gazed down at her, noting the curve of her jaw, the shape of her eyes and nose. She stared back defiantly, then he walked away through the piles of ash-coated autumn leaves.

When he reached the river crossing, he saw Stone Ghost standing at the edge of the water, wet up to the knees. The bottom half of his turkey feather cape hung around him in drenched folds.

Browser carefully made his way down the trail to him and said, "Worried that I might have fainted in the trail, Uncle?"

Stone Ghost smiled. "A little."

Browser locked his trembling knees. Placed a hand on his uncle's shoulder to steady his balance. "Obsidian knows who the woman is who helped to kill our Matron. She even knows what she looks like, but she won't help us to find her."

Stone Ghost took his arm in an affectionate grip and guided Browser into the river and back toward the village. He waded the current slowly, a step at a time, to keep his balance.

"But you already know what she looks like, Nephew. You've seen her several times in the past nine moons. You just thought she was Obsidian."

Browser halted and peered down at his uncle while memories flashed: Obsidian that day on the trail. Obsidian in his chamber. And many other times when she had seemed to be a different person.

He said, *"Twin pendants for twin daughters?"*

Stone Ghost nodded. "I think her mother lied about her age when she came to the Longtail Clan, hoping no one would make the connection with what happened here thirty summers ago. She told people her daughter had seen seven summers, not ten, and claimed that her other daughter had died. In a very real way, of course, she was dead. Outcasts are dead to their clans." He rubbed his forehead before continuing. "But I think it goes even deeper, Nephew. It seems that each of his daughters has one of those pendants. Ash Girl had one too, didn't she?"

Browser stiffened. The cold river swirled around his legs. "She told me she'd found it in Talon Town, and that's what she told Hophorn when she gave it to her."

"I think she wished to be rid of it. I can't say why she chose to give it to Hophorn. Perhaps she thought Hophorn was more powerful than the evil creature that lives inside the pendant."

Browser looked back at the Witches' Water Pocket. The pool shimmered.

Obsidian was gone.

"Blessed gods, you don't think...if there is any chance that was Shadow Woman, I should go after her!"

"No." Stone Ghost tugged Browser back. "This is not the day, Browser. Today, she will kill you."

"Not if I get a war party—"

"She hasn't survived this long by being foolish. If she thinks for one instant that you suspect, she will kill you, me, Catkin, and anyone else you might have confided in, and then she will vanish forever."

They continued walking. Stone Ghost stepped out onto the bank and steadied Browser's arm while he picked his way across the slick rocks to the sand.

Browser fought through a dizzy spell and forced himself to take deep, slow breaths. His headache had grown almost incapacitating.

Stone Ghost said, "Let me help you back to Dry Creek camp, Nephew. You must sleep and eat."

Browser nodded, said, "Thank you, Uncle," and allowed Stone Ghost to lead him up the trail.

A group of small boys from the Dry Creek camp ran up the riverbank in front of them, laughing and playfully shoving each other into the water.

Stone Ghost turned to watch them; his turkey feather cape, buffeted by the wind, flattening his shirt against his bony chest. "When you are better, I would like you to help me do something, Nephew."

Browser looked at him through one squinted eye. "Crossbill has ordered that everyone pack up their remaining belongings and be ready to leave for Dry Creek village tomorrow morning. This thing you wish to do, can it be done from Dry Creek village?"

"It does not matter where the journey begins. The task will require several days travel, maybe longer."

"Where are we going?"

Stone Ghost tenderly clutched Browser's arm, then gazed up at the ash-coated cottonwoods along the river. The streaks of sunlight slanting through the branches dappled his face and fell upon the water below like flakes of gold. "A place that I am not even sure exists, Nephew. A place of legends."

~

As I listen to the children running along the river trail above me, I pluck a grasshopper from the stones and use a stick to mash it flat, then I scrape the grasshopper from the rock and put it in my mouth, chewing patiently.

Seven children.

One of them lags behind the others, panting, coughing.

I stop chewing and silently squat on my haunches. I am hiding in the old eroded hole in the bank, waiting to see the lagging boy come into view beyond the brush to my left.

Ah, there he is. Thin and pale, the little boy staggers more than he runs. He wears the yellow cape of the Dry Creek villagers.

A smile tugs at my lips, and I feel the growl rumbling deep in my throat. I am the Summoning God.

I step back into the shadows, my black eyes glistening, and chew again. But not today.

Not today...

Bibliography

Acatos, Sylvio. Pueblos: *Prehistoric Indian Cultures of the Southwest,*
trans. *Die Pueblos* (1989 eds.). New York: Facts on File, 1990.

Adams, E. Charles. *The Origin and Development of the Pueblo Katsina
Cult.* Tucson, AZ: University of Arizona Press, 1991.

Adler, Michael A. *The Prehistoric Pueblo World A.D. 1150-1350.*
Tucson, AZ: University of Arizona Press, 1996.

Allen, Paula Gunn. *Spider Woman's Granddaughters.* New York:
Ballantine Books, 1989.

Arnberger, Leslie P. *Flowers of the Southwest Mountains.* Tucson, AZ:
Southwest Parks and Monuments Assoc, 1982.

Aufderheide, Arthur C. *Cambridge Encyclopedia of Human Pale-
opathology.* Cambridge, UK: Cambridge University Press, 1998.

Baars, Donald L. *Navajo Country: A Geological and Natural History of
the Four Comers Region.* Albuquerque, NM: University of New
Mexico Press, 1995.

Becket, Patrick H., ed. *Mogollon V.* Report of Fifth Mogollon Conference, Las Cruces, NM: COAS Publishing and Research, 1991.

Boissiere, Robert. *The Return of Pahana: A Hopi Myth.* Santa Fe, NM:
Bear & Company, 1990.

Bowers, Janice Emily. *Shrubs and Trees of the Southwest Deserts.*
Tucson, AZ: Southwest Parks & Monuments Assoc, 1993.

Brody, J. J. *The Anasazi.* New York: Rizzoli International Publications,
1990.

Brothwell, Don, and A. T. Sandison, *Disease in Antiquity.* Springfield,
IL: Charles C. Thomas, 1967.

Bunzel, Ruth L. *Zuni Katcinas.* Reprint of 47th Annual Report of the
Bureau of American Ethnography, 1929-30, Glorieta, NM: Rio
Grande Press, 1984.

Colton, Harold S. *Black Sand: Prehistory in Northern Arizona.* Albuquerque, NM: University of New Mexico Press, 1960.

Cordell, Linda S. "Predicting Site Abandonment at Wetherill Mesa."
The Kiva (1975) 40(3):189-202.

—. *Prehistory of the Southwest.* New York: Academic Press, 1984.

—. *Ancient Pueblo People.* Smithsonian Exploring the Ancient World

Series, Montreal, and Smithsonian Institution, Washington, DC: St. Remy Press, 1994.

—. and George J. Gumerman, eds. *Dynamics of Southwest Prehistory.* Washington, DC: Smithsonian Institution Press, 1989.

Crown, Patricia, and W. James Judge, eds. *Chaco and Hohokam: Prehistoric Regional Systems in the American Southwest.* Santa Fe, NM: School of American Research Press, 1991.

Cummings, Linda Scott. "Anasazi Subsistence Activity Areas Reflected in the Pollen Records." Paper presented to the Society for American Archaeology, 45th Annual Meeting, New Orleans, 1986.

—. "Anasazi Diet: Variety in the Hoy House and Lion House Coprolite Record and Nutritional Analysis," in Kristin D. Sobolik, ed., *Paleo-nutrition: The Diet and Health of Prehistoric Americans.* Occasional Paper No. 22, Carbondale, Il.: Center for Archeological Investigations, Southern Illinois University, 1994.

Dodge, Natt N. *Flowers of the Southwest Desert.* Tucson, AZ: Southwest Parks & Monuments Assoc, 1985.

Dooling, D. M.. and Paul Jordan-Smith, eds. / *Become Pari of It: Sacred Dimensions in Native American Life.* San Francisco: A Parabola Book, Harpers; New York: Harper Collins, 1989.

Douglas, John E. "Autonomy and Regional Systems in the Late Prehistoric Southern Southwest." *American Antiquity* (1995) 60:240-57.

Dunmire, William W., and Gail Tierney. *Wild Plants of the Pueblo Province: Exploring Ancient and Enduring Uses.* Santa Fe, NM: Museum of New Mexico Press, 1995.

Ellis, Florence Hawley. "Patterns of Aggression and the War Cult in Southwestern Pueblos." *Southwestern Journal of Anthropology* (1951) 7:177-201.

Elmore, Francis H. *Shrubs and Trees of the Southwest Upland.* Tucson AZ: Southwest Parks & Monuments Assoc, 1976.

Ericson, Jonathan E., and Timothy G. Baugh, eds. *The American Southwest and Mesoamerica: Systems of Prehistoric Exchange.* New York: Plenum Press, 1993.

Fagan, Brian M. *Ancient North America.* New York: Thames & Hudson, 1991.

Farmer, Malcolm F. "A Suggested Typology of Defensive Systems of the Southwest." *Southwestern Journal of Archeology* (1957), 13:249-66.

Frank, Larry, and Francis H. Harlow. *Historic Pottery of the Pueblo Indians: 1600-1880.* West Chester, PA: Schiffler Publishing, 1990.

Frazier, Kendrick. *People of Chaco: A Canyon and its Culture.* New York: W. W. Norton, 1986.

Gabriel, Kathryn. *Roads to Center Place: A Cultural Atlas of Chaco Canyon and the Anasazi.* Boulder, CO: Johnson Books, 1991.

Gumerman, George J., ed. *The Anasazi in a Changing Environment.* School of American Research, New York: Cambridge University Press, 1988.

—. *Exploring the Hohokam: Prehistoric Peoples of the American Southwest.* Amerind Foundation, Albuquerque, NM: University of New Mexico Press, 1991.

—. *Themes in Southwest Prehistory.* Sante Fe, NM: School of American Research Press, 1994.

Haas, Jonathan. "Warfare and the Evolution of Tribal Polities in the Prehistoric Southwest," in Haas, ed., *The Anthropology of War.* Cambridge, U.K: Cambridge University Press, 1990.

— and Winifred Creamer. "A History of Pueblo Warfare." Paper Presented at the 60th Annual Meeting of the Society of American Archeology, Minneapolis, 1995.

—. *Stress and Warfare Among the Kayenta Anasazi of the Thirteenth Century A.D.* Field Museum of Natural History, Chicago, 1993.

Haury, Emil. *Mogollon Culture in the Forestdale Valley, East-Central Arizona.* Tucson, AZ: University of Arizona Press, 1985.

Hayes, Alden C, David M. Burgge, and W. James Judge. *Archaeological Surveys of Chaco Canyon, New Mexico.* Reprint of National Park Service Report, Albuquerque, NM: University of New Mexico Press, 1981.

Hultkrantz, Ake. *Native Religions: The Power of Visions and Fertility.* New York: Harper & Row, 1987.

Jacobs, Sue-Ellen, ed. "Continuity and Change in Gender Roles at San Juan Pueblo," in *Women and Power in Native North America.* Norman, OK: University of Oklahoma Press, 1995.

Jernigan, E. Wesley, *Jewelry of the Prehistoric Southwest.* Albuquerque, NM: University of New Mexico Press, 1978.

Jett, Stephen C. "Pueblo Indian Migrations: An Evaluation of the Possible Physical and Cultural Determinants." *American Antiquity* (1964) 29: 281-300.

Komarek, Susan. *Flora of the San Juans: A Field Guide to the Mountain Plants of Southwestern Colorado.* Durango, CO: Kivaki Press, 1994.

Lange, Frederick, et al. *Yellow Jacket: A Four Corners Anasazi Ceremonial Center.* Boulder, CO: Johnson Books, 1988.

LeBlanc, Stephen A. *Prehistoric Warfare in the American Southwest.* Salt Lake City, UT: University of Utah Press, 1999.

Lekson, Stephen H. *Mimbres Archeology of the Upper Gila, New Mexico.* Anthropological Papers of the University of Arizona, no. 53, Tucson, AZ: University of Arizona Press, 1990.

— et al. "The Chaco Canyon Community." *Scientific American* (1988) 259(1): 100-109.

Lewis, Dorothy Otnow. *Guilty by Reason of Insanity. A Psychiatrist Explores the Minds of Killers.* New York: Ballantine Books, 1998.

Lipe, W. D., and Michelle Hegemon, eds. *The Architecture of Social Integration in Prehistoric Pueblos.* Occasional Papers of the Crow Canyon Archaeological Center, no. 1, Cortez, CO, 1989.

Lister, Florence C. *In the Shadow of the Rocks: Archaeology of the Chimney Rock District in Southern Colorado.* Niwot, Colorado: University Press of Colorado, 1993.

Lister, Robert H., and Florence C. Lister. *Chaco Canyon.* Albuquerque, NM: University of New Mexico Press, 1981.

Malotki, Ekkehart. *Gullible Coyote: Una'ihu: A Bilingual Collection of Hopi Coyote Stories.* Tucson, AZ: University of Arizona Press, 1985.

— ed. *Hopi Ruin Legends.* Lincoln, NE: University of Nebraska Press, 1993.

— and Michael Lomatuway'ma. *Maasaw: Profile of a Hopi God.* American Tribal Religions, vol. XI, Lincoln, NE: University of Nebraska Press, 1987.

Malville, J. McKimm, and Claudia Putnam. *Prehistoric Astronomy in the Southwest.* Boulder, CO: Johnson Books, 1993.

Mann, Coramae Richey. *When Women Kill.* New York: State University of New York Press, 1996.

Martin, Debra L. "Lives Unlived: The Political Economy of Violence Against Anasazi Women." Paper presented to the Society for American Archeology 60th Annual Meeting, Minneapolis, 1995.

— et al. *Black Mesa Anasazi Health: Reconstructing Life from Patterns of Death and Disease.* Occasional Paper no. 14. Carbondale, IL: Southern Illinois University, 1991.

Mayes, Vernon O., and Barbara Bayless Lacy. *Nanise: A Navajo Herbal.* Tsaile, AZ: Navajo Community College Press, 1989.

McGuire, Randall H., and Michael Schiffer, eds. *Hohokam and Patayan: Prehistory of Southwestern Arizona.* New York: Academic Press, 1982.

McNitt, Frank. *Richard Wetherill Anasazi.* Albuquerque, NM: University of New Mexico Press, 1966.

Minnis, Paul E., and Charles L. Redman, eds. *Perspectives on Southwestern Prehistory.* Boulder, CO: Westview Press, 1990.

Mullet, G. M. *Spider Woman Stories: Legends of the Hopi Indians.* Tucson, AZ: University of Arizona Press, 1979.

Nabahan, Gary Paul. *Enduring Seeds: Native American Agriculture and Wild Plant Conservation.* San Francisco: North Point Press, 1989.

Noble, David Grant. *Ancient Ruins of the Southwest: An Archaeological Guide.* Northland Publishing, Flagstaff Arizona: 1991.

Ortiz, Alfonzo, ed. *Handbook of North American Indians.* Washington, DC: Smithsonian Institution, 1983.

Palkovich, Ann M. *The Arroyo Hondo Skeletal and Mortuary Remains.* Arroyo Hondo Archeological Series, vol. 3, Santa Fe, NM: School of American Research Press, 1980.

Parsons, Elsie Clews. *Tewa Tales* (reprint of 1924 edn.). Tucson, AZ: University of Arizona Press, 1994.

Pepper, George H. *Pueblo Bonito* (reprint of 1920 edn.). Albuquerque, NM: University of New Mexico Press, 1996.

Pike, Donald G., and David Muench. *Anasazi: Ancient People of the Rock.* New York: Crown Publishers, 1974.

Reid, J. Jefferson, and David E. Doyel, eds. *Emil Haury's Prehistory of the American Southwest.* Tucson, AZ: University of Arizona Press, 1992.

Riley, Carroll L. *Rio del Norte: People of the Upper Rio Grande from the Earliest Times to the Pueblo Revolt.* Salt Lake City, UT: University of Utah Press, 1995.

Rocek, Thomas R. "Sedentarization and Agricultural Dependence: Perspectives from the Pithouse-to-Pueblo Transition in the American Southwest." *American Antiquity* (1995) 60: 218-39.

Schaafsma, Polly. *Indian Rock Art of the Southwest.* Albuquerque, NM: University of New Mexico Press, 1980.

Sebastian, Lynne. *The Chaco Anasazi: Sociopolitical Evolution in the Prehistoric Southwest.* Cambridge, UK: Cambridge University Press, 1992.

Simmons, Marc. *Witchcraft in the Southwest* (reprint of 1974 edn.), Bison Books), Lincoln, NE: University of Nebraska Press, 1980.

Slifer, Dennis, and James Duffield. *Kokopelli: Flute Player Images in Rock Art.* Santa Fe, NM. Ancient City Press, 1994.

Smith, Watson, with Raymond H. Thompson, ed. *When Is a Kiva: And*

Other Questions About Southwestern Archaeology. Tucson, AZ: University of Arizona Press, 1990.

Sobolik, Kristin D., ed. *Paleonutrition: The Diet and Health of Prehistoric Americans*. Occasional Paper no. 22, Center for Archeological Investigations, Carbondale, IL: Southern Illinois University, 1994.

Sullivan, Alan P. "Pinyon Nuts and Other Wild Resources in Western Anasazi Subsistence Economies." *Research in Economic Anthropology, Supplement* (1992) 6: 195-239.

Tedlock, Barbara. *The Beautiful and the Dangerous: Encounters with the Zuni Indians*. New York: Viking Press, 1992.

Trombold, Charles D., ed. *Ancient Road Networks and Settlement Hierarchies in the New World*. Cambridge, UK: Cambridge University Press, 1991.

Turner, Christy G., and Jacqueline A. Turner. *Man Corn. Cannibalism and Violence in the Prehistoric American Southwest*. Salt Lake City, UT: University of Utah Press, 1999.

Tyler, Hamilton A. *Pueblo Gods and Myths*. Norman, OK: University of Oklahoma Press, 1964.

Underhill, Ruth. *Life in the Pueblos* (reprint of 1964 Bureau of Indian Affairs Report). Santa Fe, NM: Ancient City Press, 1991.

Upham, Steadman, Kent G. Lightfoot, and Roberta A. Jewett, eds. *The Sociopolitical Structure of Prehistoric Southwestern Societies*. San Francisco: Westview Press, 1989.

Vivian, Gordon, and Tom W. Mathews. *Kin Kletso: A Pueblo HI Community in Chaco Canyon, New Mexico,* vol. 6. Globe, AZ: Southwest Parks & Monuments Assoc, 1973.

Vivian, Gordon, and Paul Reiter. *The Great Kivas of Chaco Canyon and Their Relationships,* Monograph, no. 22, Santa Fe, NM: School of American Research Press, 1965.

Vivian, R. Gwinn. *The Chacoan Prehistory of the San Juan Basin*. New York: Academic Press, 1990.

Waters, Frank. *Book of the Hopi*. New York: Viking Press, 1963.

Wetterstrom, Wilma. *Food, Diet, and Population at Prehistoric Arroyo Hondo Pueblo, New Mexico*. Arroyo Hondo Archaeological Series, vol. 6. Santa Fe, NM: School of American Research Press, 1986.

White, Tim D. *Prehistoric Cannibalism at Mancos 5MTUMR-2346*. Princeton, NJ: Princeton University Press, 1992.

Williamson, Ray A. *Living the Sky: The Cosmos of the American Indian*. Norman, OK: University of Oklahoma Press, 1984.

Wills, W. H., and Robert D. Leonard, eds. *The Ancient Southwestern*

Community. Albuquerque, NM: University of New Mexico Press, 1994.

Woodbury, Richard B. "A Reconsideration of Pueblo Warfare in the Southwestern United States." *Adas del XXXIII Congreso Internacional de Americanistas* (1959) II: 124-33. San Jose, Costa Rica.

—. "Climatic Changes and Prehistoric Agriculture in the Southwestern United States." *New York Academy of Sciences Annals* (1969) vol. 95, art. 1.

Wright, Barton. *Katchinas: The Barry Goldwater Collection at the Heard Museum.* Phoenix, AZ: Heard Museum, 1975.

A look at Book Five:
Bone Walker

From *New York Times* bestselling authors W. Michael Gear and Kathleen O'Neal Gear comes part five in their prehistoric mystery series.

Ancient evil stalks the Southwest when Dusty Stewart's adoptive father and world-renowned anthropologist, Dr. Dale Robertson, is found brutally murdered in Chaco Canyon—buried upside down and mutilated, with a hole drilled in his skull. Bonded by grief, Dusty and Maureen Cole work to uncover links between Dale's ritualistic death and a seven-hundred-year-old string of disturbing Anasazi murders.

As Dusty and Maureen's search uncovers long-buried secrets of past love affairs, deceit, seduction, and betrayal, *Kwewur*—the mythical Puebloan "Wolf Witch"—is one step ahead of them, watching from the shadows and drawing his next victim into his twisted lair of perverted Spirit Power.

In the ruins of a dying empire, War Chief Browser and the woman he loves—but dares not touch—face defeat. To win, he and Stone Ghost must hunt the perverted witch, Two Hearts, and his psychopathic daughter. But as Browser tries to save his beloved Katsinas People from extermination, he unknowingly engages in a cat-and-mouse game with Two Hearts. But who is hunting whom?

Can Dusty and Maureen finally unveil answers to the mysteries that have shrouded their past and put an end to an ancient reign of terror?

AVAILABLE DECEMBER 2023

About W. Michael Gear

W. Michael Gear is a *New York Times, USA Today,* and international bestselling author of sixty novels. With close to eighteen million copies of his books in print worldwide, his work has been translated into twenty-nine languages.

Gear has been inducted into the Western Writers Hall of Fame and the Colorado Authors' Hall of Fame —as well as won the Owen Wister Award, the Golden Spur Award, and the International Book Award for both Science Fiction and Action Suspense Fiction. He is also the recipient of the Frank Waters Award for lifetime contributions to Western writing.

Gear's work, inspired by anthropology and archaeology, is multilayered and has been called compelling, insidiously realistic, and masterful. Currently, he lives in northwestern Wyoming with his award-winning wife and co-author, Kathleen O'Neal Gear, and a charming sheltie named, Jake.

About Kathleen O'Neal Gear

Kathleen O'Neal Gear is a *New York Times* bestselling author of fifty-seven books and a national award-winning archaeologist. The U.S. Department of the Interior has awarded her two Special Achievement awards for outstanding management of America's cultural resources.

In 2015 the United States Congress honored her with a Certificate of Special Congressional Recognition, and the California State Legislature passed Joint Member Resolution #117 saying, "The contributions of Kathleen O'Neal Gear to the fields of history, archaeology, and writing have been invaluable..."

In 2021 she received the Owen Wister Award for lifetime contributions to western literature, and in 2023 received the Frank Waters Award for "a body of work representing excellence in writing and storytelling that embodies the spirit of the American West."